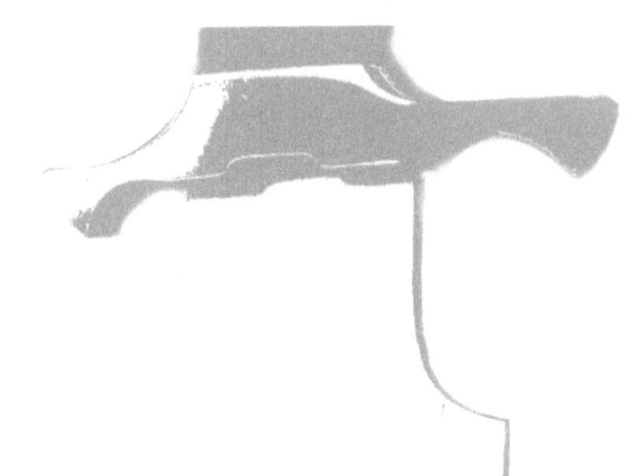

RECLAMATION

BETHANY A PERRY

ISBN: 978-1-7344692-0-2

To my mom, Johnny, Robin, and Benny, my very best friends.

And Jensen Ackles, for being an incredible artist, and inspiring
me to love something enough to finish it.

THE VILLAGE

CHAPTER 1

om puts you to bed every night with a giant knife clutched in your hand. Not even big enough to tie your shoes, when you have them, smoke from the nightly campfire crawls up your nose. Mellow mesquite embedded in your brain.

Mom quizzes you. "Now, Adelaide, where do you hit them?"

"In the head," you say.

"And if you can't?"

"Run away and hide. Be quiet."

She snuggles close. "That's right, jellybean. Silent as the grave."

Dad hugs you both and curls up next to the fire with you. "Mike and I can take the first watch, ladies."

You giggle. You're just a little kid, not a lady yet.

Mom stiffens. "Jack."

Dad sits up. "I know, Melinda. I can smell them."

And so can you. Putrid, maggoty meat and coppery blood clotted like spoiled milk.

"Stay with the kids. I'll go," Mom says. Before Dad can argue, she's out of the clearing.

He stands, machete drawn, firelight flickering across his cheeks. "Michael, stay with your sister."

"You got it, Dad."

Eyes wide, you take in short, silent breaths. Mike's bigger than you, but you're just as quick.

You sit up. The haft of your knife is slippery with sweat. "When are they coming back?"

Crowbar held out, Mike shushes you. "I don't know. But when they do, I've got a root beer sucker with your name on it."

The dead come stumbling into the clearing. Mom and Dad crash through the trees, but the dead are here now.

Clutching your knife, the first birthday present Mom ever gave you, you jump up and start stabbing. The blade cuts the air as you breathe through your nose and stay silent. Silent as the grave.

* * *

One foot catching the back of its mate, Adelaide tripped down the next two stairs and lost her grip on the box. Cursing her own feet for the hundredth time today, she snatched the handrail. The box tumbled end over end into the driveway.

"Ah, hell."

Jane chuckled and leaned over the box. Sheaves of red hair fell in her face. "Addy, you're the smoothest person I know." Box loaded in the truck, she used knitting needles to secure her hair at the nape of her neck.

Addy favored her with a sour grin. "Shut it, woman. I'll go get the next one." She turned and ran face-first into her dad.

"Whoa, little girl. Slow down." Dad raised both hands, palms out. "Let me help you."

Addy backed up a step, steeling herself for him to argue, again, for her to stay. "I got it, Dad." She patted him on the shoulder. "We're almost done anyway."

"I could use some help, Mr. C.," Jane said, leaning against the truck.

He smiled but turned to Addy before she went back upstairs. "Addy, wait. Listen—"

Addy brushed past his outstretched hand and went up the side stairs to the second floor.

Staring at the last two boxes sitting on a strangely empty floor, she fought off the melancholy. Her brother had moved out forever ago, and now her dad would be kicking around the house alone. When was the last time he'd been alone?

Addy picked up another box. Blinking a lock of her brown hair from her lashes and failing, she started for the door. And there was Dad again, trying to take the box.

"Dad. Really. I got it."

He didn't let go. "I really wish you'd reconsider. They found a Dead Head in the village just last week."

"One. Dad. Really. When's the last time one 'Head was a problem? Besides"—she eased the box back into her arms—"we've been here, what, three years? We've seen less than five inside the walls. Plus, there's always the Cure." She patted a black pouch hanging off her belt. "Pretty sure me and Jane will be perfectly safe in our new place."

He gave her half a smile. "So headstrong. Just like your mother. Makes sense, you got those brownzel eyes of hers."

Addy softened. Leave it to him to try and guilt her into staying by bringing up Mom.

"Dad." The handle of her machete clanked against the box as she shifted it to her hip. "By the time you were my age, you had two kids already."

"Almost. I was twenty-four when you were born."

"Whatever. Look. I get it. I miss her too. But we can handle it."

Glancing out the window, the light turning his blue eyes almost white, he frowned. "I just hate you being so far away."

"It's just down the road." Addy stepped around him, trying to put the melancholy behind her. She managed to make her way down the stairs without tripping this time—small miracles—and set the box in the truck.

Jane grinned. "We about done?"

"What's this 'we'? You've hardly moved more than two boxes."

"That's because I don't live here."

"May as well," Dad said, coming down the stairs with a box resting on one hip and the butt of his gun slapping against it with each step. He didn't even look down. He never missed a step.

Jane took the box from him at the bottom. "Thanks, Mr. C." Standing on tiptoes, reaching as far as she could, she set it on top of the others.

He reached over her head and gave it a push. "Jane, why don't you just call me Jack? I don't think we need to stand on ceremony anymore."

"You got it. Tell Michael hi for me."

Addy held out her hand. Her feet hurt, her arms hurt, her everything hurt. "Keys, please."

Jane handed over the keys, green eyes dancing.

Dad stepped back. "I'll come check out security at this new place tomorrow, Addy."

"If you have to." Addy hopped into the truck. After the third try, she stabbed the keys home and started it.

Jane leaned out the window. "We'll be fine, Jack," she said, a bad imitation of Scottish brogue dripping off her tongue.

He crossed his arms. Curls on the back of his neck bouncing in the slight breeze, he nodded. "Take care of each other. You're always welcome back here."

"You worry too much, Dad," Addy said, letting off the brake. As they rolled down the drive, a whole world of freedom before them, she leaned over. "Dead Heads or no, we are not coming back here."

Jane watched Jack recede into the distance. "You said it."

***

Jack coughed in the dusty rooster-tail Addy's truck had created.

There went his youngest, off to face the world on her own. What he wouldn't have given to stop her. But she was twenty-three, well into adulthood, and he couldn't treat her like a child forever. No matter how much he wanted to. At least they had the Cure.

Swallowing, swiping at his eyes, he turned for the stairs. After securing the gate at the bottom, he trudged up the stairs and repeated the process with the second gate. At the top, he swiveled a handle on the wall. Trip wires popped up along every other step, but the handle squealed as it spun.

With a grimace, he brought out the oil from inside and dripped a bit on the handle. He went to spin it again.

The crunch of gravel under a foot stopped him.

His hackles rose in painful pricks along his spine. The base of his skull tingled. Hand hovering over the grip of his gun, he waited for the owner of the foot to round the corner.

The feet took regular, measured steps, and Jack relaxed a millimeter. Only the living walked with a purpose.

As a portly, balding man stepped into view, Jack sighed and pulled his gun anyway.

"Whoa, hey Jackson, good morning," the newcomer said, peeking through the lower gate.

Jack shook his head. "You can call me Mr. Cooke, Wade."

Wade grinned, fleshy lips pulling back from his teeth. "OK, Mr. Cooke. Can I come up?"

Jack holstered his gun once again. An audible sigh from the bottom of the stairs followed him into the house.

As the door snicked closed, Jack exhaled, shoulders falling. The man might be a worm, but he was Mayor Worm. Frowning, Jack opened the door again. Eyes narrowed, he spun the trip wire handle and clomped down the stairs. Dust assaulted his nose as he reached the bottom and he all but sneezed in Wade's face as he opened the bottom gate.

Wade threw up a hand, spittle covering his palm as he did. "Whoa. Hey, Mr. Cooke, are you OK? Getting a cold?" His pleasant expression rippled, becoming something predatory, reptilian. His hands disappeared behind his back.

All at once, Jack noticed the bulge beneath Wade's armpit. The pommel of a knife peeking from his belt. He peered at the man, reassessing. "Just dust. Always happens this time of year."

The little man nodded, empty hands reappearing.

Jack shook his head and scratched at his salt-and-pepper beard. Only little more than stubble, it could use a trim. He'd been so preoccupied with his soon-to-be-empty home, it'd slipped clean off the map. "Come on up."

Following the mayor up the stairs and resetting the trip wires, he locked and barred the front door.

"Never too many precautions, huh, Mr. Cooke?" Wade bounced on the balls of his feet, hands clasped in front of him.

Jack stared through him. "No."

Wade bounced.

Jack stared.

Wade shuffled a foot. "Do you think I could get some water or something, please?"

Another "no" on the edge of his tongue, Jack led him into the kitchen.

Wade took a seat at the kitchen table, chair creaking under his considerable ass. He sighed, a smile stretching his lips, and Jack filled a glass with cold water and ice.

Setting the glass in front of Wade, Jack sat across from him.

Wade took a swig, clapping a hand to his forehead as he set the glass back on the table. "Brain freeze." He tittered.

Jack's mouth twitched, but he wasn't sure if it was a smile or a frown. He pressed his lips together. Leaning on the table, he sucked a labored breath through his nose. Exhaled. "What can I do for you, Wade?"

Wade took another sip from his glass. "Well, Jackson, um, Mister, Mister Cooke, I—that is the I who is mayor—was wondering if you wanted to be on the Security Committee."

Chuckling, Jack leaned back in his chair and crossed his arms. "You're joking."

"Oh no. About town matters, I don't joke."

As Jack exhaled a laugh, Wade picked the glass up again. His fingers slipped, sending the glass sliding toward the floor.

Jack stuck his hand out in time to stop it falling and set it back on the table, no more than two or three droplets escaping it.

Wade pointed. "See there? That's one of the things I—that we—want you on the committee for. You're so quick." At some point, the little man had begun to sweat, upper lip beaded with dirty, salty drops of it. "Not to mention the, uh, incident the other day. Not that any of us are ill-prepared to deal with Dead Heads after almost twenty-five years, but it does make one reconsider security matters at a time like this." Wade wiped his lip with the back of his hand.

Jack lifted his own lip. While Wade was right about reconsidering security matters, just being in a room with him and his slippery ass made Jack want to jump out the nearest window. He cocked his head, tightening his crossed arms. "No."

Wade sighed, knocking back the rest of the water like it was a shot of vodka. The ice cubes crunched and squeaked between his teeth.

Nails on a chalkboard.

"Jackson. Jack. We need your help. You're a great benefit to this community, and we need you to take part in its safety." Reaching to his face, Wade chuckled at his hand and glanced at Jack. "Heh. I forgot I got contacts again. It's been so long since I had them, I keep trying to adjust glasses that aren't there."

Jack grunted.

Wade stood, sliding the chair back under the table with a prissiness reserved for actors. No one else could be that over-the-top with it.

Herding him to the front door, Jack flinched when one of the floorboards creaked.

At the door, Wade stopped. "Listen. We're working really hard here on rebuilding this community. The state. Hell, the planet. We need everyone's help. You have a skill," he said, motioning to the bar on the door. "We need your skill. It's been a long time since we were able to have stability. Security. But it's here now, and you can help us maintain it. You can help us improve."

Jack frowned down at him, nose itching. He couldn't get that damned 'Head off his mind. No one had been hurt, but what if they had? What if they'd been bitten? Still, what Wade proposed sounded like the kind of old-world bureaucracy he did not miss.

Rather than answer, Jack reached past the mayor, unbarred the door, and motioned for Wade to take his leave.

Repeating the process of entry in reverse, without all the flying spit, Jack slammed the gate and locked the chain.

"The next city council meeting is today. It's at city hall, noon," Wade said.

Jack grunted, sun-warmed lock gripped in a tight fist. He glanced up, meeting Wade's eyes. "I'll think about it."

CHAPTER 2

Addy pointed to the porch of the old barracks building. "Is that the couch?"

Jane squinted. "That's it. Let's get it inside." They each took an end.

Dad might be nervous about their new digs, but he had no reason to be. Not only did each door inside their apartment sport shiny new locks, the three barracks sat ringed in chain-link. With razor wire rolled around the outside and top of it. Plus, a guard tower squatted by the gate, manned all day and night.

Dad had always loved gates. He'd probably throw a party when he saw this.

Fumbling her end of the couch, Addy stumbled up a step.

From somewhere above her, Jane cursed. The couch jumped forward as she yanked it higher.

"Sorry, sorry," Addy said. She squeezed her fingers beneath it. "It's heavier than I remember."

"I miss the days of not having to move furniture up and down stairs," Jane said, voice muffled.

Peering over the couch, all Addy could see was the top of Jane's head. "It's better than what we had before we got here."

"Straw in a bag and some clean dirt? Yeah. But it's heavier."

Reaching the top of the narrow staircase, they pivoted their way into the hall. Jane set her end down.

Lowering the couch, Addy couldn't find a good way to set it down without crushing her fingers. She sat it on her toes and tried to ignore their screaming.

Jane stood. "We get in here, I'm taking a shower. Immediately."

A voice floated up the staircase. "If we help you with the couch, can we stick around?"

Two guys appeared from the stairwell. One, a short and freckled redhead, sketched a timid wave and stood back to watch the other pass.

Taller, leaner, and muscular, he shook shoulder-length brown hair out of his eyes and crossed his arms while grinning at Jane.

Addy's mouth fell open. He could've been broken off one of those Greek statues her mom had shown her once. Chiseled from marble.

"Tim," Jane purred, swinging her hips toward him. She laid the Scottish accent on again and grazed his arm with her breasts. "You and Louis move the couch for us, and we'll talk about it."

"Sure, sure," he said, pointing Louis to Jane's end. Spinning, he smiled at Addy. "I'll get that from you. Can you get the door, um, I'm sorry," he said, pausing, "have we met?"

She stuck a hand out. "Adelaide Cooke."

Taking her hand and brushing his lips across the back, his round brown eyes widened. "Not Mr. Cooke's daughter?"

Her cheeks tingled. "The one and only."

He locked his eyes on hers. "I'm guessing you have your mother's eyes, then, because those are certainly not his." He leaned forward. "And they're far prettier."

She flushed.

The blood crawled up his cheeks. "Well," he said, working his fingers under the couch, "please. Allow me." Leaning his shoulder into the inside of her calf, he lifted the couch. "Say, you want to go target practicing tomorrow, after you get all this moved in?"

It took her four tries to open the door.

***

Once she closed and barred the door, Addy dragged her feet to the couch.

"I have done a lot of things in my life," she said, flopping down next to Jane. "Fought hordes of Dead Heads. Run for hours at a time. Helped build a house from the ground up."

"True," Jane said. "Point?"

"I have never done something so exhausting as moving."

Laughing, Jane stripped off her shirt and dumped it in the floor. "I'm going to take a shower."

"I'll never get used to that."

"What, showering?"

"No," Addy said, shaking her head. "Yes. I mean, whenever you want to, just taking a warm shower."

"Yeah," Jane said, wiggling out of her shorts and dumping them on the couch. "I will. Watch this." She pulled her knitting needles from where they held her hair and stuck them into the floor. Their deadly points pierced it with a woody thump. Without another word, she walked into the bathroom.

As the water slopped onto the floor of the shower, no doubt a catastrophic flash flood for whatever insects lived in the pipes, Addy unwrapped and set up the TV.

Her big brother, Michael, had scrounged it for her while he'd been out, working to repair radio and cell phone towers. He might be a pain in the ass, but sometimes he came through.

Digging a thumb-sized memory stick out of her pocket, she plugged it into the back. There was always the chance one of the things wouldn't work. The TV, the port, her mom's legacy on the little memory stick.

Crossing her fingers, she held her breath and turned it all on.

Picard screamed the intro of Star Trek from the TV.

"Jesus girl, turn that down!" One towel around her body and one around her hair, Jane left a trail of water from the bathroom to the couch.

Eyes wide, Addy stabbed at the TV's buttons. "Sorry, sorry…"

Picard's screaming went on, uninterrupted.

She hit it right, and the little white line on the display inched down to nothing, muting Picard. Finally.

Addy exhaled. "Sorry."

Perching on the couch, Jane shook her head. "Not even a full day in, you got the Star Trek going already."

"And?"

Chuckling, Jane pulled a ball of yarn out of the bag next to the couch. Unsticking her needles and sweeping her shorts onto the floor, she leaned back into the couch and began knitting.

A hat? Scarf? Mittens? Who knew.

After raising the volume to a reasonable level, Addy flopped next to her. As Data, the android, came into view, she watched his flat expression.

Now, there was someone she'd like to be. Strong, full of life. But without emotion. Detached from it all, yet completely human.

Instead, here she was, sitting on a couch that once belonged to someone from a different world. For no reason, on the edge of tears and gazing at the ceiling of a room that had been barracks for young military men. Now apartments for people like her, who'd never seen the world the way it once was. Who never would.

And the thought running back and forth through her mind, wearing a trench in the floor from its pacing, circled those people. The ones who'd lived here before their world went to shit. Had they lost their families? Had they been lost? Or were they, like her dad, still out there somewhere? Fighting through the constant pain of loss, blood, and death?

CHAPTER 3

The door creaked open on hinges screaming for oil. Jack winced, stepping into what used to be a classroom.

From his perch at the head of the room, Wade beamed. "Glad to see you could join us."

Jack looked over the seven other people in the room. People he'd seen around but didn't really *know*. All seven sucking in their guts, squeezed into desks meant for middle schoolers.

Wade sat at what once could have been a teacher's desk. The chalkboard behind him displayed an organizational chart with one name under the Security section.

Jack's own.

He frowned. Wade was some kind of special.

"Wade," Jack said, with one curt nod. He stalked to the front of the room, all eyes glued to him, and picked up the eraser. In one swipe he eliminated his name from the board and set the eraser back in the tray with a puff of chalk.

Taking a seat near the window, he twisted the desk to face the room instead of the front and leaned against it, arms folded. He stared up at Wade.

Who was sweating again. Of course.

"Well. Welcome anyway, Mr. Cooke."

Jack nodded.

"Um. Yes," Wade said, shuffling and stacking the papers in front of him, "we were just getting to the business I'd spoken to you about. Given the unfortunate incident with the Dead Head two days ago, we need to improve security."

Jack stabbed a finger toward the board. "You should ask before you put my name on that board, Wade."

"I apologize, Jackson. You were nominated to lead the Security Committee by three sitting council members. The vote was unanimous. No further discussion was needed, so we added you to it."

"What if I wanted to decline the nomination?"

"Is that why you're here?"

Jack hesitated, brow furrowed. There was no backing down now.

"No. I'm here to sign up for it."

Wade grinned and stood, chair legs scraping across the laminate floor, and finished the job of erasing Jack's name. He rewrote it in decidedly girlish handwriting. Removing a kerchief from his pocket with a flourish, Wade wiped his fingertips, refolded it, and slid it back into the pocket. "So, Mr. Cooke, who would you like on your committee?"

Jack scoffed. "You want me to nominate more people for this bureaucratic nightmare?"

Wade reached for his face again, trying to adjust glasses that weren't there. Eyes sliding to his hand, he swallowed. He picked up his pencil instead and twirled it between his fingers.

Jack got the distinct impression the other people in the room were watching them like they were combatants in a heated tennis match.

"Yes, I would like for you to fill out your own committee. You have the instincts this council is looking for when it comes to who is best to fill these roles."

Jack re-crossed his arms and stared at the floor. He already knew who he wanted. But … "I'll talk to them myself. I'm not going to sign them up for some committee or whatever without talking to them first."

Wade shook his head. "Maybe you don't understand the function of the Security Committee."

Jack opened his mouth to interrupt, but Wade raised a hand in his direction.

Blowing air through his nose, Jack closed his mouth and resettled his arms.

"The committee is being created to oversee all aspects of security," Wade said. "Our constabulary is robust, but there are other aspects of security that are lacking. The purpose of this committee is to ensure the fences are sound, the alarms are maintained, and that the Dead Head Task Force remains ever vigilant. That last one is the most important. It is easy to become complacent in these peaceful times, as we have seen." Wade paused, almost adjusted his imaginary glasses, and sighed.

He went on. "The Task Force is our best line of defense against the dead. They are trained, unafraid, and experienced. I'd like the Security Committee to oversee their continued training, discipline, and weaponry." Wade shuffled some papers in front of him and glanced up. "And whatever else you, the head of security, require of them." He swallowed, swiping at his dripping brow with a shirt cuff.

"In short, your job is to oversee any and all aspects of security. Bring all aspects of security under one umbrella, as it were. Any violations of policy shall be reported back to me, the mayor, immediately." Pursing his lips, he nodded and raised his eyes to Jack's.

Jack stood, put his back to the room, and stared out the window.

The village beyond the window, a fragile little creature, beat with the living hearts of the people in it. Down to a man, they depended on each other for food, shelter, safety. Seemed like he'd been in this position for a while now, without being named.

May as well put a name to it.

He spun. "Let's do this."

***

Addy's phone rang.

Jerked from sleep, she spilled from the bed and knocked her head on the floor. Rubbing her face, she reached up on the nightstand with the other hand and felt for the screaming thing.

Before bed, all the detritus from her pockets had wound up there, and as she fumbled for the phone, something hard bounced off her skull.

She snatched the phone and flipped it open. "What the hell?"

"Hey, bean. Didn't mean to wake you."

"Don't call me that, Michael. It's the middle of the night. What did you think was going to happen?"

Mike sighed. The line crackled. "I'm sorry baby sister. I needed to test the lines. This tower has been nothing but a thorn in my side."

Addy wiped her eyes. "You've always been good with machines. You'll get it."

Crashing through the bedroom door, Jane crouched, a knife in each hand.

Addy flapped a hand at her. "It's just Mike."

Jane grunted, sheathing the knives in dark places. She smoothed her hair. "Tell Michael hello. Since your dad obviously didn't."

"Is that Jane?" The line crackled again.

Addy nodded, realized what she was doing, and answered aloud. "Yes." She shouted toward Jane's retreating back. "She says hi."

"What's she doing there tonight? Do her parents know she's spending the night?"

"Jesus Christ, Michael. I am twenty-three years old. We are not having a sleepover."

She flipped the phone closed.

***

Sleep destroyed, Addy waited until she heard Jane's regular breathing through her door. It was a thick door, but Addy's mom once taught her to sit and Listen.

* * *

"Now, what do you hear?"

"I don't know. My heartbeat," you answer.

Your mom shakes her head. "Not that. The rest."

A whooshing in your ears wants to take over everything in sight. You breathe deep, and it's like coming up for air. Your ears pop and the whooshing is gone.

Ragged breathing.

As you Listen, your mom stands on silent feet, but for the scuffle of one stealthy heel.

You grin because you bet she didn't think you'd hear that. But you're learning already and—

BANG! The door rattles in its frame. The sound of Mom's knife unsheathing.

You finally open your eyes and leap up. Your right foot is asleep from sitting crisscross applesauce all that time. You stumble on it, limping into the wall.

Now you can do more than hear it. You can smell it. The stench of fetid meat and crusted blood. Past coppery and into smelling like rust tastes.

You're only eight, but you're pretty sure that's how everyone's going to end up eventually.

Blood pooled in the fingers until they're blackened claws. Blood pooled in the feet until they swell and split. Shredded chunks of bone holding up the rotted flesh of the dead as it wanders around, remaking everything in its image.

And it crashes through the door. But it's just the one.

Mom takes it on alone. In silence.

You Listen, and all you hear is breathing. Hers and its, wrapped in a complicated dance of life and death. Buzzing gurgling from it, and your mom's short, sharp exhales.

You almost have time to be scared, but she stops its buzzing, jamming a knife through its ear, and closes the door again.

Made of iron, she scoops you up and runs you away from the stench and the blood.

Everybody might end up that way in the end, but not her.

Everybody but her.

* * *

The melancholy from the morning seeping into her night, Addy's restless feet carried her downstairs and outside.

Heavy clouds blanketed the full moon, its bright circle just a dim, diffused haze. Two streetlamps painted everything below them a garish and cartoony orange.

Leaping from the side of the porch, quiet feet poofing a small cloud of dust from the ground, she crept past the building and eased around to the pitch-black west side.

She caught the whisper of one stealthy heel over the scrubby grass.

One hand fingering the black pouch on her belt—Dad's handiwork and packed with her dose of the Cure—she unsheathed her giant Bowie knife with the other.

Taking one silent step after another toward the fence, she Listened.

In a place this well armored—with the Cure five years old and the hordes rounded up and smoked, embers and ash blown to the four corners—it seemed crazy there could be two breaches in as many days.

But there it was.

Ragged, labored breathing. Senseless.

Because they never lay down, never went to rest, the blood had nowhere to go but down. Sometimes, when death was close behind them, something that had only just taken them and twisted them into this walking pile of murder, it would pool in the bottom of their lungs. It would bubble when they breathed. It sounded like a coffee pot, percolating over a fire.

In front of her now, out in the pitch-black, one bubbled.

Her toe hit the fence, the tip of her nose cold on the chain-link.

And it bubbled out there, shuffling closer. Its feet still had shoes, their heels scuffing the gravelly dirt.

Chain-link rattling, the timbre of the bubbling shifted. As though it were sniffing through the nose, drawing air down empty sinus cavities and into bloody lungs.

If the clouds moved, she'd find it right in front of her. It had to be.

Movement behind her.

She caught her breath as a guard rounded the corner of the building, red-beamed flashlight aimed low.

The guard inhaled, a sharp breath drawn over their teeth. They lifted their light, splashing it over her face and onto the fence behind.

Addy tracked the red beam into the desert beyond the fence.

Nothing but trees and rocks.

***

Clutching her bow, Addy stepped into the morning sun, squinting.

Tim looked her up and down, a grin dimpling his cheek. "Brought your bow today?"

"Yeah. What'd you bring?"

He held a rifle to port. "Two .45s and this bad boy," he said, seesawing it. "Old M-16. Army-issue."

Reaching for it, Addy asked where he'd gotten it.

Tim chuckled, tucking a stray hair behind an ear. "A girl has her ways."

His impression of a coy teen girl endearing, somehow, she smiled and dropped her hand. "So where are we going?"

With the barrel of the rifle, he pointed south. "There's a range a mile or so that way, if you're up for the hike." Eyeing the Bowie knife on her hip, the machete on her other, one side of his mouth raised. "Think we brought enough weaponry?"

"No. My dad always says there's never enough."

"Does he. Your dad's smart. Shall we?"

As they reached the fence, the gate guard stepped up. The freckled redhead from yesterday.

"Louis," Tim said.

He unlocked and rolled the gate open. "Hey, Tim. Going out shooting?"

"Yeah, just me and Adelaide." Tim smiled at her. Dropping her a wink, he touched the small of her back.

Her stomach dipped to her toes and back.

Louis grinned. "Say hi to Jane for me, Addy."

Attempting to sketch a salute, she just missed smacking her temple with the bow. With a nervous chuckle, she lowered her hand. If she were any smoother, she'd be sandpaper.

"We'll be back in a couple hours, tops," Tim said, waving her through the gate.

Louis rolled the gate closed. "Have fun."

Just beyond the barracks, a road curved away from the mountain. Following it, they passed an old cemetery.

Addy peeked through the fence surrounding it.

An irregular circle of burned dirt and grass in the middle, the odor of dead flesh and charred bone wafted out.

"The cleanup crew disposes of the dead ones here," Tim said.

Addy nodded. She'd seen it enough times to know you never got used to the stench.

Chewing a nail, she walked in silence. She'd spent her whole life in a small group of less than ten. Her family and a few others, mostly. Being around this many people in a group, what Dad called "civilization," fit like pants that were one size too big. Almost right, but with a belt that cinched in all the wrong places. What was she even supposed to talk about?

Passing through an abandoned housing development, an empty playground caught Addy's attention. Paint peeling back to reveal naked metal sent a hollow spike through her. Wind pushed through her skin and into the void inside. Whispering across the absence of everything. The emptiness.

Tim cleared his throat.

With a start, she glanced up.

He'd stopped ten feet ahead, hand on a hip, brow cocked. "We going?"

A piece of hair flew in her mouth as she drew breath to speak. She spat it out and shook her head. "It's. Well," she stammered.

"It's what?" An edge in his voice.

"Nothing." She jogged to catch up to him, stomach twisted. Throat thick.

They walked in relative silence, through three more developments slated for demolition and a valley where a rappel tower had once touched the sky, now little more than four gigantic poles and a few scraggly boards. Over a hill and down into the tall grass and mesquites.

At what Tim called range number five, they stopped. He handed Addy the rifle and walked downrange to set up their targets.

Sitting in the dirt, she crossed her legs and laid the rifle over her knees, considering its flat black finish. Its deceptive light weight. The heavy business end.

Dust puffing under his feet, Tim stopped next to her and smiled down. "Did you know," he said, pointing to a spiky plant nearby, "virtually every part of a yucca plant is edible?"

She stood and handed him the rifle. "I did. Edible plants are, were, my job. Did you know," she said, poking him in the shoulder a little harder than she meant, "you can eat the seed pods of mesquite trees?"

Smiling, he poked her back.

Her organs cringed.

He offered her the rifle again. "Wanna go first?"

CHAPTER 4

Jack locked the lower gate and hopped in his electric golf cart.

The crunch of gravel under a foot. Again.

Hand on the hilt of his knife, he put one foot back on the ground and scented the air. Whatever was out there carried no stench. No bubbling. Even so, on the assumption prepared was better than the alternative, he unsheathed the knife and gripped the haft.

"Just me," a voice whispered.

Sheathing the knife, he exhaled. "Celia."

A dark-haired wisp of a thirty-something woman stepped out from behind the house, displacing less dirt than should be possible.

Jack frowned. "Where have you been?"

"Out." Beneath heavy lids, her brown eyes flashed and dared him to question her further.

He motioned her into the golf cart. Jack drove them down the street, swerving to avoid the potholes and cracks, and tried anyway. "It's been three months."

"I told you. I've been out."

"You have to be careful out there. Cure or no, it could still be dangerous."

She bounced along in the passenger seat, hand holding the shade next to her head, mouth pulled into a grimace.

"Celia."

"I'm all growed up, Jack. You don't need to order me around."

"I know that. If I didn't worry, who would?"

Half her mouth turned up. "So, what's been going on?"

Just like that, the conversation about where she'd gone was over.

"I've been roped into heading the Security Committee," he said, brow scrunched.

"Wadeling. *Puta.*" The distaste dripped from her voice like oil from a leaky engine.

"Yeah. We found a 'Head in town a few days back. Also, I figure it'll be easier to keep an eye on his slippery ass like this." Jack squinted up at the mountains.

Celia chuckled. "He figures the same thing about you."

Jack nodded, an image of Wade reaching to readjust non-existent glasses popping into his mind like a jack-in-the-box. *Pop goes the weasel.* He let his foot off the accelerator. "You want to unofficially be an unofficial member of the committee?"

"Thought you'd never ask." Smiling, Celia slid out of the seat. "Sounds like a blast. I'll watch your ass, and you won't even know it."

"Most importantly, Wade won't know it."

Turning to leave, she paused. Swallowed. "You're too late. Something has already started."

The smile that had started on his lips froze. His gut screamed it knew that. But his mouth was slow to catch up. "What're you talking about?"

"I don't know, Jack. Something is going on. It smells around here. Something smells."

"You sure?"

"Just be careful. Watch your back for when I can't." She walked away, speaking over her shoulder. "Don't get so busy being annoyed at him you can't see what's really going on. Keep your nose up."

With that, she crossed the yard of the closest house and hopped over the retaining wall into the ditch before Jack could so much as say goodbye.

He clicked his teeth, sucking air across them like he was tasting wine and repeated her words to himself. "Keep your nose up."

***

Jane kicked a rock. "So Addy, how'd the date go?"

Addy shrugged, walking ahead. "Good. It was good."

She closed her eyes as Jane jogged to catch up, feet slapping the ground.

"Adelaide, are you serious right now?"

Without looking, she pictured Jane's crossed arms. "Don't give me that look."

"What look?"

"That one."

Jane sighed. "I'm not giving you a look." Stopping, she touched Addy's arm.

Addy turned.

She was giving her *a look*. "It's just. Every time, Addy. There's a guy. He's cute. You go out with him. He's not cute anymore."

"That's not even— No I don't." Breaking eye contact, Addy picked at a spot on her shirt. She definitely did.

"Yeah, OK. I'm just saying, if you don't figure this out soon," Jane said, pausing to grip Addy's shoulder with light fingers, "you're going to get left behind on this whole 'repopulating the human race' thing."

Frowning at Jane's hand, Addy shrugged.

"I mean, don't get me wrong," Jane said, walking on. "I'm all for trying out a wide variety, seeing if you can find the best fit."

Addy chuckled. "True."

"But Addy, you have to get past first base. You have *to* get to first base, for god's sake."

"What does that even mean?"

"Figure of speech. That's not the point." Jane elbowed Addy in the rib. "You know what I'm saying."

"Tim's nice, Jane. I like him. Really."

"Promise me you'll try a little harder?" She stopped again.

Glancing at the sun as it continued its march up the sky, Addy sighed. "You'll be late for work. We should go."

Jane kicked another rock. It flew into the dry, brown grass on the side of the road. "That barn stinks like horse shit."

"It's a barn, Jane. It's *made* of horse shit."

Speaking of, the barn came into sight. Just an old airplane hangar, really, but everything had once been something else.

Jane paused, hand on the door. "Did I tell you my parents are coming over tomorrow?"

"Yeah? What's the occasion?"

"They think it's my birthday." She scuffed the ground with a heel.

Jane's frown catching, Addy matched it. "Already? How old will you be again?"

"The hell should I know? It's what they say is the anniversary of the day they found me. That's been sixteen years, I guess. I was like seven or eight or whatever when, you know." She glanced at the horizon. "I lost my other parents."

"We'll make them something special."

"If you're talking about cooking up something special, you know that's all you. If I can't beg or trade it—"

"I know. I know. Then we're not eating it. Yeah. I know, Jane."

Nodding, Jane disappeared into the barn.

Addy spun. And ran face-first into her dad. "Oh! Geez Dad, where did you come from?"

He frowned at her, brow furrowed.

Backing up a step, she saw he wasn't alone. "Hey, Liz, how're you?"

A woman about Dad's age nodded at her, her blonde ponytail swinging. "Good, Adelaide. You?"

"You know."

Elizabeth turned to Dad, hand on his arm. "See you tonight." As she reached out to open the barn door, it swung open with enough force to break her nose. She leapt back and it missed her by an inch.

"Whoa, whoa, whoa, Beth." The raven-haired man stepping out of the barn held his hands in front of him, letting the door close on his shoulder rather than lower them.

Elizabeth slapped him on the other shoulder, one hand on her gun. "Gerald, I don't know how many times I have to tell you not to charge through this door like a bull."

He smiled, showing what seemed like each and every gleaming tooth.

Addy found herself smiling just watching him do it.

"At least one more," he said, smiling at her then Addy as he stepped out of the door's range. It slammed into the frame with a screaming creak of metal.

It set her teeth on edge, hearing that scream resonate through the walls of the barn. But even the ungodly racket didn't distract her from noticing her dad watching Elizabeth watching Gerald.

An uneven feeling rolled through Addy. Had Dad really noticed another human woman?

Drawing her out of her reverie, he touched Addy on the arm. "How's the new place, little girl?"

She gave him a thumbs-up. "There's more guards than we thought. Security twenty-four seven. Isn't that what you say? Twenty-four seven?"

"Mmmm." Dad ran his fingers over his beard where it angled down his chin. Gripping the back of his neck, he rubbed the curls at the base and peeked at Elizabeth again.

Addy cleared her throat.

Dad turned back to her. "I'll come and see it later."

"Jane and I'll be home around dark."

"Maybe tomorrow then. Tonight's the first meeting of this Security Committee thing I'm doing." He nodded to the barn. "Elizabeth's the first official member. And hopefully—"

He waved Gerald over. As Ger walked over, Dad followed Elizabeth's entry into the barn with his eyes.

Addy frowned.

When had Dad become an adult person and not just Dad?

***

Jack parked his cart in front of an adobe building with tiny windows ringing the top and GYM painted on the side in blocky, teal letters.

Funny what they'd brought back since they didn't have to run from the dead every day anymore.

Inside, half a dozen people worked on weights. A couple tossed a medicine ball between them.

He spotted a large blond man toward the corner, jumping rope.

"Andrew," Jack said, angling over.

Hopping on one foot, Andrew spun a circle. He kept spinning the rope. "Jackie. Hey, come to spot me?"

"Not today." Jack sat on the closest weight bench and watched the spinning rope. The thick scent of sweat crept up both nostrils. A bit like grilled onions. "Got a favor to ask you."

The spinning rope slowed. "Sure. Anything." Jaw tight, Andrew angled his chin at his muscled shoulder. A silvery bite mark covered in sweat pinched and lengthened as he spun the rope.

The blood crawled up Jack's cheeks. "You don't owe me anything, Andy."

The rope sped up again. "I do. I always do."

Jack nodded, glancing at the mirrors ringing the wall. Across the open room, someone ran laps back and forth. Back and forth. Practice, preparation, or habit? "I'm doing this Security Committee thing."

"You in it, or in charge of it?" Andrew crossed his arms and the rope in front of him, sweat flying almost far enough to hit Jack.

"In charge of."

He chuckled. "Course you are." He skipped the rope a few times, switching feet. "OK."

"OK?"

"I'm in. Whatever you need."

Jack nodded at the weights next to him. "I need your muscle."

The rope stopped. "Got it. You got it, Jackie." Andrew sat on the bench, bringing a towel with him. Wiping his face, he frowned. "Didn't think you'd ever get involved with that kind of stuff. You didn't seem interested."

His stomach twisted, full of snakes and knots. "I'm not. But the situation arose. And you know as well as I do, they could use someone more security-minded to keep this place in shape."

"I don't know. That thing the other day is a rarity. Otherwise, seems like we've done pretty well so far. Don't you think?"

***

"Yo, Adelaide!"

Shading her eyes, Addy looked for her brother. No one else said *yo*.

Standing on the roof of a house just down the block, he waved an arm over his head.

"Michael? What are you doing up there?"

He crouched, booted feet crunching over the sunburned shingles to a ladder. It hopped against the eave as he swung down onto it, bouncing and taking two rungs at a time.

"Hey, little sis. How you doing today?" Breathless, he grabbed her into a bear-hug and squeezed.

Squeezing him just as tight, even as the breath oozed from her lungs, she closed her eyes and smiled. She'd missed the jerk.

Not that she'd tell him that. Instead, she let him go and stepped back, squinting. "What are you doing back? I thought you were on a cell tower miles away."

Michael nodded, curly dark hair falling onto his forehead. "My boss brought me in. Woulda been here sooner but we had to swing wide around the old hospital."

Addy scrunched her brows, jerking her head back and squashing her chin against her neck. "Why? There's no 'Heads there. Not anymore."

"I know. He says he won't go near the old hospitals. I told him it's totally safe, and anyway, we're big boys. He wouldn't do it. So we're later than we could have been." He clapped Addy on the back, hard enough to make her stumble.

Big boys, indeed. He might be six years older, but sometimes Addy imagined someone got their birth order wrong.

He grinned, bouncing on the balls of his feet. His baby blues, both just like and nothing like their father's, shone. "We got all the towers in the area working. Cell reception should be up to ninety percent."

"I know. You called me last night, remember?" She gestured toward the road. "I've gotta go to work. There's always houses to be torn down. Walk me?" She hooked her elbow, and he snagged it.

The rows of houses they walked between had been readied for demolition. Any appliances and furniture that hadn't rotted to dust had been hauled away for recycling. Paintings, sculptures, knick-knacks too. Though many of the paintings were catalogued and kept in the cool, dry depths of art storage.

Addy had been down there once or twice, helping box and store them. Her dad told her it was important to save them. She wondered why they wasted the kindling.

"I guess with all this power we don't need it," she mumbled.

"What's that, bean?"

She scowled. "Don't call me that. Nothing."

Mike released her arm, digging into a pouch on his belt. Identical to the black pouch on her own belt, it held extra supplies besides just his dose. Fishing out two suckers, he offered her one.

Head shaking, she grinned as he unwrapped one and popped it in his mouth.

"Mmm. Watermelon. I love these," he said, muffled voice sticky as it rounded the edges of the sucker.

"Why are you always wrong about everything? Sour apple is the best." She slapped him in the back of the head.

He punched her shoulder. "Hey! You can't hit your older brother."

As she cocked back to come in for another swing, she caught movement from the corner of her eye. She took a few steps toward it.

"Addy, what—"

"Ssssshhhhhh." She held a finger to her lips.

Mike froze, one foot in the air, eyes wide. He sniffed. "Do you smell it?"

Addy nodded, closing her eyes and breathing deep.

The wind puffed in her face, bringing with it the smell of rot, decay in the black fingertips. Maybe even split, spoiled, and rotting feet.

What it was doing here, another one inside the walls, was a great question.

One she didn't have time for as she pulled her machete from its leather sheath. It whispered into the air, sharp enough to cut it, and she raised it over her shoulder.

Michael produced a crowbar, pointing at the house to their right. The paper stick of the sucker protruding from his mouth.

In silence, they flanked the house with a large cottonwood tree in the back. Addy waited six breaths, long enough for Mike to round the other corner, and peeked out.

Somehow, the Dead Head had gotten tangled in an old dog chain. It bit at the tree as though its next meal was coming from it, and sure enough, as Addy followed its gaze, she spotted a treed cat.

Its shiny tortoise-shell coat gleamed, whiskers beaded with blood. Half a mouse hung from its mouth, and it growled from deep in its throat.

In response, the 'Head groaned, a cicada-like buzzing rattling its chest.

Just buzzing. No bubbling. Seventy-two hours at least. Seventy-two hours since this thing had last taken a living breath.

In its nightclothes, it pulled at the dog chain, links clanking. Long, straight white hair hung down its back in listless sheets, and the skin of its neck was mottled with yellow and purple horizontal stripes.

And it was too far gone to administer the Cure.

Addy swallowed back the gloom that wanted to pop up. Somehow, the 'Head alone in this yard was a little too much like the empty playground from the morning.

Creeping, she and Mike closed in from either side.

The thing looked up at the last moment. Had the eyes been green? They were black now, blood dried in the vessels, the sclera shattered and dead. Like the backs of old puzzle pieces.

Addy raised the machete, ready to chop a leg from under it, when the dog chain lost its grip, releasing the 'Head back into its natural habitat. Coming at Addy's throat.

Off guard, Addy stumbled back, tripped over a hidden sprinkler head, and fell ass over teakettle. The machete skidded away, and a swollen, blackened foot clouded all her vision. The stench of rot unbearable.

She gagged. She always had.

Dry heaving, she kicked at its lower legs. Her foot glanced off one, enough to knock the dead woman back a pace.

Rolling to the machete, Addy snagged it. She stood and swung a full circle with it. Centrifugal force and gravity pulled the blade into the arm of the thing, and at the last second, she flicked her wrist. Just like her mom had taught her.

It stuck in bone, and she wiggled it, ignoring the thrumming handle.

Stinking breath, filled with rotting blood, pushed itself up her nose and down her throat.

As she bent sideways, fighting another dry heave, Michael swept across with the crowbar, hooking the thing across its shoulders. He produced a hammer in the other hand, and as he jerked the crowbar, he hit it in the jaw with the hammer.

It fell, taking the crowbar with it.

The buzzing cicada sound never wavered. Never stopped. It buzzed and buzzed as it fell. It rolled its head in the dirt, scraping half the skin from a dead cheek.

Mike, freeing the crowbar, raised the claw side of the hammer for another blow to the head.

Addy held a hand up and worked her machete free.

His breath ragged and strained, Mike smiled around the lollipop still wedged between his teeth and cheek. "Be my guest, bean."

"Don't call me that," Addy said, using gravity to drive the machete into the skull.

The buzzing continued.

She pried it loose and dropped it again. Repeated. It was a bit like cutting buzzing wood.

The blood had been seeping away from the head for days, and each time she hit it, it sounded like a dried-up pumpkin. Days past carving.

Thunk. No more buzz.

Addy lowered the machete into its skull one more time for good measure, clipping herself on the knee.

As she inspected the new cut, bloodying her favorite pants, she caught movement in her peripheral. Using only her eyes, she tracked the cat scratching its way down the tree.

It planted the dead mouse at her foot and sat.

Chapter 5

Jack nodded to his guests.

Except Celia, who had opted to attend the first Security Committee meeting from outside. Across the street. Via binocular. He'd even dug up and set out a baby monitor for her so she could listen in.

Elizabeth sat next to Jack, one leg cocked up onto the corner of the kitchen table. Gerald and Andrew took up the other side of the rectangle. Before each of them was a glass of cold, clear water. With ice cubes.

Might not ever get used to having cold, iced water again.

"You all know why we're here," Jack said, standing to pace.

His feet like balloons inside his busted cowboy boots, his heels echoed too loud off the tile. He sat again. "Wade's asked me to head the Security Committee, and the first thing we need to do—"

He broke off, looking out the window. Sunset was coming again. Too soon for the night to fall. But it did every day. Every day…

Andrew cleared his throat.

Jack began again. "Wade's asked me, in his official capacity as mayor and in consideration of the 'Head they found a few days ago, to head the Security Committee. Mostly we're to oversee the Dead Head Task Force, make sure their training is current, run them through drills, that sort of thing."

Gerald sat back, chair creaking. "That doesn't sound terribly exciting."

"No, Ger, it doesn't. But I don't expect it to take too much time away from doctoring the animals."

"That's a full-time job in itself," Gerald said.

Elizabeth frowned. "I've got doubles to work, Jack."

"Not anymore. I got your shifts changed. Just regular shifts from now on."

Her leg jumped from the table, heel stomping the floor. Jack winced.

"Someone has to clean the horseshit out of the stalls. Someone has to bathe them. Brush them. Who the hell else is going to—"

Jack laid his hand over hers and squeezed. "It's OK, Liz. It's OK." He lowered the register of his voice, rubbing the back of her hand.

Glaring at him, she balled her fist. But she closed her mouth, flared her nostrils, and sucked a breath in. "Fine. Fine."

Jack nodded, glancing to Andy and Ger.

"We're here because I wanted everyone to know what everyone else was doing. Give us all a chance to check in with each other. Make sure the air is clear." He paused, eyes landing on each of his friends in turn. These were the people he trusted most, with the exception of his kids.

Still, he hesitated. Dropping his eyes to study the scratched surface of his kitchen table, he scraped it with a thumbnail.

"What is it?" Ger asked, tilting his head to the right. Like always.

"Wade wants us to report any lawbreaking or transgressions to him immediately. What I want from you, above all the other jobs I just talked about, is your eyes and ears."

Elizabeth made a noise deep in the back of her throat. "You want us to be Wade's spies? Are you joking?"

"I'd like to think you all know me better than that. No. I want you to be *my* spies. Andrew, you're my muscle."

Andrew, nodding, crossed his massive forearms. "'Course I am."

Jack turned to Elizabeth. "Liz," he said, touching her hand again, "you are so fast with a weapon you make my head spin."

Make my head spin for other reasons, too.

"And you know when to watch, when to listen, and when to act. I need you in this," he said, leaning forward.

Half a smile ghosted her lips. "You got it. You know that."
She pointed at Ger. "You want him because he's got the skills."

Ger laughed, leaning toward her. "Skills that pays the bills,
sweetheart." Pointing a finger at her, making an invisible gun, he
clicked his tongue and winked.

Andrew chuckled. "You're an idiot, Ger."

"Beat me to it, big guy," Liz said, smile in her voice
apparent.

"Yeah, yeah," Jack said, shaking his head. He smiled.
Something electric crackled in the air when they were together,
filling him with light. A sense of purpose.

"Gerald," he said, "you're the best investigator I know. And
you never know when we'll need medical knowledge. I know
you're a vet, not a doctor. But you're smart. Listen." He crossed
his arms on the table. "I think something is going on here. I
don't know if you can smell the under-stink, but it's worse than
balls on a summer day. We've got—"

A light, rhythmic clicking began in the living room, inside
the cavern of the dead grandfather clock. A tiny echo.

Jack sat up straight, sniffing and holding a finger in the air.
The wait-a-minute finger.

The clicking continued, just above audible.

From behind the fridge, a small red light flashed in time with
the clicking. One tiny LED.

He spoke from the side of his mouth.

"Proximity alarm."

***

Standing at the window, fidgeting with her Bowie knife, Addy
tracked Michael and another man through the gate outside. Sun
slanting through the trees, the man walking with Mike was little
more than a shadow. Mike carried a bundle in his arms.

They disappeared inside.

Jane spoke from the couch, knitting needles clicking. "Tell
me again why you haven't told Jack about the 'Head."

Addy grimaced, staring down into the darkening yard. "You know as well as I do, he'd just freak out. And try to make me move back in." Her stomach clenched. She'd spent her whole life under his watchful eye. And it was great. She was alive. But for months, all she'd wanted was a little time to figure out life as it was now, in this village, with these people. And all he wanted was for her to stay in her room where it was safe.

The wooden floor of the hallway creaked.

Knock.

Pause.

Knock knock.

Their secret knock. About as imaginative as Mike, but also as sturdy and agreeable. Predictable but comforting. Just like Mike.

Passing Jane on her way to the door, Addy bumped the couch. "You're closer to the door, you know."

Jane chuckled. "Not anymore."

Addy swung the door wide. "About time you got here."

"Bean!"

"Don't call me that." She squinted. "Is that my cat?"

The sound of Jane's needles ceased. "Your what?"

Addy pursed her lips. "My cat. I can't help it. She adopted me." She took the cat from Mike and glanced at the stranger.

Tall, green-eyed, silent stranger.

She motioned them inside as the cat began to purr.

The newcomer closed the door behind them., Bolted it. Bolted the second lock. Put up the chain. And the crossbar.

Addy frowned. "We usually save the whole production for bedtime. Um, who are you?"

Mike started, "Sorry, Addy. This is Dean, my boss I mentioned before. Dean, this is my sister Adelaide, our friend Jane over there on the couch. Addy's cat you've met."

Scratching the cat between the ears, Dean stuck out his other hand.

Taking it with the wrong hand, the one not holding the cat, Addy offered a jittering shake to his firm up-and-down pump.

It was a good handshake.

His. Not hers so much.

Awkwardness accomplished, Addy sat the cat down. "Come in, guys. Have a seat. I was just about to make some food. You hungry?"

"Oh no, we couldn't—" Dean began, his deep tenor tinged with an accent. Southern, maybe.

"That sounds great," Mike said, heading for the couch. He tapped Jane's foot.

She moved an inch.

He shrugged and sat.

"Ouch! That's my foot, Michael."

"You didn't move it, so I sat on it," he said. But as he spoke, he lifted up enough for her to pull her feet out.

"Your dad tell you I said hi?" Curling her feet under her, she went back to the knitting.

Idly curious if it was a scarf or a hat she was making, Addy walked into the kitchen. Between the cabinets and countertop, all she could see of Dean was a stiff torso wearing a pea green Army-issue jacket. He fidgeted and cleared his throat.

She leaned down onto the bar, head beneath the cabinets.

Those green eyes turned to her again.

"You can come in here if you want. I'll just be a few."

Getting two dishes out for the nameless cat, she filled one with water. Turning to set them in the floor, she ran the bowl directly into Dean's midsection.

She gasped, water flying.

"Whoa," he said, holding his hands out.

She grabbed the towel hanging over the side of the sink and patted his shirt dry. "Where did you come from? Why were you standing so close? I—" She paused, looking up. "Oh crap, I'm so sorry."

He smiled.

It was far sunnier than she'd imagined it would be.

"It's OK, Adelaide. Here." He took the towel, drying his face. "You do…whatever it is you were doing. It's my fault."

Glancing down, she noticed she'd even managed to soak his boots with cat water.

Cheeks flushing, she chattered about whatever her mind spit at her.

"So, the Dead Head, right, it's all stuck in this dog chain. Which, now that I think of it, is kind of hilarious because there's this cat up in the tree, just like if it had been a dog on the chain, and it's got this mouse. Like, half chewed with guts and all, and the 'Head is just down there, like, you know, doing that thing they do, and—"

"Adelaide. Addy. Hey, whoa," Dean said, reaching for her hand.

She'd been trying to get the bowl back to the sink but had gotten so distracted with her ramblings she'd been talking with her hands, waving the bowl everywhere and spraying the kitchen with what water remained in the bottom of it. And some had splashed his face. Again.

She dropped her arms, frowning at the ground. One day maybe she wouldn't break everything she touched.

Her cat sauntered into the kitchen and wound around her ankle.

She patted her, scratching all the way to the base of her tail. "Oh, I know."

"What do you know?" Jane called.

Addy stood.

Jane and Mike were on the couch talking, probably didn't even notice what had happened. Typical.

"Beverly. Her name is Beverly."

***

"Jack," Andrew whispered.

Still facing the living room, Jack cocked his head.

"How close do they have to be to trip the alarm?"

"A hundred feet from the outer front door. Fifty feet from the walls downstairs. The only way upstairs is the one door. We're cut off from the bottom floor." He eased from his chair and crept to the living room.

His friends followed, no louder than mice.

Removing his gun from its holster, he counted clicks. Five, a pause, five more.

"It's the front," he whispered.

Orange light fell through the blinds, carpeting the floor in a zebra-striped arc-sodium glow. Tiptoeing around the light, Jack paused. "Andrew. Check the periscope. See who's out there if you can. I'm going to the front window. See if I can get a clear line."

It's not even a Dead Head anyway, Jackson.

He frowned. His dead wife didn't talk to him as much as she used to, but when she did, she was always right.

Still. Can't be too careful.

Yes, you can. Don't be stupid. You're going to shoot someone you know one day.

She'd been gone what. Eight? Ten years? Twelve? Time just wasn't the same anymore. Let's see. Addy was now twenty-three, and she was twelve then, so—

"It's Adelaide," Andrew said, his voice muffled by the wall.

Jack lowered his gun. It had been pointed directly where Addy would be standing at the foot of the steps. The sun had set, his daughter just another shape out there in the dark.

As usual, Melinda had been right.

He holstered his gun and stalked to the door on tent poles. Disabling the alarm, he nodded to Andrew, stepped past him, and unbarred the door. Unbolted a dead bolt. And the other. Pulled the bolts from the floor and top of the door.

Of course, none of it mattered if the dead got all the way up here, not really.

But they didn't generally get inside the village. That's what the Task Force was for. That and the walls, the fences, the traps.

And the Cure.

Peeking out the door, he shone his penlight down the stairs. Addy and a man he didn't know stood at the bottom. He spun the handle and the silent hinge lowered the trip wires. He stepped onto the porch, shining the light into the man's eyes.

"Addy," Jack said.

The strange man put a hand up against the light, squinting. Muscular shoulders hid under his green Army-issue jacket, the outline of a gun poked from under his armpit. The pommel of a knife stuck out of his belt.

Well armed. So there was that.

"I need to talk to you, Dad. Come open the gate. I don't have my key anymore."

"Good thing, too," Jack said, opening the top gate and descending. Leaving the light pointed into the man's eyes, he frowned. "I might've shot you before I knew it was you."

"How many times have we talked about this? Think first, shoot later."

Jack stopped on the bottom step and sighed. Lowering the light, he opened the gate.

"Dad, this is Dean. He—"

"He better watch his ass. Dead Heads aren't the only thing I shoot. Men who mess with my daughter got a bullet with their name on it, too," Jack interrupted, eyes narrowed.

Addy put a hand on his wrist. *"Dad."*

Jack glowered at Dean a moment longer, then glanced at his little daughter, face smoothing.

She was twelve when she lost her mom. Eleven years ago. Closing in on twelve.

About time to be getting on with your life, Jack.

Addy squinted at him, smiled, and lowered her hand. "This is Mike's boss, Dean. He wouldn't let me come alone. Mike is back at the apartment with Jane. I need to talk to you about something Mike and I saw today. Can we come up?"

***

Staring out the kitchen window with her arms crossed, Addy relayed the story of the Dead Head, ending with the cat. "So anyway, I guess I got a cat out of it. I named her—"

"Little girl," Dad interrupted, "when did you plan to tell me this?"

Addy met his eyes. Heat rose in her cheeks. "Tomorrow, I guess. Dean, he thought we should come tonight. So. Here we are."

She glanced at Dean, who stood in the corner of the room, leaning against the wall. He hadn't said more than four words since they'd come in, mostly about how he'd rather stand, but she could feel him watching. His bright green eyes never stilled, always searching for input.

She wished he'd sit. She couldn't stand to sit if everyone else wasn't. It made them feel uneven somehow. On different levels.

"Adelaide," Dad said, "I'm in charge of security now, for one thing. You should definitely have told me. You ought to have come sooner. Dean did the right thing."

Addy felt more than saw a shift in Dean's posture. He loosened maybe three micrometers. Praise from her dad could do that to people.

She gripped her upper arms, turning away from them all again. "It was no big deal. One 'Head, tangled up. It took us like five seconds."

Gerald jumped into the conversation, his voice low and soft. "How fresh was it?"

"Three days. Give or take an hour or two."

"Are you sure about the time?"

Addy's mouth opened, but her dad cut her short.

"My daughter knows this better than any of us, Ger. If she says three days, it was three days." A smile raised one side of Dad's scruffy beard. "She's got a talent for it."

"I'd like to take a look at it, Jack. Would that be OK?" Ger asked.

"We are not going at night, Gerald. Not all of us." Dad glanced at Addy, eyebrow cocked.

Addy stepped away from the window, fist balled. She didn't see Dean move, but there he was, holding a hand toward her.

"I see you wantin' to fight. But go with him on this one."

She glared, mouth turned into an upside-down U. "You stay here if you want. I'm going."

Dean reached for her.

She snatched her arm away and glared at her dad. "I'm going."

Dad stood. "Andrew and Dean will stay here with you. Just tell us where you found it, exactly. We'll take care of the rest."

Addy exhaled, a long, slow, thoughtful affair. Her dad could be as stubborn as she was when he wanted.

Someone had to give first.

With a grimace, she explained where they'd been, drawing an imaginary map on the table with her finger to illustrate.

"And don't forget, there's a big, noisy cottonwood in the back yard."

***

Addy gnawed at a thumbnail. Tiny little shards poked her in the tongue.

Dean paced. He must've been good at it; he hadn't stopped since her dad left.

From the depths of her favorite chair, the only thing she'd left behind, she sighed. "Could you maybe sit down?"

He stopped, hand on his chin, staring down at her.

"Please?"

He sat on the couch. "Sorry, I'm just. I wish I'd gone."

She shrugged. "Dad's got it."

He shook his head. "Your brother, Mike, he's a smart guy."

She glanced up to find him staring at her, brow raised.

"Uh. Thanks?"

He kept staring like he was expecting something else. More.

She nodded.

He chuckled and leaned back. "He tells me you killed it. Practically took it apart, from what he says. You do that?"

Addy grinned. Mike telling stories again. "Yeah. I guess. It really wasn't a big deal. It was all bound up for most of it anyway."

"Yeah, but it was pretty fresh. Three days?"

Addy nodded.

Dean leaned forward, palms meeting between his knees. "Where do you think it came from? Only three days? It couldn't have been far."

Her brow creased. Not that she hadn't thought of it like that, but…she hadn't thought of it like that. She sat forward too, elbows on her knees and chin on her fists.

Dean leaned so close she felt the heat coming off his leg.

"Damn, I don't know. The old town?" She shook her head. Even as she said it, it made no sense.

"Adelaide, you know that doesn't make sense," Andrew piped in from behind her in the kitchen.

She jumped two feet if she jumped a day. She'd forgotten he was in there. Nodding, she combed through options.

"It could have been—"

"Someone from the village," Dean finished for her.

She let a smile just touch her lips. "That's true. But that doesn't make sense either."

"Sure it does. The question isn't how did someone from the village get to be a Dead Head."

"The question is, how did they go unnoticed for three days?"

Dean leaned back, throwing his arm over the back of the couch. The spot where his lower jaw met his upper bulged and contracted as he clenched and unclenched his teeth. "This is a pretty small village. I don't live here half the time, so I don't really know everyone. But there aren't so many people that everyone doesn't know someone."

Addy nodded, leaning back and closing her eyes. "Someone missed her. Someone noticed." The inside of her eyelids stung.

She blinked three or four times in quick succession and leaned into the back of the chair as far as she could go, pressing her head into the cushioned shadows.

"So the other question is, why didn't someone say something?" Dean asked.

A chair in the kitchen creaked. "Maybe they did," Andrew said, his feet clunking on the tile until he reached the throw rug in the living room. His steps turned into muffled thunks. He stopped next to Addy's chair.

She brushed both hands up her face, for all intents looking like she was rubbing it as she dried the corners of her eyes.

Dropping her hands, she stood. "Yeah, maybe. Don't you think my dad would have heard of it, though?"

Andrew shook his head. "Addy, I think—"

Dad's proximity alarms began their soft alert. *Tick tick tick.*

Dean sat up. "Do you think it's them?" In one motion, he stood and unholstered, his gun in his hand before Addy had really seen him draw.

Admiring his speed, she gripped the handle of her knife.

"Could be," Andrew said. He towered over them both as he strode to the front door, squinting through the periscope. "There's no one." He peeked out the closest window. "It must be in back."

The sound of muffled gunfire, the echo itself louder than the shot, drove them all to the ground.

Addy bumped her head on the floor, the carpet padding the worst of it. She grunted.

Dean, brow creased, mouthed, *"You OK?"*

She nodded, rubbing the spot she'd bumped.

The clock *tick, tick, ticked.*

Andrew crawled to the window and stared down at the driveway. Fogging the glass in front of him, he exhaled through his nose. "They're coming in hot." He crouch-walked to the door, reaching for the bolts.

"There's no time for that," Addy said, banging her elbow on the ground, jumping to her feet, and running into the kitchen while bent at the waist.

Dropping her knife on the tile, whenever it was she'd unsheathed it, she opened the cabinet below the sink and pulled out a bundle of chain. She called for Dean. Someone might be close, but her dad needed this ladder more than she needed to be quiet.

"Yeah." Right behind her.

"Open that window," she said, pointing to the one over the sink. As he did, she crawled under the sink and hooked the ladder to a thick metal pipe that ran the length beneath it. She backed out, unrolling the first rung. "OK, help me with this."

Dean grabbed one side of the ladder, helping her unroll it toward the window.

Once they reached the sill, she gave a quick three-count and they tossed. It unrolled, chains clinking against each other, the side of the house, and finally the ground.

Addy leaned over the sink and poked her head out the window to watch them approach.

Her dad in the lead, Ger and Liz just behind, Ger's hand between her shoulder blades.

Addy opened her mouth to shout at them, but someone gripped her shoulder. Stumbling back from the window, she ran into the table.

She rounded on Dean. "What do you think you're doing?" Whispering be damned.

"We don't know where that shot came from. Or who's out there. You need to stay back." He'd dropped the whispering too, but refrained from shouting.

As she stood, rubbing her hip where it'd smacked the table, the chain clanked against the house. Elizabeth appeared in the window.

Andrew pushed Addy out of the way and pulled Liz through the window in one motion.

The ladder clanged against the house like it was in a hurricane.

Gerald fell into the windowsill, blood soaking his shirt high up on his shoulder. Andrew helped him through, and Addy waited for the clanking chains to reveal her dad.

And waited.

Waited.

Where was he?

The chains stayed still.

She approached the window, shrugging Dean off when he tried to grab her again. She peeked out.

Dad stood, one foot on the ground, one on the first rung. As one hand held the rung above his head, the other pointed his gun into the dark. Not moving, he seemed to taste the air.

Addy glanced into the night, the air silver and still. No movement had followed them back, no sound, no smell. She opened her mouth to shout down, reconsidered, and closed it. Her dad would know when to come up.

***

Before crossing the sill and climbing into the kitchen sink, Jack glanced out to the horizon again and sniffed.

"Dad."

He turned his head, his sweet baby daughter staring at him with her eyes wide and looking like her mom. So beautiful yet hard. Harder than even he probably was. This Dean better look out.

"Yeah, baby girl, help me in." He stuck a hand out, and she took it, hauling him in with strength and speed. He felt more than heard his shoulder scream against the strain.

As he hopped off the counter, his knees almost spilled him to the floor.

Andrew, with the speed of a snake, caught and steadied him.

Jack patted him on the shoulder. "Thanks, man."

Nodding, Andrew let him go and sat.

Accounting for everyone, his eye fell on Liz.

She chewed a nail, staring at Ger with undisguised affection and concern in equal parts.

And now he saw what he should have seen before. He wasn't alone in his regard for her. And it was Ger she'd noticed, not him.

Getting old and slow there, Jackson.

He stared at the blood drenching Ger's shirt. "You alright, Ger?"

Ger nodded, hands already busy. He yanked a small syringe from a pouch clipped to his belt and bit down on the plastic tip.

He unsheathed the needle, the tiny syringe sparkling with a calm, golden liquid.

The room stopped as Ger lifted his shirt and delivered the intramuscular dose of Cure.

Jack didn't know he'd been holding his breath until a slow, hot exhalation escaped over his tight lips.

Ger slumped into a chair, head hanging between his knees.

"Let's get these shades closed," Jack said.

Andrew and Dean pulled the ladder in as the rest of them prowled the kitchen and living room, drawing the blackout shades.

As Andrew stowed the ladder back in its place under the sink, Jack watched the yard. Celia was still out there, impossible to spot.

He removed the penlight from his pocket and tapped "*come in*" in Morse.

Her light flashed back. Long, long, long. Pause. Long, short, long. "*OK*."

Lowering the shade, he spoke to his daughter. "Are you sure it was dead?"

Addy blinked. Nodded.

Of course she was sure. Stupid question.

He stalked to the front door, dropped the trip wires, and opened both gates. He waited, the night smelling of green mesquite.

Celia appeared from the dark, holstering her handgun. She followed Jack up the stairs but didn't enter the house until he'd locked back up and preceded her into the living room.

Andrew exhaled through his nose, Liz sighed, and Gerald laughed.

He'd had his reasons to keep her involvement quiet, and they had all presented themselves at the same time. Exasperation, disapproval, and incredulity.

Much as he loved each of his friends, none of them liked Celia.

"Mmm. My favorite people." Celia sighed, throwing her legs over the arm of the couch one at a time. Sitting on the arm, her boots hardly depressed the cushion.

Addy sat next to her, throwing an arm over Celia's knees.

Celia grinned. "How you been, kid?"

"You know."

Celia nodded.

Elizabeth, taking a seat as far away from Celia as she could, narrowed her eyes.

Gerald followed, pulling the chair from under the desk and straddling it backward.

As Jack took Addy's chair, Dean and Andrew fought over who would get to stand.

Beating Andrew to the punch, Dean sat in the floor.

Jack's suspicions of Dean grew. Clearly, he already liked his little girl. Otherwise, he would have sat next to her.

Addy, oblivious, leaned back into the couch and crossed one leg over the other. "What happened out there, Dad? We heard a gunshot, and the proximity alarm went off before you ever got close."

"About the alarm, little girl, I don't know. But I think Celia can tell you about the gunshot," he said. He glanced at the small woman.

Staring, resting bitch face turned up to eleven, she sighed. "I got to where you and Mike saw that 'Head before your dad did. There was nothing there."

Jack nodded.

Addy shot to her feet. "That's not possible. Where did it go? We left it there. Dad?"

"I don't know, honey. That's why I asked if it was dead."

"There's a lot of things I'm not very good at. But killing Dead Heads is something I am good at doing." She swallowed. "It was dead. I'm one hundred percent."

"I believe you," Jack said. "I just had to ask."

Gerald gave him a single, crisp nod. "I'll go over there during the day. There should be some clue. I'll run it down."

Addy crossed her arms and sat. "Then what was that gunshot?"

"Celia's a good shot," Jack said.

Celia grinned with one corner of her mouth. "There was a 'Head behind them. I doubled back to tail them, and almost got it in time." She gestured at Gerald. "It bit him before they saw it. Sneaky fucker."

Gerald shrugged, blood oozing from the bite. "I'm good. I had my dose of the Cure ready. No big deal. For all your faults, Jack's right. You're a good shot."

Celia scowled, heavy lids low.

Addy opened her mouth.

Jack beat her to the punch. Sometimes it was the only way to get a word in. "I promise you, we will find out where they're coming from. And we'll plug the hole." He smiled, struggling to let it reach his eyes. "This is your Security Committee now. We won't let anything happen. To you, or to this village."

Addy frowned. "You don't know that."

His throat began to close around a lump that hadn't been there a moment ago. He'd made the same promise to her mom eons ago.

He had to promise her, though. That's what you did. You made the promise and you did everything you could to keep it.

"Dean," he said.

Dean stood. "Sir."

"Make sure my daughter gets home safe. It's dangerous out there tonight."

CHAPTER 6

Addy and Jane stood in the window, following Mike and Dean's exit across the parking lot and out the gate.

"Girl, that Dean could polish my knives any day," Jane said.

Flopping on the couch, Addy clicked her tongue. "I bet he could."

Chuckling, Jane dropped next to her and picked up her knitting. "What'd your dad say about the 'Head?"

"They didn't find it."

For once, Jane's needles stopped. "They what?"

Addy relayed the story from start to finish, leaving out all the times she'd run into things. Or fallen down. Hit her head.

"Jesus, Adelaide, is Jack OK?"

"Dad's fine. He's fine. They're all fine."

Exhaling through her nose, Jane picked up her needles again.

"Jane."

She nodded.

"Why are you making a hat in the middle of spring?"

Jane's lips drew into a fine line. "I get cold easy."

Addy lay her head back and closed her eyes. A warm lump hit her in the lap and began purring.

Scratching her cat, Addy floated, flashes of light going off inside her eyelids.

$$* \, * \, *$$

Lying in the grass with your eyes closed, the insides of your eyelids are red where the sun hits them.

The shadow of the tree above you interrupts the sun sometimes and it goes dark.

Mom hums, clothespins going snip-snap *as she hangs clean sheets and clips them into place. They ripple in the wind, and you catch the scent of fresh, sun-warmed soap.*

Basket empty, Mom lies in the grass next to you.

You turn to her, grass scratching on your cheek. There is no concept of time in your mind as you lie there, studying her pretty face in the sun.

She takes your hand and you both lie there, the smell of sheets and sunshine in your nose. Light as the air that blows through the flapping sheets.

But then.

The smell.

Interrupted by the smell. You know the one. The one that's always there.

Always been there.

Will always be there.

The one you wish you could scrub from the inside of your brain. You'd use steel wool if you thought it would help.

Rotted death, come to tear down the sheets and your life and your happiness and your innocence and everything you love.

It's quick, but your mom is quicker.

The fence is broken again and now there's bloody finger claws in the clean sheets.

But bouncing on your mom's hip, you're inside before it even has time to know you were there.

It's quick, but your mom is quicker.

She's always quicker.

* * *

Addy opened her eyes.

Beverly slept on her lap, still purring.

And Jane next to her, knitting the ear flaps on that ridiculous yellow and brown hat.

With a frown, Addy booted the cat off her lap. "I'm going to bed."

Jane's mouth turned up, the tiniest of smile lines appearing next to the right corner. "Make sure you know who you want to dream of, my dear. Tim or Dean. I'll take the other one."

Addy grinned back. "What about Mike? I thought you liked him?"

Jane's needles stopped moving. Lowering the hat to her lap, she stared down at it. "I don't want to talk about it."

Addy's brow creased, her stomach doing a flip-flop. Usually, the girl would crack a joke, become Scottish, something. Considering silence was a new one, Addy wasn't sure how to take it. But Jane hated pussyfooting.

"Jane, look, I know he likes you. He's liked you forever."

Jane shook her head, hair falling in her eyes. She threw it aside. "I don't want to talk about it," she repeated.

"Really Jane, I—"

"I don't want to talk about it, Addy," she said, knocking the knitting aside. It fell to the floor as she stood, glaring. She marched into her room without another word.

Addy watched Beverly, who batted at the yarn ball. It rolled across the floor.

"The hell got into her britches?"

***

"Need to get that cat a litter pan."

Addy snorted, lifting her chin from her chest. The sounds of the Enterprise D played in the background on a loop.

Jane leaned over the back of the couch, her face sideways. "Fell asleep out here, huh? Left that thing on, too," she said, angling her chin at the TV.

Addy wiped drool from her chest and rolled her neck. She grinned. "Been a long time since I've fallen asleep on the couch." She uncrossed her feet and set them in the floor. One of them was pins and needles. Best to sit for a minute instead of trying to walk on it.

Jane bumped the couch, unbarred the door, and walked out with Beverly cradled in her left arm.

Addy rubbed her leg, the blood rushing through nerve endings, the pins and needles so painful she hesitated to move. Slapping at it, the pain reassured her she was still alive.

It was good to feel alive. Most of the time.

Grumbling, Jane came back up alone.

"Did you leave her down there?" Addy shook her foot.

"You're damn right I did. You can bring her in. But I was not standing there"—she pointed out the window—"waiting for her to do her cat business. She might be the prettiest damn calico cat I've ever seen, but I am not waiting for her to get it done." Her nostrils flared, eyes lighting up. The blood rushed to her face, reddening her pale cheeks.

Addy chuckled. It was fun to get her all riled up. But she relented. "OK, alright, we'll get a litter pan."

After breakfast, Addy scooped some leftover eggs into a bowl. As she put on her boots, Jane laughed from the kitchen. A soft little laugh Addy wasn't sure she was supposed to hear.

"You know what Mike told me last night?"

Addy's fingers paused over her laces. "No. What?" Maybe this was what led to Jane's outburst before bed. Addy held her breath.

"He said they used to buy eggs from the store all the time. They were already a month old when they got them! Can you imagine?" She snorted.

Addy sighed. She finished tying up her boots. "How did you not know that?"

"Never came up."

About half a million things went through her mind. How Jane and Mike talked about weird things. How Mike was stupid about her, and about how Jane always seemed to like him. Telling their dad to say hi to him all the time. Why had she gotten so upset at the suggestion of a relationship with him?

She didn't actually say any of it. What she said instead was, "I'm going to go get the cat. See you in a minute."

Outside, the bright sun cast long morning shadows Addy hurried to get into. Their apartment, with its north-facing windows, had to be at least twenty degrees cooler than it was in the sun.

Creeping around the same corner she'd last seen in the dark, she called the cat. "Beverly, kitty kitty," she said, her voice lilting up and down in a singsong. Something her mom had done the few times they'd had animals. They'd had a cat when her mom—

Well.

It'd been a while.

Tapping the side of the bowl of eggs, she crunched across dry grass.

Ah, here was a mess of feathers. The pile of feathers in one place, they formed a semicircle around what used to be a round little body. Wings and head were all that remained.

Addy knelt and picked up a feather. Sniffed it. Checked the quill. With the blood still wet, the cat couldn't be far.

"Kitty kitty kitty?"

Back here on the west side, it was all shadow and morning. It still smelled fresh, the dirt not yet hot and baked like it would be in a few hours. The sky was as clear as clean glass, not a blemish in the perfect—

"Mrow?" Beverly called back.

Addy smiled. She approached her cat and neared the spot where she'd stood the other night, listening for something that bumped against the chain-link, stinking like the carcass of a dead fox who'd lain in the woods three weeks too long.

The cat rubbed against the fence, up and back, up and back, arching her back as Addy approached.

Setting the bowl of eggs down, the stench of rotted flesh brushed past her nose.

Addy stopped and looked at the fence.

Caught between some of the razor wire on the other side, a chunk of flesh.

Dead, blackened flesh.

Her pins and needles came back.

***

Jack leaned on the shiny metal table. "So what you're telling me, is this one, the one that bit you last night, is less than three days dead."

"That's what I'm telling you." Gerald lowered the disposable doctor's mask, leaving fingerprints in rusty-colored blood on the paper.

Rather than wasting a paper mask, Jack had tied a bandanna around his nose and mouth.

He hid behind it. Just looking at the putrid mess on Gerald's autopsy table was enough to make him want to back out, puke first.

He swallowed. "OK. So what I need to know is one, who was it?"

Gerald nodded. Not in a gesture of knowledge, but more of a go on.

"Two, how did it get dead?"

Same nod.

"Three, find out who's missing him. Someone is. You cover the first two. That last one I'll do."

Gerald's close-cropped black beard pulled into a grimace. He cupped his chin and stared, his other hand trailing across the patch under his shirt.

"Hey, Ger, your gauze is soaking through." Bites took forever to heal, bleeding almost constantly for a day or two. Something about anticoagulant in the saliva.

At least, that was the running theory.

Ger frowned, turning his head at an awkward angle to look at his bleeding shoulder. He grunted. "Let me change this. Then I'll get into this autopsy."

"I'm going to get some interviews done and check in on the Task Force." Heading toward the door, Jack stopped. "You charge your phone today?"

Gerald chuckle-snorted, nodding. "Never thought I'd see those stupid things again. But yeah," he said, pulling an ancient flip phone halfway from his front pocket, "I got it with me."

"Good. My son has most of the towers around here working, so we should be able to use them pretty consistently." Jack turned back to the door.

Without invitation, the scene around the kitchen table last night splashed across his mind. Ger giving himself the shot. Elizabeth watching him with concern. Affection.

He stopped, one hand on the knob, and stared at the door. "So, you and Liz."

Autopsy tools clanked. "Yeah."

Jack nodded, still facing the door, heart pounding in his chest. He didn't have to see the smile to hear it in Ger's voice.

"Good. That's, that's good."

"Sure. She's a wonderful lady. I'm a lucky man."

Jack closed his eyes.

His mind had picked a fine time to finally remind him there were women in the world besides Melinda. A fine time to tell his heart it was alright to let go of his dead wife and move on.

He looked over his shoulder. "You are. Call me when you have something."

Jerking the door open, the rectangle of light blinded him. He stepped out into it, pulling the door closed without another look at his friend.

He could be, should be, had to be happy for him. Ger deserved it.

***

"Mrow?"

Adelaide, knees in the spiky grass, pushed her face against the cold chain-link.

Sniffed.

The dead skin flapped in a slight breeze, wafting the somehow sweet scent of decay into her nostrils.

It had come from a 'Head. Two days dead at least.

The cat rubbed against her leg, destabilizing her. Addy tried to shoo her.

"Addy?"

Distracted, she lost her balance, ass falling to the dirt. Sharp, dried grass poked its way through her jeans and into her legs.

Scowling, she glanced up.

A handsome young man reached a hand down.

She took Tim's hand and stood, managing to keep her cheeks from flaming completely into magenta. Brushing the back of her pants with one hand, she considered what to do with the other.

Tim still had it.

Take it back? Leave it? Kinda, just, twitch it and see what he does? And now it was sweating. Of course.

"Tim, mornello," she stuttered.

The corner of his mouth raised, brows drawn together. Squeezing her hand once, he let it go.

She wiped her palm on her jeans, desperate to dry the sweat. "I mean, good morning. Hello." She sketched half a wave.

His brown eyes cool, he crossed his arms.

Her brain suddenly convinced her knees even though he liked her, it didn't mean he didn't laugh at her when she wasn't around. Half her mouth smiled, her stomach slick.

"Addy, what are you doing back here this morning?" He smiled again. Nothing but pure sunshine.

She stuffed the doubts. "Oh, just looking for my cat."

"You have a cat?"

"She's new. She ate a bird, wanna see?" Addy pointed, feet moving toward the desiccated pile of feathers.

"Uh, no thanks. Good to know she's a hunter," he said, fingers grasping Addy's sleeve. He locked his eyes on hers. "A survivor. Like you."

Addy's heart skipped up into her throat. She might have smiled, but it wasn't exactly like she could feel her face. Maybe? She could be making the puking face right now. She'd never know.

Tim leaned close to her, close enough for her to smell the soap on his skin.

So strange they all took showers so often. Who had started that? Probably people her dad's age. There had been showers every day for them, before the dead took over. Now they'd taken things back from the dead and it was showers all the time again. It—

"Adelaide."

Her wandering eyes snapped back.

Inches. He was inches from her face. He'd put an arm around her while she'd been off woolgathering.

She stiffened. People weren't often this far inside her bubble.

He leaned closer, and lips like the silk of a rose touched her eyelid.

He definitely did not tell jokes about her to his friends. She closed both eyes.

He kissed her other eyelid.

In the dark behind her eyelids, half a mouse was laid bare.

A gory pile of feathers, beads of blood still wet on the quill.

A dead woman. Not even out of her nightclothes. Dead for three days before she was killed again. Too many to bleed anymore, not enough to stop stinking.

His cool lips touched hers.

Her gorge rose, but there was no graceful way out of his embrace. Besides, even on the edge of throwing up, on the tip of blood and rot making everything into its image, the kiss was nice. Tim's smooth lips were like a waterfall. Refreshing.

She kissed him back.

Her mind never stopped its race from the gory to the grotesque, from the memories of the dead to the smell of them, but she kissed him back and let it all break up into cobwebs.

The chain-link rattled in the breeze.

She snapped back, concentration broken. Pulling away, she twisted her mouth into a smile.

He smiled back. "Can I come see you later?" he whispered, kissing her on the cheek.

She flushed again. Definitely magenta this time. "Yeah, OK. You know where I'm at," she said, backing up.

For a moment, the arm wrapped around her remained firm. Then it softened, falling back to Tim's side.

Addy stepped back and tripped over the cat.

Pinwheeling her arms, she reached out to Tim as he tried to grab her. Just out of his grasp, she tripped over a patch of grass and probably some air and fell into the fence.

Tim reached for her again, but she held out a hand.

"I'm alright," she said, scooping up the cat. She smiled at the purring furball. Without raising her eyes, she told Tim she'd see him later and dashed inside before she could fall down again.

***

Parking his cart under a large mesquite, Jack took a deep breath.

Dust, mesquite, gunpowder.

He hopped out, the sound of small arms *pop-pop-popping*.

A young man sitting on a rock waved. "Mr. C. Come down to do some target practice with us?" His mellow skin gleamed in the sun. He ran a hand through deep black hair, standing it up at all angles.

Jack shook his hand. "Not today, Ricardo. Just checking in on you guys. You heard I'm your boss now?"

"*Sí.*" Ric grinned, the lack of smile lines giving him away as a teen. His eyes, hard and flat, could have belonged to someone twice his age. Still, they danced when he smiled. He hopped up. "You want to see the boss? Um, the other boss?"

"Lead the way."

They passed a row of boys in foxholes, aiming what looked like M-16s downrange. Paper targets fluttered with the passage of bullets. The sharp crack of ammunition assaulted Jack's ears.

Ric tapped him on the shoulder and handed him a set of over-the-ear earmuffs. The kind you might wear in cold weather. Not much for keeping you from going deaf, but he slipped them on anyway.

It helped. A bit.

Ric pointed at the foxhole in front of them. "Tim's the lead this week."

Jack nodded and gave him a thumbs-up. He walked up behind Tim and watched his target practice.

For whatever reason, Tim fired from a single-action bolt rifle. After each shot, he pulled the bolt back. The brass casing popped out, he slid another bullet in, loaded, and fired. Though methodical, the process took him less than three seconds.

Jack glanced downrange.

Even at a hundred feet, Jack caught daylight on the other side of the target. As he watched, more of the center disappeared.

He hated to cut such a demonstration short, but speaking of daylight, he was losing more every second he dillydallied. He stepped into the sun, casting a shadow over Tim.

Tim stopped firing and glanced up, unpleasant curl in his lip. As his eyes met Jack's, his expression softened. "Mr. C.!" He pulled off his own earmuffs. "To what do I owe the pleasure?"

Jack knelt, knees screaming at the rocks pressing into them. "Just doing my rounds as head of security."

"I heard about that." Tim smiled from ear to ear. "I'm so glad someone else will be in charge of these ruffians." He waved at the rest of the range. Their rifles still *pop-pop-popping*. "And I'm even more glad it's you, sir."

Jack frowned. "It's good you're happy. Do you guys need anything? How are you set on supplies?"

Tim held up a finger and laid the rifle against the sandbags in front of him. Grasping the side of the foxhole, he leapt up and out with an agility Jack could only envy.

They walked away from the range and into some swaying brown grass.

"I'd like to get them more training. We could always use that."

Jack pulled the earmuffs off. "Are you stocked for target practice?"

Tim nodded. "Wouldn't mind taking a few of these guys 'Head hunting, though. Just for moving targets and all."

Stomach in his toes, Jack shook his head. "Let's not go leaving the village if we don't have to. We have walls. Let's worry about them instead."

"You're the boss." Tim smiled.

Frowning, Jack glanced at the mountains next to them, standing sentinel over the village. He shuffled his feet, weighing his next words. If he told Tim about the 'Heads from yesterday, Wade might hear about it. But if he didn't, he wouldn't be able to use the Task Force for the very job it'd been created for.

He blew out through his teeth. "Listen, there have been a couple more sightings."

Mouth open, Tim gaped. "Inside the walls?"

Jack nodded. "Which is why I think we need to start with the walls. Check for breaches. Anywhere they could get in."

Tim dug a notepad from his pocket. His expression hardened, eyebrows drawn so far, his eyes almost closed. "Can you tell me where?"

Jack pulled a map from his hip pocket and opened it, shoving the paper clip holding the ancient thing closed into his shirt pocket. "Near my house, for one."

Tim scribbled. "What happened to it?"

"On Gerald's autopsy table as we speak."

More scribbles. "Others?" His jaw worked.

Jack hesitated. Addy didn't need to be dragged into this mess. Not any more than she already was. "The southwest side, in those abandoned houses." He pointed to the area.

"Who reported it? What happened?"

He cleared his throat. "My anonymous source says it's been taken care of."

Clenching the notepad, Tim frowned again. "I'll get my guys on a perimeter check just as soon as we're done here."

With a nod, Jack handed the earmuffs to Tim. "I'll expect a report this evening."

"You'll get one."

***

The door slammed behind Addy, and as she made her way up the stairs toward their apartment, darkness descended inside. Lit only by the red exit signs, the light cast onto the slim staircase was thin at best.

Silver lining. A day of work had erased all thoughts about the dead woman. About the cat. About Tim and his round, brown eyes. Manual labor, she'd found, was the best remedy for a busy mind.

But this dark staircase closing in on her like a dank cocoon, the stink of her own sweat crowding her nose, forced the memory of the dead woman and so many others to the front of her mind. Like pushing to the front of a horde, they scratched at the inside of her skull.

She trudged up the steps and watched one stair eat the other as they fell behind her.

Nearing the top, she felt more than saw a presence.

She dropped her hand to the haft of her knife.

The shadow at the top shifted, the shape familiar.

She exhaled. "Oh god, Dad. What are you doing here?"

"Came to check in with you, little girl."

"You're out late. It'll be dark soon." She took another stair.

He squeezed her shoulder. "I know. But I wanted to check in on you, and we need to talk about the Dead Head you saw."

"You could've called."

Dad nodded. "I could've."

Addy smiled. "It's good you're here, I guess. I wanted to tell you about something I saw this morning."

A warm weight hit Addy in the ankles and she stumbled, flailing at the banister. Scratching at it with her nails, she caught it just as Dad grabbed her arm. She looked to her feet.

"Beverly. You dumb cat." She picked up the purring cat and cocked her head in a follow-me gesture. They headed down the hall. "The other night, I thought I heard a 'Head outside the fence," she said, shaking her keys from her pocket.

There were so many of them. Why didn't they just invent touch plates like in Star Trek?

"And this morning, I found a chunk of skin on the razor wire."

Dad grabbed her shoulder, pulling a quick breath over his teeth. "Adelaide, are you sure?"

"Two days dead at the most."

His eyes skipped back and forth. "So that's three, unless it was one of the ones you or I have already seen. Counting the first one, that's four in a week, inside the walls."

"There haven't been that many since we moved here, have there?"

"No. In the three or four years since we came here, there's been one. One."

She lifted her brows. "That's what I thought. Something doesn't feel right."

Dad crossed his arms. "This is more than coincidence. Something is going on." Scratching his chin, he leaned close again. "Does Jane know?"

"I haven't really gotten a chance to tell her much yet. She knows about the 'Head Mike and I got, but not the rest."

He pointed at the apartment door. "You need to tell her. But no one else."

Addy scratched the cat. Dad confirming her intuitions an unexpected boon, her stomach still twisted around itself.

"Adelaide," he said.

The door downstairs slammed again.

He looked around, then back at Addy, cupping her chin with two fingers.

Making her feel both safe and like a little girl. His super-power.

"No one," he repeated.

She nodded as Tim appeared from the stairwell.

Oh, goody.

CHAPTER 7

Addy's flashlight cast a bouncy circle of light in front of them. "You know, for people who are supposed to stay in after dark, we don't do a very good job of it, do we?"

Jane exhaled through her nose. "Yeah, well. Someone has to bust my parents' balls for not showing up. And bring them all this extra food." She shrugged, jiggling the pack on her shoulder.

"I wonder why they didn't call."

"My parents don't have phones."

Addy grunted, sweeping the road with her flashlight. One would think the older generation would have been all over phones.

"So Jack and Tim went well, you think?"

Addy sighed. "Just because Dad was nice doesn't mean anything."

Jane chuckled under her breath.

"It's not like I've brought a lot of guys home. Any. Whatever. He's, well," Addy's feet slowed. She paused.

Jane walked a few feet before she stopped. Her own flashlight swept back and forth.

Addy took a breath. "He's overprotective."

Jane laughed. "That's one way to put it."

Putting one foot down in front of the other, Addy laughed back. "Psychotic. That's another way." She grinned, picturing her dad squeeze Tim's hand so hard he might break it. Tim weathered it well, smiling more than grimacing, before he was allowed to have his bloodless hand back. Attempting to be subtle about shaking the life back into it, he'd mentioned something to her dad. What was it?

"Hey Jane, what did Tim say about reports?"

"Mmm. I wasn't listening."

"Liar. What did he say?" Tensing her side before Jane hit it with a bony elbow, she dropped the flashlight.

Jane snatched it up. "Jack said something about guard reports and perimeter checks. You think he was talking about the whole village?"

Addy considered. He'd been made head of the Security Committee. Scuffing a pebble, she shrugged. "He might've. I mean there's been three Dead Heads in town the last couple days. Maybe four."

"Three. Please. You, me, Jack and Mike, my parents, we took on an entire horde a few years back. Three is nothing."

"Still. That was forever ago. The Cure's been out for like five years. This town has been around at least that long. To have them here, now, that's…"

"That's a little strange, lass."

Addy nodded. Not that Jane could see the nod in the dark. "Yeah, it's weird. I wonder why he wants to keep it so quiet?"

Jane scoffed. "People are starting to settle down. I mean, the apocalypse lasted twenty years. But now they're together, there's the Cure, people are fed and happy. My mom—" Jane's voice caught. Her foot skipped a step. "Nancy always says people want to be fed and happy. They don't like the status quo to be upset. Those people, they won't want to change. They'll resist. But first…" She stopped, the constantly moving flashlight coming to rest on Addy's face. She sighed. "They'll get scared. They'll be stupid. They'll fight."

Addy nodded, eyes closed against the light.

Husks of houses leaned toward the road, empty but for the sighing eddies of wind.

Empty empty empty. Wind and walls.

And a squeak.

Jane broke the spell. "So, I think he—"

"Sshhhh."

There it was again. The squeal. A screaming hinge. Followed by… What? A thump?

Jane grabbed her arm. "Adelaide. Is that my front door?"

Again, Addy nodded.

Useless gesture though it was, Jane didn't wait to not see it. Ditching the pack in the road with an unceremonious shrug, she took off toward the only occupied house on the street.

Addy broke into her own gallop to catch Jane, flashlight bouncing from the ground to the sky. Ground, sky, ground, sky.

The dark had come, and they were out in it.

***

Crouched back to back with Addy behind a decorative granite boulder, Jane produced no less than three throwing knives. The tails of her jacket flapped in the spring breeze.

As Addy clicked her flashlight off, the beam reflected off the handles of at least three more. The girl carried more pointed weapons than most people knew existed. And still, her wardrobe was skintight.

How did she hide them all?

The hinge screamed. The door thumped against the frame.

Addy's skin popped goose bumps on every exposed inch. Her scalp crawled. She cringed each time the door slammed into the wood.

Jane tensed against her back as Addy pulled out her own blades. The machete and the Bowie knife, their handles cold in her palms. Warming to the touch as she breathed deep and opened her ears.

And there it was. The breathing. Bubbling. Rattling. Stinking.

"It's close," Jane whispered.

Addy did no more than nod, her blood running like icewater.

It was in the house. Jane's parents' house.

The door slammed into the frame. Splintered wood.

The question was—

"Where are my parents?"

Addy shook her head, the pit in her stomach turning her gut inside out.

Jane shifted. "I'm going in there, Addy."

"Of course you are. I'm going with you."

"You don't have to, lass."

"Yes I do. Don't be an idiot."

Jane turned half her body and peeked at Addy with her peripheral.

Addy peeked back, wide eyes locking on Jane's half-lidded ones. She had to hand it to her, the girl was cool under pressure. Addy felt like she was going to simultaneously throw up and explode, shooting sweat from under her arms like a busted pipe.

Standing, backs against each other, they stepped onto the walk. The moon a searchlight in front of a sky full of stars, the splintered door frame glowed white as bone.

Squeeee…crack…squeeee…crack. The door bounced in the breeze, the bubbling just inside it.

Thump.

The bubbling paused as the 'Head bumped into a wall. The sound changed as it altered its trajectory and stumbled deeper into the house.

Easing toward the house, the breath in Addy's nose ran hot. The skin on her arms cold. Her stomach in knots.

But her hands remained steady.

Jane cocked an elbow. She spoke over her shoulder. "Got your Cure?"

"Yeah. But it won't do us any good if we get our jugular ripped out."

"Be fucking careful, then."

Addy exhaled through her nose. No sense arguing that logic. "Aim low. They're fresh. Might be able to save them if we can get them to the hospital."

"Got it," Jane said, her clenched teeth turning it into more of a hiss.

The broken cement of the sidewalk angled from the driveway and swooped around to the front door. A pointy, bushy yucca stood next to the walk. Now almost the size of a tree, it was probably a tiny baby when the house was built.

Blood glistened on some of the spines.

Jane in the lead, they mounted the small porch. The door thumped the frame again, and they waited until it swung open to squeeze in.

It thumped behind them.

Silver moonlight fell through the blinds. A trail of blood wobbled around the room, pooling every now and again where the 'Head had run into something and changed course.

The stench of it filled the room and curled Addy's nose hairs.

She stowed her machete and pulled out the flashlight. Aiming it into the flesh of her arm, she peeked at her friend.

Jane nodded, her eyes slits.

The soft click of the light didn't cause a change in the bubbling. Addy brought it away from her arm in small, slow increments, allowing their eyes to adjust. The tiny LED cast a glow that may as well have been daylight inside the black house.

A few things in the living room were broken, pictures had fallen over, the fishbowl had been smashed with little, dried goldfish in the bottom. Add that to the splintered door frame and things did not look good for Jane's parents.

Addy sighed through her nose.

Jane stepped toward the hallway, following the wobbly trail of blood.

Addy Listened.

It bubbled in the kitchen, bumping into the table.

They crept down the hall and inched toward the kitchen, bloody tile in front and behind.

***

Jack, hand on his gun, watched the door to the autopsy room creak open.

Elizabeth and Celia entered and latched the door behind them.

Gerald, who had donned his paper mask and gown, said hi to Liz.

She blushed and said hi back.

Next to Ger, Andrew hulked in his own paper gown. It flapped around his thighs, thinking about coming close to his knees and reconsidering halfway. He'd been assisting Ger, putting the old boy back together.

"So Gerald," Jack said, "did we find out who this was?"

Gerald nodded, blood-stained mask covering his mouth, muffling his answer. "We did." He stopped, eyes roving over each of them, lingering on Liz. "It's why I wanted you all here. Even you,"—he angled his head—"Celia."

She sketched a curtsy in her army boots. Her smile was more grimace than grin. "So. Spill."

Gerald took a breath. "It's our deputy mayor."

Heat seared Jack's side like a cattle prod. He'd seen the man. Not two days ago. When Wade had roped him into this stupid committee, he'd been there.

"Daniel," Elizabeth said. His name sighed out of her mouth like she'd been punched in the gut.

Jack nodded. "Yeah. Pencil mustache. Solid face. Didn't cause any trouble."

She frowned. "Question is, how did he get here?"

"And how did Wade not know already?" Celia asked.

"He had to have," Liz said.

Jack, hand under his chin, tapped his cheek with one finger and looked from one woman to the other. Wade had to have known. Had to have *at least* known the man was missing. Why had he not said anything? To the head of security?

Of course, he hadn't told Wade about any of this. Looked like it was a two-way street.

Hand over his mouth, he mumbled from behind it, "We should probably tell him now."

Gerald inhaled. "I thought we were keeping this to ourselves until we knew more, Jack."

"We were, Ger. But this"—he gestured toward the table—"was the deputy mayor. Second-in-command. If Wade finds out we knew and didn't tell him, well." He stopped, hand on a hip.

Celia cleared her throat. "It wouldn't be good for us."

"He won this one," Andrew added.

Jack fished his phone from his pocket and dialed Wade.

***

Addy and Jane followed the trail of blood to the kitchen. It pooled around the doorjamb, where presumably the 'Head had gotten hung up before bouncing off the frame and moving on into the next room.

So much blood. Injuries, the hospital could deal with, but they had to be survivable.

Addy's stomach turned over. Her chest tensed. The likelihood of this being one of Jane's parents intruded on what should be a cool head.

She shook it. Stay cool or die?

Stay cool.

The bubbling, rattling breath shook the chest of its owner not three feet to her right.

She linked her left arm with Jane's and clenched the knife in her right. Waist height.

Aim low. Bring them back.

As the Dead Head bubbled up from the dark recesses of the kitchen, neither girl jumped, though Addy's heart tripped a beat before beginning to race. Even a lifetime of training could not erase the primal feeling of prey and predator.

As the 'Head entered the light, chomping its monstrous teeth, a little girl screamed in Addy's head.

Her steady hand lashed out. She knocked the dead fist away.

Jane's dad, come to try and eat them both. His breath stinking of copper and what could only be described as sewer sludge, he lunged at Jane.

Only he could use just one hand. The other had been lost when his arm had been torn from his body. Half his shoulder ripped away with it, a shiny collar bone jutting from the gaping hole. From armpit to ankle, chunks of flesh and blood upon blood upon blood soaked into his shirt and pants.

There was no surviving that much blood loss, no matter how much blood they had in the bank. No surviving.

As Addy's flashlight traced the wound, Jane sucked a breath over her teeth and sliced the air in two with one of her knives. It buried itself in what was left of her dad's shoulder. Not so much as a drop of blood escaped the dry wound.

She sobbed. Just once.

The next knife sank up to the hilt in his eye.

Yanking a knitting needle from her hair, she grunted. It sailed through the air and plunged into his ear. For good measure.

The bubbling stopped.

The body crumpled in a slow slide to the floor. It took forever if it took an inch.

As it came to rest in its own pool of blood, what was left of it, Jane extracted her blades. Three insignificant popping sounds followed them out of the dead flesh. Careful to avoid the blood herself, she sank down next to the body and breathed heavy. Her chin sank to her chest.

Addy traced the path of blood to the stove.

Ah, indoor cooking. An interesting convenience. Not as easy as using a cook fire, but Dad always called it a marvelous invention.

Either way, blood tracked up the side of the stove. Dried to the color of weathered wooden patio furniture, it flaked and peeled like the red paint they sometimes slathered on it.

She turned to Jane. "We have to find your mom, Jane."

Jane pulled one strained breath after another through her nose. "Adelaide. They're not my parents. They never were. You know that."

Something hard lodged itself in Addy's throat. She tried to swallow past it, but all she got for her trouble was pain. Her eyes prickled.

Dammit not again. She was not going to cry again. "I know it, Jane. But they loved you."

Jane nodded but made no move to stand.

Addy swept the rest of the kitchen with the flashlight. The only sounds were the whooshing of her own heart and Jane's breathing. No movement.

Swallowing again, she crept back into the hallway. Approaching the second, perpendicular hallway that led to the bedrooms, she paused to Listen.

Nothing.

Knife held at port, flashlight at her shoulder, she rounded the corner.

The beam fell on a face.

She gasped. "What the—"

"Ah! Get that thing out of my eyes!"

Addy stumbled, back hitting the wall behind her, knife dipping.

The light from the flashlight jittered. Expectations of an empty hallway shattered, it took her a moment to process the face.

She breathed, slowing her heart rate. Pointing the light at his chest, it clicked into place when she saw the pea green jacket.

"Dean?"

CHAPTER 8

J ack flipped the phone closed. "Wade is on his way."

Celia blew out a breath. "I'm leaving."

Jack called to her retreating back. "Celia."

She stopped, hand on the crossbar. One eye peeked over her shoulder.

Jack sighed. "Be careful."

Celia scoffed, unbarred the door, and slipped out.

Liz barred the door behind her. "She's wild as a cat, that one." Equal parts condescension and respect.

He turned to Gerald. "What else do we know, Ger?"

"Like what?"

"Do we know how he died?"

"That's been hard to pin down."

Jack's brow creased. He stepped to the table and stared down at the stinking, rotting body. "What do you mean?"

"There's no external injuries, save for Celia's gunshot. He wasn't turned by a bite." He shrugged.

Jack blew out a breath, long and slow. His whisker hair tickled his nose. He rested a hand on the table and leaned down. What Addy said about the one she had found crossed his mind. Again. "Bruising on the throat?"

His skin crawled getting this close to the body. Though it'd been headshot from 400 yards, and logic dictated it had finished its cycle of death and reanimation, Jack's hindbrain still reported it could sit up at any moment. Start breathing. Bite him in the face.

He swallowed and leaned closer.

"Nothing I could see," Gerald said. "Here, let me get you some more light." He turned another lamp on.

As little flecks of blood on the skin came into sharp relief, bits of dirt in the neck creases showed up. Nothing remarkable about the skin stood out. No finger marks, no bruising, nothing that would indicate—

Wait.

Was that a pore? Or…

"Ger, do you see that?" Jack didn't point with his finger. His eyes pointed to a small area, just a millimeter or two in size, near the base of the stiff's neck.

Gerald knelt and aimed a penlight at the spot. "Is that a needle hole?"

Jack nodded, nose brushing cold skin.

His heart squeezed in on itself at the thought of what a needle hole could suggest. And not one where an addict would put it.

It was where a murderer would put it.

A slick arterial delivery of quiet potassium chloride. Window cleaner. Air. Anything. It would have been simple.

And then open the door and turn the new Dead Head loose.

Jack took two slow breaths. "Whoever did this wanted to create panic. Destruction."

Andrew inhaled. "*Did* this?"

Jack glanced up, Andy towering over the autopsy table. "Yeah. Someone did this on purpose. That needle hole," he said, pointing, "was made by a murderer. Without testing, we won't ever know what did it. But they left the hole in a visible place."

"They thought we wouldn't find it," Liz said.

Jack tapped his chin with a finger. Looking around at the three of them, he frowned. "Something is going on here. I don't know if it's simple murder or something else."

Silence from his friends. Three pairs of eyes watched him.

He began to pace. The back of his neck prickled as their eyes followed him. "We have to assume the worst. Someone could be trying to cause an outbreak."

Andrew gasped.

Liz cursed.

Gerald, jaw clenched, leaned on the table like he needed it to hold him up. "What the hell would that do?" he asked, the wind knocked out of his words.

Jack stopped pacing. "Besides create chaos, I have no idea."

He felt his phone buzz before the ringing began. He picked it up halfway through the first ring. "It's Adelaide," he said, flipping the phone open.

"Dad? Where are you?"

His daughter's voice made him uneasy in a way he couldn't specify. She sounded off her footing. If it had been his eldest, he would have said scared.

But Addy didn't scare easy.

As he opened his mouth to tell her to come meet him here, a rattling knock at the door all but made him jump out of his skin.

He nodded at Liz and angled his chin toward the door.

"Jackson," Wade said as he entered the room, oiling through the door like some kind of well-fed snake. "What exactly is going on?"

Jack, putting the phone back up to his ear, gave Wade the one-minute finger.

Wade bounced on the balls of his feet, nodding and favoring Jack with a lopsided leer.

"Addy, baby girl, go home. I'll come meet you later. Promise."

***

Jane yanked the door closed behind the three of them, the splintered wood cracking, and laid a palm flat on the face of it. Holding the knob with her other hand, she laid her forehead on the door and breathed.

After about thirty seconds, she drew a breath through her nose and freed a knife from her belt.

For all Addy knew the same one she'd used to end her adoptive dad.

Jane carved a giant X into the door.

Addy sniffled, tears she'd cried for Jane as she watched her carve now drying on her cheeks.

The pain rested in the set of Jane's shoulders. It twisted her spine, bending her almost double.

Addy sniffled again. "Dean, are you sure, double sure, triple sure there was no one else in the house?"

He stared at Jane. "I'm sure."

Addy sighed. "Jane."

Jane turned, her beautiful, tiny, little, fragile face contorted into a scowl Addy hadn't seen on her in years. Her lips pressed into a white line. "Yeah."

"What now? Should we head back to the apartment? Call my dad?"

Jane exhaled like she'd been gut-punched. But she bobbed her head. "Yeah. Call Jack."

"Let's get off this porch while we do," Dean said.

Addy handed off her flashlight to him as she pulled her phone.

He switched it on and flanked her as Jane lit the other side. The three of them walked into the street.

Addy dialed. "Dad? Where are you?"

"Hey, little girl, I'm at Ger's."

"Security Committee stuff?"

"You could say that. You OK?"

"No. We're pretty far from it, Dad."

"Where are you? Are you home?"

Before she could answer, the phone bumped. His voice became muffled, far away.

"Dad? What's going on over there?"

Someone cursed. More muffled voices. Dad's own, echoing inside his lungs.

"Dad, we're coming—"

He spoke into the phone. *"Addy, baby girl, go home. I'll come meet you later. Promise."*

The line went dead.

Addy scowled at the phone, closed it, and slid it back into her pocket. She glanced at Dean and Jane. Considered. Reconsidered. "He's at Ger's. He said come meet him there."

Dean stopped, swinging his flashlight to point at her hips. "He said go home."

She rounded on him, stepping up close enough to feel his breath. She lowered her voice. "Dean. You were eavesdropping." Red waves radiated from her ears. Little spots danced in front of her eyes.

She took a breath to lower her blood pressure. Let it out. Swiveled her eyes to his. "And you think we should go back to the apartment."

"It kinda sounded like he had his hands full. He wanted you to go home." He lowered his tone and reached toward her shoulder.

She flinched. Voice shaking, she lowered it again. Almost a whisper. "So you follow us to Jane's parents' or whatever, now you want to tell me what I should do?" At least the spots in front of her vision had gone. She took another deep breath and drew her machete.

Dean glanced at the weapon and lowered his hand. "Addy, I wasn't following you. That's not— I saw you guys. Look. We don't have time for this. Let's get out of the open," he said, making a point to look around them, "and get you home. Come on."

"I'm not going anywhere with you." Addy spat out the words, twisting the wrist holding her machete.

To his credit, Dean didn't back up.

She scowled, not admiring his bravery at all. Really. Instead, she turned to her friend for support. "Jane, do you think—"

The space behind Addy was empty. "Jane?" She spun a circle.

The darkness had swallowed Jane.

She turned back to Dean, mouth falling open. Her angry calm vanished as her voice rose two octaves. "Where is she?"

Eyes wide, he swept the flashlight's beam into the distance. Movement just on the edge of the light, maybe 50 yards, could have been Jane's retreating back. Headed in the direction of Ger's. Fast.

"Crap, Dean, we have to catch up to her."

"No argument from me."

They took off after Jane.

***

Jack folded his arms.

Wade, hands clasped behind his back, sweat beaded on his lip, bounced on his toes beside the autopsy table.

Jack watched him mince around. How many times would he have to wonder how this man had made it through the apocalypse? He narrowed his eyes. "Wade, I'm sure you recognize Daniel."

"He's my second-in-command, Jackson. Of course I do." Wade stopped circling the table and leaned over what was left of Daniel, lips pursed.

When he squeaked out the question of what happened, Jack explained as much as he was able. Leaving out the part where Addy had been there. Dean and Celia, too. No need to drag any of them into this.

Wade sniffed at the body and stood, producing a clean, white hankie from his pocket. He wiped his brow and lip, patting at his pursed mouth. He stowed the kerchief in his pocket again and reached for glasses that weren't there. His fingers touched his temple before he sighed and lowered his hand. Bouncing on the balls of his feet again, he gazed across the table and made eye contact with Jack. "What about the other one?"

Jack shook his head. "What other one?"

The light in the room seemed to breathe, closing down to a spotlight that fell just on Wade and Jack.

Jack clenched his fists, palms slick with sweat.

"Someone killed another one yesterday. It was killed with a machete," Wade said.

Jack's stomach clenched, saliva dumping into his mouth. Wade knew. He was sure. But he couldn't swallow. Couldn't betray a movement that nervous. Instead, he shook his head. "News to me. I'm the head of security. Why wasn't I told?"

"Don't play that game with me, Jackson," Wade said, taking a step around the table. Leaning toward Jack, hands still clenched behind his back, he sucked a squealing breath through his teeth. "Your daughter Adelaide uses a machete, does she not?"

The muscles on Jack's face didn't so much as twitch. "A machete is a pretty common weapon."

Wade nodded. "It is, it is." He bounced one more time, looking down at the corpse.

Most of the blood had congealed inside the sack of skin. Very little fluids ran down the trough to the drip pans. It smelled like fucking three-day-old roadkill.

Wade sniffed. "I didn't come here to argue with you. Either tell me what you know, or—"

"Or what?" Andrew interrupted.

All at once, the light came back up, and there were five people in the room again. Andrew had stepped between Wade and Jack, looming over the tiny, little mayor.

Jack touched him on the shoulder. Bring it back, big guy.

Wade, shaking his head, pulled the hankie out again.

Were those monogrammed initials? Were they really Wade's? Who had time for any of that pomp anymore?

Wiping his brow and sweaty upper lip, he clicked his heels together and all but pranced to the door. He knocked twice on it.

A rumbling growl began outside.

Wade removed the bar, unlocked the door, and opened it.

The growl approached the building. Light streamed in from the night, blinding Jack.

He raised his hand to it and made out headlights. The headlights of a tall truck. Like the military ones they'd found a garage full of. Shadows moved through the lights.

"What is this?" Jack had to raise his voice almost to a shout to be heard over the rumbling engine.

Wade stepped to the side of the door and waved someone in. "You've been trying to undermine me since you moved here years ago, Jack."

Jack, glancing at Andrew, took a step back. "That's crazy, Wade. I'm just trying to live here."

Two men came in, rifles held to port. As they got close enough to block the light, their young faces materialized.

Jack stared. "Ric? What are you doing here?"

The teen shook his head and glanced at Wade.

Wade nodded.

Ricardo pulled handcuffs from his belt. "It'll be easier if you just put these on, Mr. C."

Jack backed up a step. He swallowed around a lump in his throat. "Tell me what this is about."

The resolve in his voice was firmer than he'd thought it would be. Good.

Wade flinched. "I'm arresting you, Jackson. And your friends. You killed my deputy mayor. You killed"—he paused and glanced around the room—"Mrs. Norton. Their teacher."

The boys gasped. Ric crossed himself.

The tips of Jack's fingers tingled. It made no sense, what was happening. Not that Wade had ever liked him, but it made no sense. Fighting to keep his voice modulated over the rumbling engines, he shook his head. "How can you say we killed Daniel? I didn't…I never even saw Mrs. Norton's body."

The stench of exhaust crept into the room. The boys looked back to Wade.

Jack glanced at his friends. He wanted to tell them to go, get out, but his tongue stuck to the roof of his mouth.

Wade approached the table again, mincing his way across the room. "Look at this body, boys. No bite marks. No nothing. Just the bullet in his head."

Oh.

Fuck.

Jack slid one foot sideways. If he could make the door, he could—

"Boys," Wade said, "he's trying to run! Don't let him escape!"

Another shape filled the doorway. With the light a halo behind it, Jack couldn't make out who it was. But they left no room for escape.

He turned back to the younger boys.

Ric held out the handcuffs.

Jack shook his head.

"Enough of this," Wade said, snatching his own .45 out of its holster and aiming at Andrew's temple. "Put the cuffs on or one less of you will be leaving this room alive."

Jack held out his wrists.

CHAPTER 9

A rumbling up ahead gave Addy pause. She stopped chasing after Jane and Listened.

Trucks. Big ones. She'd seen them driving around town before, taking supplies here and there after coming in from runs.

"Dean," she said, reaching for his arm.

He stopped with her, mouth set in a frown. "Are those trucks?"

Addy nodded. Dammit. In the dark again. "Yeah." She paused. Swallowed. "They're parked at Gerald's. What are they doing there at this time of night?"

"I don't know. Let's catch up to Jane. I've got a bad feeling about this."

Addy nodded again, already moving. Dean's bad feeling matched her own.

They rounded the corner. Ger's house screamed, bathed in headlights.

He'd taken more of a warehouse than a house. He'd converted a large bit of it to do his vet thing out of, and it was big enough for dogs, horses, you name it. Flanked by the trucks, it looked like a tiny toy as they imposed themselves over it.

A chill worked its way down Addy's spine. Her feet slowed, one forgetting to get in front of the other. She all but tripped over it.

Dean caught and steadied her. He led her to the bit of cover he could find, a bushy mesquite. Scant cover, but better than nothing.

Addy crouched, gnawing a nail.

Someone got out of one of the trucks, swinging into the light and standing in the garage door.

She narrowed her eyes. Something about that shape.

But then a handcuffed man, forced through the door of the garage, stumbled into the headlights.

Dad.

She tensed.

Before she could jump up, Dean caught her by the shoulder. "Addy," he whispered, "no."

His voice stopped her for a moment, soothing something she hadn't known was knotted up inside. It unraveled into her gut, and she exhaled.

That might've been the first time she'd exhaled since they had gotten here. She did it again, breathing in and out.

After her head quit screaming, she peeked around the tree again.

***

"Jack!"

He faced the dark beyond the trucks. Who was out there? It was a short list.

"Jack! No!"

Whoever it was closed in, coming at a dead run.

"Stay back!" he shouted into the dark. What little good it would do.

Scrambling feet stopped just outside the light.

He felt more than saw his guards raise their guns.

Adrenaline dumped into his gut, spreading to his thighs and up his shoulders. Cuffed behind his back, his arms ached.

He struggled against the cuffs. She couldn't. She had to go.

She stepped into the light, hair gleaming like a ruby, a knife in each hand. And one in her teeth. Their deadly blades reflecting pinpricks of light into his eyes.

His legs shook. He might stop breathing. He stopped struggling and stepped between the guns and the girl, looking down at her.

Knife still between her teeth, she stared up at him. Locked onto his eyes. Shook her head.

"Jane, leave now," he whispered. "Please don't get involved in this."

Her eyes never left his. Again, she shook her head. She flipped a knife around, slipping it through her fingers like it was on rails, and raised her arm to throw it. Her eyes never left his.

Hands like steel bars gripped his wrists. Twisted.

He shouted, driven to his knees, eyes clenched shut. His arms, wrenched up between his shoulder blades, burned.

Something cold and hard pressed onto the crown of his head.

"Drop the knives." The voice came from far away, outside the lights.

A voice he knew. Someone from the Task Force. Someone who should've been watching for Dead Heads but was here instead.

The boy gripping his arm twisted again.

Jack inhaled through his nose, sealing the pain behind his lips. He'd be damned if he'd give the kid the satisfaction of another sound.

He opened his eyes and there she was again. Her eyes still on his.

She lowered her hands, crouching and laying the knives on the ground. With exaggerated slow movements, she removed the knife from her mouth and laid it on the ground.

A small, freckled boy stepped over, stood her up, and told her to turn and put her hands on the side of the truck.

"Hey, Louis. How's tricks, kid?" She breathed at him, leaning toward him instead of away.

He stepped back and aimed his gun higher, level with her neck. "Put your hands on the truck, Jane. Feet apart."

She smiled, a cat inspecting its prey. "Sure thing, sweetie." She spun.

The boy groped more than searched, pressing her against the truck with his body and removing her weapons.

Jack, kneeling in the dirt, rocks biting into his kneecaps, clenched his teeth. Red spots danced in front of his eyes. He'd have a heart attack if he wasn't careful.

He took slow, measured breaths, and memorized the boy. Louis. Not someone he was about to forget. Or forgive.

***

"Adelaide, you can't," Dean whispered, his hand encircling her bicep.

She clenched and unclenched her fists.

Her father, on his knees in the dirt. Her best friend, suffering indignity at the hands of an adolescent.

"Addy," Dean said. A little louder.

She scowled.

"There's too many of them. We can't do them any good going over there."

"I can't just let them take them god knows where. We have to do something about it. I can't just— I can't." She tensed her legs, trying to stand.

He held his grip. Firm. Not tight, not digging into her arm. Just firm.

She stayed low.

"We'll help them, alright? I promise. But we can't do anything right now. Addy," he said again, using his other hand to touch her opposite shoulder.

She relaxed, sitting in the dirt. Tiny little pebbles bit into her ass.

"We'll get them back."

She nodded. It had been too long of a day to argue.

Besides, she'd counted at least a dozen of them, rounding up her father, her best friend, and her dad's friends. Loading them into the trucks. Not that she'd admit it, but Dean was right.

The trucks backed up, cracking gravel under their tires.

They watched as the trucks pulled away.

THE ROAD

CHAPTER 10

You're tucked into a fetal position. Your ears ringing.

Your mom leans over you. "You're going to be OK. Just breathe."

Her whisper into your ear stops the ringing. She's right.

Surrounded by bodies, black blood sprayed across the ground and your arms and everything you can see, the woods are still.

Her voice, the most soothing sound in the world, brings you back. Your breathing slows.

Light fingers stroke the back of your head. "Us one, them zero," Mom says. "We got this."

You look up, staring at the berries you were picking when the horde came. They're spilled all over the ground, leaking their juice into the dirt.

Mom looks around with you. "We'll get more. Sometimes you have to let the berries go. Sometimes you can't stop them from spilling. We'll get more."

She's right, but still. They were good and sweet. And now they're ruined.

"We'll get more," Mom says again. "Would Captain Picard give up?"

You smile. "No."

"That's right, jellybean. Let's go. We'll find more berries and get them back to our boys."

* * *

Addy opened her eyes, ringing in her ears subsiding, and looked at Dean.

He spoke into the phone. "Yeah, Mike, we're comin' to you. You're what? Where?"

The voice on the other end crackled.

Dean frowned. "Say again."

More crackling. Addy caught something that sounded like "south tower."

One side of her mouth turned up. It was probably best they collect Mike. They should be together. If nothing else, so she could keep him out of trouble.

And even as scared as she was about her dad and Jane, Jane's needles flashed in the headlights as they loaded her onto the truck, tucked in her hair. They'd be OK. For now.

Dean hung the phone up and pocketed it. "Let's get to Mike." Standing, he held out a hand to her.

She stood without taking it and brushed the back of her pants. "Where is he?"

"He's out working on the south tower. It's pretty much under control, but there were a few details to finish up out there. Sealing it off, that sort of thing."

Addy nodded. Since he'd started working on them, she'd wanted to see a tower up close. She had never been close enough to one to find out much about it, even scattered about the country as they were.

Dean clicked on the flashlight and headed south.

She frowned. "Are we walking?"

"Till we get out of the village, yeah. Once we get outside the wall, I've got some transpo."

"Transpo? Who talks like that? What are you, ninety?"

Dean opened his mouth, closed it, opened it again. Sighing, he turned. "It's this way. Come on."

***

Jack looked around. "Is everyone alright?"

Dust settling, the back of the truck lit by whatever working streetlamps there were, he strained his eyes to count bodies and scrutinize faces.

"Yeah, Jackie, I think we are," Andrew said. "I should've done more."

"This isn't your fault, Andrew."

"It's no one's fault," Elizabeth said across from him. Leaning against Gerald, she tented her legs.

Blood rushing to his cheeks, Jack's forehead tightened. "Of course it is. It's mine. I shouldn't have taken this stupid job in the first place."

"Could someone tell me what you're on about?" Fake Scottish accent laid on thick, Jane leaned against the tailgate. Illuminated orange as they crossed under a working arc-sodium, she struggled against her bonds.

"If you move away from that tailgate. It could come open," Jack said.

Mouth and eyes popping open, she stopped struggling. But she scooted her ass and moved away from the tailgate, bobbing as the truck bounced. Wobbling back and forth with the motion of the truck, she closed her mouth, lips compressed to near invisibility.

Jack hadn't seen her this worked up in quite a while. It wasn't unusual for Jane to have an attitude, but damn. She was livid. Was it the boy who searched her for weapons? Or was there more? He considered sealing the question behind his lips, but it came out anyway. "Jane, is there something wrong? Besides," he said, looking around the truck, "this?"

She shook her head. "Don't avoid the question. What is going on?"

Admiring her determination, he shelved the question. For now, he explained in as few words as possible about Wade and their first, and seemingly only, twenty-four hours as Security Committee.

She chuckled. A small, tight little laugh just audible over the sound of the truck's engine.

"What's funny?" Ger asked, his head leaned back and eyes closed. The shadow on his shoulder growing again.

Damn but those bites took forever to heal.

Thank god for the Cure.

Jane glanced at him, then back to Jack. "You're right," she said, angling her chin. "You shouldn't have taken the job."

Jack nodded. Responsibility for whatever was happening right now, and whatever was about to happen, fell squarely on his shoulders. He took two slow breaths, breaking eye contact with Jane and staring out the back of the truck.

So if it was his fault, what could he do about it now?

The trucks slowed to a crawl, pulling into a gravel drive. They'd taken more turns than Jack could keep up with, but they were still within the village. Somewhere.

A zipper from the front unsealed a flap and Wade stuck his face through. He sniffed. "Yes. Well. Here we all are."

"Yeah, Wade. Here we all are," Jack said, sliding toward the cab. "Wherever here is."

Bumping Jane's leg, he paused as she sucked a breath through her nose. "Sorry, Jane."

Pressing her mouth back into the tight frown, she shook her head.

He scooted until he was up at the window and stood on his knees. "What is it we're doing here, Wade?"

To his credit, Wade didn't retreat. He stared at Jack, though he didn't quite make eye contact. He took two breaths before answering, the second hand on his watch setting the theme music. "There are…unanswered questions."

"Specific."

"I'm sorry, Jackson. Mr. Cooke. I can't be any more specific than that."

Jack looked around the truck and paused on Jane. "There's no reason for her to be here," he said, still looking at her.

Wade clicked his tongue. "She got involved when she pulled a knife, knives, on my men."

"Yeah but that wasn't—"

Wait. What?

Jack turned his head, tendons in his neck creaking. "Your men? What do you mean, your men?" A pit formed in his stomach, bleak and empty.

Wade chuckled, an oily gurgle. "Of course they're my men, Jackson. Whose did you think they were?" Laughing, he zipped the flap closed. A moment later, the door to the front of the truck opened and closed. Then the door to a building.

Silence fell.

Jack's abs ached as though he'd been throwing up. He leaned against the side of the truck and knocked his head back. The canvas side bowed.

It didn't make him feel any better. He stomped a foot. It helped a little.

Liz whispered from a world away. "He set us up."

Jack's gorge rose. His forehead burned, skin across his cheeks tight. He'd been played a fool.

"Jack."

Someone scooted close.

He glanced over.

Starlight bounced off the knitting needles in Jane's hair as she inched closer. Her eyes held such blind trust, it was all he could do to swallow the puke creeping up his throat.

God help him, she smiled. "Jack, it's OK."

He shook his head, mouth clamped over the taste of bile.

"Look at us, Jack."

With a grimace, he glanced around the truck, taking in each of them.

Each face, lit with starlight, held resolve. Confidence. A lifetime of experiences that built their mental strength even as it honed their muscles. There wasn't a single one of them who hadn't saved his life and vice versa at least a time or two.

Meeting Jane's eyes, he frowned. "There's no one else I'd rather be in the shit with than all of you."

"Good thing then," a voice said from the dark outside the truck, "because you are in some shit."

Jane stiffened. "I know that voice," she whispered. "I can't place it. But I know it."

The speaker chuckled. "I'm sure we'll talk more later."

Footsteps crunched around the truck and as the door of the cab opened, the door to whatever building they'd parked next to also swung open.

Boys outside the truck grunted.

Jack scooted his ass to the end of the truck and leaned out as much as he thought he could without being seen.

Several people loaded wooden boxes into the other truck. What looked like weeks' worth of supplies.

When they were done, the engines started again, a dull roar in the desert night.

***

Just outside the outer wall, Addy took in the rusted, crooked heap wedged between two mesquites. "This? This is your, ahem, transpo?"

Dean's shoulders slumped. "She ain't pretty. But she's mine. Did the solar job myself." He gestured at the hood.

Addy had seen worse. The small, flexible solar panels on the hood were even with the corners. Laid flat and well-spaced, their wires showing where they needed to and no more.

Peeking into the bed before she got in, she saw two rows of boat batteries. "Wired together in series to increase voltage, huh?"

Dean grinned. "I take it you know something about solar?"

"Kinda have to, Dean."

He nodded, chuckling as he turned the engine over. Rather than comment, he smiled again, mouth turned down at the edges, and dropped the truck into gear. He pointed off to their right. "This used to be the east gate, but it hasn't been used for a while. Gonna be a little rough until…we…get…" He trailed off, the truck's forward momentum petering to a halt.

Addy, frowning, followed his gaze out the windshield.

Two trucks, a lot like the ones her dad and best friend had been loaded onto, pulled up to the old gate. Someone stepped down from the closest one and opened the gate. The gate appeared rusted, unusable, overgrown, but it opened like it was on greased ball bearings. The trucks, their gasoline engines belching, crawled through the open port. Exhaust pouring into the air, they waited as the boy closed the gate and arranged the foliage to look natural.

Addy covered her nose. The exhaust stench was unbearable. Acrid and thick and nauseating. It'd been going on a decade since she'd seen a gasoline-powered vehicle running, besides these. Hell, vehicles were a thing in and of themselves. There'd been more and more these past couple years, but her dad once told her most people didn't even walk regularly anymore when the disease first began spreading.

Her dad.

As the trucks passed, the one working streetlight at the gate illuminated his face staring out of the rear truck.

"Dean." She grabbed his arm, her heart pounding the inside of her ribs hard enough to bruise. "My dad. Dean, they're in there. Where are they going?"

"I don't know." He watched the trucks drive down the hill.

In silence, Addy watched with him.

At the bottom of the hill, both trucks turned left and disappeared.

Addy's breath crowded her throat, each lungful a chore. Her heartbeat pounded in her temples.

Covering her face with her hands, she slowed her breathing. Taking measured, full breaths, her heart rate dropped back to a semblance of normal.

She lowered her hands, glancing at Dean.

He sat watching her, arms draped over the wheel. Waiting.

"Let's go get Mike. We'll figure out what to do after that," she said.

Dean goosed the accelerator, the whine of the engine ratcheted up a notch, and they rolled down the hill in the same direction the trucks had taken. He left the headlights off, and they rode in the silent dark, stars glittering overhead. Most of the moon hung over the mountains behind them.

As they neared the intersection, their momentum slowed.

Addy glanced left. Red pinpricks of taillights receded into the distance.

"Definitely heading out of town," Dean said.

Addy, head full of so many thoughts she couldn't pin one down, pressed her lips together.

Dean let the truck roll straight through the intersection, and then they were flying around a curve, crisp air blowing through the open windows.

Addy's hair flew back from her temples, her eyes wide as saucers. Flying in darkness, headlights still off, the Milky Way cast the light of ten billion stars onto the empty road—the sheer size of the galaxy was something her mom had always loved to talk about.

Cleared by a village crew to serve as a firebreak and to maintain visibility, the smooth road unrolled before them like glass.

Addy closed her eyes. In her mind, she could see the air as though it were colored smoke, flying over them and rippling out behind.

Still, Dean went faster, easing into another wide curve. As they straightened, the engine whine decreased.

"Hang on here, it's gonna get a bit bumpy," he said.

Gripping the handle above the door, she opened her eyes.

Now he turned on the lights, illuminating chunks of pavement in piles. Carpeted in greenery.

"There's nothing left of the road up there," she said, breath light.

Growing up, her life had been all broken pieces and bloody ground. Here, outside the village, in the world from which she'd come, no clean surfaces stood. If it wasn't knocked over, blown up, or blanketed in dirt and dandelions, it was smothered in blood and offal.

Still, after having been in the village for a while, it jarred her senses to see it again. A deep part of her craved the order of whole walls and flat roads. Maybe it was all the TV. Things were always clean and polished on the Enterprise.

But this? This was the wasteland. The wilds.

Grunting, Dean bumped them through a hilly parking lot behind what used to be a sprawling metal building. At the edge of the lot, a cell tower loomed. Easing the truck up next to it, he flashed the lights once, paused, and flashed them twice more.

Just like Mike's knock.

He shut the truck down and opened his door. "Come on, we're here."

***

Addy gazed up the tower.

Dean cupped his hands around his mouth. "Mike, you up there?"

Mike's answer floated down from the top. "Yeah, boss. Give me a sec."

As Michael knocked and bumped his way down the tower, Addy kicked at a piece of demolished asphalt. The hairs on the back of her neck tingled. Her back naked, exposed, she turned it toward the wall and leaned. One hand gripped the handle of her Bowie knife, unsnapping the restraining band on its holster. Her eyes widened, drawing in as much light as she could. She sniffed.

Clean, fresh night air.

"Hey, Dean?"

He turned from the door, eyes wide, brows lifted.

"What were you doing at Jane's house?"

He crunched on a heel, his turn agonizingly slow. As he opened his mouth, the door in front of him swung back.

"Bean. Hey, what are guys doing here? Never mind," Mike said, waving them in, "get in here."

"Don't call me that."

Dean followed her in, and Mike locked them inside the roofless block enclosure surrounding the cell phone tower.

"It ain't much, but I've got a fire. Somebody gonna fill me in?" He held a hand toward the fire, a one-man tent pitched next to it. The flaming mesquite wood sent sparks ten feet into the air, where the wind whisked them into the desert.

On her way around the tower, Addy craned her neck, following the line of the built-in ladder to the top. "How tall is it?"

Dean laid his hand on the side. "About sixty feet."

"That's a long way up." Settling down next to the fire, she caught the faint scent of burning meat. Her stomach rumbled. Nothing in the world existed like fire-cooked meat.

Mouth watering, she asked her brother if he had any food left.

Mike flopped down across from her, a cloud of dust poofing up around him. He shot her a lopsided grin. "Yeah, bean, I got some food left. Just like you, eatin' up all my food."

Addy grinned back. He could complain all he wanted, but he'd hand over the food.

As Dean stuck a booted toe in the fire, nudging the coals, Mike sailed a hunk of meat over it.

She caught it, fumbled, and snatched it just before it hit the dirt. She raised a fist in triumph. "Ha!"

As she chewed the meat, salty, a little gamey, but juicy and flavored by the mesquite fire, Dean explained the situation to Mike. He stood with his hands in his pockets, bending over once to load another slim branch on the fire.

Mike glanced at her several times as Dean spoke. As he finished the telling, ending with them pulling up next to the tower, Mike stood and gaped at them both.

"So they just took Dad and Jane? Where are they going?"

Dean shook his head. "We don't know. But I think I can find out."

Addy started, dropping her last bite in the dirt. Dammit. Picking it up, she brushed it off and asked Dean just exactly how he was going to do that.

He held up a finger and pulled out his phone. "What's the use of being a cell phone network supervisor if you don't have the phone number to all the towers?"

Addy chewed meat and dirt, watching him as he walked away. The dirt crunched between her teeth.

She asked Mike for some water.

"I bet he'll be up there all night now," Mike said. He handed off the water to her.

"What do you mean?" She swished some of the dirt from between her teeth.

Mike nodded toward the tower. "He's going up there for better reception," he said. "Probably call everyone on our team." He sat next to Addy and snagged the water.

Dean's boots clanged against the ladder as he ascended.

Her brow wrinkled. "Why would he do that? He hardly knows us."

Mike chuckled low in his throat. "It's the way he is, Addy. We've worked together for a while now. He takes care of his people."

"So we're his people now?"

"I am. So now you are too."

"Just what I always wanted. A new babysitter."

CHAPTER 11

J ack lifted his face from the cold metal bed of the truck. Cheek flattened and slick with drool, he questioned his ability to fall asleep in such a rumbling beast.

Sitting up, he rolled each shoulder, upper arms strained and tired. Being tied for so many hours wasn't something his muscles nor joints took kindly to.

However many hours it had been.

The sky still dark, the air smelled like sunrise. And exhaust. What a stench.

"You OK?" Jane had all but disappeared into the shadow next to him. She'd curled up into the corner of the truck and had worked her arms around under her feet and into her lap.

Jack rode a wave of envy. She must be double-jointed to pull off such a thing. He shrugged. "Just a little sore. How long was I out?"

"Not long. You didn't start snoring yet."

"And how long does that take?"

"How should I know? A while? All I know is you do. Your kids say you could wake the dead."

Laughing into his chest, he dried his cheek on his shoulder as best as he could. "That is patently untrue."

She chuckled, scooting toward him. "Turn around. Let me see if I can get your hands free."

He obliged, eyes sliding across and over Elizabeth and Gerald. They'd fallen asleep on one another, his lap her makeshift pillow.

Good for them, really. He might've been slow on the uptake, but he couldn't begrudge Ger the chance.

Before Jane prodded him into action, he finished his turn. His ass had fallen asleep during his brief nap and was like sitting on a potato. A dead, dumb, senseless thing.

Jane cursed.

"What?"

"You've got on handcuffs. I don't have anything to pick them with."

"I should. You'll have to look in my front shirt pocket."

As he spun to face Jane, she stood on her knees. The truck lurched over a bump, sending her face-first into his chest.

His stomach flip-flopped. His nose reported she smelled a bit like fresh flowers and light sweat.

He asked his nose to kindly butt out.

Jane got her hands in front of her and pushed off his chest, a butterfly taking wing, and squatted instead. As she felt his shirt for the pocket, her breasts all but pushed up into his nose, he inhaled and exhaled with caution. And concentration.

"Ah, got it. Jack," she said, leaning back.

He lifted his eyes and a corner of his mouth. "Jane?"

"Why do you have a paper clip in your pocket?"

"Never know when you might need a paper clip."

She sat back on her heels.

"Alright fine, I stuck it in there this afternoon when I was going over the map with Tim."

Tim. Huh. If Ricardo was there, and the other boys from the Task Force, where was Tim?

"OK, mister, turn around again," Jane said, holding out the little bent paper clip.

He did as he was told.

He could feel his ass now, not that that was a good thing. The floor of the truck was cold, hard, and unforgiving. Something that bothered him more than it would have just a few years ago.

The cuff on his right wrist released its pressure. He pulled his right arm around with care, letting the deep pins and needles do their business. As the blood rushed back into his upper arm and shoulder, he stifled something between a groan and a sob behind clenched teeth.

Scooting around, Jane folded his left arm up for him, laying it over her shoulder and rubbing it hard enough to help the circulation, but soft enough not to cause pain.

Well. Any more pain than it was already in.

He glanced at her hair. "Those are weapons, too, right?"

She nodded, pulling the needles from her bun and holding them out to him. Her hair unraveled, falling in her face and over her shoulder.

Taking them, ignoring the fresh scent of shampoo wafting away from her, he stared at the needles.

On the blunt end of one, blood crusted around the top. As he stared, wondering whose blood it was, his mind adjusted to the fact he could see it.

The sun was rising.

He held them out to her. "Jane, whose blood is this?"

"It—"

The truck downshifted, sending her rolling into him again. Before she connected, before he had time to think about his reaction, he threw an arm out and held the needles away from her body as she wobbled.

Eyes widening, she missed getting her hands up in time again. Her face connected with his collar bone.

"Ouch." Even muffled by his chest, pain rode the edge of her voice.

Helping her sit up, he glanced around the truck again.

Andrew, settled with his back in the opposite corner, stared and grinned with half his mouth. Liz and Ger had woken but not moved.

"Where the hell are we, Jack?" Ger asked.

"I think that's what we're about to find out." He handed the needles to Jane.

She re-knotted her hair with them and sat, biting her lip.

***

The fire crackles and you sit wedged between Mom and Dad, smothered in warmth.

They're laughing, joking, smiling with each other. Your dad says something funny, and Mom laughs and oh, how it's like bells. Like wind sighing through the leaves. Beautiful, light, full of breath and life.

Her arm floats across your vision to touch your dad, and you hear them kiss over your head.

"Ew," your brother says. He's on the other side of the fire, and he's making fun, but he's laughing too. Chewing on his food and laughing. You smile, and he turns to you. Says, "Don't you think you're a little old to be all smooshed in with Mom and Dad like that?"

Shaking your head, you laugh. You might be twelve, but no one's too old for a good smoosh.

Mom hugs you, cocooning you in warmth. "I wish the solar panel was working," she says. "I'd kill to watch some Trek."

You smile. It's your thing with her. No one else likes it. You hug her back.

Dad says how he'll try to get the panel fixed in the morning. And he tells you to go to sleep because he and Mom have the watch covered.

Drifting off, the sound of the fire popping and crackling, enveloped in the heat from your parents' bodies, no cold fingers can touch you here.

* * *

Addy's lids fluttered, the rising sun just breaking the horizon.

Still cold inside the concrete bunker beside the tower, the tip of her nose numb, she rubbed her arms under the blanket.

Wait, blanket?

She looked down at the two blankets which had, at some point, been laid over her. No wonder she'd dreamed of being warm.

Pushing them aside, she glanced across the fire. Mike slept on, light snores emanating from inside the tent.

You'd think he'd learn to sleep quietly, but he'd learned from the best. Their dad could wake the dead.

She looked over her shoulder and found Dean leaned against the tower itself. Too far away from the fire, he'd crossed his arms and feet, rested his chin on his chest, and fallen asleep sitting up. With no blankets.

As she stood, her foot scraped across some gravel. No louder than a mouse.

Dean started, arms and legs uncrossing. Losing his balance, he threatened to topple over. Instead, he put a hand down, rebalanced, and bounced to his feet.

He was quick, she'd give him that.

"Hey, just me," she said. Holding a hand out, she stood, fell over the skimpy pile of mesquite, and wobbled.

Before she could faceplant in the rocky dirt, Dean grabbed her under the arms and hauled her back up.

She shook him off, drawing her brows together. "I got it."

He let go. "OK, alright. You got it."

Crossing her arms, Addy kicked at a rock. It pinged off the tower.

She looked all the way up.

The morning sun bounced off the antenna, and while it was still broken in places, pieces had been added back to it. It looked like a patchwork quilt, but apparently, it did the job. Speaking of the job…

"What did you find out?" she asked.

"I know what direction they're going. We can catch them."

"Are we taking your truck?"

"No," Dean said. "Well, yes. But no."

"What does that even mean? Yes or no?"

"We'll take it out to the river. From there, we've got, well, you'll see."

"Mike," she shouted over her shoulder, "shag your ass. The sun's getting high."

She turned back to Dean, brows drawn down. "What are we waiting for? We're wasting daylight then."

***

Dean pulled off the winding road about a mile after they'd crossed the river.

Addy frowned. River. A funny term for little more than a stream. Her dad told her most of the water was underground. Somehow, she always pictured a riverbed just like the one she could see. With less sunlight and some sort of cavernous, underground beach. White water surging between the banks.

"It's just up here," Dean said, unloading bags from the truck. "Hey, Mike, grab that, would you?" He angled his chin at the last bag.

"I'm perfectly capable of helping, Dean," Addy said. She stepped between Mike and the truck, lifting the bag that had to weigh seventy-five pounds if it weighed an inch. She didn't stagger, but she clenched her fingers, knuckles whitening, and her knees knocked together once.

Dean raised a brow. "You got it?"

"Mm-hmm. Ungh." *Yeah, yeah, let's go.*

He nodded at Mike, half a frown pulling the corner of his mouth down, one tiny dimple next to it. "Grab a couple of those batteries, would you?"

Mike nodded. "Here," he said, "I'll do you one better." Dumping the contents of his bag, he loaded five of the batteries into it, packed stuff around the edges and sides of it, and rolled the rest up in his sleeping bag.

Addy's shoulder screamed to put the bag down. She shifted the weight and considered dropping it on the ground.

"You can put that down for a minute before we go," Dean said.

She narrowed her eyes. Heat rose in her cheeks, and she ground her teeth. "I've got it."

To prove it, she hefted the bag farther up her shoulder. Her arm might be going to sleep. Didn't matter, she wasn't going to put this bag down until they got where they were going.

She wobbled toward the vague direction Dean had pointed when they got out. The guys mumbled behind her, but the wind blew across her ears, not unlike the way it sounded when she blew across an old Coke bottle. Her own labored breathing, loud as a bass drum, took up the rest of her hearing. What winter was left in the spring breeze froze the tips of her ears.

With cold ears came an aching head.

Of course, a headache was a wonderful thing to have with these two guys behind her. All but fighting over who got to tell her what to do next. And what was with the rocks that must be in this bag? Why did it have to be so heavy?

She opened her mouth to ask Dean why he needed to bring *all* of his barbells.

Her open mouth, breath sucking in over her tongue, caught the scent first. Just before an arm appeared out from behind the cottonwood next to her. There it wasn't, there it was. Grabbing at her hair.

She dropped the bag. It landed on her right foot. She exhaled with a *woof*.

The 'Head grabbed for her again.

She extricated her foot, losing her balance and falling back onto her elbows.

Attempting to unsheathe the knife, she forgot to unsnap it and it snagged.

She rolled away from the 'Head's arm as it fell. Bony fingers grasping air where she'd been not two seconds ago.

Finally unsheathing her knife as the 'Head stumbled and reached for her again, she stabbed toward the neck.

The knife sunk into its shoulder.

She half expected dust to fall from the wound as the thing loomed over her again. Heart beating in her ears, she swallowed the taste of copper in the back of her throat.

Fear wasn't something there was time for. She might have a dose of Cure in her pouch, but it would do her no good if she let it rip her throat out.

Its claw-like fingers grasped at her and it leaned, falling into her face. Air, breath if you could call it that, exhaled from its mouth. It stank like the black wings of buzzards after feeding. Coated in decay and moldy flesh. The creature writhed over her body in some sort of grotesque imitation of intimacy.

She grimaced. Her nerve endings tingled. Blood rushed through her veins, fighting for its very life. She never felt more alive than she did fighting one of these things.

Even as it snapped at her nose, her arms holding it just out of reach, she grinned.

Running feet crunched over the dried undergrowth.

Dean kicked the Dead Head, sending it flying off Addy. It landed five feet away with a thud. He leapt over her and nailed it to the ground, impaling it with his machete. Taking a quick and dirty aim with his sawed-off, he blew its face into a thousand tiny pieces of blood and gore.

The head split like a rotted melon, the edges caving in like a week-old jack-o-lantern.

And then Mike was next to Addy, offering her a hand up.

Dean stepped over and offered his hand as well.

Addy exhaled, stood without touching or making eye contact with either of them, and brushed the front and back of her pants clean of leaves and dirt.

"I didn't need any help." Sheathing her knife, she stalked to the too-heavy bag and hefted it back onto her shoulder. "Let's go."

Dean passed by her, turning his head and opening his mouth.

She glared.

He closed his mouth and led the way.

CHAPTER 12

One of the boys, no more than fifteen, pointed a rifle into the back of the truck.

"Come down, Jack," Wade said.

Jack couldn't see him, but he was out there. He'd be the first one Jack got his hands on.

Hands that were free of the cuffs, thanks to Jane. He'd had just enough time to return the favor.

But he kept them clasped behind his back, waiting for the child with the gun to climb up here.

"He said come down, Mr. Cooke," the boy said, pointing his rifle in a vague upwards direction.

Jack glared down at him. "We're going to need some help. With our hands tied, we can't get down very easy."

"What are you waiting for, boy?" Wade asked. "Get up there. You! Get over there and help."

The boy with the rifle slung it over his shoulder and hiked himself into the truck. Behind him, Ricardo shuffled into view, his own rifle slung over his shoulder.

Before the first boy could get a foot up, he found his hand cuffed to the truck.

Jane punched him across the jaw.

He fell limp, arm suspended over his head.

Jack jumped down, Andrew thudding into the dirt beside him a split second later. Andy's hands remained tied behind his back, but that had never stopped him before.

"Down," he grunted at Jack.

Crouched low, Andrew's sweeping kick ruffled his hair.

Andy's boot connected with the side of Ricardo's head, sending the kid into the dirt.

Still crouched, Jack grabbed the rifle. He checked the safety. It was on.

One corner of his mouth turned up. At least one of these kids wasn't a bloodthirsty idiot. And Ricardo had always seemed nice.

He flipped the safety off and aimed at the side of the truck. "So, about that conversation, Wade."

"Jackson, I just want to talk to you." Wade's wheedling voice drifted around the side of the truck. And his voice oozed sweat.

Behind Jack, Ger, Liz, and Jane crawled down from the truck.

Liz crouched in his peripheral. "This asshole."

Jack grinned, nodding. "What is it you want to talk about, Wade?"

"You killed my deputy mayor. You were coming for me."

"That's nonsense. You know that."

"I know nothing of the sort, Jackson. I know you've wanted to take my position since you moved into our village."

Jack snorted. "Nothing could be further from the truth. All I ever wanted was to live in peace with my family."

"Ah, yes. Your children," Wade said, voice oily. "Do you have any idea how lucky you have been, Mr. Cooke, to have both of your children with you, still?"

Jack's stomach lurched. "Of course I know. Your point?"

"His point is, he's trying to distract you," Jane hissed.

Jack glanced behind him. Ger and Liz crouched with him. Andrew stood, back to the truck, eyes darting in every direction while Jane worked his ropes.

She was right. What was all this talking doing? He raised his voice again. "Wade, why don't we sit down and talk this out?"

A voice spoke in Jack's ear. "I don't think so."

Stifling a nervous jump, Jack snapped his head right.

A figure, suspended from the undercarriage, grinned. A fist lashed out.

Cracked in the chin, Jack's head spun. He fell to his stomach. The rifle skittered away.

Breaking his cover, Andrew grabbed at it.

A shot split the air.

Shouting, Andrew fell to the ground. He clutched his shoulder, blood seeping between his fingers and soaking into the asphalt.

"I don't want anyone else hurt," Wade shouted. "Stop this now!"

Tim lowered himself from the undercarriage, smiling. His eyes flicked to either side of Jack.

Swallowing, Jack sat up. Held both hands in the air as the boys surrounded them again.

"Cuff 'em," Tim said.

Shuffling feet. Iron fists pinning Jack's arms behind him again.

Bubbling, gurgling, moaning.

He turned, heart pounding a rhythm inside his ribcage hard enough to break bone.

A Dead Head shuffled closer, hands raised. Stinking, blackened teeth gnashing.

He jerked, yanking at the metal bands wrapped around his wrists. "Get these cuffs off me!"

Tim cleared his throat. "Stand down, men."

The boys lowered their weapons. As they retreated around the trucks, one of them grabbed Ricardo and dragged him along.

"Andrew. Andrew, get up," Jack said, backing into his friend.

Together, they stood, backs against the truck. Gerald, Elizabeth, and Jane backed up to the truck with them.

Jack pointed left with his chin. "Go. Go that way."

Tim appeared in the open space. He leveled a rifle at them. "No. I don't think so."

Still the 'Head shuffled closer. Buzzing. Gurgling around something stuck in its throat.

The stench of rotted flesh left out on a warm day wafted over Jack's senses, his nose burning.

"So this is really you," Jane said, taking a step toward Tim.

He looked down, eyes bouncing from her cleavage to her face. He licked his lips and the tip of the gun wavered, even as it remained aimed at her heart.

She stepped closer.

"Jack," Gerald said. "Jack, we've got to do something."

Jack watched the tip of the rifle, and the brave girl staring it down. "Ger, what have I gotten us into?"

Slow but steady, the 'Head stumbled toward them.

Ger pressed his shoulder into him. "Jack, that 'Head is getting closer. Obviously, Wade wanted you out of his way, and he's about to get it."

Elizabeth stepped in front of the 'Head as its black fingers grasped for Jack. "If you want them for breakfast, you gotta get through me, first." She raised her bound hands to push it back.

Mouth an open maw, it moved with sudden alacrity. Teeth clashing together, it took a chunk out of the underside of her bicep. Blood-drenched skin dripped from its nightmare teeth.

Screaming, she tumbled into Jack, knocking him into the truck.

His head clanged against metal. His ears rang, a white flash of light from behind his eyes blinding him. He fell, and Elizabeth fell with him.

She writhed on the blacktop, scraping her face and screaming so loud her voice cracked.

The Dead Head fell to the ground and crawled along the trail of blood, licking at it.

Gerald kicked the side of its head, knocking it off course.

Jack found himself staring into its deadened, blackened eyes. Blood in the capillaries long since coagulated.

It hissed and jumped forward, surprising strength left in its wasted muscles.

Jack, head pounding, ears ringing with Liz's screams, backed away. Backing through molasses. Like it was a bad dream and he couldn't wake. Couldn't crawl away even as the 'Head inched closer. As it lapped up the blood Liz had spilled. As it reached out for his leg.

A red and green streak landed on the 'Head, shouting from deep in her throat. Jerking the needles from her hair, Jane impaled it through the temple with them both. Sheets of her hair hung in her face as she yanked the needles from its cranium. She stabbed it again and again, rotted gourd of the 'Head thunking with each impact. Brain sludge dripping through the widening hole.

She screamed herself hoarse. Covered in sweat, dirt, and its stinking blood. She stabbed it again and again.

Tim snatched her arm and pulled her off it, throwing her to the ground.

Jack found his voice. "Don't you touch her!"

Instead, Tim stared him in the eye as he laid a boot heel over Jane's throat.

Her struggles quieted.

He pointed the rifle between her eyes, resting the sights on her forehead. "Try me, Jack."

***

Adelaide, standing inside what looked like a caboose, glared out the front window. "So this train car runs itself?" Arms crossed, she rocked with the uneven tracks.

"Yeah. All solar, all electric," Dean said.

Piloting the train, he sat in what Addy had already dubbed the Captain's Chair. One small window next to him, he was otherwise surrounded by screens, buttons, lights, and levers.

She nodded. "You do this one yourself too?"

"Nah. The company gave me this one."

Mike spoke up from the back, reclining on the bed. "Dean's pretty important to the company, Addy."

She glanced at Dean. "That so?"

"That's so, sis."

Dean shrugged.

Wobbling, she joined Mike in the back, lowering herself into a chair that rocked with the train. "So, tell."

"It's a pretty big operation, getting all the cell towers back up," Mike said. Setting his feet in the floor, he leaned forward, elbows on his knees. "Our company, Iridium Flare, started in California. It's taken a lot of work to get our feet under us. IRF has slowly moved east." He nodded at Dean. "Dean was there, in the Mojave, when they got the first ground station back on line."

Addy watched Dean's back and the screens in front of him.

Must be pretty smart to work all that stuff. Her mom had shown her a thing or two, but really the most she knew about old technology was how to use a TV.

Speaking of TV.

"Hey, Mike," she said, turning back to her brother, "we gotta pick up some Trek at some point."

"Oh my god, Adelaide. You and your Trek."

"Michael. You know I need it."

"I know you need your head examined."

Addy felt the top of her head, frowning. "What does that even mean?"

He smiled. "Nothing. Say, is your cat going to be OK?"

"I left her out." She flashed on the pile of bloody feathers. The desiccated mouse corpse which had been her first gift. "She'll be fine."

"Mike," Dean called.

Mike winked at Addy and joined Dean.

Addy sat back and took in the small space.

Latching cabinets with glass fronts held neatly stacked bowls, plates, and cups. A long-barreled rifle laid across a coat rack by the back door, a quiver of arrows hanging beneath it. Inside a stand on the floor, the tips of a baseball bat, a bow, a staff, a machete, and what looked like it could be considered a katana peeked out. She hadn't seen a sword like that in ages.

Opening her mouth to ask Dean if he was any good with it, her eyes fell on a small picture frame. Almost small enough to miss, it hung on the wall above the tiny bed. Two boys, the older with an arm hooked around the shoulders of the younger, smiled out. Sweaty, dirty, happy boys.

The eldest couldn't have been more than ten in the picture. The other six or seven, probably.

They looked so happy.

"Dean," she called, the question about who was in the photo on her lips.

He turned away from some joke her brother had been making, corners of his eyes crinkled in a smile.

Her heart stopped.

The eldest boy in the photo was him.

But the youngest boy wasn't here. Hadn't been spoken of.

She swallowed around the lump in her throat.

"What's up, Addy?"

"I, um, nice…nice train." Oh god. Now what was she saying? *"Nice train"? Smooth, Adelaide.*

He smiled, and the corners of his eyes crinkled again. His teeth, white and straight, peeked out from behind his lips. "Thanks. Make yourself at home. There's food," he said, motioning over his shoulder in the vague direction of the kitchen area. He went back to driving.

Addy sat back, heart racing. She stared at the picture. Who took it? Where were they now? And where was the younger boy?

Face burning, she closed her eyes and leaned her head back.

The rocking of the train carried the slick feeling in the pit of her stomach out and away. She drifted off.

***

Gerald struggled against his bonds. "They didn't give her the Cure, Jack. Why didn't they give her a dose?"

Jack shook his head. A useless gesture. A lot like whatever it was he'd been doing for the past few days. He yanked his arms, tweaking his shoulder.

That was useless, too. Not only had they re-cuffed him, they'd also bound him to the side of the truck. He couldn't even move around.

"Because they're a bunch of sick fuckers, and Tim is their captain," Jane said.

She lay on her side in the floor of the truck, trussed like a hog. She hadn't been given her needles back, of course, and her hair hung across her face, obscuring all but her mouth. She flipped her head, but most of the hair stuck to sweat. She pushed and pulled against the ropes holding her wrists.

Seemed Jack was the only one lucky enough to get actual cuffs.

"Jackie, we gotta do something about this." Andrew's large shoulders bunched.

Jack opened his mouth, inhaled to speak, and exhaled nothing but breath.

Andrew's face crumpled. "I haven't been much help. Some 'muscle' I turned out to be."

"Hey, no. Andy, this isn't your fault." Jack paused, searching for words that could bring the blame back where it belonged. His mind felt like a butter knife. Like an ancient silent movie with Vaseline over the lens. Old and fuzzy.

He glanced at Andrew's shoulder with fresh, white gauze stretched to the breaking point. In an unusual gesture of mercy, Wade had ordered the graze cleaned before they got underway.

Elizabeth groaned.

Jack narrowed his eyes, focusing on her ragged breath.

She wasn't dead, but she was still bleeding from the bite. She would bleed out if the wound didn't get dressed. Not only that, the fever sweat had already begun on her face. Before long, it would cover her body. Her chest heaved as she struggled for each breath. Even if she didn't bleed out, she'd turn soon without a dose of the Cure.

"Liz," Jack said, "hang in there. We're going to fix this. We're going to—"

The zipper between the rear and cab rasped, flap dropping open. Wade's sweating face appeared in the hole. He stared at Liz.

Jack cleared his throat. "Wade."

"Jackson, I, this isn't supposed to be this way," he said, eyes still on Liz.

"Wade, look at me."

The mayor, with what seemed like a Herculean effort, averted his eyes from the dying woman.

"You need to help us," Jack said. "She has to get a dose. She needs her wound dressed. You can't just let her die back here."

Wade nodded as Jack spoke, eyes flicking between him and Liz. He opened and closed his mouth twice before any sound came out. "We can't stop right now, Jack. I'm sorry."

Jack kicked out, stretching to smack Wade in the face with a boot heel. He missed, but the little man recoiled.

"Got a onetime offer for you, Jack," Tim said. His face out of sight, his voice alone made the offer. "I got one dose of Cure here. For your girl. But," he said, floating a hypodermic filled with amber liquid in the window flap, "she's got to get it herself."

"You son of a bitch, you can't do that," Gerald said, voice on the ragged edge. He wriggled toward the window and leaned in, speaking from deep in his throat. "Please. Let me."

Tim chuckled. It was low, barely discernible over the engine noise and wind. But it was there. "You're all tied. She's the only one with her hands in front. Has to be her."

Wade's face appeared in the window again. "This isn't what I wanted, Jack."

"Shut up, you sniveling freak," Tim said.

Wade's face disappeared again.

The balance in power teetered. Jack felt it wobble.

Again, the syringe floated in the window. "Here's your chance, honey. Take it."

Shivering, Liz opened red-rimmed eyes. Sucking snot up her nose, she struggled to her knees and began to shuffle toward the window. Gerald hopped back over to her and knee-walked behind her. When she fell, which was at least twenty times if it was one, he was there, catching her with his chest. She'd nod, and he'd lean her back up again to shuffle a few more inches.

Just in front of the window, a coughing spell wracked her body. She shivered from her toes to her spine, teeth clacking. Hacking and bleeding, she ended up on her ass.

Once she'd gotten the coughing under control, she pushed to her knees.

The hypodermic floated just within reach.

Extending her bound hands, she wobbled back and forth. Shaking like she had the DTs.

"You got it?" Tim's disembodied voice echoed from the front.

Shivering, teeth chattering, Liz formed her lips around the word no.

"OK, you got it!" Tim shouted. It was a gay sound. A shout you'd hear at the circus. If there had still been a such thing.

He opened his fist, letting go of the syringe.

Liz dove to catch it, bloodying her nose and mouth on the floor of the truck.

The dose fell, bounced off the open flap, and disappeared between the cab and the truck. Into the open air between.

Gone.

***

Addy stood, swaying her way to Dean and Mike. She pointed over Dean's shoulder. "What's that?"

Dean squinted at the middle display, lips pursed. A red dot flashed. "Something on the tracks." He punched a few buttons, turned a handle.

Addy and Mike rocked as the train slowed.

Mike started to the back. "We gotta clear it, Addy."

Addy unsnapped her knife. As she reached to unsheathe her machete, Dean's hand fell over hers.

Why? Why would that give her butterflies? Alright, he was pretty. But there were lots of pretty men. Tim, for one.

"Let Mike and me handle this," he said.

She flushed from her forehead to her toes and jerked her hand away. "You're the one who knows how to steer this thing. You have to stay here." She spoke through clenched teeth. "I'll help Mike clear the tracks."

"That's not true," he said. The chair creaked as he stood. "Mike knows how to drive it. Don't you?"

"Sure do. But Dean, you're not suggesting—"

"That's exactly what I'm suggesting."

Addy spun on a heel.

Dean, hand on Mike's shoulder, guided him to the Captain's Chair.

She opened her mouth to protest, but Mike turned toward her, his face an apology.

Lungs contracting, forcing the breath up and out, her heart clenched into a fist. She took a gulping breath, watching Mike's face. His open, trusting face. So sweet. Innocent, even.

Yeah. He should stay here.

Dean opened the back door and grabbed his own machete. "Come on." He stepped out and beckoned Addy with a wave.

"It's hard to believe there's only one car on this train," she said, joining him. She stood on the little porch, too small for two people, really, and eyed the dull silver sides of the caboose.

Dean nodded, checking the other side. "Sometimes I pull stuff with it. Tower equipment, that kind of thing. But one is all I need," he said, patting the side of the car. Glancing over his shoulder, he smiled. "It's clear. Let's get this over with." He hopped down and extended a hand.

Ignoring his hand, Addy jumped down, wobbled, grabbed the stair railing, and righted herself. Small miracles.

As they crept past the front of the train car, she looked at the engine. A separate piece attached to the front, it even had its own set of two wheels.

"I've never seen anything like this."

Dean came up next to her and patted the train again. "She may be ugly, but she's my baby." He looked up the side of the car, the sides of his eyes crinkling in a smile again.

Addy watched him pat the train car, calculating. Between this train, his truck, and welding cell phone towers back together, his days must have been full. "You stay busy, huh?"

"Yeah. I do. Come on," he said, motioning at the track, "let's get this done."

He'd stopped the train about 500 feet from the obstruction. As they approached, Addy squinted. "Looks like a tree." She unsheathed her machete.

"Careful though," Dean said, holding a hand out. He didn't look, and his arm almost clotheslined her.

She rocked back on a heel. "Whoa, geez, Dean. Knock a girl over why don't you?"

"Sorry." He looked over his shoulder, lowering his arm. "Sorry, but do you see something besides tree?"

Addy knelt, sniffing. The tree was downwind. Her nose wouldn't help. She closed her eyes and laid a hand on the track.

The rail thrummed. If it had been audible, it would have sounded like buzzing. As it was, there was no sound. Only the thrumming under her hand.

"It's old, slow, crippled probably," she whispered.

"No reason not to be careful."

"Well, then. Let's get this done." Addy opened her eyes and stood.

Creeping up on the mostly intact tree, just its crown bent across the tracks, the 'Head pinned beneath it reached for them. It wheezed like a bagpipe losing air.

Dean hacked at the small branches with his machete. "Wonder what happened. This wasn't here a week ago. Hell, it wasn't here three days ago."

Adelaide shrugged, raising her own machete to chop away branches.

The commotion spurred the 'Head into movement. It struggled against its woody prison, buzzing louder.

Addy smiled. There was no way its wasted muscles were strong enough to get out from under the tree. It was pathetically hilarious, unable to get out from under a few branches.

They were dangerous when they surprised you, deadly in a group. But like this? Laughable.

Even so, the sound of its buzzing disturbed her. Set her teeth on edge. She had to mask it.

"So Dean," she said, pitching her voice high.

He continued to hack. "Mm-hmm."

"How long have you and Mike known each other? He's been out on the road for a while, but I don't remember him mentioning you last time he was home."

"Oh, I don't know. Six months probably. Why?"

Because I needed to ask you something, and who is in that picture over your bed seemed like a bad ice breaker. "Just wondering. You guys work well together?"

Dean stopped, machete buried in a thick limb. "Yeah. We do. Your brother's a good guy."

"He's…yeah. He's— Yeah."

"He's what?" Dean asked, returning to chopping.

The 'Head buzzed in the background. Static on a TV.

Addy shivered, kept chopping. "What can I say? He's my brother. I mean, we got through the apocalypse together. He's a tough guy."

"But."

"But. He's pretty smart but sometimes he needs my help. And he's a little. Well. Naive."

Dean chuckled. "No, he's not always quick on his feet. Although he doesn't fall over them as much as you—"

"What? Hey!" Addy kicked out at Dean's ankle, missed, and kicked the rail. "Ouch! Oh, piss upon a flat rock!"

Dean chuckled again.

She hopped away from the tree, cursing. Once her toe quit throbbing, she hobbled back over and resumed cutting. They grew ever closer to freeing the 'Head.

"He's a good guy to have around. I wouldn't want anything to happen to him," Dean said, reaching down to grab the last branch off the 'Head. He looked up at her, green eyes twinkling. "You ready?"

She nodded.

He pulled the limb off the 'Head.

On unsteady arms it pushed itself from the ground, black fingers digging in for purchase. It lurched to its feet and lunged at Dean, who took a backhanded swipe at it with the dull side of his machete. It staggered back, its cloudy, wasted eyes falling on Addy.

How they saw anything out of those eyes was a mystery she might never have the answer to.

She swung her own machete low, connecting with it in the midsection. It hit home and she both tugged and twisted.

Intestines like shriveled sausages snaked out and splattered to the ground.

"Oh, Addy. Gross," Dean said, swinging hard enough to chop the hand reaching for her clean off. It flopped to the ground, spilling some kind of black ichor from its ragged end.

"Mine was better," she said, swinging for its other arm.

Dean laughed as she pinned the arm to its side, slicing halfway through it.

"Yeah, but mine was more *save your life*," he said, smacking it in the head with the flat side of the machete. The force of the hit knocked it off its feet, torso on the tracks. Its head hung over the rail. Without hesitation, Dean swung hard enough to behead it in one.

The disembodied head rolled away from the tracks and down the hill. He watched it go.

"Looks kinda like a tumbleweed," he said.

Addy burst into laughter.

***

The truck downshifted, jarring Jack from his reverie. He lifted his chin from where it'd fallen on his chest. His neck screamed. He muffled the groan creeping up his throat as best he could.

"You OK?" Jane whispered from her corner.

"Yeah. How's Liz?"

"It's been almost twelve hours," Andrew said.

Jane sighed. "She'll turn soon."

Jack's stiff neck creaked as he lifted his head to peek across the truck.

On one of their stops for food, water, and bathroom, they'd finally allowed Liz's wound to be dressed. Wade had even been magnanimous enough to allow Ger to have his hands tied in front. He sat with her head in his lap, stroking the hair from her forehead.

The hair stuck to her pasty, pale face in limp, wet strings. Her breathing shallow, dark circles ringed her eyes. Her lips, the only spot of color on her face, had turned a deep, cherry red. She'd been chewing the inside of them for hours.

Every muscle in her body twitched at once, as though she were falling asleep. Her shallow breathing slowed.

"Jack," Jane whispered, eyes wide as dinner plates.

He met them, and in them read the thought screaming in his own head.

She's turning. And we're tied up next to her.

"They gotta stop this truck, Jackie." Andrew scooted out of the back corner and put himself between Liz and Jack.

"Hey!" Jack called. The shout scratched against the inside of his throat like cat claws.

Liz twitched again.

"Get away from her, Ger," Jack said, leaning to the side. The cuff caught him halfway over. He glanced at Jane and Andrew. "Stop the truck on three."

They nodded.

Jack counted down, and they shouted in unison.

The truck downshifted again, the brakes squealing.

"Thank fuck," Jane breathed. She was still hog-tied and couldn't seem to wriggle free. Lying in the floor of the truck must have been akin to being in front of class naked. Exposed, helpless, nowhere to hide. Yet she'd weathered it well. Had kept her wits and her smart mouth about her.

A corner of Jack's mouth turned up.

Her strength and beauty made a magnetic combination. One he'd never taken account of. And shouldn't.

The truck rolled to a stop.

Heels scraping, Ger scooted away from Liz and toward the front of the truck. Streaks marred his cheeks where tears had cut tracks in the dirt. "I think she's gone, Jack."

Jack hung his head, their history as friends playing like a film on fast-forward. All the fights and flights.

"Jackie, it's not your fault."

Jack scowled, brows knitted. He opened his mouth to deny it but didn't get a sound out before Tim appeared at the back of the truck.

The tailgate lowered and Tim peered in. "Ah. Has she turned?" Frightening clinical detachment flavored the question.

"We think so," Jack said. "You've got to get us out of here."

"That'd be one thing to do," Tim said, hand on his chin.

Jack felt more than heard a shift in the atmosphere.

It was waking.

The hair on Jack's arms stood, painful goose bumps raising at once on his legs and arms. A chill raced down his spine. He mustered all the command in his voice that he could. "Tim. Let. Us. Out."

"Yeah. Let's do that. Boys," Tim said, motioning to the boys flanking him. "Make it quick."

"Jackie."

Jack shook his head. "You go. I'll be right behind you."

Andrew shuffled to the back, shrugging off the help Tim's soldiers offered. He landed on his feet behind the truck.

Ric approached Jack with a key. "Lean forward Mr. C., so I can unlock you."

Jack shook his head. "Get her first," he said, cocking his head in Jane's direction.

Ricardo shrugged. "Whatever you say. Help me out, Brian," he said, speaking to the towheaded boy climbing in.

The boy, one Jack had seen at the firing range, kicked Jack on the way past, connecting with the side of his knee.

Jack fought a gasp of pain, biting the inside of his lip. Whatever had happened to these boys had been happening for a while, right under his nose. They hadn't turned against him like this overnight.

"Jackson."

Swiveling his eyes, he caught just the top of Wade's head visible behind the truck.

He clamped down on the inside of his lip.

"I'm sorry about your friend, Jack," Wade went on.

"That's an unexpected sentiment, coming from you. You could have given her a dose of Cure. Anytime, you could have. You still can. We've got another sixteen hours."

"Why is that? Sixteen hours. So precise. What a strange number."

Jack opened his mouth to respond but closed it as the boys carried Jane past.

The sinews of her arms stood out as she strained against her bonds. They'd released the rope tying her hands to her feet, but both her hands and feet were still bound. As they passed her out of the truck, she said something about watching their fucking hands.

Ric hopped back in the truck, key in hand.

Liz jerked. She took a rattling breath.

"Beth?" Ger whispered.

Jack, eyes wide, sweat popping up on his forehead, shook his head. He cut his eyes to the boy. "Ric, unlock me."

The boy stared at Liz, who jerked again and began to sit up.

"Ric, look at me," Jack said.

"Beth, you're OK," Ger said, scooting toward her.

"Ricardo, unlock me," Jack said, dropping the whisper.

The boy's mouth hung slack, his hand drooping. The key began to fall.

"No, Ric, don't drop that—"

The key clinked to the floor.

Liz snarled.

Ger stopped scooting, no more than a foot away from her. He tried to smile, the muscles in his cheeks twitching his lips up and down. He spoke from the side of his mouth. "They say they can retain some memory this close to the change."

Liz snarled again, her throat bubbling. Like she had a bad cold and couldn't cough.

Ric leapt from the truck.

Jack tore his eyes from Ger and flung his leg out, trying to hook the key with his heel. He pitched his voice low. "Ger, you need to get away from her. It's not her, not anymore." He missed the key and tried again. It moved toward him an inch and got hung up in a crease. He kicked at it.

Liz turned to him, snarling and bubbling. Her open eyes, bloodshot and yellow, the color of sick death, looked through him. Whatever she was, whoever she had been, was gone.

"We can still get you the Cure, baby," Ger said, reaching for her shoulder.

"Ger, don't touch it," Andrew shouted. He bounced, trying to get back into the truck. With his hands tied behind him, he couldn't climb. "She doesn't know you! That's nothing but a lie, man."

Panting, Jack kicked at the key. It jumped a few more inches toward him.

"It's not a lie," Gerald whispered. He reached for her shoulder. "Baby? Baby, I know you're in there. Stay with me. We'll get you cured."

Jack paused his attempts to drag the key and stared, open-mouthed, as the Dead Head turned away. As it did, was there, maybe, some little recognition that wavered across its face? Like the ripple of a stone cast into a still lake.

It turned to Gerald. Mouth hanging open, saliva mixed with blood seeping from its mouth and dripping to the floor, it snarled and bubbled.

Jack flinched as its lifeless eyes settled on his friend's face. He fought the urge to close his own.

Far away, Jane screamed his name.

He couldn't turn to find her, though. He was entranced.

Ger smiled. A sunny, wide smile. He reached for Liz's shoulder, bringing both bound hands up.

Her teeth sank into his wrist, crunching down into bone. A high-pitched wail erupted from Gerald's throat.

The sound of Ger's heart breaking deafened Jack, made his ears ring. His own heart thumped in his chest, a stuttering bass drum knocking against his ribs. Muffled voices shouted from far away, but in here there was only the sound of bone crunching, teeth scraping over the marrow as they crushed with a strength only the dead possessed.

Still, Gerald screamed, his face a mess of tears and snot. Screamed her name.

She released his wrist.

Time slowed. Jack watched a single drop of blood-infused saliva drip to the ground. Splash.

"Jack!" Jane's shout broke through, brought him back to reality. The sound of it ripping all the way from her toes, coming through her throat so loud it must have been tearing her larynx to shreds, jarred him into movement.

With slow precision, he hooked the key with his heel and pulled it close. The key was all that mattered. Whatever was going on with Gerald would have to take care of itself. The key was all that mattered.

An eternity that lasted five seconds passed. A limber back he'd forgotten he ever had bent in ways he hadn't thought of in years.

And there it was, the key in his hand.

As one cuff unlocked, the world came back into sharp focus.

Before he could move to free his hands, the Dead Head leapt. It ripped and tore at Gerald, sinking its teeth into the soft space between his shoulder and chin. It snarled and gurgled, blood spurting into its face and hair.

Painting it with humanity's oldest dye. Cain's favorite pigment. The color of murder.

Even as the Dead Head ripped, energized by Gerald's struggles, Ger lifted a tired, bloodless arm. At some point, the rope had given way, and with both arms free, he wrapped them around her. He pulled her in close. His crimson lips moved.

Jack couldn't hear him, couldn't read his lips. It wasn't necessary.

Eyes on the grotesque parody of lovers, he got into motion again. Switching hands to unlock the other wrist, the key fell.

He pulled the still-cuffed wrist free, chain clinking against the truck.

Liz snorted, lifted her sanguine face to the sound.

Though Jack froze, she moved. For a moment, Ger's grip held her. She snarled, breaking the rope binding her and crawling across his limp body, bloody handprints painting the bottom of the truck. One hand gripped Jack's ankle, pulling with a strength he'd forgotten.

It had been years since he'd seen one so fresh. Their strength seemed to grow in the first hours. Become inhuman. Preternatural even.

His back against the wall, he couldn't run. He pressed against the side of the truck, kicking the 'Head in the face with the other boot.

Its head rocked back yet it crawled forward. It bit into his ankle, ripping his jeans open.

Jane screamed. Something incoherent.

A shot rocked the 'Head, flung it off him.

He scooted to the rear of the truck, pushing feet slipping in blood.

Another shot deafened him as strong hands grabbed him under the arms and hauled him to the ground. As he fell, someone spoke.

"Don't kill it, we need it."

"What do we do then?"

"Just aim…here, give me that."

Jack's ears rung. Someone crouched next to him. She smelled like flowers, sweat, dirt. His head swam.

"You're OK, you're OK," Jane repeated over and over in a mantra.

Another shot. Someone cursed. Feet pounded the ground next to Jack's head. The smell of coppery blood and gun smoke filled his nose.

"Ah, dammit, she's getting away," someone shouted.

"Well go after it!" Wade. But from far away, inside a box. Like he was hiding in the other truck, shouting through a cracked window.

A commotion followed the retreating Dead Head. If it had instincts to run away from gunfire, then maybe the rumors were right. Maybe there was some memory after all.

Jack kept his eyes closed. A warm cheek touched his.

"You're OK," she whispered in his ear.

CHAPTER 13

Addy sat watching the country slide by. She'd never seen so much of it pass by in such a hurry. It was sickening. "Dean?"

He peeked over his shoulder. Smiling.

"Are we almost there?"

"Wow. Didn't take you long to start asking *are we there yet.*"

Addy sighed. Whatever that meant. "Just yes or no, really, would be fine."

He chuckled, turning back to the screens and punching up a map. "Yeah. Take a look."

She joined him at the front of the car.

He traced a finger across their route. "OK, so there are some tracks that aren't on the old maps, which I hope our friends don't know about. The company has put a lot of work into the tracks. Some of them didn't connect, some had to be replaced. They did really well following the old tracks, but some of it"— he pointed to a moving dot—"like the one we're on? Brand new."

"Fascinating."

"It is," he said, missing or ignoring her sarcasm. "Now, according to my sources, the people that have your father and the others are using a supply road. It's some interstate but mostly two-lane blacktop."

"Well yeah. Even now, the old cities are a wreck. Best to swing wide."

"Right. So the supply road, I'm told, goes all the way east."

"What?" Addy leaned on his shoulder, peering at the map. "I had no idea."

"Besides IRF, someone has been rebuilding the roads. We don't know who." He shrugged. "Someone certainly helped with Cure distribution. IRF didn't do it alone."

"Were you part of that?"

"Me? No. That was before my time."

"What does all this mean? How far are we from Dad, Jane, and the others?"

"According to my guys, we're not far." He pointed to the map near what had been the Texas border. "We're about to meet back up with the interstate for a stretch. We should be able to get close."

"When should I wake Sleeping Beauty?"

Michael snored from Dean's bed.

Dean chuckled. "Go ahead. We're close."

Addy swayed to the rear of the car, dropping to a knee next to the bed. Reaching to shake her brother, her eye caught the framed picture again. Dean, and a boy younger than him. A boy who wasn't there.

"Michael," she said, shaking his shoulder. If this were their dad, she'd shake and jump back. He often came up swinging. Mike was much gentler.

"Hey, baby sister," he said, stretching and smiling. "We there?"

"Dean says we're close." She glanced at the picture.

Mike followed her gaze. "Oh, yeah. His little brother. He had him almost until the end."

A weight dropped into Addy's gut. She leaned in to whisper. "Do you know what happened?"

Mike shook his head, round blue eyes wide. "No. He doesn't talk about it. All I know is his name, Cameron. And that he almost made it. But didn't."

Addy glanced at Dean's back.

He punched buttons and pulled levers. Their momentum slowed. "Hey guys, we're here," he said, standing. "You two go ahead outside. I'll call my guy, make sure your dad is where he's supposed to be."

Addy checked her weaponry, snagged the bow and arrows, and followed Mike out the door. As she pulled it closed, she glanced at Dean. He stood by the sink, one arm leaned on the counter, supporting him.

At this angle, Addy could see he was thinner than she had taken him for, but the lines of his muscles stood out under his shirt. He was as strong as they came.

Surprisingly funny, too.

He caught her staring, gave her a tight-lipped grin, and turned his back, speaking into the phone.

She closed the door.

Turning, she all but ran into her brother.

He leaned against the railing, watching the western horizon through binoculars.

"Hey, let me take a peek," Addy said.

Mike turned, binoculars still in front of his eyes. "Whoa, Addy, did you gain weight?"

She fought a grin, snatching at the spyglasses.

Mike jumped back, hopping off the steps with grace. Even though they were behind him.

Taking a moment to appreciate his dexterity, she stepped down, gripping the rail. Landed on both feet. Awesome.

She poked out her lower lip. "Seriously, let me see them."

Mike shook his head. "I'll give them to you when we get closer. I don't want you to break them."

"Oh my god, Michael, I'm not five."

"Addy, you broke my compass last week."

"That was an accident."

"Hence," he said, taking a step away and wrapping a hand around the binoculars, "why you can use these under supervision only."

As she cocked back to slug him, the door to the train opened and Dean stepped down.

"They stopped. We'll have to backtrack a bit. Come on."

***

Sitting up on his elbow, Jack caught sight of Wade, mincing his way down from the other truck.

"Timothy, we need to have a word," Wade said.

Jack worked to sit up.

Jane untangled her arms with the same speed and dexterity as before. She put a hand under his arm and helped him.

He smiled. "Thanks, Jane. Thanks for looking out for me. Back there."

She frowned. "I didn't do anything. You've been bitten."

"You did everything. I couldn't move. I froze. You brought me back. Look," he said, pulling up his bloody pants leg, "she bit my boot. I'm fine. This isn't my blood." Ger's blood, smeared across the side of his boot, swirled within Liz's fingerprints. He pushed the pants leg back down over his boot, tugging too hard at the hem.

He'd see Ger's twitching, hopeful smile in his dreams for weeks.

Jane sighed. Sitting back on her heels, eyes closed, she wobbled, in danger of falling. "I think I'm gonna be sick."

He lifted a hand to catch her. The cuff dangled from his wrist. "Shit. Jane."

She opened her eyes. Stared at his free hand. "Jesus, Jack. Untie me."

She held her wrists in his lap and he worked the knots, watching the boys. They'd all turned their backs. Eyes on Tim and Wade.

His fingers slipped, rope burning the tips. "Dammit. Almost got it."

All at once, the rope slipped free. Without a pause, Jane flipped her feet from under her and went to work on the rope binding them. Sweat popped on her brow as she strained against the ropes.

He watched a drop of sweat roll down that long, graceful neck, between her breasts, and disappear down her shirt.

Whoa, cowboy. Take a step back.

He inhaled, looking away before Jane could catch him staring.

Casting his eyes about as Jane freed her feet, he found Andrew. Next to the truck, watching whatever was happening with Wade and Tim. It sounded like an argument.

Wade's voice, raised and shrill, floated above the wind. "This was not what we agreed upon, Timothy!"

"I told you there might be some collateral damage."

Jack couldn't see past the row of boys who'd gathered to watch the fight, but he imagined Wade bouncing on his toes, agitated.

Scratch that. He could see feet. One pair, circling the other in a wide arc. The other, bouncing on its toes.

"There's to be no more *collateral* as you call it. This has got to stop. I don't know what you've planned with these people, but if it's more of this, I do not condone it."

"Hey, Wade, you're preaching to the choir. But they want what they want. Neither of us can change that. We've got what they want now. Speaking of which." The feet paused their circling. "You two. Get that body in a body bag. We don't want it going anywhere. Make sure it's a new bag, so it can't chew its way out. Get to it!"

Two boys jumped into the truck.

Body bag? They were saving Gerald? For what purpose? Having bled out, he needed a bullet to the brain and that was that.

Jane gripped his shoulder, pointing to the trees behind him with the other. "Jack, did you hear that?"

Attention split between the men arguing and the small copse of trees behind them, he shrugged. Was that movement, there behind that tree?

"I can go no further, then," Wade said. A declaration.

"Suit yourself."

A shot split the air.

Jumping, Jack spun.

Wade fell, half on the pavement.

The circle of boys parted, and Tim emerged, seating a revolver in its holster.

"Well, Mr. C. Here we all are."

***

"Adelaide, slow down," Mike called.

She'd gotten fifty feet ahead at least, plunging through the tall grass.

She waited for them to catch up with a hand on her hip. "Why are you taking so long?"

"Addy, seriously, I know you want to get there," Dean said, catching up to her, "save them. But we have to be smart about it."

She grimaced, nodding. Of course they did. Picard wouldn't have had it any different. Neither would her mom for that matter.

Neither of them was here, though. And Dean wasn't them.

It was her dad up there, and Jane, and they both would come in, guns blazing, knives flashing, shooting first and asking questions later.

Dean snagged her arm just above the elbow before she walked away.

Stopping, she glared at his hand. Made eye contact.

He lowered his hand and pointed ahead of them. "Look, we'll get into that bunch of trees and see what's what. They should be just over the next hill."

As Addy nodded, a scream floated over waves of grass. "Jack!"

Without thinking, Addy crouched. Dean and Mike crouched with her, all three scanning the area around them.

"To the trees," Dean whispered.

Keeping low, the three of them ran to cover. There were more shouts from ahead, but mostly Addy's friend, flat-out screaming for her dad.

Her heart beat a quick staccato in her chest. "Michael."

"I know, I hear her."

They rushed through the trees. Addy took each piece of cover three at a time, waiting as Dean and Mike flanked her. Once they'd caught up, she leapt again and surged forward, feet just touching the ground. As she paused once more to let them catch up, something crashed through the undergrowth ahead.

She stopped, taking cover behind the nearest tree, and holding a fist in the air to signal Mike and Dean to stop.

The sound of their movement ceased.

The crashing from ahead continued.

Addy held her breath, unsheathing the Bowie knife. Opened her ears just like her mom had taught her.

It gurgled. Not bubbling yet. By god, it was fresh. Less than an hour. If it was turned from a simple bite, it could still be turned back.

Leaning the bow against the tree behind her, she felt her belt for her emergency dose of the Cure. Dad always said not to leave home without it. It was there, tucked inside the little black leather pouch he'd made her.

She unsnapped the top and waited for the 'Head to pass. When they were this fresh, a frontal assault was suicide.

It grew closer, ripping through brambles, snarling at the trees it hit.

The gurgling came into sharp focus. Just a few steps away.

Addy tensed. Ready to jump.

It passed her, leaves sticking out of its hair, blood splattered down its legs.

Her breath caught. Her dad and Elizabeth had been friends for years. Long enough for her to recognize the profile as it sniffed the air, even at this mostly oblique angle.

The rest of her adrenaline dumped into her stomach.

More crashing from the direction of the road. They must've been chasing her. It.

It took off, away from the pursuers.

Addy crouched, glancing to Mike as she did. He stood, back to a tree, halfway around it and staring at her with his saucer eyes.

Palm down, she patted the air and lowered herself. Mike followed suit. She glanced to Dean.

He was nowhere in sight. Damn, he was good at hiding. First, Jane's parents'. Now, here.

Pulling the bow down, she made herself tiny under a bramble.

The pursuers drew closer.

But they didn't stop to inspect. They sprinted after the Dead Head, blowing by like a hurricane. They never even slowed near Addy, Mike, or Dean.

Adelaide waited, eyes closed, nose lifted to the wind. As she decided no one else was coming and stood, a stick broke to her right.

She lifted the bow for striking.

"Hey, just me," Dean said, empty hands held up.

"Jesus, Dean. Sounded like an elephant parade."

"Addy." Mike peeked from behind the tree. "What's going on?"

She shrugged. She was supposed to know? "Let's get closer, see what we can."

As they crept through the brush, the voices from the road got louder again. More shouting.

Her heart reminded her it was there, and capable of beating at an accelerated rate of speed. She swallowed the knot in her throat.

A shot split the air. Silence followed.

She crouched and snuck forward. The trees broke just ahead, the trucks about fifty feet from that. Give or take ten feet. Hard to tell when her heart beat so hard it jiggled her eyeballs.

Swallowing again, she knelt and stuck a hand out. Mike laid the binoculars in it.

One truck. Two truck. Five boys. A tall, muscular blond. Could be Andrew.

Where were they?

There. Dad. Jane. Separated from the group. Maybe it would be possible—

The small half circle of boys opened, and Tim walked through, holstering a gun.

What the hell?

Whispering, she described the scene to Mike and Dean.

Tim spoke to her dad, waving at the boys behind him. One wrestled Andrew into a truck. Two of them handcuffed Dad and Jane together. Tim's mouth moved, but they were too far to hear what he said. And she'd never been very good at lipreading.

"I can't tell what they're saying. Dean, are you any good at that?"

"At what, Addy?"

"Lipreading."

"Oh. Yeah. Hand 'em over."

She passed him the binocs and watched him as he watched them. He clenched and unclenched his jaw six times in three seconds. Clenching, unclenching.

"Adelaide." He lowered the spyglasses.

Instead of answering him, she lost her balance and flung a hand out, reaching for air to stop her from falling on her ass.

Dean caught her hand and steadied her.

A line of butterflies raced from her toes to her crown.

Swallowing, she pulled her hand back. "What?"

"We've got to get them out of there."

***

Cuffed together, Jack and Jane sat in the dirt at the side of the road and squinted up at Tim.

"Anyway," he said, "I think we could come to an understanding."

"I don't know what you want, Tim. But I don't think we can work together," Jack said.

Tim shook his head. "You might want to rethink that strategy, Mr. C. You saw what happened to your friends. We only need one fresh Dead Head alive. We've got your friend for that. What was his name?"

Brow drawn, Jack looked at the road. What did that mean, they needed a Dead Head alive? Who was this "they" he kept talking about? And instead of taking the bait Tim had thrown, Jack asked his own questions.

"Why did you kill Wade? Weren't you on the same side?"

Tim chuckled. Bubbly, like a child. "No, we weren't on the same side." He covered his mouth, giggles growing. After a moment, he laughed aloud, doubled over with belly laughter.

Jack scooted back, pressing into Jane and turning so he was fully between her and Tim. His stomach clenched. Madmen laughed that way.

As Tim's laughter subsided, he leaned down until his face was almost in Jack's. "You know nothing about this. Nothing." He motioned to the others. "Get them back in the truck. We've got a lot of ground to cover."

The boys helped Jack and Jane to their feet, an uncertain process now that they were linked together. Side by side, they started toward the truck. Tim held out a hand.

"Jane, dear," he said, caressing her chin.

She jerked it from his hand, eyes on fire and mouth drawn into a cruel scowl. She cleared her throat, and for a wild moment, Jack thought she was going to spit in Tim's face. Instead, she spoke. "Where are we going?"

Tim opened his mouth, and an arrow planted itself an inch from his toe.

As he leapt back, Jack flinched, and Jane turned away from the trees.

She glanced at Jack. "Did that come from over there?" She pointed with her forehead. West of the direction it had really come from.

As she pointed, a cacophony of noise sounded in the same direction, and some sort of commotion began to the east.

Tim scowled. "You two, go check it out. You two," he said, pointing to Ric and another boy, "go that way. You," he said, and Jack recognized Louis. Couldn't forget that face. "Come with me."

All the boys dashed off, leaving Jack and Jane standing in the middle of the road, alone.

"Great planning," Jack whispered.

Jane exhaled half a laugh. "He's not the brightest bulb in the shed."

Jack grinned. "Where'd you get that one?"

"From me," Addy said, approaching from the trees.

Jack stifled a shout. No. No, no, no. "Adelaide, what are you doing here?"

"Saving your asses, whatsit look like? Come on, I don't know how long they'll be gone."

"Addy, I," Jack began. He faltered, fear and anger at equal proportions. "I don't have the handcuff key." A lame attempt, but his mind was just not up to full speed. She was not supposed to be here, miles and miles from home. What was she doing out here?

"Dad, we can pick a handcuff. Let's get out of here. Jane?"

Jack glanced at the woman handcuffed to him.

She shifted her weight from one foot to the other.

He rifled through excuses. "Andrew. We can't leave him."

"I'll do whatever you need, boss," Andrew said, from inside the truck.

"I'm not leaving you, man," Jack said.

"Dad, we have to go. We've got a ride home. Let's get you out of here. Andrew," Addy said, jogging to the truck, "let's go."

Jack's brain slipped into gear and took off at a thousand miles an hour.

Who were *they*?

Why did *they* want a fresh Dead Head?

What were *they* planning?

Were *they* responsible for the murders back home?

Too many unanswered questions. He had to know.

"Adelaide, I'm staying," he said, reaching for his daughter with his unbound hand.

She clutched it. "No, Dad. No. You've gotta come with us."

"Us?"

"Me, Mike, and Dean."

Jane laughed. It tinkled like a bell. "Oh, girl. You got Dean with you?"

"Not now, Jane. Will you come?"

Glancing at Jack, she stretched out a hand to Addy.

Adelaide stood between them, holding each of their hands in hers.

Jane shook her head. "I'm staying here, lass." She laid the Scottish brogue on as thick as she could get it. "I'll be fine."

Adelaide squeezed both of their hands. A tear dropped to the dirt. She lowered her voice to a whisper. "You don't know that."

Little hands squeezed Jack's heart. He hated to cause his baby girl pain. He pulled her in and hugged her, arm around her shoulders.

She vibrated against him, shaking.

Kissing her on the top of the head, he swallowed around the lump in his throat and lied through his teeth. "I promise, we'll be OK. Go home, Addy."

She stepped back, her eyes puffy and red. Tears streamed down her cheeks. "Dad. Jane. I—"

Tim shouted, approaching. "Louis! You and Ric get that body out of the road! We gotta go." Faint, but growing closer even as he spoke.

Jack's heart sped up again, racing in his chest. "Adelaide, go."

With one final squeeze of their hands, she disappeared into the trees as though she'd never been there.

Tim sauntered around the truck, hands in his pockets.

"Well Jackson, I don't know. This arrow had to come from somewhere," he said, yanking it from the ground. He turned it over, staring at the feathers. "Whatever." He sighed, tossing the arrow on top of Wade's body.

Jack glanced down at the little man, never again to bounce on his toes. A monogrammed handkerchief hanging half out of his pocket. One small, perfect hole in his forehead, just above his right eye.

"Why, Tim?"

"I can't tell you that yet. Not telling you is the only reason you stuck around, isn't it? You two could have run quite easily during all that ruckus."

Jack shuffled a foot. Wouldn't do him any favors to agree with the boy.

"Get in the truck, Jack. You too, beautiful," Tim said.

Ric stood by the side of the road as they loaded up, staring at the body. Tim approached him.

"Hey, Ric. Don't think on it. Look," he said, grabbing the younger boy by the back of the neck and giving him a comradely shake, "we're the Task Force. We're the top of the food chain, man. Nobody can tell us different."

Ric glanced up at him, a smile reaching one side of his mouth. "Yeah."

Tim slapped him on the back, but Ric's smile never touched the other side of his mouth.

Jack followed Jane into the truck and waited to see where it would take them.

CHAPTER 14

"Adelaide! Slow down!" Michael shouted from somewhere behind her.

Addy's running feet carried her another thirty yards before slowing. She picked one foot up, tripped over it, and fell on her face.

Someone stomped to a halt next to her. "Bean, what are you doing?"

She closed her eyes and breathed. The grass, warmed by the sun, smelled sweet like hay. She let the smell and the heat from the sun envelop her in a tight cocoon. Far away from the broken heart of letting her dad go. And Jane.

Mike sighed. "OK, drama queen. Let me know when you're coming." He left, feet beating the ground.

The grass next to her rustled. Dean spoke, voice soft. "Addy, what happened back there?"

She sighed. Cracked an eyelid. Dean sat in front of her, legs crisscross applesauce. "I don't know, Dean. They decided to stay." A tear seeped out the corner of her eye, wetting the grass against her cheek. Rising on an arm, she frowned and swiped at her face. "I don't know. They didn't want to come." Her voice broke, and she looked down into the dirt.

Some ants trudged by, most carting large grass seeds. Simplicity guided them to and from their home. The need to feed and reproduce. If only life were that simple.

She sat up and brushed dirt from her arm. Cleared her throat. "There's something my dad wants to know. Some mystery that needs solving. I could see it in his eyes," she said. "And he won't give up until he knows the answers."

"What about Jane? And your dad's friend, the big guy?"

"She didn't want to come, either." More tears streaked her cheeks.

Jane didn't want to come. Her dad, he could be expected to sort of do his own thing. But why would Jane choose to stay?

Dean pitched his voice low and soft. "I'm sorry they didn't come. But it's good your dad has backup."

She swiped at the stupid tears again and frowned, brows drawing into a wrinkly V. "I guess." She glanced up.

Eyes round, he frowned and touched her knee. "I'll help you. Whatever you need."

Wiping the rest of the tears, she nodded. Her face still flushed and hot, she dropped her hands in her lap and stared down at them.

Dean sat still and quiet while she collected herself.

Once her face dried, she uncrossed her legs. "We're going to keep following them. Maybe we'll have another chance to help."

Dean nodded and stood, offering a hand.

Taking it, she stood and made her way back to the train with him. As she put a foot on the step, Mike poked his head out.

"Who was that guy?"

"What guy, Michael?"

"The one who had his gun out when he got there. Did he shoot the mayor?"

Addy, hand on the rail, lost her balance and fell back as a stone dropped in her stomach.

Dean, directly behind her, caught her with his body. Hands on her shoulders, he helped her stay upright and left a hand on one shoulder as she sat on the step. "You OK?"

She closed her eyes. "Oh my god. Tim."

"Which Tim? Not the head of the Task Force," Dean said.

"Yeah, and Addy's boyfriend," Mike supplied.

If Addy's skin didn't take that moment to flush a deep shade of brick red, she'd have been more surprised than anyone. Crawling under the train car would have been another acceptable response.

"Do what now?" Dean asked.

"How do you know him?" Addy asked over top of him.

Dean, clearing his throat, opened his mouth. No sound came out.

Glancing at him without making more than half a second of eye contact, Addy asked again.

"I, uh, I deal with the Task Force quite a bit coming in and out of town, much as I do," he said. "Now you mention it, I've seen some of those other boys before too."

"Good," Addy said, standing, "Now that that's settled. Let's go."

***

Andrew, eyes closed, leaned against the side of the truck. The side where nobody died lately. None of them sat there.

"So, Jackie, the fuck happened back there?"

Jack shook his head, resting the hand cuffed to Jane on the floor between them. "I have no clue. It seems we were led down the same path Wade took."

"Look where that got him," Jane said.

"Dead, that's where it got him," Andrew said.

Closing his eyes, Jack nodded. Concentrating on the hum of the engine and singing of the tires quieted the cacophony in his head. "All that stuff Tim said to us. About getting 'there' and seeing what's really going on. The power was never with Wade. It's not with these idiots, either."

Jane tugged the cuff.

He peeked at her.

"If they're not the ones with the power, then who is?"

"That's what I intend to find out."

Jane, grimacing, shook her head. "We should have gone with Addy."

"She's probably right, Jackie."

"I don't know guys," he said. Imitating Jane, he tugged the cuff. "I appreciate you guys sticking with me. Backing my play. Means a lot."

"Sure," Jane said. Her smile brightened her face. "Couldn't leave you alone with these animals."

Grinning, he glanced out the back of the truck.

The sunset had turned purple. Staring out at it, Jack shook his head. "I can't figure out what they're up to. They're just kids. They can't be in charge of anything."

"Jackie, they're older than you think."

"How do you mean?"

"When you were their age, what were you doing?"

Jack frowned. "Going to school. Getting zits. Thinking about getting laid."

Andrew chuckled. "Not in that order."

Jane laughed aloud.

Jack, blood rushing up his neck and into his cheeks, nodded. "Yeah. So. What's your point?"

"These kids are different, Jack. They have a whole list of new concerns. Staying at the top of the food chain is one."

"Trust me, getting laid is still at the top of the list," Jane said, eyes on the waning sun.

"You'd know, Jane," Andrew laughed.

She turned, face set in stone. An alabaster statue. "I mean it. Procreating is at the top of the list. Rebuilding the human race. It's priority number one. Everything else is in service to it."

"Interesting theory."

"It's true. I read a lot. One of the things I read is textbooks. Psychology is dry as all hell but useful."

Jack tugged the cuff again. "Alright, Jane. You're right. But what are their secondary plans in relation to us? And keeping Ger in a bag?"

"You're not immune, Jack."

Everything blushed, starting at his toes. Thankfully, it was getting dark inside the truck. "That's not the conversation we're having."

Jane, frowning, put a hand under her chin and went back to watching the sunset. Venus had popped out at some point. Bright as a diamond, it shone in the indigo sky. "What we are talking about, then, is that they'll do anything, literally anything, in service to that. Up to and including murder."

Jack scoffed. "Jane, I know the world is different than it was when I grew up. It's impossible not to know that. But murder? Isn't that counterproductive?"

"Jackie, you saw it with your own eyes."

Turning to Andrew, he scowled. "What I saw was a madman. Leading a group of impressionable but ultimately good young men down a path carved by his own madness. But he, he has a goal."

Jane faced him. "And that goal is procreation. You mark my words, Jack."

CHAPTER 15

ndrew snored.

Jack jumped awake, yanking his arm. It met with resistance.

He stared down at it, fuzzy sleep mind trying to work out why he was cuffed to a slender arm.

Jane cleared her throat.

Right. Life was a nightmare and she was in it.

"Jane, you make this nightmare bearable," he heard himself mutter.

"What was that?"

He cleared his throat. "Nothing. How long was I out?"

"I don't know. I nodded off. You tried to pull my arm out of its socket. Hard to sleep through."

"Shit, sorry about that."

"No worries, Jack."

He shifted, sliding off his numb ass and onto a hip. Which then cried out in pain, grumbling about how hard the floor of this damn truck was. "Jane. You haven't called me Mr. C. in forever."

"And?"

"No and. Just an observation." He leaned toward her. "I'm very observant."

She chuckled. "Indeed. When you want to be."

"What's that supposed to mean?"

She leaned in and whispered. "That I'm observant too."

He laughed, sitting back. Shifted a hip again. "Well. Thank you again for staying with me. I wish you hadn't, but I'm glad you did."

She cocked a leg up and wrapped an elbow around it. Leaning her cheek on her knee, she smiled. "Same here."

"What's the second thing on your list, Jane?"

Her forehead wrinkled, a fine line appearing between her eyebrows. "What do you mean?"

"If the first is procreation, what's the second?"

She turned, and he followed her gaze.

A tiny sliver of moon hung in the sky near the horizon, and the Milky Way projected the light of a billion stars onto the landscape.

When it became clear she wasn't going to answer, he tried a different tack. "Jane, whose blood was on your needles? Where were you before?"

"I'd really rather not talk about that."

"What else are we going to talk about?"

"Anything."

"You're the one reading psychology books. You know you should talk about it."

She sighed, turning back to him. "Can we talk about procreation or something instead?"

He shook his head. "No, we can't."

She sighed again, looked up, then blinked rapidly ten or fifteen times.

He jumped. "Hey. Hey, are you OK? I can't remember the last time I saw you cry."

"No, no, I'm not," she said, voice cracking. A tear fell as she dropped her head to look at him.

Grabbing the hand he was cuffed to, he slid closer and wrapped the other arm around her.

She stiffened but allowed him to pull her in. Lying her head on his chest, she shook with silent sobs.

Staring out at the Milky Way, Jack considered who it could possibly have been to make her cry like this. Cry at all.

He rifled through the slim options. His breath caught.

"Jane," he whispered.

She snuffled, lifting her head. Red-rimmed, tired eyes peeked out from her puffy face.

The back of his throat hurt. There was no way to fix this. He asked the question that had to be asked. "Was it one of your parents?"

Opening her mouth, that fine line appearing between her brows again, she hesitated. Cleared her throat. "It was my dad," she whispered. "It was Bill."

The bottom dropped out of his gut. "Oh my god, baby. I'm so sorry," he said, squeezing her against him.

He and Bill had been friends since before the village. Saved each other's asses on more than one run. Sat around a fire on watch more nights than he could count.

They'd lost a lot of that since coming to the village. Bill and Nancy had withdrawn, shying away not just from Jack and his kids, but the rest of the village as well. In a way, he'd lost his friend years ago.

But Jane. Jane had just lost him. Had to do it herself.

He pulled her closer.

She cried for a while, and between snuffles told him what happened.

His mind seized upon Dean. What had he been doing there? He had a million questions. None of which would have comforted Jane. And she was here, now, hurting. He left the questions for another time.

After her tears slowed, her breath returning to a regular rhythm, he landed on a different question. "Tell me something good about him, Jane."

She laughed, sitting up and wiping her face. Only after drying it did she turn to him.

"He loved nut trees," she said.

Jack smiled. "Why? Did he like nuts?"

"Oh, god no. He hated them."

"Then why did he like nut trees?"

"He liked to feed squirrels."

Jack threw his head back and laughed. Jane chuckled with him.

"A squirrel enthusiast? I knew the guy for years. How did I not know this?"

"He would've kept them as pets if my mom would've let him. He loved the furry little idiots."

"Wow. But all the times we ate squirrel? I mean sometimes it was the only meat."

"He pretended it was rabbit."

Jack laughed again, something close to a giggle. His insides suddenly glowed with airy light. Like blue skies.

"Your turn," Jane said.

"Something nice about your dad?"

"No, silly person. Something nice about someone you've lost."

His smile faltered. Well. He started it.

"She loved the stars."

"Your wife?"

"Melinda. Yeah."

Jane smiled. "Addy doesn't talk much about her. Tell me."

He pressed his lips together. Forced himself to think about her face. It was tough. Like looking at someone through a frosted window. You could see the shape of them, but not the features.

Jane stared at him, eyelashes still wet. If it would make her feel better to talk, he probably should.

This was how he could fix it.

So he talked, and he told her about Mellie's fascination with space. How she'd been grateful for the end of light pollution. Her affinity for sci-fi and cooking and weapons, and how she'd passed those things on to Addy.

Things he hadn't thought of in years. Wouldn't let himself.

Also how her laugh was like tinkling bells. How she fought. A beautiful mother, a fierce warrior.

"How did you get over losing her?" Jane asked. "Addy doesn't talk about that either."

"Well," he said, glancing at his feet, "you never really do. It's just something you, I don't know, you kind of learn to live with. It changes, shifts, from bright red to dull pink."

Something else he hadn't spoken of in years. That pain. If he'd ever talked about it at all.

Something tenuous trembled inside him. A dam threatening to break.

She shifted, knees pointed toward him, head leaning on the side of the truck. "I don't remember my parents."

His head snapped up. She'd never, not once, spoken of her real parents. He held his breath.

"When my second parents, I don't remember their names, when they found me, I couldn't even tell them my name. I was either too little or too traumatized. I don't know," she said, sniffing.

In the dark, her eyes twinkled like stars. He faced her the way she faced him, knees pointed toward her, head leaned on the canvas side of the truck.

"So. They called me Jane."

He laughed without humor. "Like Jane Doe."

She nodded, looking at a finger and picking at her nail. "I guess, yeah. Anyway," she said, glancing at a sleeping Andrew, "I have a few memories. Like five or six. I think it's my real parents." She sniffled and sighed. "But I don't know. I don't know, Jack. I don't even really know how old I am. I can guess, but what does it even matter?" She shrugged, her hands slapping her legs.

He reached out and grasped her fingers. "It doesn't. You're strong, Jane. One of the strongest women I've ever known."

She squeezed his hand. "Thanks for saying that." She smiled.

And they talked. About the nature of life, about how Jack remembered the world before. About Jane's dislike of any sort of time telling, about whatever popped into their heads.

After a while, the heavy feeling around Jack's heart lifted. The hopelessness over what had just happened to Liz and Ger. The horror of losing people. He hadn't lost anyone since Melinda. It stung. It stung a lot more than he wanted to admit.

But talking to Jane? Somehow, the cloud dissipated like fog in the face of the rising sun.

They talked, all night, until the sky lightened.

"It's morning, Jack," Jane whispered. Her eyelids drooped.

His own eyes, full of sand, fought to stay open. To watch the western sky lighten with the eastern sun. To see her face light up, her smile come back.

But sleep dragged them down. He opened his mouth to agree with her.

Instead of talking more, he found himself waking. She'd lain her head on him and fallen asleep. The sun rose higher in the sky. He checked his watch. Six o'clock.

Of course, they'd changed time zones. It must be at least eight, judging from the light.

He slid down into the floor, arm around Jane so she wouldn't get jostled, and repositioned her so her face rested in the hollow of his shoulder.

She shifted her body, cuffed arms the only thing between them, and stilled.

Smiling, he let his eyes fall closed again.

***

Addy chewed a nail to the quick, watching Dean talk on the phone.

Mike, steering the train, glanced over his shoulder. "Stop chewing your nails, bean."

"Don't call me that."

He reached into his black pouch. "Have a sucker."

She shook her head but took one. Stuck it in her mouth. Grimaced. "Michael, I hate these root beer ones."

"Sorry. Out of cream soda."

She shrugged. The flavor was awful, but root beer was Mike's favorite. It reminded her of being a child, eating these things before their expiration date had passed. "How do you never run out of these?"

"My little secret, bean."

* * *

You pull on the sucker. The flavor is awful but it's your brother's favorite. You humor him as your parents talk.

"The solar panel is broken, Jack."

"Mellie, we'll be alright without it."

"We need it, babe. I'll go alone. You stay with the kids."

"We don't need it. And I won't let you go alone."

You smile around the sucker. Your mom is tough. Headstrong. Gets what she wants, every time. You'll go with her to get the new solar panel. You're twelve years old, after all. Big enough to hold your own against the hordes.

You pop the sucker out of your mouth, the aftertaste of sticky root beer clinging to the back of your tongue. "I'll go with you, Mom."

Dad sighs.

Mom grins at you. "Well, that's settled then. We'll go together, jellybean."

* * *

Addy threw the sucker into the trash. "Don't call me that. I hate this fucking flavor." She wobbled away, the back of her throat burning with the aftertaste of root beer stuck in it.

Sitting on the bed, she glanced at the framed picture. The boys in it were so happy.

She smiled. What must it have been like before the world changed? Like it was now? Worse? Better?

Lying down and covering her eyes with an arm, she eavesdropped on Dean.

"OK, well, you find out where it ends." Nothing. "Mm-hmm. Yeah. Awesome. Mm-hmm." Another pause. "Yeah. I'll get back. Might be text." His phone flipped closed. Footsteps. The chair across from her creaked.

"So, Dean, what's up?"

"Thought you were asleep."

"No."

"Fair enough. My guys say the convoy is taking the long way, but they're still heading east."

She sat up. "Do you know where they're going?"

"Not yet. But most of the roads dead-end before they get to the coast."

"Hm. How are the tracks between here and there?"

"Clear. We've got a big choice of routes. The East Coast is riddled with tracks," Dean said.

"So we'll just keep going, right?"

"Right."

She exhaled out her nose, closing her eyes and rubbing her elbows. Turning, she gazed out the window behind her.

The sun had long since set. The Milky Way twinkled at her, its clouds of stars burning with warmth. Her eyes fell on the picture again. She turned to him.

His green eyes smiled.

"Can I ask you something?"

"Sure thing, Addy."

"Tell me about this picture." She hooked a thumb over her shoulder.

He closed his eyes, face falling into neutral. "I can't do that."

"Can't or won't?"

"Both."

She frowned. If he wouldn't talk about his dead people, she wouldn't talk about hers, either. Sighing, she watched the night landscape pass.

"So that Tim guy," Dean said. "He your boyfriend, like Mike says?"

Grinning, a tight and uncomfortable production, she shrugged. "I don't know. No."

He touched her on the knee.

She eyed him. His raised brow and soft eyes, they melted the ice in her heart. A bit.

"Which is it?" he asked.

"I don't have any idea what's going on, Dean. I don't know, I guess."

"I hope, once we catch up to them again, we can find out."

"Me too," she said. "I need to know what happened. Did you see Liz?"

"Your dad's friend? You mentioned her."

"Yeah. She was…" Addy choked, grunting from deep in her throat.

Dean pulled a breath over his teeth. "Addy. Was she the Dead Head that ran past?"

She nodded, eyes closed. The color red clouded her mind, and tears wet her cheeks. Again. "And I saw Andrew, but not Gerald."

"I saw a body. They had it in a body bag and threw it into the other truck."

"Oh god. Oh god, Dean. The hell is going on?"

"I don't know. But look, we can follow them. As far as the tracks take us."

"Then on foot if we have to. We'll find them."

He nodded, squeezing her knee.

Laying a hand over his, she squeezed him back. They sat like that, swaying to the rocking of the train, for more than a minute.

Addy broke eye contact after a few moments and stared at the back of her hand. Thinking of Tim roiled her gut. There were so many questions. But she'd already started seeing him, and how was this supposed to even go?

Dean, handsome and sincere, had been nothing but helpful since the moment she met him. Even when he was overprotective, it was obvious it came from a place of caring. But who was he, really?

Her stomach bubbled, her mind some kind of sludge/spaghetti mix. How could Jane stand dating? It seemed hopelessly complicated.

She pulled her knee from under his hand and curled her leg onto the bed, trying on a grin. It didn't go exactly as she planned, but the corners of her mouth raised.

He smiled back, Cupid's bow of a mouth tight across his teeth. "We'll figure this out, Addy."

She nodded. Glanced at the picture. Happy kids.

Dean's phone rang. Leaning back, he took the call.

She watched him as he spoke, and he stared at her, face rippling through emotions every few moments. After a few nods, his raised brows drew together and he frowned.

"It's what now? You're sure?"

A few more nods, then he snapped the phone closed.

"Well, Addy. Hope you packed your swimsuit."

"My what?"

"You don't know what a…never mind. Get some shuteye. Next watch I'll teach you how to drive this thing. If we don't stop, maybe we can beat them there."

"Where?" Addy sat up, feet back on the floor.

He crooked a finger. "Come up here, I'll show you."

They wobbled to the front of the car. Dean laid a hand on Mike's shoulder.

Addy's forehead tightened like she was just on the edge of vertigo. Drive this thing? He was out of his mind.

Dean pulled up a map and pointed. "It looks like they're headed here," he said, zooming in on a tiny landmass just off the curve of the coast. "A city next to what used to be called the Outer Banks."

"Those islands?" Addy gripped the back of the Captain's Chair, leaning over her brother's shoulder.

Mike turned, putting a hand on hers. His eyes wide and round.

"It's cool, Mike. We'll get there first, head them off. Right, Dean?"

Dean nodded. "Like I said, I'll teach you to drive this bucket on the next shift. We'll drive non-stop. Get there first. My guy says there's a small settlement nearby. We'll pull in here," he said, pointing again. Just at the tip of the land.

Addy patted Mike's shoulder. "Good plan. I'll get some sleep."

***

"Ain't that sweet," Tim cooed.

Again, Jack jerked awake.

He'd curled his free arm around Jane, and she was squeezed up next to him. Long, regular breaths warm on his collarbone.

Tim stood just outside the stopped truck. Sun streamed in, the air heavy with humidity.

"Here," Tim said, pitching a canteen into the truck. It sailed in a flat arc toward Jane's head.

Jack rolled to snatch it before it hit her, flexing the cuffed arm so her head wouldn't hit the floor as he did. Catching it just before it hit her, he looked down and into her open eyes.

Brown flecks danced in the green of her irises. Her pupils dilated.

"Sorry. You OK?" he asked.

"Um."

"Here." Setting the canteen behind him, he helped her sit up. Disentangling his arm took a bit of work, considering it was asleep from the elbow down.

Worth it.

I mean. No. Water.

He snagged the canteen and held it out to her.

Eyes widening, she took it and spun the cap off. It fell, bouncing across the floor. She swigged, closed her eyes, and swigged again. A bit escaped her mouth, and when she took the canteen from her lips, she wiped her chin and handed it to him.

He wasn't sure what was better. The taste of the cold, sweet water, or watching the drip escape the corner of her mouth.

Dammit, Jack. You're too old for her. Stop.

He frowned at Andrew. "Here you go, man," he said, handing off the canteen. They'd left at least half of it for him.

Andrew downed it, tossing the empty container at Tim's head after he finished.

Tim ducked as it flew past, laughing. "So sassy. Let's go, Jackson. Need to palaver with you." He nodded, then Ric and Louis climbed into the truck.

Jack scowled at Louis as he leaned in to unlock the handcuff.

Louis caught his scowl and flashed a wolfish grin. "Here, Mr. C. I'll unlock her and Ric can help you down. I'll just keep an eye on her while you're gone." He pulled a handgun from his belt.

"Touch a hair on her head, boy, and—"

"What, like this one?" Louis asked, using the sight of his gun to brush a hair from Jane's temple. His finger rested on the trigger.

"I'll be alright, Jack," Jane said. She growled at the boy.

Jack, chest tight and throat burning, slid away. He glanced at Ric.

The boy had the decency to look disgusted.

As Jack stood to crouch-walk to the end of the truck, Ric approached from behind, grabbing the cuff and clipping it to Jack's other wrist.

Bound again.

He slid out of the truck without help, landing on both feet. His knees were touch and go for a moment, but neither gave in. He grinned with the corners of his mouth turned down. "So Tim. Here we are again."

"Let's talk over here," Tim said, holding an arm away from the truck.

They walked west down the road, side by side.

"I guess you have some questions for me," Tim said.

"A couple."

"Shoot."

Jack scoffed. "And you'll answer?"

"If I can. I'm not an animal, Jackson."

"I like the way you've started calling me Jackson, Tim. What happened to Mr. C.?"

"That's what the people back home are probably saying, right now," Tim said, half a grin curving his lip.

Jack stopped. He hadn't considered what people might be thinking back home.

Tim continued, stopping five feet ahead. He turned back. "I'd like to keep walking. Been a while since I stretched my legs."

Jack jogged to join him. It did feel good to walk. The creaks and complaints from his joints subsided as they stretched, blood flowing back into them.

But damn, he felt good all over. The sun shining warm on his head, the scent of water in the air, blue sky above.

It had been years since he'd felt so good.

He smiled. "So, Tim. Questions?"

"Ask away." With the sun beating down on his head, not a drop of sweat marred Tim's brow.

"Do you know who's responsible for the murders back home?"

"Murders? You don't say."

"Answer the question."

"Yes." Same half smile playing on his lip.

"Yes, you'll answer, or yes, you know?"

"Yes," Tim said, stopping and turning, "I know."

Jack nodded. He'd assumed as much. "Can you, will you tell me?"

"I can tell you who's responsible, or who did it. But not both."

The cogs began to turn, Jack's eyes flashing back and forth. "You mean it's not the same thing," he said. A statement, not a question. He narrowed his eyes and smirked at the boy. "Who told you to do it, Tim?"

Mouth falling open, the smug grin left Tim's face for the first time since he'd shown up, hanging under the truck in ambush. "How'd you figure…you know what"—he flashed the grin once again—"it doesn't matter. The general gave me orders. I followed them."

"General? Are you saying there's some sort of military organization behind all this?"

Tim stopped, clasping his hands behind his back and spreading his legs. "That's a question better left for when we get where we're going."

"And where's that?"

"East."

Jack tilted his head, considering. "How far east?"

"All the way east."

Jack smiled. He hadn't been to the ocean since before the kids were born. They'd been planning a beach trip since Mike was a baby. But it never happened. "Maybe we can avoid holiday traffic."

Tim snorted. "I don't even know what you mean by that. But I assume it was a joke."

"Yeah, Tim. Your powers of deduction are stellar."

Tim walked away. Jack jogged to catch up again.

"One more question, Jackson," Tim said, "then we have to get going again."

"Why did you kill Wade?"

Tim stopped again. His face clouded. "He wanted you out of the way. Thought you were some kind of competition. It was easy to manipulate him into getting these trucks. But in the end, he refused to meet the terms he agreed to." He stopped, squinting into the distance. "The people we're going to see, they insist on terms being met. There is no wiggle room. I won't be caught in the company of someone refusing them. And I won't be part of it."

"So you killed him so you wouldn't get in trouble."

Tim eyed the horizon. "Something like that."

"Who are they? What do they want?"

"Sorry, Jackson. That's two questions too many. Back in the truck with you."

CHAPTER 16

Dean pointed at a flashing light on the screen in front of Addy. "Hey, get that."

Addy slapped at his hand. "Yeah, yeah. I see it." She scowled and pulled the lever to correct their speed. Getting on the last nerve she had was a line Dean had crossed hours ago.

He raised both hands. "Sorry, just trying to help."

"Well don't. You taught me how to drive this thing more than a week ago. I've driven at least half the distance since then. I think I got it."

"Doesn't hurt to have an extra set of eyes, is all I'm saying."

She put her back to him. The screens flashed. Before this godforsaken train, she'd never seen this many working screens next to each other. Learning how to read them all at once was a bit much.

But it sounded like he thought she couldn't handle it. "I'm fine. Go take a nap."

Without turning, she could sense him still standing next to her. Probably with his arms crossed. Looking tough and working his jaw. Fine jaw that it was.

After a bit, the little hairs on the back of her neck reported he'd walked away. The overstuffed chair in the back creaked.

She drove, peeking out the window from time to time.

They'd been in the East when she was small, but it was always so crowded there. So many people fighting over resources. Dead Heads fighting over their own resources; all the people. They'd moved west before she had very many clear memories of this place.

The sheer number of trees was a bit overwhelming. The land had spooled up like one of those little paper blowers her mom had found once. Man, they'd played with those for weeks before they just fell apart.

Overhead, the sky she'd grown accustomed to seeing every night, stars shining like little flares, had become tinier and tinier till there was only a little strip left. All the trees and the teeny little sky felt like they were boxing her in. Trapping her in some prison of land and sky.

But as the day lightened, the sky began to unfurl. It was gradual, but the sky opened and the trees grew shorter.

She slipped the window open. The cool air flowing in had a salty feel.

She whispered, "I don't think I've ever been this close to the ocean."

Someone fell in the floor behind her.

"Michael, I swear to you. We don't strap you in and you fall out of bed. Every time."

He stumbled up the train, bouncing off the counter, the chair, the stove. From above her head, he smacked his lips. "Coffee."

"You know where it is. I'm driving this thing, you madman."

He shuffled away.

A loud beeping began from the floorboard by her foot.

She called her brother over her shoulder. "Mike, what did you break?"

A red light flashed from the floor. It was like—

"Proximity alarm!" She shouted, pulling on the brake and pressing both feet into the floor. The screen in front of her flashed red. The whole thing. It was coming from everywhere.

The open window agreed.

The smell of rot mixed with dead fish wafted into the cabin.

"Addy, what the hell?" Mike asked. Sounded like from the floor.

Ignoring him, she inched up to the window. Sucked in a breath of stinking air. Slid the window closed. Slow. Slow.

"Adelaide," Dean whispered.

She finished closing the window, latch making barely a snick. Silenced the alarm like Dean had shown her. Setting the brake, she turned around.

Now those things were taken care of, her heart began to thump against her ribcage. It took up all the room in her chest. There was no room for breath.

"Addy, breathe," Dean whispered, sliding closer.

She opened her mouth to tell him what was out there. Closed it. Opened it. You needed breath to speak, to force the words out. She still didn't have any.

She reeled, toppling from the chair. The floor rushed at her but didn't rush. Like a dream. Strange, slow, with the focus all wrong.

Dean slid under her and she landed on him. He grunted. "You OK?"

Still, the breath didn't come. She'd never, never seen that many. Not in one place. Not ever.

That was a lie.

Probably the last one she'd ever tell herself. Even if she started breathing again, which was looking less and less likely, there was no way out of where they were.

Surrounded by a horde.

***

"Adelaide, I need you to breathe."

She stared up at Dean. The light fell from behind him, giving him a halo. If he were an angel, that was probably OK.

I mean, he is bossy. But pretty angelic.

"Addy." He gave her a gentle shake. His face worked its way through frustrated, angry, worried.

Her eyes had dried out. Better close them.

"Addy!"

He shouldn't be shouting. Not through water like that. Very dangerous for the…

Surrounded.

Don't scream.

Don't breathe.
Just slip. Under the— Slip.
Sssshhhhhh.
Stop.

Stop.

Rubbing.

My.

Arms.

"Dean?" Her voice echoed like someone had sent it to her through a tube.

Her back, warm from his hands, tingled. Her arms pins and needles.

He gripped her biceps, pushed her away, and stared down at her. His eyes flitted from one eye to the other, from her forehead to chin. Crushing her against him again, he rubbed her back and arms. Creating friction and heat. Calling her blood back from her toes. "Addy, breathe. It's OK. We're gonna be OK. I need you to breathe for me," he whispered, breath hot in her ear.

She nodded, the warmth spreading from her back and arms to her cheeks and forehead.

Heart beating hard but regular, she pushed away from him and sat up.

"Are we surrounded?"

He grimaced. Nodded.

"Shit. Shit, shit, shit." She paused, grabbing for Michael's hand.

He clutched her.

"Alright," she said. "We're going to be alright. Dean, do you have flares?"

"I do."

"OK. Alright. We can do this. When we get up, we do it slow. Dean, get the flares. Mike, get in the Captain's Chair. We can do this."

They nodded. She squeezed Mike's fingers and dropped them.

Dean gripped her shoulder. "You sure you're alright now?"

"I'm sure. Thank you," she said, bobbing her head. "I don't know what happened. I haven't…" She paused. Bit her lip. "It's been a long time since I've seen a horde like that."

Dean frowned. "You're right. We can do this. Meet me at the back. I'll get your bow ready."

"It's your bow, Dean."

"Yours now, Addy. I saw how good of a shot you are."

"I meant to hit him."

Dean shook his head. "No you didn't. No time for arguing. Come on."

He crept to the Captain's Chair and opened a panel in the floor behind it. He pulled out the flares.

Mike sat in the chair, releasing the brake with a steady hand.

These were good men to be in a corner with. Calm, cool, not unlike her dad. Mike was basically the softer, younger version of him, after all.

Dean was…well he was something. Hard one moment, soft the next.

Her cheek should have been stinging. Mike had slapped her, hard, one time when she'd gone into shock like that. She thought that was how you came out of it.

It seemed Dean had brought her out of it with sheer force of will. That was something, alright.

Addy crept to the back, meeting Dean and taking the bow and quiver. "How many flares do you have?"

"Ten."

"We'll use four. Shoot them in five-second intervals, over the track behind us. I'll clear stragglers. We're going to inch forward as they move."

"Right. Good thing this is a quiet freaking train."

"Got any better ideas?"

"No, Addy. This is good. Let's do it."

Addy, taking her station at the front window across from Mike, nodded to her brother.

Dean shot the first flare.

It sailed into the daylight. Orange glow pale against the sunny sky, it left a thick trail of smoke.

The horde began to shuffle as one. A few of them ran into the front of the train. Bounced off. Ran into it again.

Dean shot the second flare.

It sailed right of the first one, catching the attention of more 'Heads.

Addy peeked at the horizon. It rippled like water. Like a moving, stinking carpet.

Good god, they were everywhere.

One turned toward the train and appeared to sniff.

She pegged it with an arrow, hitting it between the eyes with a meaty thump. It dropped like a sack of rocks.

Nocking another arrow, its end jittered as Dean fired the third flare.

The undulating mass followed the smoke trails.

The rail ahead began to clear. She nodded to Mike.

Letting off the brake and squeezing the accelerator a touch, Mike crept the train forward.

Another 'Head turned toward the movement.

Dean fired the last flare.

Addy beaned the 'Head. It dropped.

The train rolled.

Moving as one creature, the horde shuffled off, following the flares.

Addy, pushing the quiver of arrows away and leaning on the bow, slumped to the floor. "I didn't think that was going to work."

"What?" Mike asked. Eyebrows raised almost to his hairline, he all but fell out of the chair.

"We got lucky," she said.

Dean sat in the floor next to her. "It was a good plan."

She laughed.

"But you're right," he went on. "We got lucky."

***

The flap unzipped and drooped down. Tim stuck his face in the window and glared. "I need you guys to do something for me."

The first time he'd spoken to them in over a week, Jack's ears perked up.

Andrew kicked at the flap. He caught Tim in the lip with his ankle.

"Ouch! You son of a bitch!" Tim's hand flew to his face. It came away bloody.

Jane chuckled. "Nice shot, big guy."

Andrew grinned. "Thanks, pretty lady."

"Well, *big guy*. You're on my list now," Tim said.

"What list is that?"

"If you have to ask, you're as dumb as you look."

Andrew scowled and glanced at Jack.

"What do you want, Tim?" Jack asked.

"This is important, Jackson. You have to agree. If you don't, we all die."

"That a threat, Timmy boy?"

"No, it's a fact."

Jack glanced at Jane. Once he'd gotten back in the truck from his little talk with Tim, he'd found her rope-bound once again. They hadn't had another night like that one, where they'd talked till the sun, but his insides buzzed when he looked at her. The time with her and Andrew in the truck, while being transported like cattle down long and winding roads, had turned out to be some of the most fun he'd had in years. Playful innuendo bandied across the truck between him and Jane, chatting with them both about whatever came to mind, even playing road trip games. Odd, but you took your happiness where you could get it in this world.

Even so, he fought with himself every night. Something had changed between him and Jane. Was maybe growing between them. But how could he pursue that? Irresponsible, at best. Even if she returned the sentiment.

Pulling his eyes away, he squinted. "What is it, Tim? What do you need?"

"Silence. From all of you. Till I say it's OK."

"Why? Are we going to get you in trouble if we make noise?"

"Trouble is one way to put it. Dead is another. Look. We're passing through some defenses. These defenses require silence."

Jack considered. If silence was needed, what about the truck engines?

"I know what you're thinking," Tim said.

"Oh?"

"Yeah. You're thinking these trucks are loud enough to wake the dead. And they are. But we have ways through these defenses. Still, I need you all to be quiet as little mice. Can you do that for me?"

Jack caught Jane's and Andrew's eyes, asking them without asking. Both nodded. "Yeah, Tim. We can do that."

"Good. These defenses are…" He paused and blew a hair off his forehead. "Sensitive." Leaning back, he zipped up the flap.

Both trucks slowed to a crawl, engines gearing down.

The first growls sounded from just beside the back wheels.

The stench of sour blood and rotted, bloated fish wafted into the truck. A hint of salt came with it, but whatever freshness the sea pushed in was overtaken by death.

Andrew dry heaved.

A louder snarl by the tire, just on the other side of the simple canvas wall, dragged its edges through the soft tissue of Jack's mind. He glared at Andrew.

The larger man nodded, burying his mouth and nose in his shoulder.

Jane inched over, back to the front of the truck, sliding across the floor in silence. Pressing her shoulder against Jack's, she glanced up at him. She met his eyes with hers and swallowed.

As steady as a rock, he gazed back. He was not going to spread fear to them. They needed a statue, and that's what they'd get.

Like an eddy current, the first 'Heads flowed in behind the truck. Though the horde's buzzing wasn't much louder than a beehive, the stench of them was overpowering.

These were the defenses Tim spoke of? Who were the kinds of people that would use a horde of Dead Heads as a defensive wall?

Small explosions rocked the air.

"Hey, hey, hey! Over here, you idiots!" Boys shouted, banging metal against metal. Sounded like trash can lids and hand grenades.

The Dead Heads at the end of the truck shuffled away.

From the continuous sound of feet, Jack estimated there had to be hundreds of them. Maybe more.

Some of them growled and snarled, but a feeding frenzy never happened.

Which was good. His calm veneer hung on by a thread. The last time he'd seen a horde that size, things did not go well.

As one could expect, when dealing with the dead.

A clang resounded, something like cattle gates maybe.

The flap unzipped.

"We're through. Thank you for your cooperation, lady and gentlemen."

Jack goggled at Tim. Slick sweat gathered on his brow, lip, and under his arms. His stomach full of snakes.

But this boy's expression was as flat as someone going to lunch. Tim zipped the flap back up. The truck jerked and began to roll again. Picking up speed, they rocked and rolled for another five or ten miles until both stopped, engines off. The front doors opened and closed.

Jack turned his mouth to Jane's ear. She leaned in.

He smelled flowers. How could she still smell so good?

"Listen, Jane, I—"

"Time to move, gang," Tim said.

She met his eyes. "Tell me later, Jack." Brushing the tip of her nose on his, she raised to her knees and knee-walked to the back. Without help, she threw her legs over and slid to the ground.

Envious of her knee walking, Jack pushed himself up and duck-walked, following Andrew, to where the boys held out their hands.

"Let's go, people. Look alive. That gate is open and they're probably headed this way right now."

"Tim, are you crazy? Are these people we're going to see crazy? That's. A. Horde. You can't just use it like a living wall."

"You're right, Jackson," Tim said, winking. "It's a dead wall. Much more useful for keeping the right sort in and the wrong sort out." He pointed east.

Jack followed his pointing finger.

A bridge spanned the sound, but it had no middle. It was useless.

"Tim," he said, turning, "you are crazy. What now?"

"We take the boats," Tim said, clapping him on the shoulder. "Let's go." Gripping Jane by the upper arm, tight enough to dig in and turn her skin a paler shade of white, he pulled her along. She stumbled, stutter-stepped, and got her feet under her again.

Approaching the sound, the stench of rotten fish grew.

It nauseated him. Made him want to throw up in his mouth. Or into Tim's mouth. Whatever.

Tim stretched a welcoming hand to two small motorboats on the beach. "All aboard the express cruise to Emerald Isle. Please keep your hands and feet inside the ship at all times."

Jack and Andrew boarded the right one. Jane put a foot inside.

"Oh no, sweetheart," Tim said. "Why don't you come with me in this boat. It's nicer. It hasn't got trash in it," he said, casting a glance at Jack.

She shook her head, shifting her center of gravity into the boat with Jack.

Tim grabbed her around the waist and lifted her over his shoulder, fireman style. The only sound she made was a small *oof* as he threw her over. He loaded her into the other boat and stepped in.

They pushed off and started the outboards, picking up speed.

Watching the mainland recede into the distance, Jack's stomach turned over. Considering where they'd been, where could they be going?

CHAPTER 17

The train rolled to a stop.

Only the sound of the distant sea broke the silence.

A closed gate stood before them, no one guarding it. No one opening it. No calls of "Who goes there?" Nothing.

"There's no one here," Addy said.

Mike opened the window and shoved his head through. "That's impossible."

With his head out the window, he sounded like he spoke from another planet.

Pulling his head in, he caught his chin on the sill. He stood and rubbed his jaw, staring at her with his dinner plate eyes. "There's got to be someone."

She stared at Dean. "What the hell is this?"

"My guy said there's a settlement here. He didn't say there weren't any people. I don't know." He rubbed his forehead.

She stood, hands on her hips. Everything about this squeezed her the wrong way. Like wearing a child's coat. It had sleeves and all, but the shoulders were all wrong and it would never keep you warm.

Slinging the quiver and bow over her shoulder, she checked her other weapons. Her dose of the Cure. Everything in its place. She nodded to Dean.

Hand on the door, he glanced at Mike. "You ready to go out there, brother?"

Mike bobbed his head. "Let's get out there, see what we can see."

Addy stepped up behind Dean. He spun, smiled, and looked over her shoulder.

Frowning, he stepped past her and took the picture down, removed the frame, and slid the photo into his breast pocket. He laid the frame on the pillow and stepped back to the door. "Come on."

They stepped out into the silent, humid, and oppressive air. Addy pulled a breath through her nose. Salty. Fishy. Stinky. Not like Dead Head stink, though.

"Dean, what is that godforsaken stench?"

He inhaled, brow wrinkled. "It's the sound."

"What sound? I don't hear anything."

"That sound," he said, pointing across the water. The tracks ran parallel to it. "A sound is what they call that body of water, between the mainland and an island."

Addy turned inland. Inside the fence, a sign stood before a collapsed brick building. "Walgreens. Wonder what they did there? I've seen those before."

"Some kind of drugstore," Mike said.

"A what what?"

"Mom used to get me Superman Band-Aids from there."

"Huh. OK. Well, Dean," she said, facing the sound, "what are we going to do?"

Mouth puckered, his eyes skipped between the train and the fence. "I'm gonna move the train. It just seems a little…obvious. Needs better camouflage." Holding up a hand, he walked away. "You guys stay here. I'll be right back."

Addy frowned, brow wrinkled. He had to be joking. "Split up? With that horde out there? You think that's an awesome idea?" She poured on so much sarcasm her teeth hurt.

He shook his head, oblivious. "No, Addy. It's not a great idea. Neither is leaving this big, shiny train out in the open. I'll be right back. Wait here."

As the train slipped backward around the bend, she eyed the gate, stomach flip-flopping. "Mike, let's go," she said, following the tracks ahead.

The gate hung by a hinge, all but ready to fall off. Addy gripped one of the poles holding the chain-link and leaned it back a couple feet. The steel pole, rough under her hand and burred with rust, opened a hole large enough for her and Mike to ease through.

She let it fall and it dragged a furrow in the sandy ground. It clanged against the fence, a hollow echo. Glancing over her shoulder down the tracks, her cheeks grew hot.

"I'll show you wait here, you son of a bitch," she murmured.

"What's that, bean?"

Casting an absent "Don't call me that" over her shoulder, she wandered toward the Walgreens. Easing up next to the building, she found piles of bricks neatly stacked. The tip of a five-foot-tall metal W peeked out from under one pile. Red glass lay sprinkled around it.

So they'd built a fence, cleaned up the place, and then what? Were they out there, part of the horde? Did they leave? Move to the island, maybe?

Why had Dean led them here? Had there ever been anyone here, or was it some kind of trick? Her dad had always said to be on the lookout for people to turn on you. They did it with such regularity, it was almost a foregone conclusion someone was going to.

While he'd say, "Don't let that mistake cost you your life," her mom would have said, "You'd be surprised what you can accomplish when people work together."

Wandering into the old building, kicking stones out of the way, feet crunching over the sandy floor, she considered which of her parents was right.

They both had their fair points. It wasn't like she'd ever seen one proved right over the other. It had been pretty much them until her mom had— You know.

Then Jane and her parents came along. It had been nice, the little group. Wasn't long after that they moved to the village in the old fort. Then it was work and eating, drinking, living behind walls, behind the Cure. The 'Heads had thinned. People worked together to build a community. Life had begun anew.

But then this? What had happened with the people they trusted? Wade, especially. What had he done?

Besides, hadn't he been murdered? Yet they continued east.

This was more than one someone, and—

An electric engine whined, just audible over the sound's lapping waves. Tires crunched over sand and gravel outside.

Heartbeat in overdrive, Addy hid behind the closest wall. Her stomach rolled again. Where was Dean? Mike?

The vehicle stopped and boots hit the dirt. Two pair. They spoke to each other, but she was too far away to make out many words. Just a snatch of one here and there.

"…look around, see…"

"…know they're here?…no one around…"

One of the voices, small, tinged with a hint of a Hispanic accent, floated into Addy's brain and made itself at home. A voice maybe she knew? Was it?

"Stop right there!" A male voice shouted, followed by a gun cocking.

Addy backed up against the wall and stood, pulling her knife.

"…whoa, OK guys, it's OK. Not here to…"

Dean.

He raised his voice. "I'm putting my weapons down, see? Look, nothing to be afraid of. I'm just here…"

The small voice spoke. She couldn't make out any words. It sounded almost like a furtive whisper.

Could they be plotting against her? All three of them on the same side somehow. Dean tricking her into a trap.

With purpose, she ran the back of her head into the wall. "Don't be stupid, Adelaide. He's on your side."

Dean called her name.

She stiffened. Caught her breath.

He called again. Called for her brother, too.

Mike called back, from just around the corner.

Through the empty doorway, she watched his boots cross in front of the building.

He shouted. "Holy shit! Addy, get out here!"

Gripping the knife, she crouched and crab-walked to the doorway. Adrenaline rushing through her arms, she peeked around the bricks.

Four people stood in what was once a parking lot.

One, a man she didn't recognize.
Dean.
Mike.
Celia.

***

Celia insisted on getting out of town.

Standing by the train, she took a hug from Addy.

Squeezing her, Addy let out the breath she'd been holding since she'd seen her. "I thought you were back home."

Celia laughed. "Thought the same about you, girl."

"Can you tell us what's going on?"

"I think so. But not here. There's boats down the beach. I suggest we get out of here. They're less than a half-hour behind us at this point. And they have tricks to getting in."

Addy swallowed. "The horde?"

"They use it for defense. It's a 'living' wall. But they have a way around it."

Celia left the tracks and brushed through the scrub next to them. Addy, Mike, and Dean followed her and the pale, red-headed man she'd introduced as Oren. The stink of the sound grew.

Addy breathed through her mouth. It didn't help.

The pops of rifles and grenades rocked the air. They all ducked as one, Mike full-on hitting the dirt.

Dean pulled a handgun from his belt and stood back up, pointing everywhere.

"It's them," Celia whispered. "They're coming through the wall. We stay hidden, wait for them to pass."

Nodding, Dean stuffed the gun back in his belt and crouched with the rest of them.

Long moments passed.

More long moments.

Addy's nose itched. She reached to scratch it and almost stabbed herself in the eye with her knife. Whenever it was that she'd drawn it.

The large trucks barreled past the Walgreens and stopped near the water.

Dad's voice floated across the beach.

At the sound of his voice, Addy's stomach roiled. It had been one constant knot since the last time she'd seen him. She swallowed and tried to stand.

Dean cleared his throat. Celia grabbed her wrist.

She looked down at Celia's small, grasping hand. Into her eyes.

Celia shook her head. She dropped her already small voice to a whisper. "I know you want to save him. So do I. But now is not the time."

"But—"

"We'll save him. I promise you. Just not now."

Addy held her hand out. "Binoculars."

Frowning, mumbling something about saying please, Mike handed them over.

She raised them and picked out two small motorboats on the shore. She'd caught the drama just in time to watch Tim throw Jane over his shoulder. Her dad tensed, like a coiled snake.

What exactly was Tim's deal? And what had happened between him and Dad?

The boats pushed off and into the sound, turned on their engines, and sped away.

She lowered the spyglasses.

"Addy, we gotta go," Celia said, standing. "They're gone and if we don't get gone, we will be gone."

Dean, feet sinking into the sand, made his way to her. He gave her one of his crinkly-eye smiles.

She smiled back. "Are we going back to the train, Celia?"

"Oh no. We've got our own boats. Not as nice as those," she said, pointing. "They're human-powered. You get to help, chica." She clapped Addy on the shoulder and sauntered down the beach.

"Dean, what does she mean by that?" she asked, as her brother jogged to catch the disappearing woman.

"Row, row, row your boat," Dean sang. Badly off-key.

"Wow. Don't do that again."

"What?"

"You know what."

"Sing? Oh, sweetheart, you shouldn't have asked me to stop."

As she walked away, following Celia to the boats down the beach, Dean sang "Row Your Boat" and followed.

***

The two motorized boats raced each other, weaving in figure eights. Jack had never been seasick, but Andrew slowly turned a pale shade of green.

"Hurl over the side if you're gonna," Jack said.

Andrew bobbed his head, mouth and eyes clamped shut.

Jack aimed a tight-lipped grin at him and watched the approaching shore. What fresh horrors awaited them on the island rushing toward them? The two boats twisted their wakes and began to separate again.

Staring at Tim as the boats passed earned him a smile from the boy. Water from the sound drenching his brow, he smoothed his hair with one hand and aimed the other at him like a gun. Winked.

If this boy ever touched Adelaide again, they were going to have words.

Water rushed under the boat the way road disappeared beneath tires. Soon a light flashed across the water.

"Slow it down, boys," Tim shouted.

Andrew wobbled, in danger of falling over the side, as the boats began to slow. Without cracking an eye, he leaned over the side and vomited. Sat up and opened one eyelid a fraction. "I don't like boats, Jackie."

Jack nodded. "You gonna be alright?"

"Once we get back on solid ground, I think so."

"Hang in there, big guy. We're almost there."

People lined the approaching dock, tossing ropes out as they sidled up to it. Much larger than an average pier, these could have docked actual ships. Long ladders led down to the water.

Throwing Jane over a shoulder, Tim whirled. "Gotta uncuff you now, Jackson, so you and your buddy can climb this ladder. Try anything, though," he said, giving Jane a violent shake, "and I throw her in the water."

Jack swallowed. Jane's hands were still bound, and on the way out, Tim had added ropes around her ankles. She'd never survive a swim tied like that. Her boots may as well have been bricks.

"Whatever you say, Tim."

Tim nodded, and someone released Jack's cuffs, their teeth rasping.

"Climb," the boy behind him said.

"Ricardo. I don't understand why we're still doing this. You can see he's unstable, right?"

Ric shook his head. "Mr. C., don't make me force you." He dropped his voice and leaned in to whisper. "Besides, I know he's crazy. He'll drop her before you can even shout. Please. Do what he says."

Jack climbed.

At the top, a small group of people greeted them. It turned out they weren't all children. A mix of ages, sexes, and races met him. There was no way to pin down what he was up against, but at least they weren't going all *Lord of the Flies* out on this island.

Probably.

Tim grunted, slinging Jane up onto the dock before climbing up himself.

Knocking her head against the ground hard enough to bounce, she stifled a cry behind her lips.

Jack offered a hand to Andrew, half his mind next to Jane, checking her wound. But he held onto Andy, pulling him onto the pier.

Still pale, but at least not green anymore, Andrew sat and panted. "Thanks, Jackie."

Jack nodded, staring at Jane.

She lay on the dock, still. Breathing, but not moving.

"Let's go, sweetheart," Tim said, shaking her shoulder. Her head lolled to the side.

"You asshole. You knocked her out with that stunt," Jack said, taking a step.

"Uh-uh," Tim said, holding a finger up. Foot on her shoulder, he rolled her over until she teetered on the edge.

Jack stopped, mouth dry. "Look. Don't, alright? If your issue is with me, take it up with me. You don't need to do that."

"Oh, Jackson. You know I do."

"Just don't, alright? Here," he said, holding his hands out and pointing them at Ric, who had climbed up last. "Put the cuffs on. Let's go."

Tim jerked his chin at the boy and reached down to pick Jane up.

Instead of picking her up, he rolled her half a centimeter toward the edge.

Jack sucked a breath through his teeth.

A slow grin crossed Tim's lips. He narrowed his eyes and jerked Jane from the ground, throwing her over his shoulder again.

"Come, Jackson. Let me show you what home really looks like."

THE ISLANDS

CHAPTER 18

Adelaide's oar dipped into the quiet water of the sound. Both pulling the water ahead of her back, and pushing the water behind her away, she delighted in manually propelling the boat forward.

"I'll take over anytime you want, little sister," Mike said.

Glaring at him over her shoulder, she caught Dean smiling.

She plunged the oar deeper than she meant. It slipped and her hand dipped into the cold, semi-salty water. "What're you grinning at, Dean?"

"Nothing, Addy. Nothing at all."

Arms crossed, one foot cocked up on the side of the boat, he smiled and swayed with its movement like an old sailor.

Scowling, she sunk the oar into the water again. It slipped out of her hand. "Ah! Crap!" Grabbing for it, she all but went over the side herself.

A small but strong hand gripped her wrist and hauled her back in. She toppled off the seat and onto the floor of the boat.

Deck. Keel. What the hell ever it was.

Sitting and stewing in her own ineptitude, she didn't notice when the dripping oar appeared next to her face. As she turned to thank Celia for saving her from spilling into the water, she smacked her nose into it.

"Dammit, sorry, Addy," Dean said. Pulling the oar back, he sat up to reach for her.

Addy took Celia's outstretched hand and lifted her stinging butt back onto the seat. Waited for him to ask if he could do the paddling for her now, big strong man that he was.

Instead, he continued to hold the oar out to her in silence.

Deflating, eyes smiling, she shook her head. "Could you do it for a bit?"

He nodded, corners of his eyes crinkling. Without a word, he dipped the paddle into the water and pushed them forward. From the front, Oren counterpointed Dean's strokes. They cut through the water at a good clip.

Addy goggled as both shores slid by. She'd never seen this much water at once, and to be surrounded by land on two sides but so far from any of it was a new and interesting feeling. It made her heart jump up and down to think the ocean would be even greater. Seeing it for the first time wasn't something she'd ever considered doing, but now that she was on the cusp of it, she could barely contain her excitement.

Movement on the island to her right caught her eye. In the dimming light, she couldn't quite make out what it was.

"Horses," Oren said from the front.

Addy jerked. "Sorry, what?"

"Horses," Oren repeated, turning around.

His red mustache bounced as he spoke, and Addy flashed on a cartoon her mom had once shown her. They'd lost that one pretty early on, but the funny mustachioed man had stuck in her memory.

"Wild horses, to be more precise. They've been here for hundreds of years. Outlast us, probably."

Watching the horses glide down the beach, she wondered what the sea spray felt like on their faces. What it must be like to stretch their legs like that and just run, free of concern.

"Wild, you say?" Dean asked, straining in the middle of the question as he rowed. "I don't remember the last time I saw wild horses."

"Oh yeah. They've experienced a sort of rebirth since the world went to shit. At least somebody did good," Oren said, turning back around and paddling.

Addy smiled. If anything deserved to profit from the crapstorm she grew up in, it was some damn beautiful wild horses. "Hey, Celia?"

Celia glanced at her without seeming to move, her silence as good as an answer.

"What's that tall building?"

Celia smirked. "Lighthouse. Have you never seen the ocean?"

All she could think to do was smile and shake her head. Face burning, she watched the building slide by. But instead of continuing to ask questions, she just made up stories in her mind about what a lighthouse was for.

She'd ask Mike but he'd probably laugh too.

Maybe Dean would know.

***

Packed into the back of a jeep, Jack did his best to stabilize a still unconscious Jane. Her head lolled against his shoulder.

"Tim."

He sat in the passenger seat, chewing a nail. "Jackson?"

They passed a half-demolished sign, once built from brick and wood. The remaining wood had warped, paint peeling and chipped. The left side of it held a few snatches of words.

Fo
Ma
Stat

"Where are we?"

Tim turned in his seat. "Ah, yes. Welcome home, Jackson. This is the former Fort Macon. We call it Shanti Station."

"What does that mean?"

"No idea," Tim said. "Anyway, I'm glad you could see it. I hope your stay is"—he lowered his forehead, staring at Jack from under his brow—"I hope it's pleasant."

Jack coughed. "Just threw up in my mouth a little bit, Tim."

Andrew chuckled.

Glaring, Tim faced front.

They crested the top of a sand dune. Waves crashed in the distance. A glimmer of light bounced off water, and the smell of salt filled the air. In the darkening day, the boundless ocean had turned a deep shade of gunmetal grey.

The ocean had always given Jack a light feeling in his chest. Something about all the water and the way it moved in a living dance. The life teeming below its surface, the life teeming on the land because of its very presence. There was something primordial about the ocean, something that filled him with a deep sense of purpose and gratitude for life.

A brief glimpse was all he had before they left the crest of the dune and followed it down, into what may have once been a parking area. Now pavement peeked out from a covering of sand, scrubby bushes sprouting from the odd surface.

"Get her up," Tim said over his shoulder. "We're here."

Scowling, Jack turned to Jane.

Light snores came from her delicate nose. A small goose egg bulged from her forehead just above her temple.

Lifting his bound hands, he leaned her back against the seat and took her face in them, rubbing her cheeks with his thumbs. "Jane," he whispered.

She took a deep breath but didn't stir.

Tim opened the back door and cleared his throat. His foot tapped the sand.

Jack tried again. "Jane," he said, the fingers on one hand slipping around to grip the back of her neck. The handcuff chain dimpled her chin.

Her eyes rolled under her lids.

He leaned into her ear and tried again. "Jane, baby, I need you to wake up now."

A sharp inhale through her nose and the way every muscle in her body stiffened told him she had woken.

He leaned back, one thumb still stroking a cheek.

Big, sleepy eyes smiled.

"Alright, let's move, people," Tim said. He stepped back and opened the door wide, bowing like a chauffeur.

Andrew glanced at Jack and slid out. Landing on Tim's foot, he twisted a heel.

With a shout, Tim punched him in the jaw.

Andrew raised his hands, one clutching the other to make a single fist.

"Andrew, don't," Jack said, releasing Jane and straddling her to jump out of the jeep. His right heel caught under the front seat and he fell, face-first into her chest. Lifting his hands, he pushed up, at the same time twisting his ankle to free his foot.

Tim and Andrew both stopped, staring into the jeep.

Guffawing, Tim all but fell on his ass. Andrew, fair-skinned and red-faced already, blushed a shade so red he could have been sunburned.

Jack followed their gaze.

In his effort to help his friend, he'd grabbed Jane in, well, an inappropriate place.

No doubt turning his own shade of alarming red, he sat back and snatched his hand away like he'd just touched a stove burner. His heel popped free, and he fell into the seat, stammering. "Oh Jane, I'm so sorry, I didn't, uh, didn't mean to um…"

She smiled, cool eyes dancing. "Just get out of the car, Jack."

He did as he was told.

Straightening, tears standing in his eyes, Tim shut the door after Jane slid out and motioned over their heads. Two people approached, both holding rifles to port, and stood to either side of them.

Glancing back, Jack took in the two adults. One, a tall Japanese man, the other, a pale, stocky woman.

Tim beckoned. "Come along boys and girls."

***

Passing into the fort, Jack smelled the air, its scent of wet earth.

Dug into the ground, the tops of the fort were carpeted in grass. They crossed a creaking wooden bridge over some sort of moat and into a rounded, cave-like entryway.

"Shanti Station was built back in the eighteen hundreds," Tim said, voice echoing off the brick walls. "We think it was used in the Civil War, but of course, all the records from back then have long since been destroyed. We'll never know the complete history, but there were still old cannons and stuff when Shanti Station was first commissioned."

"Commissioned by who?" Jack asked.

Tim shook his head. "Not for me to tell you. But I will say," he said, pausing and turning around. He stuck a finger in Jack's face. "It's the same people I spoke of before, and they will not tolerate any crap." His eyes jumped left and right.

Heart dropping, Jack hesitated. Tim was afraid of these people, whoever they were. And if someone like Tim was afraid, it could not be a good thing.

"Anyway," Tim said, returning to his formerly bright tone, "it's a perfect setup we have here. The drinking water is a little stale, but you get used to it."

Salty air greeted them as they entered an open, grassy courtyard. Jack had almost been expecting some sort of modern prison with brightly lit hallways and plastic, shiny cells. This ancient fort was more of an earthen palace. Humid, salty, and cool, and it was mostly outdoors. There were worse places to be imprisoned.

"This is where I leave you for now," Tim said. "Please enjoy your stay." He looked over their shoulders, nodded to their silent guards, and vanished into a room on the left.

Jack glanced right. The stone walls were lined with barred doors and windows. Dozens of people stared out the windows.

Dozens upon dozens.

Where did all these people come from? Why were they being held here? In fact, why had any of them been brought here?

Their captors marched Jane, Andrew, and himself across the grassy yard.

"Look alive, old man," the large guard said, prodding him in the back with the stock of his rifle.

Giving one last look to the silent mass of people across the way, Jack walked through the open door in front of him.

Fire crackling in a fireplace set in the left wall, the long room had a low, rounded ceiling.

Jack's chest tightened. Small spaces had never been a favorite of his. There'd been a reason he'd moved west.

"Oh good, more new people." A little man sat behind a desk, eyeglasses flashing in the firelight. Before him, a ledger spread its pages, weighted with ink in a close script.

The sight of the studious man—one who reminded him too much of Wade—the ledger before him, the cells full of people outside, it all set Jack's teeth on edge.

Forcing him into a chair, the male guard held him down while the woman took a vial of blood. Quick and painless. Clean.

Why would they want a vial of blood? What the hell?

The guard gripped him under the arms, shoved him aside, forced Jane into the chair, and repeated the process.

The recordkeeper sighed and produced a pen from inside his jacket pocket. Uncapping it, he looked up, brows lifted. "Well? Name? Age? Height? Etcetera?"

"Jackson Cooke. Forty-six. Five-foot-ten. One-fifty-something, I guess."

The man nodded, writing Jack's name and details in the ledger. His glasses pressed into the sides of his head, creating what would be a white line if they should be removed. But where Wade's eyes had carried some modicum of caring and concern, this man's beady eyes conveyed only impatience. Cold, detached, hostile little rat eyes.

As he wrote, Jack did some mental calculations. Based on the size of this room, he figured there could be as many as a couple hundred people in the cells he'd seen outside. Estimating the pages before him held about a hundred names, some with check marks next to them, Jack did more quick math.

All told the ledger could hold thousands of names before his.

But there were only hundreds in the cells outside.

So either there were more cells, or…where were the rest of the people?

Taking Jane's and Andrew's details, writing them in a cramped, slanted script, the recordkeeper's impersonal manner did not welcome questions or back talk.

Didn't stop Jane.

"Oi there, laddie," she said, laying on the Scottish accent again. "What're we doin' here?" She sat on the desk, wood creaking.

His pen skidded across the page. He sighed, capping it once again. It disappeared into his coat.

"Get them out of here," he said, waving his hand.

Their guards came forward, menacing with their rifles. Jane hopped from the desk, giving the little man a wink, and sauntered to the door.

Andrew followed, face blank.

Jack took the rear. By the door sat three file boxes, stacked on top of one another. The lid was off the top one, and what Jack saw inside as he passed turned his guts to ice. He took in a breath but couldn't let it out.

The box was filled to the brim with ledgers.

***

Oren roped the boat to a floating platform. Addy put a shaky foot on it.

Dean leapt onto the platform, sending the boat rocking. Before Addy had a chance to go ass over teakettle into the black water, he caught her and lifted her onto the small dock.

Heart thumping, she took a few deep breaths. Glanced at the three-quarter moon high in the sky. Considered asking him to kindly remove his hands. Rethought it. The firm hands wrapped around her weren't so bad. Instead, she smiled. "My hero."

Silver shadows on his face flickering, he grinned. "Anytime."

"Welcome to Harkers Island," Celia said. "This way. Stay on the boardwalk. We're in a swamp." Handing Addy a flashlight, Celia turned on her own and clunked away across the boards.

Dean released Addy but kept his fingers on the small of her back.

She wobbled on the floating dock and followed Celia, Mike between them.

"Michael," she called.

"Hm?"

"Isn't it a little crazy we ran into Celia, all the way out here?"

"Little sister, it's what I like to call luck. The universe sent us some help." He stopped. "I've always told you, but you never listen. The universe sends you help all the time. You just have to open your eyes to see it." Winking, he followed Celia.

Addy spun around. "You believe him?"

Dean shrugged. He stepped closer. "I'd be lying if I said I didn't think it was a little weird," he said. "But I'm also not one to look a gift horse in the mouth. Let's roll with it."

She frowned.

He beat her to the punch. "But we'll keep our eyes open."

Warmth spread from her head to her toes. He'd finally agreed with her.

Silent, Celia led them through the marsh until they came to a dirt road. Trees closed in over them like a canopy.

Addy shivered, holding her arms.

Dean walked next to her. "You OK?"

"Yeah. Just not used to being closed in like this. Do you feel how thick the air is?"

He looked around. "I do. Once we get out of these trees, it'll open up again."

"If you say so. I guess I'm not used to being able to feel the air, you know?"

"Desert rat."

"Yes. Yes, I am."

"Come on, Addy. Enjoy it. Maybe tomorrow we'll go see the ocean."

Her chest tingled. "I'd like that. Get closer to the horses, maybe."

"It's a date," he said, walking away.

It's a what?

She tripped over a root, the flashlight flying.

Oren, pulling up the rear, hooked her in the armpit and hauled her to her feet. He snagged the flashlight and held it out to her. "Watch the ground around here. It can be tricky." Red mustache bouncing.

"Thanks." She took the flashlight and brushed her pants. Eyes on the beam, she walked next to him. "Hey, Oren."

"Mm-hmm."

"Do you get Dead Heads out here on the island?"

He grunted. "Not usually. A straggler here or there. But they don't normally make the trip from the mainland. Not intact, at least."

"Ew. What do you mean not intact?"

"First thing to go when a body gets waterlogged is the feet," he said. "They just fall right off. The current pulls them all the way out here, they ain't really capable of locomotin' anymore."

"Oh. Easy to track then."

"Yup. 'Cept for a couple times, they ain't really been a problem out here."

Addy fingered the pouch with her dose of Cure. "Good. That's good to know."

They walked in silence for a bit before she thought of another question. The first one she should have asked, probably. "Hey, Oren."

"Yup."

"Have you guys been here since before?"

"Oh yeah. The island's always been pretty safe. Once everything died down, haha, people started showing back up here."

"Are there other islands?"

"Oh yeah. But we pretty much just all keep ourselves to ourselves, you know?"

Addy nodded.

In the dark. It was like she'd never learn.

"Yeah, I know." She considered. "How do you know Celia?"

"Cee? Practically grew up with her."

"Wow, really?"

"Yeah. Why? How long you known her?"

Addy stopped. Tilted her head, considering. How long had it been? They'd known her about as long as Jane, probably. Since before the Cure, at least. "About seven years or so, I guess."

"About the time we had a food shortage, then," he said, walking on. "She started leaving the island after that. Couple, three times a year, she disappears for a few months."

Frowning, Addy stared at Celia's back. Of course, she'd always been one to disappear for weeks on end. But to go all the way to the East Coast and back? Before the Cure was available? Multiple times a year? She'd never considered such a thing. The woman was a mystery.

Ahead of them, the trees broke. A paved road curved off in both directions. Celia, Mike, and Dean stopped to wait for them.

Addy considered jogging to catch up, thought about her spill back there, and walked with a quick step instead.

"Big House is up ahead," Celia said. She took the road to the left.

As Mike and Oren followed, Addy hesitated.

Dean hung back. "What's up?"

"I'm not sure," she said. Her head hurt. Chewing a nail down to the quick, she spat it on the ground. Aimed her flashlight at the three retreating backs.

"I'm not sure."

***

The Big House, as Celia called it, was a sprawling creation of grey boards and green shingles. It may have been a showpiece of some kind once, but now the sides and roof were patched with whatever had been available. A crow's nest stuck out the top of the roof, made of the same weathered wood. It held a simple beauty.

Just inside sheer curtains, people walked back and forth. Coming, going, not caring who could be outside looking in.

Or what.

Addy shook her head, trying to slough off the feeling of unease that'd settled over her heart since they'd encountered that horde. Everything had felt sideways since then, no matter what Mike said.

Oren let them all in, closing the door behind them. It had a bar, but he didn't drop it in. Instead, he motioned to some couches in a semicircle around a fireplace.

Before the fire sat a single chair, someone's feet sticking out of it and resting on the hearth. They had a hole in one sock. Celia approached them, leaning over the chair back and whispering.

As the man put his feet down and stood, the firelight glanced off his silver hair.

The young face beneath it jarred Addy. When had his hair had time to go grey?

Smiling, he extended a hand and crossed the room.

Sometimes, without thinking, meeting someone made you straighten your hair and pull up your pants. This was such a man. If Jane were here, she would have already told him he was a drop-dead ten.

He took Dean's hand first.

"Scott Miller," he said. His voice, light but firm, sounded the way roses looked.

"Dean Ross."

Nodding, Scott shook with Mike.

"Michael Cooke."

"Not—" He glanced at Celia.

She nodded.

A wide grin split his face. "Why, we've heard all about your dad! And so you must be"—he turned to Addy—"Jack's daughter Adelaide!"

He took her hand with a furious up-and-down shaking. Her teeth clacked in her head.

"OK," she said. Her cheeks hurt, and when she lifted a hand to one of them, she found a smile as wide as Scott's. Turning to Mike, she pulled her lower lip up and scrunched her forehead.

He shrugged.

Scott finally released her hand.

The blood rushed back into her fingers. "So, um, Scott? What do you—"

"Please," he said, extending a hand toward the couches, "sit. Oren, bring some tea for our friends."

Sitting, Addy looked around for the redhead. He was already gone.

Scott crossed to the fire again and turned the chair. It scraped across the hardwood floor as he pulled it closer to the couches. He sat and smiled, leaning an elbow on his knee and planting his chin in the palm of his hand.

His eyes, soft and happy, had calculating written all over the back of them.

What did he know about them? "So, Scott," Addy began again.

"Michael," he interrupted, "tell me about your journey. Did you see the horde? How did you get here? Don't you live in Arizona?"

Addy trailed off, frowning.

"We do," Mike said. "I guess Celia told you about our dad?"

Scott nodded, smiling, and leaned back in the chair. "Oh yes. Cee told me all about him. Much about the two of you, too. And your village, all the way out there in the desert. Tell me," he said, leaning forward again, "is it incredibly hard to get supplies out there?"

Mike shook his head and opened his mouth.

Addy jumped in. "No. We're quite capable of getting more than adequate food and water for the whole community."

Smiling, he glanced at her. "I see. I'd love to hear more about it. But first I'd really like for Dean to tell me about the phones. Celia says you work on them with Michael?" He turned away, leaning over the arm of the chair.

Oren brought the tea, pouring cups for everyone.

Cup to her lips, Addy glanced at Dean. She whispered over it. "I'd kill him for some coffee."

He spit his tea in his lap.

Laughing, miraculously not spilling a drop, she drank her tea and watched Dean clean his lap, apologizing.

The fire crackled, and her mouth watered from the smell of burning wood. Every time she tried to shoehorn her way into the conversation, Scott would find a way to get back to speaking to the men on either side of her.

As her sense of infuriation increased, so did her calm. Curious new feeling, that. But she was not about to be bossed around by this man in front of her, drop-dead gorgeous, silver-haired devil though he was.

She excused herself and found Celia leaned against the wall across from the fireplace. "So what's going on here, 'Cee'?"

"Walk with me."

They left the main room and followed a hallway that had no right to be as long as it was.

"I'm from here," Celia started. She cleared her throat. "I'm not getting into details, OK, I'm just telling you. I went west a few years back because we were having a supply shortage. Kept going. Got lost. Jack found me."

Addy nodded. She remembered the story Dad had told her of finding the half-dead, dark-haired girl in the woods, armed to the teeth. Mean as a wolverine, he'd said. He brought her back to camp anyway, and Addy, Mike, and Jane got along pretty well with her. They'd had fun.

One day she'd disappeared as fast as she'd come, and they thought that was the last of her.

A few months later, she appeared again, saying she'd been "out." And that was it. That was how it was with her.

"I don't know, maybe I got wanderlust," Celia said, stopping in front of a window and hooking a curtain with her finger. After peeking out, she moved on, hands holding her elbows. "Some people don't like me for that. Whatever, it's their deal, not mine." Stopping again, she turned. "Scott's good people. He's held this place together for a long time." She cleared her throat. "I don't know how to tell you this."

"Tell me what?" So many possibilities crowded Addy's head, she all but had to shout to be heard over them. "What's going on here?"

Celia looked up. "Your dad, Jane, Andrew, they've been taken to some kind of prison."

"That doesn't surprise me to hear."

"Sure. Thing is, people don't come out of that prison, Addy. They become part of the horde."

All the wind fell out of Addy's lungs, and she crashed to the floor. A table came with her, some kind of vase knocking her on the head as it did.

She rubbed her head, eyes stinging. "Celia, what are we going to do?"

The small woman knelt. "These people," she said, looking around, "they fight for what's theirs. That's why I brought you here. We're going to take out that prison and get all those people free."

Addy stood. "I want to help."

***

The barred door closed behind him. Jack turned a circle.

"Well, Jackie, here we are," Andrew said.

"Yeah, Andy. Here we are. So where is here, and why?"

Someone cleared their throat. "Hey, you, move away from the door, would ya?"

They shuffled to the wall, Jack asking two men if they could spare some space. The men scooted.

"Jackie, have I told you lately I'm allergic to wool?"

"No, why?"

"It's these socks they gave us. They're wool."

Jack glanced down at his own red-carpet-ready jumpsuit. Plain tan, brown socks, tennis shoes.

The tennis shoes. That was weird. There'd been a whole room full of them in racks. Like these people had robbed a shoe factory.

"Shit, Andy. Maybe somebody's got cotton socks you can trade."

The man next to Jack leaned over, touching his shoulder. "Nobody's got cotton socks 'cept some of the girls. I don't think you're gonna get girl's socks over those size sixteens your friend's got."

Chuckling, Jack shook his head. "No, I don't think so. I'm Jack, he's Andrew. You?"

The man gave him a lazy shake. "Paul."

"Good to meet you, Paul. How long have you been here?"

"I don't know, new friend Jack. Six months? More or less?" Paul seesawed his hand, a well-worn pink ribbon tied around his wrist.

"What kind of place is it?"

Paul shrugged. In the low light, he could have been thirty or sixty. His hooded eyes drooped. "They don't give us beds. But the bread is fresh and hot every day. You can smell it cooking in the mornings. They cook it right down the row."

"Back up. There's nowhere to sleep?"

"Just the floor, new friend. Although"—he leaned in, lowering his voice to a conspiratorial whisper—"if you get yourself to the infirmary for 'some reason' you get a warm bed and a hot meal before they send you back."

Jack glanced up. Andrew had wandered off. "Andrew?"

Paul pointed at the back wall. "Your friend prolly went into another room. There's three for us. Three for the girls. One door between us."

"Thanks, Paul," Jack said and stood. At the end of the long, domed room, he found two doors. On the left, another barred door, the right, an open archway. Wandering through the open arch, he found an identical room. With identical men, in identical jumpsuits, doing identical things. Sitting along the walls, mostly, some lying down with an arm under their heads to sleep. But no Andrew.

The last arch brought him more of the same. Except…

Andrew stood next to a barred door in the next archway, Jane on the other side of it.

He exhaled a breath he didn't know he'd been holding since they'd been separated. He hurried to the door, heart in his throat.

"Jane," he said, gripping her fingers through the bars.

She squeezed his hand. "I am so glad to see you guys," she said, looking back and forth between them. She leaned forward. "It stinks like women in here."

Andrew's brow furrowed. "What does that mean?"

Jane, laughing, reached her other hand through the bars and slapped him on the shoulder with the back of her fingers. She glanced at Jack.

"Don't look at me. I know what you mean. I have a daughter, and I was even married once."

He smiled, but a shadow fell across Jane's face. She dropped his hand and put it behind her back. "Dammit, Jack. Do you think Addy's alright?"

"Yes, but I think we've got bigger fish to fry."

"Hey, Jane," Andrew said. He fingered the zipper on his jumpsuit.

"Yeah."

"Did you have to take a cold shower too?"

"Oh god," she said, laughing, "was that awkward. That guard, the lady, acted like she hadn't seen a naked girl before in her life. Like she never looked in a mirror."

Jack opened his mouth to reply but was instead assaulted by his brain. Unbidden, he pictured the room in which he and Andrew had been hosed down, but superimposed Jane, stark naked, being playfully sprayed by a shy but otherwise smiling woman.

Really, Jack? Really? Knock. It. Off.

He sobered. "At least it was a real shower room, with actual water."

Jane asked him the question with her eyes.

He looked between them. "World War II? Nazis? Ring a bell?"

Andrew nodded, recognition dawning. His eyes widened.

Jane shook her head.

Opening his mouth, Jack hesitated. How much to tell her? A crash course in the Holocaust, or just the basics?

"We're in some real trouble, guys. I don't know exactly how bad. But we need to figure it out before we get gassed, shot, or burned alive. Because those are shaping up into very real possibilities."

CHAPTER 19

Addy narrowed her eyes. "Does this hallway never end?"

Celia smiled over her shoulder. "Always with the sassy questions."

"You know it."

"Yeah. Here, let's go in here. Someone you need to see."

Brow creased, Addy followed Celia through a swinging set of double doors with red crosses painted on them. The acrid smell of antiseptic and bandages wafted through the doors. "Oh, is this the hospital?"

"More infirmary than hospital but whatever. Semantics. Over here," Celia said, crooking a finger over her shoulder.

Most of the beds sat empty, but two at the end of the long row had screens set up around them. As they approached, someone moaned from behind the one on the left.

Addy jumped, lip curled.

Like a 'Head but lower-pitched, the person buzzed. The sound grew until the person coughed, and the buzzing stopped.

She grabbed Celia's shoulder before they rounded the screen. "Celia. Are these…did these people get the Cure after turning?"

"See for yourself." Without waiting, she rounded the curtain on the right.

Addy followed, swallowing hard enough to hear her dry throat click. It'd been years since she'd seen anyone turned, then cured. Knowing it was possible, and seeing it in front of you, well…

"Oh my god, Adelaide," a voice croaked from the bed.

Inhaling, Addy backed into the screen and knocked it over. "Elizabeth?"

The woman on the bed nodded. Clean of the blood Addy had last seen her soaking in. Nose red and raw. Eyes sunken. But human again.

"Give me a hug," Liz croaked, holding her arms out. An IV needle taped to one, the line stretched to a sack full of purple-red blood.

Addy picked up the screen and tried to set it right. As she let go, it toppled over. Again.

Celia grabbed it. Making eye contact, she nodded toward Liz.

Addy stepped closer and crossed her arms. "Are you, um, how do you feel?"

Lowering her arms, Elizabeth pressed her lips together in a thin smile. "I've been better. But I guess I've been worse. So there's that."

Addy perched on the bed, careful to avoid Liz's feet. Opening her mouth, she drew in breath for a question. Closed it. Opened it again.

"What was it like, that's what you want to know, isn't it?"

Addy nodded, eyes on the floor.

"That's the question I've gotten the most. And I tell you what, Addy," she said, reaching for her hand.

Addy let her take it.

Her hand was warm. Alive.

Elizabeth smiled, but it was tight and pained. Like it hurt her throat, but also like it hurt her heart. "I don't remember much between when I was bitten and when I turned, and I don't remember much after Celia found me and cured me. I just remember waking up here." She cleared her throat. "But the middle part. It's so clear. You can't believe how clear. Like the kind of nightmare where you know you can't run fast enough, but you can't even make your brain think to move. Much less run."

Liz stopped, clearing her throat again. It buzzed. Grabbing a tissue, she coughed until some kind of clot released and flew into it.

Stomach gurgling, Addy tried not to watch as Liz balled it up and threw it into a tiny trashcan full of the same.

"I couldn't try to stop it," Liz said, continuing. "There wasn't that much of me left. But I remember it. Clearly. Like watching a movie."

"Well, that's…" The words dried up. Opening her mouth did not boot them out. They just weren't there.

"Awful. Terrible. Horrific. Completely and in all ways fucked," Liz supplied.

Nodding, Addy lowered her head again. Tears fell before she could stop them, hot on her cheeks. They splashed onto her jeans and soaked into them, leaving tiny wet dots.

"Addy," Liz croaked.

Adelaide raised her head again.

"If there's fight left in you, you have to fight. You have to get Jack and Andrew and Jane back. They're, uh—" Her voice cracked and wavered. She cleared her throat and tried again. "They're the only ones left."

Addy frowned. "Oh, I'll fight. We will get them back. We'll bring them home."

Liz nodded, leaning back into her pillow. Her eyelids slipped shut.

"She needs some sleep," Celia said, tugging Addy's sleeve.

Taking one last, long look at Elizabeth's lined face, she stepped out of the screen and followed Celia back to the hallway.

Addy leaned against the wall, trying to catch her breath. It felt like she'd just run a mile. "I can't believe she's OK."

"If you want to call it that."

"I mean, she's better than the last time I saw her."

"Yeah. I guess. Addy." When Addy looked up, Celia went on. "She killed the man she loved. Ripped his throat out. She can't remember who did this to her, what happened, but she remembers that. Ripping his throat out. The blood spurting into her face."

Addy swallowed, throat clicking again.

"Adelaide, she remembers how it tasted. How good it tasted. That's pretty damn far from OK."

"Jesus, Celia." Addy slid down the wall, her dry throat forgotten. She worked to suck one breath in after the other. "I can't. What is this?"

"Your dad has been taken by the people that did that to her. We cannot fail in getting him back."

Looking up at Celia put a crick in her neck. "I know. Why are you telling me this?"

Celia squatted next to her, arms stretched over her tented knees. "I guess I just really need to know that when it comes down to it, you're fully with us."

"Of course I am."

"Because we're not just getting your dad back. We're destroying that whole place."

"I realize that."

Celia sighed. "Addy, there's something you need to know."

"What?"

"It's not easy to tell you. But before we go in there, I have to."

"Adelaide! There you are!" Scott charged down the hallway, Dean and Mike in tow. They'd each switched from tea to beer.

The girls stood. Celia crossed her arms. "Scott. We're talking."

"Great. Talk over. Adelaide, if you would," he said, crooking an elbow.

Without consulting her brain, her hand reached out and took his arm.

He whisked her down the hallway, and Celia was gone.

***

Scott opened the door of a squat, metal building onto a room full of rowdy men and women. Tinny music played through speakers over the makeshift bar. The bartender raised a hand to Scott and disappeared to the other end.

Overwhelmed by the number of people, the haze of smoke, the cacophony of sound, Addy took a step back.

Scott tugged her arm, and she stumbled over the doorjamb. Dean and Mike followed them.

Coughing, smoke creeping down her throat, Addy glanced over her shoulder.

Dean grimaced and took a pull from the beer. He leaned forward. "You OK?"

"What?"

He leaned closer, raising one warm hand to cup her chin and pull her ear to his mouth. "Are. You. OK?"

Turning her head, she found his eyes next to hers. She gulped everything down, everything Liz had said. Shoved it down as far as it would go. "Fine."

Her arm jerked. "Addy, I want you to meet some people," Scott shouted.

The next hour may as well have been three. Addy met so many people she couldn't keep track of their names.

What she could gather, between the drinks Scott shoved at her, were that these people were good and honest people. And they all wanted to take the prison down. Between smoking, drinking, and playing cards, it was all they talked about.

Finding herself at the end of the whirlwind, she sat on a stool. The round bartender stood in front of her, eyebrows raised.

"Sorry, what?"

"I said, you want a drink?"

She looked down at her empty beer. When had that happened? And how many was that? "I've never seen so much alcohol. It's illegal where I come from."

"Welcome to Harkers Island, my friend. Where the hooch flows free."

"I'm, um. I'm sorry. What's your name?"

He stuck out a hand. "Christian."

She shook. "Adelaide."

He smiled, walking away to serve someone at the other end.

Eyes closed, she laid her head on the bar. The fuzziness in her head almost drowned out the horror of what had happened to Liz.

"You're sure you're OK."

She jumped and smiled with her eyes still closed. "You scared the crap out of me, Dean."

"I move quiet. What can I say. I'm Batman."

"Who?"

"Adelaide," he said, hitting her arm, "do you really only know Star Trek references and nothing else from before?"

"No. I also know Star Wars."

"This will not do. It's untenable."

Smiling, Addy lifted her head and leaned on her elbow, resting her head on her hand. "Well, I guess you'll have to teach me."

He grinned. "That can be arranged."

Her stomach lurched. The blood left her head.

She plastered the smile on her face. This was just too nice after the flurry of activity and strangers and Scott's pushy introductions.

"Alright. You're not OK," Dean said, leaning in and staring into her half-closed eyes.

"No, no. I fine. Let's keep—" Her head slipped off her hand and smacked into the bar. "Ah shit," she said, rubbing the spot she'd hit.

"Addy, whoa. Alright. Let's get you, um…" He stood, glancing around the smoky room.

At his urging, she threw an arm over his shoulders, and he wrapped his arm around her.

"I'm pretty sure you're getting some boob there, Dean," she said, laughing.

"Oh god, Addy, sorry," he said, bobbling her as he slipped his hand lower on her waist.

"I didn't say you had to move it."

"Well. Now I'm sure of it. You're drunk. Let's get you a place to lie down."

CHAPTER 20

Morning beat down on Jack's head. He cracked an eyelid. Tiny little daggers of light stabbed his eye. He sat, rubbing his face, and glanced around.

Most of the men were waking as well, doing about the same.

The scent of freshly baked bread floated through the cell. His stomach rumbled.

Gripping it, he glanced at the barred door between the cells. Jane slept just on the other side, one slender arm stretched under it.

Reaching for her hand, he paused. Watching her sleeping face was a small miracle in itself. With the birds chirping outside, the faint sound of the ocean cresting and coming ashore, her perfect eyelashes could have been something out of a Disney movie.

There's no such thing anymore, Jackson. Stop staring.

But he didn't. Not right away.

She inhaled, fluttering her eyelids. Smiled. "Good morning, Jack."

"Morning. Sleep well?"

"Oh yeah. Like a bag of rocks."

"I don't know if that's good or not."

"Friend Jack."

Jack glanced up.

Paul stood over him, frowning, hand extended.

With a glance at Jane, Jack took it and stood. "Morning, Paul. What's up?"

Paul looked over his shoulder and smiled at Jane. "I'm sorry, but we can't talk to the women."

Jack glanced at Jane.

She asked the question. "What do you mean, we can't talk?"

Paul shrugged. "Just one of them things, sweetheart. Pretty as you are, we still can't talk to you." His eyes met Jack's. "Move away, if you know what's good for you, my friend. And for her."

With a last glance at her, Jack turned his back and walked away with Paul. With the rock sitting in his gut, the smell of the bread wasn't so pleasing anymore. He put a hand on Paul's shoulder. "So why would they put the door there if we can't talk to them?"

"It's just one of the rules." Paul shrugged. "The guards make the rules, but they don't tell us what they are. I've been here a year. Most guys, they come and go in a couple months or less. Girls too. I think I figured 'em out though." He leaned in and lowered his voice. "Just do what I tell you, you'll make it."

A megaphone, one of the old electric ones, crackled from the opposite end of the cells.

"LINE UP, MEATHEADS. TIME TO GO TO WORK."

All the men headed to the front of the cell and formed a single file.

Turning to find Jane, Jack instead found empty space on the other side of the door.

Stomach a mess of knots, he followed Paul to the line. "What is this?"

Speaking out of the corner of his mouth, Paul whispered back. "We gotta work on the jetty this week. Needs shoring up, I guess. We might could talk more on the beach."

Andrew joined them in line. "Beach day, Jackie?"

Jack shrugged. "Seems that way. Keep your ears open today, will you?"

With a nod, Andrew followed Jack and the others out of the cell and into the warming sun.

***

"Hey, sleepyhead."

Addy shuffled out Celia's front door, closing it behind her. "Morning, Dean. Thanks for taking care of me last night."

He smiled. "My pleasure. You ready to go see the ocean?"

The inside of her temple pounded out a bass rhythm, but it was nothing compared to before Celia had nursed her back to consciousness with water and coffee. She'd also told her Scott wouldn't be available to talk about the invasion plan until later in the afternoon. "My morning is all yours."

"Just what I like to hear. Milady," he said, bowing and stretching an arm toward the road.

They followed the same road they'd come in on and clanked out the same wooden boardwalk to the canoes.

"So, does anyone know we're going, or are we stealing?"

"Does it matter?"

She frowned and narrowed her eyes. Overexaggerated a thinking finger on her chin. "Nnnnnooo. No, it doesn't."

He handed her an oar. "You have to help, though. So no dropping the oar."

She resisted the urge to hit him with it as he stepped into the boat. But it was a close call.

They paddled around the side of Harkers Island, and Dean pointed the boat toward the lighthouse. As they crossed the sound, Addy sweated out the last of the alcohol. Her arms, shoulders, and abs ached by the time they tugged the boat ashore, but it was a good ache, and her head was clear.

"You ready?" Dean asked, stepping from the boat.

"Ready as I'll ever be. Is it that way?" Addy pointed over the dune.

"Course it is." He set off, trudging through sand.

"Race you!" Addy shouted, taking off. The sand ate her feet up to the ankles, but it didn't matter.

She was flying. Up and up, to the top of the dune.

And there it was. The vastest living thing she'd ever seen. It breathed like a sleeping giant. The sun glinted off a cresting wave near the horizon.

Dean bumped her shoulder on the way past. "You snooze, you lose, slowpoke!" He continued down the dune, sand spraying from his heels.

"Dammit. I don't think so," she murmured. Uneven as it was, the sand was easier to run in than she'd thought it would be. In fact, as she picked up speed, she seemed to almost rise above it and run along the tops of the tiny little dunes under her feet. The salty spray pushed into her face and she sucked in a breath through her nose, nostrils open as far as they'd go. Her lungs filled with salty, humid, fresh air.

Stopping just short of the waterline, she waited for him to catch up and met his eyes. "I have never smelled something so alive in my life."

He grinned, a sunny smile stretching from ear to ear. "I'd forgotten how amazing it was." But it wasn't the ocean he watched as he spoke.

She smiled. "Let's go in the water."

"Addy, we don't have swimsuits."

"Just up to our ankles. Prude." She winked, leaning over to take off her shoes and roll up her pants.

He did the same, and they walked into the water.

Cold water splashing around her ankles, for the first time in her life, the ocean surrounded her legs, pushing its way to shore, then sucked on her feet as it washed back out.

It was the most magnetic and majestic thing that had ever happened to her.

"Come on," Dean said, reaching for her hand. "A little farther."

"It's so cold, Dean. I didn't know it'd be so chilly."

"You'll get used to it." He tugged.

She stepped farther out, holding his hand for balance as a wave crashed into her shins. As it sucked itself back into the ocean, unknown things touched her calf. "Something's tickling my leg."

"Sand, seaweed, jellyfish. Don't worry about it. The ocean is full of things."

"Life. It's full of life."

He watched the horizon. "That it is."

She licked her lips and tasted salt.

Scooping up a handful of water, she drank in a mouthful. Let the rest drip through her fingers. Drop by drop, becoming part of the ocean again.

A wave broke onto her knees, pushing her back. Pinwheeling, she grabbed Dean and shouted. The shout escaping her mouth was something she hadn't heard from herself since she was a child. Since before her mom died. Something she'd forgotten existed.

A shout of joy.

Grabbing onto his arm, she laughed. And laughed.

And he laughed, holding her close as the waves washed over their legs.

Closing her eyes, she rocked with the push and pull of the sea, all the while holding Dean for support.

When she opened her eyes, she found him staring at her. So close, she could feel his breath on her chin. Smiling, she released him. "Race you to the lighthouse!"

***

Walking down the dune toward the ocean and finishing the fresh bread they'd been handed as they left the fort, Jack's spirit lifted. Strange though it was, given the circumstances, the delicate butterfly wings of joy whispered against him.

Seeing the ocean, feeling her great massive pull, was a forgotten pleasure he'd let go for too long.

One of the guards pointed to Paul. "Make some groups. Get to it," he said, retreating to stand with his colleagues. They didn't point the rifles they held. Didn't have to.

Jack, picked for Paul's group, left Andrew to head to the other side of the beach.

Piles of rocks sat above the high tide line. Jack positioned himself next to Paul. "So tell me," he said, pulling a boulder close and picking it up, "where do the women go?"

"Laundry."

Trudging through the sand fifty pounds heavier was no easy task. By the time Jack got to the water line and dropped off the rock, sweat had drenched his everything.

After catching his breath, he jogged to catch up to Paul. In the sun, it was clear Paul was at least thirty years Jack's senior, but that didn't seem to slow him down any.

"What else is there?"

"Got a lot of questions, don't you, Jack?"

"I like to know things."

Paul stopped, pointing a finger to the sky. "Rule number one. Knowing things gets you killed."

"What about you?"

With a sigh, Paul trudged back up the beach. He picked up a rock and passed Jack without a word.

Hurrying to the rock pile, Jack slowed picking up another rock. Now would not be the time to put his back out.

"Paul," he said, quickstepping as best he could through the warm sand, "tell me what's over there. I'll take the responsibility."

Paul huffed and looked over his shoulder. Through his thinning white hair, the top of his scalp had already begun to redden in the sun. "You look like that kind of guy. I'll tell you, but it's on you if they come asking questions."

"I'd never name you."

Paul nodded. "I believe that, friend Jack. Over there is the hospital I told you about." He pointed across one of the dunes. "There's the dock you probably saw. But there's also quarters for the guards," he said, chin pointing toward them, "and the general. She's a different story."

"General? Is she the one running this place?"

"Yeah. And the hospital."

"So, is she a doctor?"

Dumping the rock in the sand and setting off up the beach again, Paul laughed. "No. She's nuts is what she is."

"What makes you say that?" Jack placed his rock on the pile, glanced at the men removing them and hauling them onto the jetty, and caught back up to Paul again.

"Look, the hospital is mainly for patching guys up, prisoners and stuff, you know. But I've heard some strange stuff about it. Stuff that makes the hair on your neck stand up."

"Like what?"

Paul hesitated.

Jack picked up a heavy rock so Paul could get a smaller one. His back wasn't happy about it, but Paul nodded.

"Thanks, friend. But I don't think we ought to be talking about it." He hefted the smaller rock.

"Paul, tell me. Like what?"

Shaking his head, Paul set off up the beach at double the speed.

He didn't speak for the rest of the morning. Once, when Jack asked him again to explain, he mumbled something about "that's how you become a Dead Head" and trudged off down the beach. Eventually, Paul traded places with one of the guys in the water and went to the end of the line, as far away from Jack as he could get.

Jack took the hint.

***

Panting, smiling, wet and sandy, Addy stopped at the base of the lighthouse and looked up. It used to be covered in black and white paint, the diamond pattern still discernible, but much of it had chipped and blown away long ago. Like so many things in this world, falling apart and going back to the land they came from.

"I haven't seen one of these in years," Dean said, catching up to her.

"What were they for?"

"Ships."

"Descriptive."

He smiled, shaking his head. "I know. Giving you a hard time is one of the finer things in life."

"Oh good lord, Dean. I have a brother for that. Don't you start."

The lines around his eyes crinkled. "There's a light at the top, or there used to be, that spins three-sixty and lets incoming ships know where the land is. For when it's dark or foggy."

"At the top? Do you think we can get up there?"

"I don't know, Addy. Judging from this paint, it's been a long time since it saw humans. I bet the stairs are falling apart."

"Let's look."

"No, I don't think—"

She walked around the tower until she found an old wooden door. Stuck in the frame, it took several pushes with her shoulder to unstick it. After three or four full-body shoves, it popped open and she fell in.

Inside, it smelled salty and stale, and a bit like rats.

"Mmm. Lovely smell," Dean said, walking in behind her.

"Isn't it. Hey, look. Stairs." Stepping onto the first one, she looked up and up. They spiraled all the way to the top. "Let's go up them"

"I don't know if they're safe. Look at them, Addy. They're like paper. They could fall over anytime."

She jumped on the next step, hopping up and down.

Dean sucked in a breath.

As he cursed, she grinned. "Look fine to me. Come on," she said, stepping onto the next stair.

"Just, dammit, hang on." He shut the door. "I don't see anything to bar this with."

Not taking the bait, Addy took another stair. So far, so good.

"Adelaide, wait for me."

"Fine," she said, stopping and turning. "Hurry up."

He wedged the door closed and bumped it a couple times for good measure.

They climbed, the gusting wind from the ocean buffeting the steady tower.

Reaching the top, Addy opened the door before her and climbed narrow stairs into a room with a full view of everything around them. Glass miraculously still intact, they were surrounded by the great ocean on one side, the sound on the other, and a narrow strip of land on two sides.

"The island looks so different from up here," she whispered. She pressed up against the glass, fogging it with her breath. Smooth under her fingers, the cool glass formed a transparent wall between herself and the world.

The hairs on her arms prickled as Dean leaned in next to her.

He laid one hand over hers.

She inhaled, swiveling her forehead to look at him.

He smiled, eyes skipping to her lips and back to her eyes.

Heart fluttering, she dropped her eyes to his hand, turning hers around and gripping it.

Catching movement from the corner of her eye, she turned back to the window.

"Oh Dean, the horses. Look, aren't they beautiful?"

"I see beauty, Addy, but it's not out there."

Eyes widening, she faced him.

He smiled, cheek dimpling, and caressed the back of her hand with his thumb.

"Addy, I—"

She kissed him, cutting him off.

After a breathless moment of hesitation, he kissed her back.

Everything inside, her stomach, her lungs, her heart, her mind, all filled with pink air. Every nerve ending tingled.

It went on forever.

It was over too soon.

He pulled away, smiling and stroking her hair and cheek.

Butterflies exploded in her stomach and her breath stopped.

"Addy, I—"

Tripping backward, looking for breath, she knocked her head on one of the giant, lopsided lenses in the middle of the room. Hand gripping her head, she stumbled.

Dean reached for her.

She tried to catch onto him. Instead, she knocked him to the ground, where he almost fell into the hole next to the old, busted light.

He managed to roll to his stomach and away from danger.

"Crap, Dean, shit, I'm sorry," she said, reaching for him.

But these cursed hands.

She sat, back to the glass, teeth clanking together, and stuffed her hands under her legs. The back of her throat burned. Swallowing, she leaned her head back and closed her eyes. Tears slipped from beneath her lids and tracked, wet and cold, down her cheeks.

Dean slid in next to her, laying a hand on her thigh. "What's wrong? Was it, um, was it me?"

"Oh god, no, it wasn't you," she said, opening her eyes and smiling at him. "You're perfect. No, it's me and my damn clumsy ass."

"It's cute, Addy."

"No." She wiped her face. "It isn't cute. There's nothing cute about what it's caused."

"Sweetie, I'm alright. What are you talking about? We're not talking about what just happened, are we?"

"No, we aren't."

"Tell me."

Swallowing still hurt. She stretched a painful smile across her lips.

"Mom, are you sure there's solar panels in that old store?"
Mom chewed a nail. "I think so, baby."
"It doesn't smell good. I think there's Dead Heads around."
"Are you sure? I don't see any."

"I was sure. I just didn't say so. I was only twelve."

Dean pried a hand from under her leg and held it. "Whatever happened, it's not your fault, Addy."

"Sure." She sighed. "The parking lot was the size of a football field. It'd been one of those warehouse-sized sporting goods stores. The kind of place we often went for supplies. Getting in was easy. There were no chains on the doors, no locks. The doors were still intact, which was a small blessing."

"Wait here by the door, Adelaide." Mom went deeper into the store. "Signal me if you hear anything."

"She disappeared into the store. I don't know how long she was gone. I looked at some stuff in the glass cabinets, and when a shadow showed up in the door, it startled me. A rack of clothes fell, crashing into a display case and breaking the glass. The sound was enough to wake…

"Buzzing from outside, growling and moaning. The stench. They were just outside the door. And it wasn't barred. I whistled. She came. But I'd already knocked over the damn rack, broken the glass. They heard us. They pushed open the door."

"Addy, get behind me."

"Mom fought them, four at a time. Indestructible. Knocking them aside with more strength than any other woman possessed, she stabbed and slashed them. All the while backing farther into the store.

"They came in waves. It was a whole horde. Where they'd been hiding as we crossed the giant parking lot was a mystery, but there they were and they came in their dozens, streaming through the door."

"Adelaide, run to the back. Get out the back door."

"But I couldn't leave her. I got out my own machete. But then I tripped. And, backing up, she fell over me. One of them, one of the stinking horde, fell with us. It opened its black maw. Mom stuck her arm in the way to deflect it, and its teeth sank into the soft flesh of her hand. She pulled down a breath. No screaming, just a breath."

"Addy, run."

"I just sat there, Dean. The horde coming, Mom bitten. I just sat there. If my dad hadn't appeared from the back… I don't know."

"Your dad was there?"

She nodded, tears streaming down her face. "He wasn't supposed to be. He told me later he and Mike followed us. Just to make sure we were OK, you know? My mom was always so confident. But my dad was always worried." Addy glanced up. Something unwound in her chest. A spring that'd been taut for so many years it was a way of life.

Dean, frowning, brow creased, licked his lips. "What did he do?"

"Get her out of here, Jack!"

"Mom, shouting, fought back a dozen more of them. She was bitten, again and again. Protecting our exit, she took off across the store."

"COME AND GET ME YOU STINKING ASSHOLES!!!"

"Dad got me out the back, Mike grabbed me, and we ran away. The last time I saw her, she was standing on top of some boat display, bloody, wailing like a madwoman. Dean, she took out a hundred of them if it was one." Though her vision doubled, she smiled. From ear to ear. "She was the toughest woman I've ever seen."

He cupped her chin with two fingers, giving it a gentle pull. She turned.

"You're pretty tough yourself. Don't sell yourself short just because sometimes you trip over your own feet." He glanced at them. "They're pretty big."

Slapping him on the shoulder, Addy smiled. "You shut up about my feet."

Dropping his hand, he smiled back and watched the ocean.

While his face was turned, she took a moment to admire him. Not that she hadn't before, but she'd never done it openly. It had been too much to admit she even wanted to, much less take the chance of him seeing.

It was pretty clear he wasn't going to tell her to stop, though, so she drank in every inch of his strong, stubbled jaw, the beating artery in his neck, his muscular shoulders.

Tip of a picture sticking out of his breast pocket.

"Dean."

"Yeah."

"Tell me about that picture."

He frowned, glancing down. Easing his hand from hers, he pushed it back into his pocket and buttoned the flap closed.

"No."

"I told you. Now you tell me."

Shaking his head, he chuckled. "Those are the rules, eh?"

"Yep."

He let a breath out through pursed lips. A tight, whistling exhale like he was blowing a balloon. "There's not much to tell, Addy." Taking her hand again, he reached into his pocket with the other and drew out the picture of the smiling boys. "My mom took this right before the virus hit. I think there were already some sick people somewhere. But it was just the flu, somewhere halfway across the world. This was our first day of summer break."

"Summer break?"

Laughing, he nodded. "Every summer, school took a break. I guess you wouldn't know about that."

"No. Not really."

"Well. Anyway. He'd just finished his first year of school. My little brother," he said, pointing at the picture, "Cameron. He was six, I was ten."

"What happened to him?"

"He and I kicked around for another twenty years together." Dean smiled at the picture.

"Till the end?"

"Almost."

She squeezed his hand.

He looked up, and there was a first. Tears rimmed the bottom of his eyes. One fell.

She opened her mouth to ask another question but watching him press his lips into a fine line convinced her otherwise. She waited.

He blinked and wiped his mouth. "Our parents didn't make it past the first six months. I raised him. Raised us both."

"Did anyone else adopt you?"

"We stayed away from everyone else. For a long time. So, no. It was just us two against the world."

"How'd you do it?"

"It wasn't easy," he said, pocketing the picture. "But I don't know. Kids are resourceful. And tough. We got to where we could take out fifty of them together without breaking a sweat. He was tough. Tougher than me. And smarter."

It was killing her not to ask. But she waited.

"He scraped his arm on a nail. A fucking rusty nail."

"Is that what…"

"No," Dean said, laughing.

The corners of Addy's mouth raised, but there was no mirth in his laugh. She frowned, eyes wide.

He glanced at her. "You have the most beautiful brown eyes I've ever seen, Adelaide. You know they change?"

She grinned. "I've been told. My dad calls them brownzel. Both brown and hazel."

Laughing, he nodded. "Cameron had eyes like that, too. Not much different from yours. Great for talking people out of supplies."

She laughed too.

Looking over her shoulder at the ocean again, Dean's laugh tapered off. "We went to the nearest hospital to see if we could find some tetanus shots. I didn't know if they'd even still be any good, but I remembered our parents getting them for us for school. Saying that if you got cut by anything rusty, you should get one or it could kill you."

"Is this the story of why you don't go near hospitals?"

"You got it, sweetheart."

"Did you find the tetanus shots?"

"Yeah. A whole rack of shit fell on Cam, including those damned tetanus shots. Also freeing about a dozen 'Heads that'd been pinned in a room by that piece of shit rack."

He cleared his throat. Opened his mouth, cleared his throat again, and closed it. Swallowed. His Adam's apple bounced.

"His foot got stuck. I think I heard his ankle break. And then they were on top of him. He pulled two of them into headlocks and told me to run. I watched them rip into him."

"Oh god. Dean."

His Adam's apple bobbed again. "I killed every single one of them and sat with his head in my lap until he turned." Tears streaming down his face, he met her eyes again. "The Cure came out two weeks later. Two weeks," he said, voice breaking.

Wiping the tears from his cheek with her finger, she pulled him into her arms.

Chest wracked with silent cries, he sobbed. She got the feeling he'd never really cried about it. The irony of it all. Twenty years lost over two weeks.

She cried for him too, kissing his forehead and whispering it was alright.

Glancing at the horses below, she watched as several ran past. At least one was a foal. They ran at full speed, one falling with tangled feet. Something jumped on it.

She gasped, and Dean's head popped up. He followed her gaze.

Mouth hanging open, she met his eyes and found her own horror reflected back.

She shouted. "How did Dead Heads get on the island? Dean, the horses!"

She leapt up, tripping her way down the narrow stairs, sliding down half of them on flat heels. He shouted from behind her.

"Addy, wait!"

CHAPTER 21

Gripping the doorknob, Addy put one foot against the wall and yanked the door. It popped free and sent her sprawling.

"Addy," Dean shouted from the stairs, only three-quarters of the way down.

Jumping up, she unsheathed her machete and Bowie knife, the only weapons she'd brought, and ran out into the sound of pounding waves.

A horse screamed. Its cries cut short, moaning, buzzing death carried over the wind.

She ran toward it.

Dean's feet pounded behind as he emerged from the lighthouse. "Adelaide!" He didn't shout, but he didn't whisper.

Another horse screamed. A piece of driftwood the size of a whole tree appeared in front of her.

She leapt over it and landed on both feet, little more than a hitch as she sprinted toward the screaming horse.

A Dead Head had one tackled, pulling its intestines out. It was dead, but the foal cried, circling.

Another buzzing, moaning Dead Head shambled toward the distressed foal, tripping over grass but continuing, inexorable, toward the baby horse.

Addy leapt, beheading it in one swift movement just as it reached for the foal. Her machete may as well have been sliding through butter.

The young horse streaked away.

Dean tackled the one feeding on its mother, knocking it to the ground. He drove a knife through its skull.

He stood and waved. "Let's get back to the boat."

"No. We have to get them all. They'll kill the horses." Without waiting for a response, she took off in the direction the horses had gone.

"We don't even know how many there are! Addy!"

The sandy ground sucked at her feet, the gusting wind from the ocean blowing her hair in her face. The salty air assaulted her, sandblasting her skin.

The problem with the ocean blowing salt and sand in her face was that she couldn't smell the 'Heads.

All but running over another, she stopped and struck it with her knife. It sank hilt-deep in the 'Head's shoulder.

The 'Head snarled and lunged at her, grabbing with its black fingers.

She jumped, but with the sand sucking at her feet, she didn't get as much air as she wanted.

The 'Head fell. Its hand scraped the front of her, catching onto her belt and gripping.

Her knife buried in its shoulder, she hacked at the arm with her machete. It was too close to get a good angle, and it glanced off.

The 'Head yanked at her belt, pulling her down.

Out of angles, she stabbed forward with the machete. It bounced off the skull.

Stinking breath in her face, the smell of it was whisked away by the ocean breeze. Its rotted, blackened teeth, tongue lolling in its dead mouth like a piece of desiccated fruit right in her face, she still couldn't smell it.

Unsettled, she gripped its wrist, reaching for her knife with the other hand.

Where in the hell was Dean?

Leaning into the thing's face, its teeth chomping at her nose, she grasped the hilt of the knife and pulled. It had buried itself in bone and slipped out only a half an inch.

Her left shoulder screamed in fire. Like nothing she'd ever felt. Pain radiated from an area just above her shoulder blade.

Sharp like a bee sting and burning like a skinned knee, only a thousand times worse.

Turning, she found herself face to face with a 'Head. One that had its teeth sunk into the soft skin high up on her shoulder.

She gripped the knife and yanked. As it popped free, she kicked the other 'Head in the face. It held her belt for a moment, but she kicked again and it flew off. Without turning, she stabbed the one biting her in the face.

The buzzing in her ear stopped. Its teeth peeled off her shoulder. It slipped to the ground.

All she wanted to do was inspect the bite. Administer the Cure. But the other 'Head was there. And the horses were still running. The beach pounded with their hooves.

Instead, she stood, snatched up her machete, and chopped at the 'Head on the ground until it stopped buzzing. Stopped groaning. Its blackened fingers stopped grasping.

Looking around, she caught Dean running down the beach.

By the time she'd caught up to him, the horses were long gone.

The Dead Heads weren't.

"Addy," he said. His face smoothed, and he took a deep breath. "You're OK."

"Yeah. And just in time to save your ass."

They circled, back to back, 'Heads closing in.

He chuckled. "There's only four of them. I could take 'em in my sleep."

"Sure you could," she said, a blade in each hand, "but then you'd think you were some kind of badass. We both know you need me."

"That might be true. But a few Dead Heads I can handle."

One of the 'Heads lurched forward. Dean stabbed it in the face.

As he pulled his knife free, another 'Head jumped. Addy dropped it with a couple hacks from her machete.

"Two left," Dean said as they circled.

The 'Heads buzzed, closing in side by side.

"On three?"

"On three."

Counting down together, they lunged.

With sea breeze in her nose and sand between her fingers and under her nails, Addy pounced on the one closest to her.

It buzzed, black fingers scrabbling. It snagged her shirt, but she hacked at the arm, severing tendons, and the grabbing hand relaxed. The arm fell useless to its side. Still, it chomped at her.

Dean shouted. "Oh! You son of a bitch!"

She smiled, hacking sideways at the one in front of her. It stumbled. She hacked again, severing its hamstring.

It dropped.

She knelt, avoiding the one grasping hand. She pushed the knife into its ear, leaning her weight on it, and listening for the *pop* as it drove through the brain.

The 'Head jerked, stilled, and was no more.

Addy grinned, releasing her knife from its head, and went to sheathe her blades.

Instead, her hands began to shake and she dropped them both. She doubled over, her whole body wracked with shaking.

Heart pounding, she checked the bite.

The wound, what she could see of it, flowed in a steady stream, caking her front and back in blood.

Her head swam, the world spinning beneath her feet. She fought to focus her eyes and glanced at Dean.

He worked his blade out of the skull of the 'Head in front of him.

"Dean?" The best she could manage was a light whisper. Which the ocean whisked away. But with her head swimming, it was probably best to lay down.

So she did.

The sandy ground, both hard and soft, warmed her cheek.

Nice to feel the warmth because she was so cold. And the sound of the ocean pounding the beach, waves breaking in the distance. Peaceful.

"Maybe I'll just close my eyes for a minute. Wake me up soon, Mom," she murmured into the sand. She got some in her mouth. Gritty between her teeth, she tried to spit it out but just got more. Grumbling, she lay on her back, face to the sun.

A shadow blotted it out.

Brow creased, she opened an annoyed eye. "What are you doing? You're blocking my light."

"Are you OK?"

"Who's that?" she asked, shading her eyes. "You look a halo. Got like an angel."

"Addy, are you bit?"

She laughed. "Yeah, hoo boy, bit. Hurt like a sonofabitch, can't describe, it was like burning, melting, scraping, twisting."

"OK. You're gonna be alright. Where's your dose?"

"Whazzat?"

"The Cure, Adelaide. Where's your dose of the Cure?"

Lifting her head, the thing that weighed about two tons, she squinted, focusing on his face. Oh, it was Dean. Of course. Boy, he was pretty. And nice. Nicer than that one guy. Made Dean ten times better.

She dropped her head back to the sand.

"Dean!" Sitting up, she grabbed his shoulder. "I've been bitten!" Her head pounded and shakes wracked her body again. The bite burned and pulsed.

Holding the back of her head, he laid her in the sand. "I know, sweetheart. I need to give you the Cure. Where is your dose?"

"Oh. Dose. Dad made me a pouch. Black pouch. On my belt." Now her eyes had sand in them. She couldn't keep them open to look at him. It was OK. She reached for his face. He grabbed her hand and kissed the inside of her palm.

"What bel…fuck it. Never mind. I'll get you fixed up. Just hang on."

Something stabbed her in the arm. Like a tiny little bee with a great big stinger.

Straight as a board, she popped up again. "Ouch! What the hell, Dean?"

"Thank fuck," he said, sitting back. Capping and pocketing an empty hypodermic, he smiled and wiped sand and hair off her clammy face. He kissed the side of her mouth.

Eyes clearing, she caught his hand. It was bloody, and there was some on his shirt.

"You're bleeding," she said. "Are you alright?"

"Fine. Come on. Let's get back."

***

Filing into the cells, their captors handed them each a bowl of soup and some more fresh bread.

Finding his way to the barred door, Jack sat and ate. How strange to have something so good in a place like this.

Paul sat not far away, dipping his bread in the soup and watching Jack with his hooded eyes. "Don't be talking to them, friend Jack. Remember, that's rule number three. No talking to the girls. They'll take you away, you won't come back."

"Thanks. I'll keep it in mind."

Paul shook his head, turning his back on Jack and facing the opposite wall.

Andrew eased down nearby. "Listen, Jackie," he said, lowering his voice, "did you hear there's some kind of crazy hospital over there?"

"I did, but I couldn't find out what they're doing there."

"Some kind of experiments, way I heard it."

"Experiments?" This looked more and more like Nazis every day. Even the asylums and prisons of the early twentieth century in America. Neither were good. "What do you mean?"

"I don't know. Injecting people with weird shit. Feeding them to Dead Heads. Or maybe feeding Dead Heads to them. There's a lot of rumors."

Jack shook his head. Injections? Poison? Just what the hell had Wade and Tim gotten them into?

It took the women until just past dusk to come back.

Jane flopped down next to the door, her own bread in hand.

"Look at these hands, Jack," she said, shoving one through the door.

The pads of her fingers wrinkled, the palm of her hand was dried and flaking.

A bead of anger growing inside his chest, he took her hand and massaged it. As he moved up to her wrist, he asked her what had happened.

"Fucking laundry by hand, that's what happened."

"Good god, Jane. Washing clothes did this?"

"All the clothes ever created by man." She laughed, stuffed the rest of the bread in her mouth, and stuck her other hand through.

He switched to it, working his way up to her elbow.

She smiled. "There was all sorts of laundry. There were sheets. Some bloody. Some with a substance yet to be identified. And the stench on those. My god. It smelled like a Dead Head, if it had been left in the sun for a week, exploded, then refrigerated."

"Ew."

"Yeah, ew. You have no idea. Almost lost my lunch a few times."

"They gave you lunch?" He worked his way back down her arm.

She chuckle-snorted. "No. Figure of speech. What were you doing all day? Taking a nap? Eating bread?"

He told her, including the things Paul and Andrew had said about the island. "I need to get into that hospital, Jane."

"Yeah, I think you do." She leaned close to the bars.

Jack leaned in, resting his forehead on the same bar she did.

"There's something going on here. It smells bad. Worse than the sheets."

He stopped massaging and held her hand. She didn't pull it back.

Which, of course, meant nothing. Or everything. *Good lord, pull it together, Jackson.*

"Jack."

"Jane."

"Have you. Uh. Do you—"

"Bitch," a woman said from across the cell, "why you talkin' to him? You tryin'a get us all in trouble?"

Mouth open, Jane turned her head.

"Pipe down, Neecy," someone else said. "Can't you see the two of them got something between them?"

Two spots of color blooming high on her cheeks, Jane turned back to him. Her mouth still hung open.

Heat rushed through Jack's body, the blood swirling through his stomach on its way to parts unmentionable. "That true, Jane?"

She slipped her hand from his.

He held his breath as she reached through the bars again.

Her fingertips slid along his jawline.

His everything tingled.

Peeking from under the bar in front of her, she smiled. A slow, sultry thing. "I was about to ask you the same thing."

He leaned against the bars again, his face inches from hers. Her breath warm on his upper lip. "Why didn't you say something?" he asked, inhaling the scent of flowers and ocean.

"What am I supposed to say?" Leaning back, she stroked the side of his cheek with her thumb. "I don't deal in feelings, Jack. How do you put something like this in words?"

His heart leapt into his throat and stuck. "Something like wh—"

"You there!" someone shouted from the front of the cell.

Jack leaned around Andrew to see a guard pointing through the window at him. "Me?"

"No, not you. The girl."

Paul stage-whispered across the cell. "Told you."

Jane stood.

Looking up at her, Jack's heart rate doubled again. He climbed to his feet.

Paul whispered again. "Friend Jack, stop."

Andrew stood, balling his fists and looking between the guard and Jack. His jaw bunched.

Louis appeared inside the women's cell, grabbing Jane by the bicep and pressing his face against the bars. "Hey there, Mr. C. Just gonna take Jane here for a little ride."

Every emotion from hate to revulsion sped through Jack's mind on the way to his fist.

He punched the bars.

Louis danced back, dragging Jane with him. He shook her. "Good try." Laughing, he pulled her away from the door.

Jack cradled his hands, his face hot, teeth clenched so hard he thought he might crack one.

One of the guards stood outside the men's cell, rifle pointed in, as another unlocked the door and barreled in.

It was the large Japanese man. He charged Jack, and Andrew stepped between them.

"Ain't gonna let you touch him," Andy said.

"Andrew. Don't."

The guard stepped right. Andrew shadowed him.

He stepped left. Andrew shadowed him again.

Jack's stomach lurched. His hand tingled as everything slipped through it.

"Don't you touch Jackie," Andrew growled.

The guard looked up into Andy's face and hit him in the jaw with the butt of his gun in one smooth motion.

Andrew grabbed his bleeding mouth. The guard rammed the gun into his belly. Andrew's breath poofed out and he stumbled.

Jack caught him and wrapped his arms around the big man's shoulders. "Stop," he whispered in his ear.

"Let go of him," the guard said.

"You don't have to do this," Jack said. Retaining his grip on Andy, he spoke over his shoulder. "We can stop this now. Just don't hurt her."

"The girl? Don't worry about her. I'm sure Louis will take real good care of her. You know he's been talking about her ever since you guys got here. Those fine tits of hers. Bet she's got a nice, tight little— "

Jack released Andrew and balled his own fists.

As he came around, the butt of a rifle met him in the jaw.

***

The boat bumped into the small wooden dock.

Addy opened her eyes. The almost full moon, low on the eastern horizon, lit the clouds over her face. The boat rocked on the gentle waves of the sound.

"Dean, when did it get so late?"

"Mmmph."

Bones aching, she sat up and cranked her neck. Lying in the bottom of a canoe was not the best way to sleep.

Dean lay slumped over the side of the boat, face splashing in and out of the water with each wave.

"Dean!" She jerked him from the water and laid him back in the boat. His dripping wet shirt was also soaked with blood.

She grabbed his hand. Clammy and cold.

"Oh crap, Dean. Crap," she said, lifting his shirt. His perfect abs also sported a perfect bite mark. Grasping his face in both hands, she shook him. "Dean, you're bit! Where's your dose? Dean!"

"Gave you," he murmured.

"You…dammit. OK, I'll get you mine."

Reaching for her black pouch, her finger slipped through a belt loop.

"What the?" Looking down, she grabbed her empty waistband. The belt, along with all its contents, was gone.

"What? No!" Sitting back on her heels, boat rocking, she frowned with her eyes closed.

"OK. Alright. OK," she said, lifting him. Heavy though he was, he wasn't entirely dead weight. Not yet. He helped a little. "We gotta walk. I'm gonna help you get out of the boat, then you gotta help me. You're alright. You're gonna be OK."

Yanking, pulling, cursing, and panting, she hauled him onto the dock. His arm over her shoulder, his feet dragged, but he put them under himself just enough to help her get him down the boardwalk and into the road.

Resting on the road, she lowered him to the ground.

He groaned.

"I know. I'm just gonna catch my breath and we'll go. We'll be there in no time."

"My hero," he whispered.

Chuckling, she lifted him again and dragged him down the road.

As they reached the Big House, lights in the front window inviting and warm, she stopped. Drenched in sweat, muscles burning, she shifted the arm across her shoulders and pulled him closer.

"We're here, you're gonna be alright. Just a little bit more, we'll get you to the infirmary."

Her stomach lurched. Thinking of Elizabeth recovering, and what she'd said about remembering being dead, was enough to send her head spinning again. That was not about to happen to Dean.

She dragged him up the walk and kicked the door, over and over.

"Let us in! Help!"

Chairs scraping inside. Commotion.

Celia opened the door. "Adelaide. Thank god you're back. You won't believe—"

"Help me. Dean's been bitten. He needs the Cure." She pushed through the door, pulling Dean in behind her.

"Addy, oh Addy, thank god it's you." Someone by the fire, covered in a blanket and dripping, stood and rushed toward her.

The sound of the heavy door closing behind her receded into the distance. Dean's weight over her shoulders lessened as her grip on him loosened. He collapsed to the floor with a grunt, bleeding onto the doormat.

Tim, sopping wet and stinking of the sound, rushed around the couch and grabbed her. Crushing her to him, he whispered in her ear.

"I'm so glad to see you, Addy. Thank god. You have to help me."

CHAPTER 22

Dean's eyelids fluttered.

Addy let out a long, slow breath. Her lungs ached like she'd been holding that breath since she'd dragged him past Tim and into the infirmary.

"Hey. That's what a man likes to see when he wakes up." She smiled. "You're OK."

Moving to sit up, he grunted, squeezing his eyes closed. He flopped onto the pillow. "Ouch. I've been better." He gripped his stomach.

Grabbing his other hand, she held it.

He smiled, eyes closed. "Not the best first date in history."

She kissed him on the cheek. "I don't know. Seemed pretty good to me."

"You don't have a frame of reference."

"You don't know that."

He laughed and cracked an eyelid. "I forgot about Tim."

Shit. Tim.

"Dean, he's here."

Bolting up, Dean cried out and grabbed his wound again. "What do you mean he's here?"

"Relax, you're going to hurt yourself. It's fine. But, yeah. He's here. He says he escaped, whatever that means." She pushed his shoulder, urging him to lay back down.

"Stay away from him, Addy. I don't trust him. He's dangerous."

"Sleep. Don't worry about me."

"It's my job," he said, head sinking into the pillow. His breathing deepened within moments, and he began to snore.

On the other side of the room, Tim and Mike spoke in hushed tones.

Sneaking off the bed, Addy crept to the door. She pushed it open a crack and turned sideways to ease through.

The door squeaked. A long, loud creak.

She winced.

"Addy!" Tim jogged across the room, weaving around beds. He'd dried off and the doc had checked him over, after tending Dean's and Addy's wounds.

"Uh. Hi Tim," she said, an uncertain grin lifting the corners of her mouth. She shifted from one foot to the other. "So, what's going on?" Holding the door open, she glanced into the hall.

"I know where your dad is. I can help you get to him," he said, smiling.

She glanced at Dean. Snoring, sleeping, angelic Dean.

Tim reached over her shoulder and pushed the door wide. "Let's talk in the hallway."

Giving Dean one more look, she ducked under Tim's arm and walked into the darkened hall.

Shivering, she leaned against the wall.

Throwing a palm against the wall behind her, Tim leaned into her space, hot breath in her face.

She tried shrinking further into the wall. Couldn't get any smaller. It didn't make sense someone so attractive could have such bad breath. "So. My dad. I saw you on the road, Tim. You had him in handcuffs."

He smiled, kissing her cheek. "Let's talk about that later. I'm so happy to see you, my dear."

Throwing up in her mouth seemed preferable, but she again ducked under his arm and walked down the hall. "We talk about it right now. Or we don't talk at all."

"Addy, I think it's best we talk about that later."

She rounded, head pounding, red spots before her eyes. In her mind, she saw herself ball up her fist, stomp her foot, and scream to be listened to. Like an angry child.

Instead, she took a deep breath. Let it out. Took another one. The spots cleared.

She opened her eyes and found the table she'd knocked over her first night here.

She sat. "What would you like to discuss, Tim?"

He sat, his mouth curved up at the corners. "Who's that you drug in here? The guy in the infirmary in there?"

"His name is Dean. He's, well, he's Mike's boss."

Tim's eyes flashed from side to side. The corners of his mouth curled further. If that was possible. "Right. Right. I know him. Works for that secret company, what's their name? Something about flare."

"Iridium Flare."

He snapped his fingers. "That's the one!"

His jubilance all wrong in the dark, chilly hallway, Addy's stomach wrapped around itself.

He leaned across the table. "There were people. They forced me to…do things…terrible things." He looked around, dropping his voice to a whisper. "They said they were gonna kill me. I had to do what they said."

"That include putting my dad and my best friend in handcuffs?"

He leaned closer still and told her, in a fervent whisper, to lower her voice.

"Why?"

He grabbed her hand, yanking her arm. "It was his company," he hissed. "They made me do everything."

Twisting her hand free, she leaned back. Her stomach flip-flopped. "Tim, are you saying—"

"I'm saying, Adelaide, your boyfriend in there is working for the enemy. Go on, ask him about it."

She stood. "He's not my…that's ludicrous. Listen, have you told Scott about all this?"

Tim, still seated, looked up at her from beneath his brows. "Yeah. He wouldn't listen to me either." He stood. "You have to believe me. I know how to get your dad and Jane out. But it has to be soon. Before…" he trailed off, looking out the window.

"Before what?"

"Before it's too late."

***

Rubbing his aching jaw and staring out at the ocean, Jack chewed the rest of his bread.

His stomach turned. What had been fresh and delicious bread yesterday was nothing more than dry crumbs in his mouth today.

Probably wasn't the bread's fault.

"Friend Jack, you're with me today," Paul said, bumping his shoulder.

Frowning, he followed him down the beach. "Paul?"

"What's the word, bird?"

"What happened last night? Where's Andrew?"

Stopping, Paul took Jack by the arm. "That Japanese guard, he knocked you real good."

Jack rubbed his jaw again. It hurt all way up into his temples. "I know. I mean after that. I remember waking up on the floor this morning."

"You got whacked, fell down, coldcocked. Your friend, he jumped on that guard and started wailing on him. Took four more of them near ten minutes to get him off 'em and tied up. Your friend Andrew, he's a tough dude."

"That he is. Got a damn lot of heart, too."

"Guards kicked him unconscious after that. Dragged him out by his feet."

"Shit." Jack's chest burned.

"Your girlfriend shouted all the way out of the courtyard. Heard that kid that took her yell a few times. She must've got in a few licks."

He stifled a grin. What a girl.

"Yeah. Well, get to work, friend Jack. Before they get suspicious," Paul said, glancing over his shoulder.

Following his gaze, Jack stared at the closest guard. He had a black eye.

Good on you, Andrew.

Now to get out of this godforsaken prison and into the hospital. See what was what, find Jane and Andrew, and figure out what to do about this place.

He hauled rocks for an hour. The sun hid behind the clouds; the spray from the ocean kept him perpetually wet. As his back began to ache, clouds intruded on his mind as well.

The sand sucked at his feet, threatening to pull him over each time he grabbed a rock to haul down to the water.

There had to be a way to get into that hospital.

After four or five more trips, he dropped a rock on the pile and stood, staring out at the ocean again. The great, moving mass of water, gunmetal grey under the cloudy sky, unfeeling and unseeing. Washing in over his feet, the current yanked at his ankles as it pulled the water back out. After a few waves, they were buried in the sand.

Paul, directing the men between the pile and the jetty, sidled over. "Friend Jack, you better get back to work. They don't like it when you stop," he said, eyes shifting over his shoulder.

The guard had already noticed, raising a hand to point.

He probably should have felt something as the guard took a few steps in his direction. Should've felt the need to act. Should've moved his feet.

Instead, he stood and felt the pull of the ocean. Let his feet get covered in sand, dug into deep holes under the surface.

Paul grabbed his arm. For an old dude, his grip was like iron. "Jack, you gotta move." He tugged.

Jack's feet popped free, sand between his toes. "Hey Paul, do you think I could go work out on the jetty?"

Nodding, Paul motioned to the guy in the middle. "If that's gonna get you motivated, hell yeah you can. Hey, Ames! Get in here!"

A man waded in. Next to the pile of rock, wood, and sand, the breakers pounded.

"Why don't you let Jack here do that. Can you carry the rocks down?"

"Sure thing, Paul," the man said, nodding to Jack and moving up the beach.

"Alright, Jack," Paul said, spinning him to face the ocean, "you stack the rocks and start filling it in with the sand we got out there. About noontime, we'll haul in some more sand. Got it?"

He nodded.

"Get to it, then. Don't stop."

Wading into the breakers, Jack wobbled when the first one crashed into his thigh. Sucking hard at his legs, the wave washed back out to sea.

The next breaker came. He leapt past it.

He should get to the hospital, try to find out what was going on over there. Try to help these people.

A wave hit him, knocking him back on his feet. Sent his head spinning.

Elizabeth ripped Gerald's throat out. Right in front of him.

Andrew, beaten bloody by the guards, while Jack lay on the floor like a dead fish.

Jane, courageous, fearless Jane, dragged off to be used and violated by a stupid, brutal, teenage idiot.

Adelaide was god knew where. Michael too. Abandoned by their useless father.

Mellie. Mellie was dead and buried.

Well. Not buried. God help him, he'd never gone back to bury her.

There was literally no one in his life he hadn't failed.

The next swell was as high as his face. He didn't turn away.

It broke at chest level, sweeping him under.

The wave tumbled him like he was in a dryer. Down was up. His face scraped the sand at the bottom.

Like a cork, he popped up farther out than he'd gone in. Bobbed up and down with a swell that broke just after it passed him.

Was that a shout?

The guard ran into the surf, pointing and yelling. Paul waved his arms. Cupped his hands around his mouth and said something.

Impossible to hear him over the crashing of the ocean, the water in his ears, his pounding heart, but it was probably something along the lines of "come back."

He intended to come back only one way. A near-drowning ought to be enough to get him into the hospital.

Slipping under the water, he listened to the breathing of the ocean.

It sang its song. It was one giant organism, and everything in it was part of it. It pulled, sucking him closer to its heart.

Rushing water filled his ears, intruded on the calm song of the ocean. It told him this was a stupid plan. One he may not come back from.

But it was all he had.

He opened his mouth wide, a bubble of air in his mouth meeting cold, salty water.

His body fought him as he blew the bubble out. His feet tried to kick him up to the surface.

Overpowering his instinct was a struggle, but before it could fight him, he sucked in a lungful of water.

Everything burned. His eyes, his mouth, his chest. His body spasmed, trying to cough out the water. It only got more water.

Limbs growing heavy, chest like it was full of rocks, he sank.

He closed his burning eyes.

The question of whether or not they could resuscitate him slipped from his mind.

His brain screamed for air while his body fought for sleep.

He'd either wake up or he wouldn't.

CHAPTER 23

Sipping coffee, Addy stared out at the morning as it rolled in behind the fog.

After her little talk with Tim, she hadn't slept more than two hours. She couldn't hear Picard's voice in her head, she couldn't go see Dean, Jane was too far away to scream for.

What a hopelessly stupid, complicated situation.

Leaning her forehead on the cold window, she whispered at it. "This is why I avoid men." The window fogged.

With the tip of her finger, she drew a heart in the fog.

Dean's face popped into her mind, and her stomach did a backflip. Everything, absolutely everything, had been right about that kiss. The way he smelled, tasted, leaned into her but not too much.

How could what Tim said be true?

With a frown, she wiped the window clean.

"You're up early."

Addy jumped, saving the coffee from sloshing. Gulping the rest down, she faced Celia. "I have to talk to Scott."

"Yeah. He missed you yesterday."

"Sure. Sure, he did. I can tell my opinions are so very important to him."

Celia laughed. "Don't take it personally, Addy. He's terrible with women."

Addy almost dropped the cup. "That's…that's ridiculous. He's drop-dead gorgeous. If Jane were here, she'd be crawling up one side and down the other of him. What do you mean he's bad with women?"

"I don't know. He just is. He's nervous is all. We gonna talk about rescuing your dad?"

"Hell yes we are."

"Great. I'm in."

After coffee, Celia led her to the Big House. Approaching the door, it opened before Addy could reach for the knob.

Dean stepped out, pulling the door behind him. He looked up, and his whole expression changed. His brows and mouth raised. "Adelaide," he breathed, reaching for her.

Tim's words had floated in the front of her head all night, but as Dean grasped her hand, they vanished. Replaced by pink, fluffy clouds.

"I didn't know where you went," Dean said. "Are you OK? How's your bite?" One hand on the small of her back, he looked her over.

"I'm OK. I'm fine. Are you?"

Celia cleared her throat.

Addy side-eyed her.

Her arms crossed, she leaned against the porch railing. "We got stuff to do. You coming with us, Dean?"

"Where?" He glanced between them.

The little pink clouds began to rain. Addy let him go, stepping back. "No, Celia, he's not going."

Dean opened his mouth.

Addy held up a finger and grimaced. Her eyes fuzzy, stomach upside down, everything about this felt wrong.

But. She couldn't ignore what Tim said. Dean had already mentioned his company. All those clandestine phone calls. Secrets.

"We're going to see Scott. I'll catch up with you later," Addy said, breaking eye contact.

"Whatever you say," he said. No anger in his voice. He opened the front door for them and stood back.

As she crossed in front of him, he snagged her hand again, lifted it, and kissed her palm.

She shivered, toes curling. With regret, she tugged her hand free and followed Celia through the door.

"What was that all about?" Celia asked.

Addy cleared her throat. "I…um. Well. We have some things to talk about. I just— He doesn't need to come get my dad."

"From what you've said, it sounds like he's a pretty good fighter. Handy to have in your corner. Why not?"

"It's nothing. Let's go see Scott."

Celia led the way through the labyrinthine house.

Addy memorized each and every turn. There were several, and the stuffed birds mounted on the walls—ducks, to be precise—made good landmarks. Eventually, a set of stairs materialized before them.

At the top, they found Scott out on the porch of the crow's nest, drinking tea.

"Morning, Scott," Celia said, breezing through the door.

"Morning, ladies. I'd offer you tea, but there don't appear to be any more cups."

Celia sat on the railing. "Not what we're here for." She held a hand out to Addy.

"Scott. We need to get over to that prison. We've got to get my dad and my Jane. My friend, Jane. His friend Andrew. Anyone else we can get."

"Addy. We're not ready for that kind of thing," he said, speaking into the fog floating off the top of the cup. "You met my people. They're all willing. But we're just not able."

"Why not?"

"For one, we don't have the manpower. And two, the armament."

Addy leaned on the railing and stared toward the sound. The one she'd crossed twice yesterday. Once as a girl who'd never been bitten. "What if I just take a small team? Bust out a half dozen people?" She turned. "Tim knows where they are. Knows the layout. He can help."

"I don't think it's wise, Addy."

"Well," she said, kneeling next to him. She leaned forward, holding his eyes with hers, though he backed up. "I don't really care what you think. I'm going. Are you going to help?"

"I—" He swallowed and glanced at Celia.

She shrugged, half a smile playing on her lips, and waved a hand in Addy's direction. "I'd do what she says."

Scott swallowed again. "I can, uh, I can get you some weapons. A couple men."

"And me," Celia said.

"And her."

Addy nodded. "That'll do."

***

Addy packed a small satchel. Extra weapons. Ammo. Water.

A low male voice floated in from the doorway. "Addy."

She closed her eyes.

"Hey, I brought you something. Where are you going?" Dean stepped into the room.

Spinning like an empty merry go round, she exhaled. "To get my dad back."

"OK, I'll get my stuff." He turned, stopping halfway around. "Well, I've got my weapons. Do you want a bow and arrow? I'm sure someone has one we can borrow."

"Dean."

He faced her, stepping into her space. "Yeah."

"You're not going."

"What do you mean? I'm fine. Aces. Top speed. Come on." He slapped his abs for emphasis and pretended not to wince.

Against the direct orders of her brain, one side of her mouth curled up. She admired his enthusiasm to put himself in danger less than twenty-four hours after being bitten.

Granted, she was too. But this was her dad. She had to.

Shaking her head, she looked up into his eyes. Closed her own. Inhaled. Opened her eyes. "Why did you come?"

"Here? To give you this," he said, holding out a small leather pouch. "I got it from the doc this morning. Saw it in the infirmary last night, and he said I could have it. I just had to mop up in there for him. Here." He pushed it toward her.

She took it, tears standing in her eyes. It was just a touch larger than the one her dad had made for her. It even had a belt loop, and as she flipped it open, she saw it was already loaded with a dose.

"Got you this, too," he said, grinning and offering her a belt with the other hand.

Instead of taking it, she stood with her mouth open.

After a moment of staring at each other in silence, Dean dropped his arm. "Is there something wrong?"

Blinking, she backed up a step. "Yeah. No. I don't know. Dean," she said, laying the pouch on the bed, "why did you come *here*." Raising her arms, she motioned to everything. "Why did you bring me across the whole freaking country? Me. A stranger. To help my dad. Another stranger. What's going on?"

"Well," he started, shifting his weight from one foot to the other. Laying the belt on the bed, he stepped into her space again.

She looked up at him, and one tear fell from each eye.

He smiled. "Mike's no stranger. And, well, you needed help."

"That wasn't the only reason, was it?"

"What are you asking me?"

"What about your company? Iridium Flare?"

His mouth hung open, on the cusp of answering or asking a question. But he did neither.

She went on. "Who are they, really? Are you here for them? On their orders?" She backed up a step. "Are you spying on me? On us?"

He shook his head. "No, Addy. It's not like that."

"Not like that? The hell do you mean by that?"

"I mean, it, there's other things going on. Yeah, it's about IRF. But not like that."

"Oh my god, Dean," she said, lowering to the bed. Only because it was in the way of the floor.

The stupid butterflies in her stomach fluttered around in her brain. What Tim had said was the truth.

"You lied to me," she whispered.

"Sweetheart, no. No, I didn't. I…listen," he said, sitting on the bed next to her and lowering his voice, "that company is up to some shady shit, OK? I've known it for a while. You heard your brother. I've been working for these people for years."

"Exactly. You're their puppet. *You're* the one doing shady shit."

"No, Adelaide, no. No, I'm trying to find out what they're doing. I'm spying on them, not the other way around."

She met his eyes. "What were you doing at Jane's house? Did you follow us? Were you spying then, too?"

He stood to pace. "This is stupid. I'm not spying on you."

"Answer the question." Her eyes burned.

He stopped, his back to her. "Fine. I followed you there."

The wind fell out of her gut as though she'd been punched. Without breath, she whispered, "Get out."

His shoulders fell.

"Get out," she repeated, louder.

He spun and grasped her hand. "I followed you there. Because I've loved you since the moment you spilled cat water on me. I couldn't let you go alone. I couldn't let you follow your dad alone. I can't let you do this alone."

Swallowing over the lump lodged in her throat, she stood. "I'm not doing it alone. But I am doing it without you. Get. Out."

***

Neon lights glared into Jack's eyes.

They'd been open for as long as he could remember. They'd always been open.

Those ceiling tiles, they looked like the room they stayed in when Michael was born. Jack had lain on the rollaway cot, staring at the ceiling, for hours after Mellie had gone to sleep.

He was somebody's dad. This tiny little baby, if cared for, fed, and taught, could turn into a man someday. He'd need his daddy to help.

His daddy.

He was somebody's dad.

"Michael! Adelaide!"

Jack jerked to sitting, his voice a deep, husky crackle against the back of his throat.

Where the fu…

Oh.

Oh! The hospital.

He fell back into the bed, a sigh of relief flooding his lungs. They hurt, but they worked.

And so had his plan.

His mouth stretched into a tight grin, and he sat up again. Gripping the side of the bed, he slipped off the edge and landed on his feet. Following a moment of uncertain footing, his legs supported him. On the other side of the room, a closed door and a large, frosted window stood between him and the hallway.

Taking a step away from the bed, hospital gown flapping around his knees, an IV line pulled him.

Grimacing, revulsion roiling his gut, he ripped the line from his arm.

The tape took half the skin with it.

He groaned, sucking in a breath over his teeth. Stumbling to the door, he pressed an ear to it.

The cold metal against his cheek, what a glorious feeling.

It was all glorious. Lights had never been brighter. Even the screaming red patch where he'd ripped the tape from his arm filled him with delicious adrenaline.

"Gotta try that near-death thing more often," he croaked, feeling for the doorknob.

The door remained stubbornly flat. There was no knob.

"Crap. Alright. Plan B."

He tapped on the little metal panel at head height.

It slid back an inch.

"Mr. C.?"

"Ri—" he croaked. His voice was like a cat's tongue scraping up the back of his throat. He cleared his throat and tried again. "Ricardo."

The small door slid fully open and Ric's happy face filled it. "I can't believe you're OK. Damn, Mr. C., you're pretty tough."

Jack smiled. "Thanks, Ric," he said, raising his scratching voice as high as he could before it dug its claws in.

"We thought you were gone for sure. For sure."

"What happened?"

"You got pulled out into the ocean. That current must've taken you by surprise. It's so strong out there."

"How did I get here?"

Ric shook his head. "One of the other prisoners, some old dude, he jumped into the water and pulled you back in. Way I hear it, he almost drowned himself. But he got you, and he did mouth to mouth. And here you are."

He owed some thanks to his new friend Paul, it seemed.

He frowned. This kid was a chink in their armor and he looked for a place to put the tip of the sword. "It didn't go exactly as I planned, but it worked out anyway."

The kid's eyes widened. "What do you mean? What plan?"

"Listen," he said, leaning into the window, "you know as well as I do, there's some stuff going on here. Plus"—he dropped to a whisper—"you saw what Tim did. On the way here. Murder, Ricardo."

The kid shook his head, mouth open.

Jack dropped the hammer again, hoping to drive the nail home. "He killed two of my best friends. In cold blood. And Wade."

What he wouldn't give to have that prancing, handkerchief using, stuffed shirt still be his biggest problem.

Ric frowned. "He scares me, Mr. C."

"I know. I know it. But you know what?"

The kid shook his head, eyes wide.

"I can't help you from in here."

Brow furrowed, Ric's eyes shifted to where there must be a handle or knob on the other side, and back to Jack.

"I can't let you out, Mr. C. It's, it's…" His eyes drifted to the handle again.

Nail that hammer, Jackson.

"It's what you have to do, Ricardo. Open the door. I'll get you out of here."

Brow smoothing, Ric made eye contact again. "There's—"

Someone shouted from down the hallway. "Ricardo!" Running feet approached the door.

Jumping, Ric slammed the window closed.

"Damn. So close," Jack croaked, leaning into the door again.

"Look alive, general's coming," said a muffled voice on the other side. A shadow passed in front of the frosted glass.

Jack tapped on the little door. "Ric?"

It stayed closed.

General? The one Paul had mentioned? THE General?

A soft, female voice made its way down the hall, speaking to several people on the way. A dull murmur through the door, Jack couldn't catch what was being said.

A shape stopped in front of the frosted window. She spoke with Ricardo. He couldn't hear the words, but its timbre held a maternal caress.

Jack crept to the window, keeping enough distance so his shadow wouldn't fall on it.

She leaned on the glass. Just a thin sheet between Jack and the person responsible for all this. The one in charge.

His throat itched, bottled with mucus.

He cleared his throat without sound. Also without effectiveness.

His lungs weren't having any more of this "being blocked" business today.

Unable to fight it, he coughed and cleared his throat, spitting a huge chunk of snotty phlegm in the floor.

Which caused him to retch.

After a few dry heaves, he glanced back up, red face cooling with each clear breath.

He was being stared at through the frosted glass. She'd put her hands on her hips. "OK in there?"

"Fine," he managed.

Did he know that voice?

"Don't go dying on me."

"Doing my best," he said.

Another coughing spell hit him, and another round of dry heaves.

When he looked up, she was gone.

Wobbling back to the bed, he swallowed several times, eyes watering. As he reached for the water cup on the nightstand, the door opened.

"You alright, Mr. C.?"

"Ric, I—" He stopped and took a breath. Just on the cusp, he couldn't overdo this. This was no longer pounding a nail, it was precision surgery. Swallowing a mouthful of lukewarm water, he smiled. "I would not recommend breathing saltwater. Doesn't work as well as air."

The kid smiled. "Good advice. Look," Ricardo said, glancing from side to side and creeping two steps into the room, "Tim is scary. Crazy scary. But her? The general?" He shook his head. "Man, I can't. She's one seriously disturbed, fucked up lady."

"Then what are you doing right now?"

"Most of the security people are paying attention to her right now. We didn't know she was coming down. Everyone's distracted. If you're getting out, it's now, or not."

Jack set the cup back on the stand. "This gown is kinda drafty. Are there any clothes in here?"

The boy pointed. "Over there in the closet. But grab 'em and let's go."

Opening the wardrobe, Jack found several jumpsuits hanging. He snatched one from the middle and balled it up. "Alright. I'm ready."

Ric checked the hallway. He motioned over his shoulder, and Jack followed, socked feet sliding underneath him. On his way into the hall, he snagged the sneakers by the door.

On tenterhooks, he crept behind the boy, breezy gown keeping his ass cold. They rounded a corner and stepped into an alcove. Its neon light flashed on about every seven seconds or so. Otherwise, it was lit only by the ambient light from the hall.

"Get dressed. Quick. We gotta get out of here."

Yanking the jumpsuit over his legs took more balance than he had. Foot stuck in a leg, he wobbled and hit the wall.

Ric, wide-eyed, snuck a glance into the hall. "I think I can get you out, but you gotta, I don't know, act inconspicuous."

Looking down at his feet, Jack shrugged. The jumpsuit he'd chosen was a couple sizes too small. It bunched in the crotch, pulling everything painfully skyward. But at least the bottoms of the legs would be dry if a surprise flood came through.

Slipping on the shoes, he jerked his chin at the boy. "Let's go."

"OK, just follow me, OK?"

"Lead the way."

Lifting his rifle to port, Ric squared his shoulders and marched into the hall.

A green exit sign hung over the door at the end of it. People milled around the edges in clumps, chattering.

Pulling down on the thighs of the jumpsuit, Jack fell in behind Ric and held his hands together in front of him. Lowered his eyes. Shuffled his feet.

Peeking out the sides of his eyes as they passed more hospital rooms, he found much of the same. Most of the rooms, designed like the one in which he woke, were empty and dark. They approached the first group of guards, their quiet murmuring growing louder.

Head down, he breathed deep. Follow the kid's lead. That was all he had to do.

"I know, but she's formidable, you gotta give her that."

"Bitch is another word for it."

One of them, a slight woman with a skeletal face, nodded to Ric as they shuffled past. "Hey, Ric, what's up?"

"Oh, just taking this guy down to one-one-three-eight."

Her lips compressed into a tight, emotionless smile. "That so?"

"Didn't you see the general stop and tell me herself?"

"Is that what she said to you?"

Ric, nodding, reached back and grabbed Jack by the arm. "Talk to you later," he said, waving with the tip of his rifle.

Calculating a stumble, Jack tripped over his feet and followed the boy.

Passing three more groups of distracted guards without incident, save one heart-stopping second when the stocky woman who'd hosed Jane down eyed him for a moment too long, they walked under the glowing green exit sign and into the stairwell.

"Smells like cat piss in here," Jack said, nose wrinkled. "Cat piss. And death."

Ric bobbed his head. "I know. It's, uh, I guess one of the hazards. We're on the top floor here. Got three flights to go down." He skipped down the first half-flight.

Jack grabbed the railing and hesitated. Scraped and bruised from his trip under the ocean's surface, his knees betrayed a slight tremble.

Rather than stand here and think about old joints, he stiffened his jaw and followed the kid.

The uneven paint of the rail scraped and bumped under his palm. He stopped behind Ric on the landing.

"Wait here," Ric whispered, holding a finger up to his lips. Creeping down the stairs, he peeked into the rectangular window in the door to the second floor. "Alright," he whispered, waving a hand over his shoulder.

More of the same chipped-paint railing. Steep concrete stairs. Stench of cat piss and death.

As Jack's foot came off the last stair, the door opened and a man in a white lab coat charged onto the landing. He bowled into Jack, knocking him back into the staircase.

Ric jumped. "Hey man!" Stepping around him and offering a hand to Jack, he glared at the man.

"Sorry. Sorry. Sorry. Didn't see you. Hey, you got a smoke?"

Pulling Jack to his feet with a strong tug, Ric shook his head. "Nah, man. I don't. You're not supposed to smoke here."

The lab type ran a hand through his hair, standing half of it on end. "Rough day at the office." He yanked the door open and blew back into the room he'd just left.

The pneumatic hinge, slow to close, held the door long enough for Jack to catch a glimpse into the white lab.

It took up most of the second floor. Just a large, white room. Beds lining the whole thing, IV bags suspended next to about half of them.

Restraints hung from the sides and ends of the unoccupied ones.

Breath catching in his throat, he stopped the door from closing.

A quarter of the way down, a big man lay crooked on one of the beds. His ankles clad in belt restraints, his feet hung off the end of the bed. He turned his head, bloodshot eyes pinning to Jack's.

"Andrew?"

The big man began to fight the restraints. As he did, plastic tubing flew. He wasn't hooked up to just a single IV, he was hooked up to six or seven. With brown, yellow, red, and unidentifiable colors flowing down into the pincushions his arms had become.

Ricardo grabbed Jack's arm and lowered his voice to a fierce whisper. "Jack, don't."

Yanking his arm free, Jack stepped into the room. He was not about to leave here without his friend. Security be damned.

Andrew jerked, straining against the straps.

And he snarled. A low, buzzing growl.

"Oh my god," Jack said, backing up and bumping into the boy. Horror and dismay gripped his heart, squeezing it against his ribs. His chest hurt in a way that had nothing to do with drowning.

"Mr. C., I told you, we gotta go." Ric tugged his arm again.

Without looking away from Andy, Jack backed into the stairwell.

The door closed on its hinge, locking the buzzing growl behind it.

Jack's throat ached as a lump rose in it. He pursed his lips, locked in what threatened to spill out, and spun on a heel. "What's going on here, Ricardo? What is this place?"

"It's…it's hard to explain. Let's just go, and then I'll—"

"Ricardo! Where are you taking that prisoner!" Heavy boots tromped up the stairs from the first floor. The owner of the voice rounded the landing.

Jack's stomach fell, even as heat rose in his cheeks.

Clomping up the stairs was the large Japanese man. Now, he sported a bruised chin and a cut above his eye. And what appeared to be a goose egg high up on his forehead.

Andy really had gotten in some good licks.

He stopped on the landing, staring at Jack. "What's going on here?"

"Uh," Ric said, dropping his eyes and shuffling his feet, "taking him to one-one-three-eight?"

"Oh, shit yeah. I'll do it for you. Let's go," he said, gripping Jack's bicep. "Buddy, have we got some posh accommodations for you. Don't we, Ric?"

The boy nodded, staring at the floor. He glanced up at Jack, made a moment of eye contact, and started back upstairs. His light brown skin had gone a dark shade of green.

"Oh boy," the guard said, dragging Jack down the stairs, "are you going to *love* this new cell we have for you. One-one-three-eight is my *very* favorite for people like you."

***

"Michael, you're staying here." Arms crossed, Addy shook her head and shuffled her feet on the wooden slats of the dock. "One of us has to make it through this. You have to stay where it's safe. Celia will let you stay here at her house while we're gone." She raised her voice. "Isn't that right, Cee?"

Her voice floated up from the boat. "Sure thing."

Smiling, Mike gripped Addy's shoulders and stared into her eyes. "Little sister, you can't order me around."

"Fine. I can't order you around," she said, brushing off his hands. "But you're staying here."

"Look, Addy. It's Dad. It's Jane. I have to come. You know I can't just sit here, wring my hands like an old lady, and wait."

He picked up his pack. "I might not be as good a fighter as you, but I'm damn good anyway and you know it."

"I know no such thing." Though she most certainly did.

"I'm coming, Adelaide."

"Fine," she said, shouldering her own pack. "So when we rescue Jane, you gonna tell her you love her? Or just stand there like a dope like you always do?"

He smacked her on the shoulder hard enough to send her flying.

"Ow!" She lifted a balled fist.

He held up a hand. "I give! OK? Sorry. I give."

"Wimp."

"True."

Dropping his pack into the boat with Celia, he stepped down.

"Gorgeous night, isn't it?" Tim jogged onto the dock. "Moon's almost full. Good lighting."

She frowned. "It's too clear. We could use more cover."

Tim kissed her on the cheek.

Her stomach revolted, and she stepped away. "Uh. Yeah. So. Come on," she said, stepping into the boat with Mike and Celia.

Oren and another man she had a vague memory of meeting at the bar climbed into the other boat. Frowning, Tim stepped into it with them. Glancing at her as he sat, he spoke out the corner of his mouth. "I'm doing this for you, you know. You could be a little grateful."

A fire began in the center of her forehead.

Jane would tell him to piss off.

But Jane wasn't here.

Dad would tell him to stop bragging.

Dad wasn't here either.

What would Picard say? Mom?

Ah, fuck it. So not in the mood for diplomacy.

"Let's go." She dipped an oar into the water.

"Adelaide! Wait!"

Her stomach dropped. It figured he'd come try and stop her. She shoved the oar at the dock, spinning the boat. "Celia," she said, giving the woman a glare that could freeze water, "untie us, please."

"Addy, please, wait," Dean said, running up to the dock. He stopped, panting, leaning his hand on a knee.

"How about no. Celia, if you would."

"Addy, what the hell?" Mike asked.

Oh, right, she hadn't told him. Now probably wasn't the time.

Glaring, she climbed back onto the dock. Crossed her arms. "What is it?"

"Are you sure I can't go with you?"

She pursed her lips. "Pretty positive."

He nodded. "Here. Take this," he said. "One last gift. Consider it a peace offering." He held out a shortbow and a quiver full of arrows.

She grinned. "I haven't seen one of these in years. Thanks, Dean. Really."

Before she got in the boat, he snagged her hand with gentle fingers. Not gripping, but not light enough to slip through. "Be careful."

"Yeah."

"I'm giving you till sunup. If you're not back, I'm coming to get you."

She tugged her hand free. "You'll do no such thing. I don't want you to come." Glancing around at the boats, she leaned toward him and lowered her voice. "I don't know what to think about this whole thing. Just, just give me some time. We'll talk when I get back, OK?"

Half his mouth raised in a smile, but his brow curved down. "It's not OK. But go."

She boarded the boat again, and this time Celia untied them. They drifted out into the sound, Dean standing on the dock with his hands in his pockets, watching.

"Adelaide," Tim called.

"What."

"You ask him about the thing?"

The other boat drifted away but the moon lit it well enough to see Tim's raised eyebrows and round eyes.

They might be pretty eyes, but she felt literally nothing looking into them. Except maybe mild revulsion.

Dammit, this was probably a bad idea.

"Too late," she whispered.

"What's that?" Tim cupped a hand around his ear.

She raised her voice, shouting across the water. "Let's get going. Come on."

*****

Instead of crossing the bridge back into the prison, Jack's favorite guard, the one he'd started thinking of as His Guard, took him up onto the grassy outer wall of the fort. Cannon emplacements lined the left side as they tromped through the sand and grass, headed toward a corner of the pentagon.

What had they been doing with Andrew? Was he turned? He growled and buzzed like a 'Head, but there was someone home in his eyes. It wasn't right, what he'd seen.

And for god's sake, where had they taken Jane?

He stared at His Guard. "Where we going, tough guy?"

"I told you. One-one-three-eight."

"What the hell does that mean?"

Hard, cold metal poked him between the shoulder blades. The sights of the rifle, no doubt a finger on the trigger as well.

Swallowing, he put both hands up, closed his mouth, and walked.

"Down the stairs."

The fading light of day just enough to illuminate a set of stairs dug into the ground, they ended in a dark hole.

He hesitated. "What's down there?"

His Guard aimed a flashlight down them. "Your new home, for now. March." He shoved Jack with the gun.

Holding his hands out, Jack descended the steep brick stairs. The smell of wet grass filled his nose. And something under it. Something not entirely pleasant.

Exiting the stairs at the bottom and passing through a locked door, they squished across sopping wet grass between the outer wall and the inner fort. Water splashed on his exposed legs. He shivered.

"Is this some kind of moat?" Jack asked.

"Yeah. Once the tide comes in through the culvert, it'll be at least four feet deep."

A buzzing moan echoed around the walls.

Jack shivered, but this time, it wasn't the chilly night. He whispered through the side of his mouth. "Are there Dead Heads in here?"

"Water and 'Heads. Keeps everybody in, and everybody out. Win win."

"Are you…is this one-one-three-eight?"

"No, in here," the guard said, pointing at a heavy wooden door wedged into an opening in the block wall. Stowing the flashlight, he climbed a set of stairs and unlocked the door. It creaked on rusty hinges. "Get in there, before the 'Heads realize we're here."

Glancing at His Guard, Jack hesitated.

"Hurry up," the man hissed.

The buzzing grew louder.

Jack climbed the stairs and stepped through the door.

It closed, plunging him into almost total darkness.

"Damn," he whispered, leaning against the door. Whatever work he'd done to get into the hospital, informative though it was, had been erased in just a few moments.

He'd lost Andrew to whatever sick experiments they were doing.

And he still hadn't found Jane.

His overactive imagination sent him frightening images of her, buried in a shallow grave on the beach, clothes ripped and bloody. Empty hand grasping at the air. Sparkling green eyes already a shade of grey, deflated and sinking into her head.

"Fuck!" He pounded the door, heat prickling his eyes. Dead Heads be damned.

In the dark behind him, a foot scraped across the sandy stone.

His breath caught.

Someone stood around the corner, breathing. The long, slow, regular breaths of a living, thinking person.

Spinning on his toes like a ballerina, he felt for the wall closest to him. As he did, the crotch of his ill-fitting jumpsuit took that moment to pull painfully on him.

He yanked down on the thighs of the suit with one hand and found the wall with the other.

One stealthy heel slid across the floor in the next room. Firelight flickered through the archway.

On sneakered tiptoes, he crept along the wall, stepping down two stairs. One of his feet hit a sandy patch and his foot skidded, crunching sand.

From the dark, someone whispered. "I know you're there."

Relief flooded every pore he had, so powerful he almost laughed aloud. The rush was so sudden and engulfing he got light-headed.

He stepped around the corner.

The last golden relics of day bounced into the cell, and there she stood, just outside one of the fading shafts.

"Oh my god, Jane." The tightly-wound spring in his chest loosened and fell away.

She laughed, stepping into the light. "Didn't know you were the religious type, Jack."

His mouth stretched into a wide grin that must've touched both ears.

Oh, you idiot. It's too late, isn't it? You're done.

He crossed and fell into her open arms, crushing her to him.

She exhaled and softened, molding herself to him. Pressing her cheek to his, she cradled the back of his head.

After holding her for what must've been oceans, he loosened his grip. Slipped a hand under her hair.

His already uncomfortable jumpsuit was suddenly almost too tight to bear.

Swallowing, he searched her face. No bruises, no scrapes, not so much as a hair out of place.

"Are you alright? Did he hurt you?"

She chuckled. "Hell no. He's too afraid of me. He brought me down here, gave me some food and water, told me to keep quiet and he'd be back. That was it."

He smiled, shaking his head. "How do you do it?"

"Do what?"

"Make everyone fall in love with you."

"I could ask you the same question."

He stood holding her, thinking about how uncomfortable this stupid suit was, and feeling her silky hair in his fingers for a full five seconds before his mind caught up with his ears.

"Jane, what—"

"Just kiss me, you idiot."

He did as he was told.

He'd never felt anything like it. Her lips were satin, the skin of her neck under his fingers like light trapped in a bottle. Every curve of her fit neatly into his own.

Pulling back, he drank in her eyes. His head swam.

He wanted to tell her a million things. How he hadn't felt like this since he was a kid. How she made him feel more alive than any near-death experience could ever do. Couldn't even touch it. How, over the last few weeks together, he'd fallen into a well of love deeper than the ocean outside. Without ever asking for it, but as unable to stop it as the tides.

The words bunched up around his Adam's apple and stuck. He drew in a breath and his knees threatened to drop him on the floor.

He pushed her into the wall, kissing her again. She tasted better than the great salty sea smelled.

Nothing held a candle to what she did to his nerve endings as she kissed him back just as fiercely.

A light tapping in the back of his mind demanded his attention. He told it to piss off.

It tapped a second time. Insistent.

With regret, he pulled away again, glancing up at the large barred window.

A 'Head wandered around out there, just out of sight. Buzzing and splashing.

"Jane," he whispered.

"Jack."

How did she still smell like flowers?

Focus, Jack.

"We've gotta get out of here. Get these people out. What they're doing up at that hospital, it's worse than we thought."

She shook her head, tracing his ear with a fingertip. "Can't."

He tugged her hand down and held it. "What do you mean? Sure we can. We're smart people."

Shrugging, she glanced at the window. A 'Head splashed by, silver light bouncing on the wall outside. "Tide's almost in, my love."

He flushed from his forehead to his toes. Grinned like a fool. Nobody'd spoken to him like that since— Well. Over a decade.

She smiled back. "That's a moat now. That, plus floating 'Heads, no weapons, dark of night? Even us smart, strong people don't stand a chance. Best to wait till morning. I'm sure if we put our heads together in the daylight, with the tide out, we can come up with something."

Nodding, he kissed her neck. Under his lips, her heartbeat fluttered like a hummingbird. He whispered in her ear. "What do you suggest we do till then?"

She shrugged. "Play cards?"

"Didn't bring a deck," he said, smiling into the soft skin behind her clavicle bone.

This damn jumpsuit, though. He pulled at the right thigh, trying to make some room in the crowded space.

Grasping his shoulders, she pushed him away. Brow lifted, she looked over the suit, taking in his exposed calves and ankles, eyes resting on the bunched fabric in his groin.

"That looks incredibly uncomfortable."

"Getting more and more so by the moment."

"Well, then. If you didn't bring any cards, I guess we really only have one option. You should take that off."

"If you think that'll help."

"Honey," she said, unzipping the front, "there's no help for us now."

CHAPTER 24

elia pointed the boat into the breakers. She shouted over the crashing waves. "Hang on, we're going in."

Addy clutched the bottom of her seat as a breaker foamed around them and pushed them toward the beach. The boat rocked as the wave passed and Celia steered into another, Mike paddling to get ahead of it.

The next one broke, and they surfed the front of it all the way to the beach.

Addy jumped out, grabbed the stern, and pulled. The sand sucked her feet, trying to keep her in the water. Mike dropped his oar in the boat and jumped out on the other side. They tugged together and dragged the boat ashore.

"Go team," Tim said, sitting in the other boat while Oren and the new guy jerked it onto the beach.

Shaking her head, Addy pulled the bow and arrows out of their canoe. What a useless lump of a person. But, still necessary. He was the only one who knew the layout of the place.

Sighing, she approached him. "Alright. Where now?"

"They're being held in the main prison. At least, when I left, that's where they were."

"They could be somewhere else?"

He looked at his feet. "I hope not."

Her stomach dropped to her toes. "What do you mean by that?"

"It's not good. Let's just hope they're still in the main one. We'll probably have to wait till the tide goes out again to get to them."

She watched the rolling breakers. The sea controlled it all. "How long will that be?"

Celia joined them. "Close to sunup. Let's stash the boats."

Boats hidden at the tree line, they walked up the beach so they wouldn't have to shout over the surf.

Guts as uneasy as the sea crashing onto shore, Addy glanced at the new guy.

For a guy of average height, he was lanky. He stood watching Tim with his eyes squinted. Resting his hand on the handle of a sheathed knife.

"Hey," Addy said.

He smiled. "Hey. Remember me from the other night?"

"Yes, kinda, I think," she said, less and less sure with every word that came out of her mouth.

Releasing the knife and sticking out his hand, he stepped toward her. His eyes, bright and round, shone in the moonlight, in contrast to his dark skin drinking it in. "Jeff."

She shook. "Right, right, I remember. Jeff. You got bull's-eyes on darts all night."

"Ha, yeah, I did. Pretty good with throwing knives, too."

"You'd like my friend, Jane," she said, smiling.

If it was possible to miss someone more than her mom, it was Jane. But she wasn't losing Jane. They were finding her and bringing her home. That's all.

"You alright?" Jeff asked, gripping her shoulder.

She swayed. "Yeah. Sorry. Anyhow," she said, staring at his knife handle, "she's pretty good at throwing knives, too. Keeps at least five or six of 'em on her at all times."

"Can't wait to meet her," he said, glancing back down the beach.

Tim stood in the surf, eyes on the horizon.

Sighing, Addy excused herself and motioned to Celia. "The hell is he doing? I wish he didn't have to come."

Celia shook her head. "But he did. Just let me know as soon as we can ditch him."

The lead ball that was her stomach thought "soon" wasn't soon enough.

Eventually, he joined them above the high tide line.

"Alright," he said, "we landed a bit south of where we need to be. There's not a lot of nighttime security on the outer walls, but there's some." He knelt in the sand and drew the shape of a pentagon with his finger. "Ocean, inlet, sound, those are the three sides with guards. One guard each at night." He drew a circle inside the pentagon. "Moat. There's about half a dozen heads or so in there, and when it fills up during high tide, fighting conditions are bad, even if you're fully armed."

"So no going through the moat," Addy said, kneeling next to him. "Got it."

He smiled, nodding. "Yeah. So inside the moat," he said, drawing another, smaller pentagon inside the circle, "is the prison proper. I mean there are a few cells along the outer walls, but those aren't really used anymore. There shouldn't be anyone there."

"Could we use them to hide out until the water level drops?" Mike asked, crouching on the other side of Tim.

"The only way to access them is through the moat. They're cut off till the tide goes out."

"Got it. How are the cells laid out inside?" As he spoke, Mike pulled out several suckers and offered one to everyone.

Jeff took one. Everyone else declined.

Shrugging, Mike stuffed the suckers back in his black pouch.

Addy fingered the soft leather pouch Dean had gotten her. Jackass.

Tim was talking, but she'd missed it. "Sorry Tim, could you repeat that?"

Glancing at her, he scowled and pointed to lines he'd drawn in the inner pentagon. "Here, here, and here," he said, jamming his finger into the sand to punctuate each word, "are the cells for the men. Did you hear me that time?"

Her blood pressure rose so quickly she couldn't see anything but black for a moment. She took a breath, exhaling through her nose. And another. "Yes, Tim. Thank you. Please go on." Able to keep her voice low and modulated, she gave herself a pat on the back. The little things.

Frowning, lips a thin white line, Tim looked away from his little map. "I'm sticking my neck out for you here. This is pretty dangerous, and if they catch me on the wrong side, I mean"—he cleared his throat—"if they catch me betraying them, the consequences for me will be far worse than whatever will happen to you."

The wrong side?

Misspeak? Or slip of the tongue?

Hard to tell.

Rather than pursue the question, she nodded. Before she could speak, Celia knelt next to her.

"Timothy, speak to her like that one more time, and you and me gonna have words."

"Sorry, Celia. I'm sorry. I'm really nervous."

"I get that. But you don't get to treat her like that. She's not your dog."

Addy bumped Celia's shoulder with her own. "Thanks."

Celia nodded.

"Alright. Ladies. Here, here, and here," he said, making three new spots in the inner pentagon, "these are the women's cells. Jane should be there."

"Good," Addy said. "What about the rest of it? Guards?"

"Around each outer door there's one, and they usually all sit kinda in the middle, playing cards and whatnot. So, there should be six guards for the cells, minimum. It's night, so," he said, making more lines on the opposite wall, "there will be more guards asleep in these rooms."

Addy frowned. "How do we get in? If we have to wait for the tide to go out?"

Tim glanced out at the ocean. "Celia said it's going out around sunup. Right?"

The small woman nodded.

"So, we position ourselves near the moat and sneak down at guard change before the sun rises. There's a door here," he said, drawing one more line, this one between the moat and the inner pentagon, "that'll lead us up into the inside."

Addy, eyes on the drawing, considered how many guards there would be. What kind of risk she was putting these people in.

She shook her head. "I can't let you guys do this. It's too dangerous. We're probably going to get caught."

Mike stood. "When the guards change, how do they do it?"

Tim stood next to him. "They make a report. Usually over coffee, inside the courtyard."

"And we're coming from the other way."

"Yeah."

"You're right. This'll never work. Let's do it."

"Michael," Addy said, standing, "no. It's just too risky. There has to be another way."

Tim glanced from Addy to Mike. "I could go in alone. Bring them out. I didn't tell them I was leaving. I doubt these guards would know I was even gone."

Addy's stomach turned, eating itself. She chewed a nail. It peeled back, exposing bloody cuticle.

"It's better than this other stupid plan," she said, scraping away the drawing with her foot.

"OK, let's do it," Tim said. He pointed up the beach. "We gotta swing wide, though. General's house is just over that dune."

"General?" Addy's eyes followed Tim's pointing finger.

"She's the one in charge of this whole shebang. Kinda nuts. Little bitchy. Strong leader. You'll want to avoid her if you can."

Butterfly wings beat in her mind, whispering against her nerves. Why should the mention of this woman make her feel off-balance?

"You got it. What are we waiting for? Lead the way, Tim," she said.

Smiling, almost a leer, he trudged up the beach.

"This plan is stupid, too," Celia mumbled, following.

Mike grabbed Addy's hand, enclosing it in cheerful warmth. "It'll work, though."

She smiled. "How do you know that?"

"Because I said so. I'm the big brother."

Nodding, she followed them up the beach. It was the best they had.

***

Moon low in the west, Adelaide and the team watched from cover as Tim sauntered through the front door of the prison.

"Addy," Celia hissed, "how do we know we can trust him?"

Addy frowned, the rock in her gut sitting on top of her intestines. Pressing down. "We don't. He told me something I thought was a lie, but it turned out to be true." She exhaled. "He's the best we got."

Michael, of course, stretched his mouth into a grin. "We're getting them back, right now, today." He grasped and squeezed her hand again.

"Mike. You simp," Celia said.

Sitting next to her, Oren bumped her shoulder. "Hey."

She frowned.

"That may be," Mike said, eyeing the fort, "but I'm a correct simp. I've got a good feeling about this."

He might have his moments of blind optimism, but his enthusiasm was hard not to catch. Try as she might to stop it, the stone in Addy's gut shifted.

As they waited, the sun began to rise, lightening the edge of the horizon with silvery pink.

"My leg is falling asleep," Jeff murmured.

Addy smiled with the corner of her mouth. "My ass fell asleep an hour ago."

As Jeff opened his mouth to respond, Tim sauntered back out of the prison. Another boy walked with him, his red hair fiery in the rising sun.

Celia leaned over. "Is that Louis?"

Squinting, Addy took in the small, freckled, red-faced boy and flashed on him blushing at Jane as he helped move their couch. Forever ago. "Yeah, it is."

"Thick as thieves, those two."

Tim stopped at the top of the dune, sending Louis along with a wave. Eyes narrowed, he stood with his hands on his hips and waited for the boy to disappear around the trees.

Once he had, he joined them again.

Celia squinted. "What's Louis doing here?"

"Addy, I have news."

Sitting up to squat, she sucked in a breath. He didn't sound like someone with good news.

"Out with it," Mike said.

"Your dad drowned yesterday."

Every bit of everything in her froze. Breath locked in her chest. Her insides, even her brain, disappeared, to be replaced by nothingness. Emptiness. The black vacuum of space.

Michael's face was a masque of neutrality. No smile, no frown, no nothing. He reflected her own gut-punched, hollow center.

Celia fell forward and smacked into the ground, bloodying her forehead.

"Shit, no, shit. That's not what I meant," Tim said, rolling Celia onto her back. "Celia are you OK?"

Addy's mouth flopped open. Closed. Open. All her spit seemed to have taken a holiday. She dug what nails she had into his wrist. "What happened?"

"The guards say one of the prisoners got him breathing again, and they got him over to the hospital. I don't know anything else. Louis is going over to check it out."

Flopping into the sand, still unable to feel her ass, Addy's organs reappeared in full force. Her heart pounded against her ribs, threatening to leap from its perch and pound the shit out of her. Literally. Closing her eyes, letting the tears that had collected there fall, she took in a few even breaths.

Mike sobbed aloud. Oren put an arm around him and shushed him.

Addy's mind's eye threw up an image of the cartoon man again, red mustache bouncing. She giggled.

She covered her mouth with the back of her hand and bit down, stifling the giggles.

"Listen, Addy, I do have a little better news," Tim whispered.

"Motherfucker," Celia said, raising a hand to her head.

Addy pressed her lips into a tight, white line. "You alright?"

Celia sat up and grabbed Tim's collar. Her face an inch from his, she growled, "He better be OK. Or it's your ass. You did this to him. You did this to all of us."

Tim raised his hands. "I know where Jane is," he said, glancing at Addy.

She watched Michael. As he sat, head lowered, arms resting on his splayed legs, a tear fell and soaked into his jeans.

"Take us to her," he said.

"Five minutes," Tim said. "I worked it out, the guards won't be around."

Addy nodded. "Five minutes."

***

The sound of an arrow thwacking into the rotten pumpkin of a Dead Head roused Jack from the deepest sleep he'd gotten in years. Even if it was half-naked on a cold stone floor, he had a beautiful woman curled up against him.

She's nothing but a child, Jackson.

That is simply not true. The tools it takes to grow up in this world are all different. Harder. Somehow altogether more. It's different. She's different.

Another body dropped onto the squishy ground just outside the window.

"Jane," he said, running his hand down her back.

She stretched, nails scraping across his bare chest and catching a nipple.

He shivered all the way to his toes. It had been so long. Was it like this before?

"Morning, love," she said, sitting up.

Running feet splashed across the wet ground in the moat.

Sitting up on an elbow, he cradled the back of her neck, pulling her down into a long, slow kiss.

Releasing her an inch, his toes still curled, he whispered into her mouth. "We're about to have company."

"No."

"Yeah. But," he said, kissing her cool, silky lips again, "they aren't taking you from me again. Not ever again."

The bolt slid back on the heavy outside door.

Pressing her forehead to his, she nuzzled his nose. "I'd like to see them try."

The large outside door opened, flooding light into the cell.

He released her, tying the arms of the jumpsuit around his waist into a makeshift belt, and stood.

Footsteps on the stair.

Turning to help her up, someone gasped behind him.

Before he'd had a chance to turn around, someone jumped on him. He stumbled.

"Dad, oh god, Dad, I thought you were dead, he told me you drowned, they didn't know where you were, oh my god, Dad you're OK."

His daughter babbled, squeezing his neck in a hug so tight he almost couldn't breathe. "Adelaide," he croaked, "you're choking me."

The pressure eased. "Sorry, sorry, I'm just so happy. Sorry."

He gave her half a smile, one side of his mouth turned down. Whatever the hell she was doing here, it was good to see her. "You're something else, baby girl."

"Jane," she said, bouncing. She grabbed her in a hug and wobbled back and forth.

Arms wrapped around her, squeezing her in a tight hug, Jane stared over Addy's shoulder at him. Brows knit. Fine line between them.

Their uncertain footing had asserted itself sooner than he'd wanted. And by the look on her face, sooner than she'd wished for as well. Frowning, he shrugged.

"I'm so glad you're both OK," Addy said, releasing her and stepping back.

Michael came around the door. His thousand-watt smile landed on Jane.

All at once, it felt as though a tiny little person punched Jack full force in the ribcage. Of course. His son was in love with her too. Had been pining over her for years.

Mike dashed across the room, hugging Jane and lifting her off the floor.

The green-eyed monster dug its claws deep into Jack's back. He fought the urge to curse. Instead, he faced Addy. "What the hell are you doing here?"

More shapes filled the doorway. Celia—that girl turned up everywhere—and a couple guys he didn't know.

"Busting you out, Dad. We gotta go."

"What...how did you get here?"

"It's a long story. Tell you on the way."

"Where?"

"Oh, it's very exciting, Jackson." A voice oozed into the room.

Jack froze. Fear creeping into the edges of his mind, clearing his eyes and narrowing his vision to a pinpoint, he whispered. "Adelaide, what have you done?"

"He knew how to get you. It was the only way."

"It's a thrilling story, really," Tim said, easing past Celia. "Chases, escapes, rebels, Dead Heads, liars. Oh, it's got it all. Even"—he leaned over Addy's shoulder—"affairs of the heart." He waggled his eyebrows.

"Get away from her," Jack growled.

Tim slipped an arm around Addy's shoulders. "Who, her? I wouldn't hurt a hair on her pretty little head."

Heart racing, Jack jumped forward.

"Not," Tim said, tightening his grip into a stranglehold, "unless you make me." Pulling a gun, he pressed it into her temple. "Please don't make me. I've just had these pants laundered, and I really would hate to get blood on them."

His brave little girl, she didn't move a muscle or make a squeak. Only stared up at him, waiting for him to make a move.

He took in the others.

Jane, staring into his eyes, narrowed her own.

Mike, hand resting on the haft of his machete.

Celia hadn't moved her feet, but she'd assumed what he'd recognize anywhere as her fighting posture.

Tim's odds, while tipped because of the gun, weren't very good.

He showed Tim his teeth.

A shadow fell in the doorway.

His Guard, followed by seven or eight more, all armed.

Tim leered. "Time to meet the general."

***

Glaring at Tim as he stripped her of her weapons, Addy held her hands behind her head, fingers interlaced. "I knew there was something I didn't like about you."

Holding up her machete, he smiled and gazed at her from the side of his eye. "Oh baby, I'm gonna ask the general if I can have you for a prize." He licked the side of her face, leaving a cold, wet, sloppy streak up her cheek.

Shuddering, she turned away but didn't wipe her face. Wouldn't give him the satisfaction.

"You're something else, Tim," Jane hissed. Hands raised behind her head as well, she'd moved next to Dad, their elbows touching.

"Jane," Tim said, licking his lips, "I know what you're up to. You keep talking, so will I."

"We going or what?" Celia asked. She'd been handcuffed, weapons stripped, and pressed against the wall with everyone else.

"Sure, sure," Tim said, groping Addy and spinning her toward the door.

"You take your hands off her," Dad said, "or I'll kill you where you stand."

"Oh, Jackson. You're in for such a treat," he said, shoving Addy toward the door. He pointed at a guard. "You, take little red and big red, the other girl and the darkie. They're not coming with us."

Behind her, feet scuffled. "You're not taking her anywhere," Dad said. A body hit the floor.

She spun.

Tim lay facedown in the cell, her dad standing over him with his fists raised.

Her stomach flip-flopped. Whether in fear or triumph, she couldn't tell. "Dad, careful."

"Don't worry about me, baby girl," he said, kicking Tim in the kidney.

Tim groaned, holding a hand to his face. "What are you waiting for, you idiots, get him off me!"

The largest guard pointed his gun at Dad's head, easing the hammer back.

Dad stood, straddling Tim, staring down the barrel.

"No, no, no," Tim said, waving his arms and standing, "don't fucking kill him. Jesus, just restrain him. Fuck's sake, why am I always surrounded by assholes and morons?"

Addy stepped toward her dad as the guard lowered his gun. Mike approached from the other side. Jane stood by the wall with Celia, eyes locked on Dad's, breathing hard.

Looking between her dad and best friend, she softened her voice. "Tim, she's part of the family. She's my best friend. She comes with us."

"You know what Adelaide," Tim said, smiling and turning to her, wiping the blood from his mouth, "I think that's a perfectly spectacular idea. In fact, I'm glad you brought it up." He spun a hand in the air. "Let's go boys. Bull," he said, pointing to the big guard, "bring tough guy, his boy, and his girlfriend."

Mike blushed. "She's not my girlfriend," he said, grinning down at Jane.

Staring at him, Jane's mouth opened and closed a few times, not making a sound.

Which was unusual. She almost always had a snarky comment. Especially when it came to Michael.

Tim, chuckling, led them out of the cell.

They walked past the prison and crossed a road, turning east into a small complex of short buildings.

One of them had been built up in several places, different colors and conditions of boards, shingles, and metal making up the additions. A flower bed in front of the porch bloomed with roses, marigolds, and some kind of bush with pink flowers. Above the railing hung a collection of tinkling wind chimes.

On the way in the door, Addy admired them.

A sun and the planets one caught her eye. The fake sun gleamed a mellow orange as the real sun shone through it.

Holding the door, Tim waved them all in like some kind of overdone doorman. "Milady," he said, as Addy passed.

She glared, crossing into the cool house. The sound of the ocean receded as they entered the homey living room.

Bull led them up the stairs and into a sparse room with two chairs.

"Keep an eye on them," Tim said. "I'll be back soon, my dear." He kissed Addy on the cheek.

She pulled back, shoving at his shoulder, but he roped an arm around her waist and pressed his face into hers, grinding his chin into her jawbone.

Exhaling as he released her and swallowing a dry heave, she plotted his very slow, very painful death.

He wandered out of the room, pulling out a knife and tossing it between his hands. The door stood open, their guard posted just outside it.

Addy sidled next to her dad, eyes on the guard. "Are you alright?"

"Yeah, sweetie. Never better. You?"

"We could take them. There's four of us. Even without weapons, we're solid fighters."

Jane nodded, her mouth drawn into a fierce grin. "You bet your ass we could."

"It's not a bad idea," he said, lowering his voice.

Narrowing her eyes, Addy stepped closer. Michael joined them, and the four of them closed the circle.

"OK, listen," Addy said, "when Tim comes back with this general, we grab the general first."

"Good idea, Adelaide," Dad said. "They all seem terrified to disrespect her. She's the head of the snake. We cut that off, and we've got a good chance of shutting this whole thing down."

"This whole thing?"

He glanced around the circle, eyes resting on Jane's upturned face. Cutting them back to Addy, he inhaled, brows knitted. "I went to that hospital. They had Andrew, hooked up to all kinds of shit. I don't know what they're doing, but there are ledgers and ledgers full of names. Probably thousands. It's all sideways."

Addy nodded. "Some of the people on Harkers Island told me you don't leave here, you become part of the horde on the mainland."

Dad cursed, staring out the window.

Following his gaze, Addy saw the peek-a-boo ocean just over the dune. A small, grey spot of salty water.

As she opened her mouth, the door downstairs slammed, interrupting her thoughts.

"…don't have time for this, Timothy." A strident voice floated up the stairs.

Addy bumped her dad's shoulder. "That the general?"

He turned his head, tendons in his neck creaking. Stared at her with round, wide eyes to match his round, wide mouth.

A fluttering of doubt and fear settled into her chest and grew wings.

"Dad?" Mike asked.

"I think it is," Dad answered, staring over Addy's head, eyes unfocused.

"Are you alright?"

More conversation floated up the stairs as feet tromped up them.

"…sorry general. I thought it was—"

"You thought, you thought. I don't pay you to think."

"You don't pay me at all, ma'am."

"Well," she said, voice low as they approached the room, "we both know that's not true."

Boot heels clacked across the hardwood floor and through the doorway.

"So, to whom do I owe…the…" she said, words tapering off to nothing.

Dad turned on a heel, sideways and slow like a broken Lazy Susan. "Saints above," he breathed.

Michael squeaked like a mouse, hands flying up to cover his mouth and half his face.

Addy, heart slamming into her ribs hard enough to bounce her eyeballs, unable to understand why this general should sound familiar, stepped around her father.

Staring at the brunette standing before them, mouth agape, was like looking in an aged mirror.

Almost all the air left Addy's lungs. Enough remained for one word to escape.

"Mom?"

THE GENERAL

CHAPTER 25

S o your dad, he says, 'Well Melinda,'" she said, lowering her voice to match Dad's, "'I think we better take these Dead Heads out before they scare away the birds.'"

Addy all but fell off her chair, doubled over in laughter. As funny as the story was, it was doubly funny when her mom imitated her dad.

They'd gathered around the kitchen table as the day waned, swapping old stories and laughing like hyenas. Even Dad laughed. More than Addy thought she'd ever seen.

For now, the miracle of how Mom was alive was secondary to the fact that she was.

Still chuckling and wiping tears from the corners of her eyes, Addy glanced at Jane.

As Addy, her brother, and her mom and dad tightened into a circle under the kitchen light, Jane became more and more withdrawn. Feet in her chair, knees drawn into her chest, she'd spent the last hour smiling vaguely at their stories and doing her best impression of wallpaper.

Guilt sliced into Addy's heart. Jane had been through three sets of parents, losing her dad less than a month ago. And here Addy was, both of her parents alive and in one piece like some kind of divine blessing.

"Jane," she said, holding her hand out, "let's tell the story of when those guys tried to come on a run with us. Remember that?"

Jane took her hand, squeezing before she dropped it. "You start." The ghost of a smile crossed her lips.

Laughter tapering off, Dad frowned at Jane, expression inscrutable. "Jane, are you alright?" he asked, scratchy voice near a whisper.

She flapped a hand at Addy, tears standing in her eyes.

Addy launched into the story, starting with how both of these boys seemed to want to fight over Jane more than they wanted to actually get supplies. Their ineptitude comical in proportions, Michael chipped in where he had lines.

Soon Addy was in stitches again, Mike and her mom laughing along with her.

Her dad stared over her shoulder at Jane, laughing less and less as the story approached its punchline.

"Anyway," Addy said, "he's lying there, flat on his back, and Jane leans over him and she says…" Turning to Jane, Addy stopped and waited for her best friend, her sister, to deliver the punchline.

Eyes darting between the four of them, tears falling with the movement, Jane stood. "I'm going to get some air," she said, voice shaking.

For a moment, her eyes rested on Dad.

Jane let the screen door slam behind her and walked out into the night.

Pit forming in her stomach, Addy turned back to the rest of her family. "She just lost her dad," she whispered across the table.

Mom nodded, looking around the table. "It sounds like you guys have been through a lot together. This must be difficult for her."

Dad lowered his hands to the table and pushed himself to stand, chair scraping across the linoleum.

Melinda laid a hand over his, fingers curling. "Let her go, Jack."

"Dad, I'll go," Addy said, standing.

The back of her throat hurt, tears for everything Jane must be feeling prickling her eyes.

Dad raised a hand. "You stay here with your mother. I'll be back." Without waiting for an answer, he followed Jane into the night, screen door smacking the frame.

Sitting, Addy watched her mom.

Mom narrowed her eyes. After a moment she looked up and favored Addy with a sunny smile. "Let me tell you guys about how your dad and I met."

Addy smiled. "Oh, Mom, I love this story."

***

The screen door slammed behind Jack, and he scanned the backyard for Jane.

She stood atop the dune, the rising full moon framing her in silvery pink.

Breath stuck in his throat, he climbed the cool sand to the top.

She stood, twenty feet away, hugging her elbows. Her cheeks shone in the moonlight.

"Jane," he called. His scratchy voice didn't get louder than the surf, and she continued staring out at the black water. As he took another step toward her, she unfolded her arms.

She stepped away and was gone down the dune.

Indecision rooted him to the spot.

His heart walked down the beach without him.

His wife and children waited in the house behind him.

The center of the puzzle just out of reach but right on the edge of his fingertips.

"She OK?"

He jumped, hands raising, and almost lost his balance. "Jesus, Mellie, you scared the hell out of me."

Her crooked grin raised half her mouth higher than the other.

"I've missed that crooked smile of yours," he said, stepping closer. "Where has it been? What happened to you? Mellie," he said, shifting his feet, sand between his toes, "I saw you bit. That was years and years before the Cure. How can this be?"

She held her hand out to him. "It's a long story, Jackson. Come back in, I'll tell you all."

Glancing down the beach again, he searched for Jane. She'd gone past the curving arc of the island and disappeared into the night.

He clapped a hand on Melinda's shoulder and squeezed. "Let's go in, then."

As the back door squealed, Mike glanced up, brows raised, and searched the empty space behind them.

Addy stood, looking out the door. "Where's Jane?"

Jack shook his head and sat at the table again, resting his head in his hands. He unstuck his dry tongue from the roof of his mouth. "She left."

Sounded so final, didn't it?

What he wouldn't give to have that prancing hankie boy still be his biggest problem.

The chair next to him squeaked, Melinda sitting on the edge. She leaned on the table.

After all these years, all this painful, long time, she'd been given back to him. An impossibility. A miracle. She'd been brought back from the dead.

And all he could think of was running out onto that beach, grabbing Jane, and not looking back.

Because despite whatever miracle had happened, anything Melinda was about to say couldn't be good.

She opened her mouth, and he held up a hand. "Mellie. Tell me you're not part of whatever is going on here. Tell me you're here against your will."

Closing her mouth, she lowered her head. "It's a long story."

"Jesus Christ, Melinda," he said, standing again. This time he smacked the chair with his legs, the seat slamming into the meat of his thigh just above his knee. It flew.

Adelaide caught it before it bounced off the floor and set it right. "Dad," she said, scooting the chair behind him.

He sat, glaring.

"Mom," Addy said, turning to her mother, "why don't you go ahead and tell us the story."

Melinda nodded.

***

"COME AND GET ME YOU STINKING ASSHOLES!!!"

I ran across the store, knocking racks over behind me and jumping over all the crap already in the floor, bleeding from a half dozen bites and crying. As my family escaped out the back, I screamed and banged and kept the dead distracted. My whole life walked out that door, and when they were gone, I don't know how I kept standing.

But I did.

Something inside seemed to snap. I went crazy. I hacked and slashed, stinking, old, black blood and guts covering every inch of me.

Eventually, they were all on the ground, bits scattered from one side of the store to the other. Pieces of them in my hair, my mouth, under my nails. I probably even swallowed some as I screamed and hacked. It stank like a cow yard, but like the shit had fermented in the sun, rotted, and then been stirred by a giant wooden spoon.

I threw up. I threw up everything. My guts were on fire, my stomach turned inside out, my throat raw.

Lying on the floor, I waited for it to be over.

But then I looked to my left, and there was my little girl's shoe. She'd lost it on their way out, when her dad had snatched her up so fast, she left it behind.

A little shoe. Almost as big as mine, really, but I crawled over to it and hugged it. And cried hot tears. If throwing up hadn't dried me all up, the crying did. I didn't have anything left.

I think I fell asleep for a while, and when I opened my eyes next, it was nighttime.

My everything screamed when I sat up. Burned. Froze. Twisted. Oh god, there'd never been pain like that. But I was still alive. I gripped that little shoe and I stumbled out of the store.

Where was the camp? Where was this store? Which way had we come?

Through the parking lot out front. I went that way. I tried to backtrack the way we'd come. Me and my little girl.

I could see them in my mind, my family.

My heroic little boy, so strong. Such a great brother. Always the one to sing a song when we were sad, or to somehow dig up some chocolate when Mom cried. Just a baby when this started. Always such a good boy.

And my baby girl. What a troublemaker. Such a smart, sassy little thing, even as a baby. But so fun to hang out with. Share the stars with. Pick berries, eat as many as we picked, get our mouths all red and go back to our boys giddy from sugar rushes.

And oh, my beautiful, brave husband. Stronger than an ox, both physically and mentally, always the one to tell me it was going to be alright even if he didn't know that. And then do everything in his power to make it alright. Practically kill himself to make it OK, if that's what he had to do. And dead sexy to top it off. A woman couldn't ask for a better partner, even if we were just kids when we started off.

We weren't kids anymore. The apocalypse had come, and we were in the shit together.

And we made it. We made it so far. We saved our babies. We pushed forward.

We made it so far.

I couldn't find them. I wandered for hours. The sun came up. I couldn't see straight, I was so cold on the inside, and I could feel my skin baking off my bones. My head was a useless mess of cotton balls.

My eyes were all blurry. They hurt. My chest was full of lead.

I was tired. So tired.

My feet tangled. I fell down. I tried to cry again, holding that little shoe. But there were no tears left. Only blood.

I listened to my heartbeat slow. So cold.

Then I was awake.

Everything was crystal clear.

There was a rushing sound in my ears. I don't know what it was. It couldn't be blood. Maybe it was thought.

But here's where it was very strange. It wasn't thought. Not really. I couldn't think to do anything. I couldn't think to want to do anything. My body moved, my chest lifted, the blood pooled in my lungs and a bubbling, groaning sound came from my mouth. But I didn't think about anything. Not where I was going, not holding onto the shoe, not anything.

The shoe. There had been people. *Food.* They had to be near.

I stumbled into trees, bounced off them. A deer bounded out of the underbrush in front of me and I grabbed at it. Meat. *Food.* Its image solidified in my eyes.

That scent went with that thing and I needed that thing.

No thought. Just *food.*

I'd like to say I was like Picard when he was turned into Locutus of Borg. I'd like to say somewhere inside I was screaming to be let out. I'd like to say there was some small part of me left that could resist tearing this poor fawn to pieces with my bare, bleeding fingers.

But there wasn't.

There wasn't anyone.

Memories remained, but the conscious mind was no more.

And after a while, even memory began to fade.

I think I was on the edge of it, the memory fading. I was covered in deer. I smelled more *food.*

The *food* had two legs. It was people. It smelled like ambrosia.

Even in life, looking back on that scent, I've never before nor since smelled something so intoxicating.

What was left of the energy in my muscles propelled me toward them. My lungs bubbled, and they heard me before I got to them.

They weren't fast enough, though. Not all of them. You know the little ones aren't as fast as the big ones?

I bet you knew that.

The rest of them escaped. I followed them as far as I could, but they'd gone away too fast for my dead legs to keep up.

I wandered. And again, I smelled *food*. I needed it.

I got close to it, so close I could almost grip it in my black claws.

But something happened, something stopped me, maybe it was a net. A tight grasp that came from everywhere.

There was pressure on my back.

It didn't matter though. I couldn't see them, but I could smell them.

And then…I couldn't. I couldn't smell them. I couldn't smell anything.

No, that's wrong.

I smelled blood. Like curdled milk.

I threw up. I threw up everything. Bits of deer and bits of somebody's baby, and blood and bile and gore and god knew.

My throat hurt. My insides twisted into some kind of knot that could never be untied.

I don't know if it ever was.

But those people, they took me into their truck and me and about a half dozen other people, they took us to some kind of hospital. Surrounded in barbed wire, earthen walls, most of it dug into a hill with one tiny little door.

Like a nightmare version of some kind of hobbit house.

It took the better part of a year to fully recover. By then, I had no idea where my family had gone or if they were even still alive. No idea, even, where I was. Who these people were. What had happened.

I couldn't remember what happened before I was bitten or what happened after they cured me for at least five years. By then, I was running my own wing in the hospital.

All I could remember for so long was what happened in the middle. I'll never leave that mother's screams behind. They follow me into sleep every single night, and I wake up to them every single day.

Crystal clear.

The people I worked for, they're the ones who made the Cure. They were running their first tests when they found me. I stumbled right into the middle of their camp. They weren't even going to catch any more 'Heads. They were just packing up.

They scrambled a dose together, imperfect stuff but it did the trick. Recovery has been an arduous trek of medications and rehabilitation. It's been a long road.

Distributing the Cure was a huge step, and I couldn't be prouder to have been part of that. So that no one has to lose their baby the way that woman lost hers.

Or the way I lost mine.

I looked for them every day since I recovered my memory. Every day.

Now they've been returned to me.

The people who made the Cure, I owe them everything.

I'm not the woman who walked into that sporting goods store with her little girl. I'm not the woman who cried with sadness and then with joy when her sweet little boy brought her chocolate and candy. I'm not the beautiful wife of a strong man who held our life together with baling wire and duct tape.

But I've tried to remember her. I like her. I miss her.

I want to be her again.

Now I can.

CHAPTER 26

Silence fell over the four of them.

Addy looked over to see her dad holding her mom's hand. Something she thought she'd never see again.

It really was nothing short of a miracle.

Why did she feel like someone had punched her in the gut, repeatedly, with a hammer?

"Jesus Christ, Melinda," Dad said, rubbing the back of her hand with his thumb, "I'm so sorry."

Snuffling tears, she glanced up at him. A tentative smile crossed her lips.

In return, the corners of his mouth drew down, brow furrowed.

"I don't understand this, Mom," Mike said, taking her other hand.

She blinked wet lashes. "What, baby? What can I help you understand?"

He sighed, looking at the floor.

Such a rare moment to see him so serious.

"So, they gave you some kind of prototype of the Cure?"

Mom nodded.

He met her eyes. "*Eleven* years ago? How? How is it possible it took them another almost seven years to give it to people? Why?"

She gripped Mike's hands with both of hers. "It takes a long time to develop something like that. So many studies, tests, failures, and more tests have to be done before the efficacy can be guaranteed."

"I don't understand what any of that means."

She swept a hair from his forehead. "Even now, there's still work to be done."

Addy shivered, slippery words walking down her spine.

Her dad's expression agreed.

"Mom," she said, "what do you mean? The Cure doesn't work?"

She gripped Addy's hand, her fingers cold. "No, honey. Well, not exactly."

"Melinda, what the hell are you saying?"

Turning to her husband, Mom smiled with her mouth but not her eyes. "I'm saying we've found there's still some holes in it."

Addy struggled to form her mouth around the word. "Holes?" Releasing Mom's hand, she scratched at the bandage on her shoulder. The bite burned, and her dressing would need to be changed soon.

"Yeah, baby, holes." She crossed her arms. "There's a pretty complex calculation, it's still being developed, but it's based on body weight, freshness of the 'Head doing the biting, amount of time since the bite, number of previous bites. So many variables. It's hard to nail down without a large sample size."

Sample size. Large sample size.

The words ran around in a circle as Addy stared at her mom, mouth hanging open and drying out.

Unbidden, the great carpet of Dead Heads they'd come through popped into her mind.

Large sample size.

Her palms began to sweat.

Dad had gone two shades paler. He looked like he might puke.

Michael stared between them, an out of place frown scrawled across his face. "Guys? What's wrong?"

Dad opened his mouth. Closed it. Glanced at Addy.

The rushing in her ears made speech impossible. She couldn't even hear her own thoughts.

"Hey, hey, are you alright?" Melinda looked between her husband and daughter, mouth tight.

Dad inhaled. "I think you need to tell us what's really going on here."

She stood.

Addy moved only her eyes to follow her, losing sight of her face behind the hanging light.

"In the morning. For now, I'll show you to your rooms. You can stay here with me. Jack, do you…"

He cleared his throat, glancing at Addy.

Why should his face make her nervous? Make the butterflies in her stomach leap around? Why was there something wrong?

But, of course, nothing was right.

"The couch is fine, Mellie."

She unclipped a radio and spoke into it, asking someone to bring fresh clothes, sheets, toothbrushes, everything. Once she was done, she stuck it in her belt and crossed her arms. "They'll get you settled in. I have some things to look after."

Without another word, she turned on a heel and clacked out of the room.

***

After changing into fresh pajamas, Addy wandered down the hall and found an open door.

"Mike?"

"In here."

Cupping her elbows, she tiptoed into the room.

He sat up in bed, feet under the covers, staring at a book. "Whatcha readin'?"

Flipping the book closed, he looked at the cover. "I have no idea. I can't see straight." He set it on the nightstand and pulled his feet up.

Addy sat where they'd been. Twisting her fingers, she took in the plain white walls. "Mike," she said, glancing at him sideways, "this is weird, right?"

"Weird, how?"

"How? Like, everything. Everything is weird. I mean, it's…" Weird compared to what? She shook her head. "I don't know. I don't have a frame of reference, as Dean would say."

"Hey, what's up with you two, anyway? You like him, right?"

She drew her toes back with such force they cramped. "That's— I don't want to talk about that." Spinning, she pulled a knee up onto the bed. "I want to talk about Mom."

"What do you want me to say, Addy? Yes, it's weird. But Adelaide," he said, slapping her knee, "we live in a world where zombies are real. Honestly, this probably isn't the weirdest thing that could happen."

"My god, Michael," she said, standing to pace, "you could be in the middle of a hurricane and be all like, 'Kinda breezy out today, ain't it?'"

He laughed. Pulled a piece of candy from the nightstand. Offered it to her.

Shaking her head, she sat again and watched as he unwrapped and ate the chocolate.

He spoke around a mouthful. "We might as well be happy about this. I mean"—he swallowed—"what the hell else are we supposed to do?"

"Do you think Dad's OK?"

He shook his head. "No. I do not."

Nodding, she chewed a nail. "Why did he decide to sleep on the couch? I would've thought he'd be over the moon at this point. And why is this place here? Where did Jane go? What the hell is Tim all about?"

"Miss Million Questions, I do not know." Throwing an arm behind his head, he scooted down in the bed till his arm rested on the headboard. "Start small, maybe we can answer them together."

"Do you think Mom and Dad will get back together?"

"Sure," he said, shrugging, "why not?"

"It's been a long time. I don't know. He's not the same. She's not the same, you know?"

He shrugged again. "I guess."

Anger flared in her forehead, and her right temple pounded. "You guess. God, you're a help."

He laughed. "I try."

"Where did Jane go? Do you think she's OK?"

Sobering, he shook his head. "No, I don't think she's OK. You said it yourself. She just lost her parents. Again. And here we are, one big happy family." He frowned. "And I mean, who knows what happened to them on the way out here. We still haven't asked Dad about it. The thing with Elizabeth, that could just be the tip of the iceberg."

Chewing the nail into sharp edges, she considered. If her own emotions had been put through the wringer, what about the emotional whiplash Dad must be feeling?

And there was still the horde out there to answer for.

"I don't like any of this, Mike."

"What's there to like? Besides Mom, there's literally nothing good about this. And that's coming from me."

Ah, there was that self-awareness. Sometimes he had it.

She leaned toward him. "Listen, don't tell Mike I said this, but sometimes he's a pretty cool brother."

He made a zipping motion over his mouth. "My lips are sealed."

Smiling again, she stood. "We gotta find Jane tomorrow. I don't know what's on the rest of this island, but I don't like her out there alone."

"Me neither, Addy. We'll find her. She's family."

***

Jerking awake, every muscle constricted, Jack fell to the floor.

Convinced he'd never sleep, the sound of the ocean through the open window behind him had lulled him like the soothing voice of a mother singing.

Now he sat, feet tangled in a blanket, ass on the cold wooden floor, shoulder shrieking from the fall.

He untangled his feet and stood, legs stiff. He wobbled out the front door and onto the porch.

He'd forgotten about her thing with wind chimes.

When Michael was born, they were nothing but kids. Just barely eighteen. Scared out of his mind but determined to help this little baby grow into a man, he'd put his best foot forward and had gotten a job and an apartment. Not that it mattered now, but he'd even graduated high school by finishing his senior year online.

God what a couple idiots they were.

But they were idiots who were in love. It was a happy little apartment, and she'd had three or four old and busted wind chimes she hung on their postage-stamp balcony for the warm summer nights. For her birthday, he'd bought her a sun-and-planets one like the one now at the end of her porch.

Not near as nice. But it chimed and it shone, and she thought it was better than diamonds.

They'd had three full summers in that apartment, a wind chime for every one. In Mike's fourth summer, the dead had come.

The apartment complex was a bloody, confusing, screaming death trap. Not many memories remained from that time—they'd been lost to so many more since then—but one stuck out.

"Just let me get my wind chime," Mellie'd said.

"We have to go now, or we never will," he told her, Mike in his arms.

She snatched up the one small suitcase she'd packed, and they left. They'd never seen the apartment or that wind chime again.

But here, she'd found another one. It was far nicer, and he'd be willing to bet it had been in some fancy store that no longer required legal tender in order to take home its treasures. Just a crowbar, if that, and desire.

Silver light from the full moon glinted through the sun. More than halfway through its night of pregnant splendor, it rested about forty-five degrees from the horizon. Dawn would come soon.

Hand tinkling the chime, he leaned off the porch to sniff the ocean; clear his head.

A shadow moved on the dune.

Melinda spoke from behind him.

"Jackson."

He jumped, knocking the wind chime into a noisy spin. It hit sour notes and tangled. "Oh, shit, Mellie. Your chime. Here," he said, reaching into the confused mess of string, "let me untangle it."

She put a hand over his. "Don't worry about it. We'll fix it in the daylight."

His heart racing, he lowered a shaking hand. "What's up? Are you alright?"

"I am. I really am," she said, smiling. "For years, I'd hoped, prayed, begged for you to be found." She took his hand and whispered. "And here you are."

Without warning, she kissed him.

Her lips, warm, comfortable, the same after all these years, were a black hole that threatened to suck him down into a place where even light couldn't escape.

The same after all these years. Of dreams and wishes and sad, desperate pleas.

All he could do was kiss her back, his Mellie.

The chime hit another sour note.

Gripping her shoulders with kind but firm hands, he pushed her back. "Melinda," he started.

"It's a lot," she said, crossing her arms. "I know, I know. I'm sorry. It is a lot. I just, well, I had to."

He dropped both hands, letting them hang by his side. "It's— I spent all these years letting you go. I can't just pick up like it never happened. I need some time. OK?"

Nodding, she retreated into the house in silence.

Glancing back at the dune, the shadow he'd seen had changed. It was just a bush or tree. That was all.

He untangled the wind chime and sat on the rocking bench until morning.

CHAPTER 27

Balancing a donut fresh out of the frying pan on top of a steaming cup of coffee, Addy opened the front door.

Her dad sat on the rocker, staring into the distance. It'd been a while since she'd seen such a thousand-mile stare.

"Morning, Dad," she said, door flapping closed behind her.

Inhaling through his nose, he patted the seat next to him. "Morning, little girl. Good night?"

"Sure, sure. Slept like a baby."

"Woke up every two hours and cried?"

"Basically."

He chuckled, taking the half donut she offered. "Baby girl. Things have changed."

She nodded, staring into the distance with him and sipping the coffee. Bitter, black, could stand a spoon up in it. The best kind. "What happened to you? On the way here?"

He rocked the bench. "Why do you ask?"

"Because Elizabeth couldn't tell me about it."

Sitting up fast enough to almost make her spill her coffee, he stared at her with his mouth open.

"Celia. She was behind us. She got to her, cured her, and now she's just across the sound. Recovering."

"I can't believe it," he said, sitting back again. He drew breath like words were going to follow. But they didn't.

"She doesn't remember being bitten, just like Mom said. She doesn't remember being cured, either. Just the stuff…in-between. I'm sorry about Gerald."

"Adelaide," he said, shaking his head and glancing at her from the side of his eye, "it was a long trip."

That grimace told her all she needed to know. Elizabeth was only the half of it. "Tell me."

Again, he drew breath like words were about to follow. Again, he closed his mouth around them.

Unease sneaked up her spine and into the base of her neck. Indecisive wasn't his M.O. "Is there something wrong?"

He stared into the distance. "Need to go over there again. There are answers over there. I'm sure of it," he said, nodding at the red roof across the road.

The unease circled her brain stem and pooled behind her eyes. "Dad?" Shaky, her voice sounded as uncertain as he looked.

"Yeah, baby girl?"

"Is Mom OK?"

Gazing at her in considering silence, he narrowed his eyes. "What do you mean?"

"I don't know. She seems different. Not like she used to be."

"I think the more important question," he said, lifting her chin, "is are you OK?"

And for no reason at all, her eyes prickled. Considering a lie, she opened her mouth. "No."

Well, so much for lying.

He nodded, wrapping an arm around her. "Me neither, honey. Me neither."

He rocked her, the ocean crashing just the other side of the dune.

He might not be OK. She might not be OK. But just like always, they had each other. Her dad had always been able to wrap her in a warm cocoon of safe, strong comfort. He could always fix anything that was wrong.

***

The front door slammed again. Jack jumped, releasing his little girl.

Such a brave girl. She'd always been so much stronger than she pretended to be.

Not unlike the woman now standing on the porch with them.

"Hey, Mellie, what's on the docket for the day?" He stood, helping his daughter up, and stared at the woman who'd been his wife.

Seemed like another lifetime ago.

Frowning, she glanced across the road. "Jackson, Adelaide, I think it's time to take you and Michael to the hospital. Explanations are in order."

Mike banged out onto the porch. The boy was the least equipped to deal with any of this. The most tender-hearted, trusting, and kind soul he'd probably ever met.

Shielding him from what was about to happen was all at once more important than finding out answers. "Michael," he said, "why don't you stay here?"

Mike grinned. "No way. You be, I be."

Jack nodded. Couldn't fault him for trying. "Melinda, lead the way."

She stepped into the sun and led them across the road.

Jack fell in next to her. "That's the hospital, isn't it?"

Silent, she nodded.

"What are we going to see there?"

She stopped. "The truth," she said, eyes still on the building.

They crossed the sun-warmed field before the hospital. As they stepped into the building, the humid heat fell from his shoulders. The crown of his head began to cool.

Even so, his heart rate bumped up a notch. Lifting his eyes to the ceiling, he recalled Andrew lying in a bed, arms like pincushions, half turned.

"What do you do here?" Pitching his voice low, he whispered like it was a library. The large entryway seemed to demand it.

Melinda rounded the front desk and pointed them to a hallway on the right. "There are about two to three thousand people on this island, besides the prison. We look after all of them here at this hospital. Especially," she said, swiping a card to open the double doors before them, "the breeding population."

The cries of babies wafted down the hallway like an ethereal blanket.

When was the last time he'd heard a baby cry? It'd been a while, but it seemed people had finally begun to really get down to doing what Jane had spoken of on the way here.

Which was procreate.

"Sounds like music," Mike whispered.

"Mmm," Melinda agreed. "The sound of babies is definitely something I missed."

Addy stepped into the ward. "How many do you have here?"

"Oh, probably about thirty right now."

"Thirty?"

"Our re-population plan and efforts here on the island are quite robust."

So clinical about it. Did she think of them as humans or numbers?

Mike grabbed her arm. "Can we see one?"

Smiling at him, a woman indulging the wishes of a small child, she took his hand. "Sure. Let's go speak to the charge nurse. She'll direct us to a suitable room."

They walked ahead.

"Addy," Jack whispered.

Stopping, she glanced at her mom and brother's backs. "What's up?"

"I— Well— Keep your eyes open."

"Yeah, sure thing, Dad. I don't think a bunch of newborn babies are going to hurt us."

One corner of his mouth turned up. "That's what you think."

You don't know their real power, kiddo.

Catching back up with Melinda and Michael, they followed them into a room.

Tim jumped up from a rocking chair in the corner, throwing down a book. Nietzsche.

"General, what a pleasure. Addy, Jack, Mike," he said, nodding to each in turn after tipping his imaginary cap to Melinda.

Addy's face went cherry red. Inhaling, she opened her mouth wide.

Jack pulled on her shirt cuff with two fingers. "Adelaide."

Brow drawn into a V, she followed his other hand, where he'd pointed at the baby sleeping in a rolling crib.

Her face melted.

Jack turned to the baby, the mother resting on the bed, the father stepping from foot to foot on the other side of them.

Melinda introduced everyone, but all Jack heard was a rushing in his ears.

Look at that teeny tiny little human.

Soft, tiny eyelashes. Flat spot in its little, oval head. Microscopic nose. Rosebud lips.

It was a goddamned miracle. A living, breathing, tiny, helpless miracle.

"Do you want to hold her?" The mother stared up at him, tired eyes expectant.

Unable to do otherwise, he nodded.

The father lifted the sleeping bundle, placing her awkwardly in Jack's arms.

He readjusted her, hand under her head, and stared into her tiny face.

And by god, if Jane hadn't been right. There was no way to deny it. He wanted another one of his own.

Before that feeling swept through him, before it had time to dig its claws in, he handed the baby off to Adelaide.

As she cooed at the baby, probably the first one she'd ever held, and doing it like a pro, a surge of pride washed through him. He'd never, ever considered her as a mother. She was his little girl.

Maybe she was growing up after all.

A shadow fell across the baby's face.

Jack and Adelaide both looked up.

Tim blocked the light. "Beautiful, isn't she?"

Lips a fine white line, Addy handed the baby to Mike. "Dad, get him out of here."

"Adelaide," Melinda said, stepping around Mike, "I think you've gotten the wrong impression of Timothy."

Jack's stomach turned. She spoke of babies like numbers. She backed a person like Tim.

This woman was a stranger.

***

Heat flared in Addy's nostrils. "No, Mom. I don't think I have."

Tim smiled, taking the baby from Mike. "Coochy coochy coo," he said, twisting the cutesy baby talk into some sort of grotesque joke. Glancing from Addy to her dad, a lupine grin crossed his mouth. "What do you guys say we talk about this?"

The implied threat enough to make Addy dry heave, she itched to grab a weapon and separate Tim's head from the rest of him.

Without waiting for the others, she stalked into the hall atop stilts.

At this point, questionable motives or no, if Dean were here, she'd ask him to punch Tim in the mouth. Repeatedly. Until all his teeth were knocked out. Seeing as he wasn't, she'd just have to do it herself.

Better than letting him speak. Better than standing here, letting him threaten babies. Better than breathing the same air.

Tim exited the room behind her parents and before Mike. Sandwiched between three of the four people in the world she'd never, ever hurt.

Even so, she balled a fist and stepped in front of him.

Her mom put a hand between them and lowered her voice. "Let's get out of the ward before you kill him. We'd hate to traumatize the neonates." Her other hand pointed the way out.

Narrowing her eyes, Addy glanced at them both. Her mom, ever the diplomat, the corners of her mouth turned just south. Tim, a dancing, grinning jester.

Careful not to stomp and scare the babies, she left the ward.

Stepping into the entryway again, she crossed her arms and tossed a hair out of her face with a jerk of her chin. Her family, followed by Tim, filed out of the ward.

"Addy, honey," Mom said, laying a hand on her crossed arms, "Tim has done more for us than you know. He's the one who engineered getting you all here. He's worked a miracle."

Dad stepped into Tim's space. "Oh, I know," he said, voice gravelly. "He's done something, alright."

Releasing Addy, Mom stepped up next to Dad, pressing into his side. "Jackson, baby, don't."

He recoiled like he'd been scorched by a hot burner. "Melinda, you don't call me that. You don't get to call me that. If you put him up to what he's done to us, you're just as guilty as he is. I don't know who you are anymore, but you're not the woman I married."

If Addy hadn't been staring at her mother, she wouldn't have seen her chin tremble. It was there and gone so fast it could have been moving at light speed.

Her heart broke, just a little, for them both.

"It's complicated," Mom said, reaching for him again.

And again he stepped away, curling his hands into fists and folding his arms. He opened his mouth.

Mike stepped up next to Addy, laying a hand on her shoulder. "Mom, Dad. Stop."

They glared at him.

He squeezed Addy's shoulder. "Mom, explain it to us. But make it fast."

Nodding, she extended a hand to the hallway on the left. "I'd like to show you our other important work. Besides breeding. Perhaps more important."

They filed across the echoing room. Mom swiped her card again and the doors opened.

Addy's pupils contracted in the light spilling out of the room before them.

Most of the wing was open, but there were several compartments set apart. Everything white, sterile, shining.

Stepping into a glass vestibule, the double doors whooshed closed behind them. The sound of rushing air followed.

"Clean room," Mom said. She pointed to the wall behind them. "Please put on the suits."

Addy picked out a white suit and hood from the ones hanging in a small closet. She pulled it on over her clothes and helped Mike zip up.

Tim grinned. "Give me a hand, Addy?"

As uncomfortable as it made her to be this close to Tim, it'd be foolish to believe her curiosity wasn't piqued. Still. "Tim, if I weren't wearing this plastic hood, I'd throw up in your face."

He pulled a frown. "Please, baby."

"No."

Laughing, he yanked the suit on, and Mom zipped the back.

Dad stood, arms crossed, watching them all. "Melinda, what are we doing here?"

"Jackson, please put on a suit. I'll explain everything. But it's best if you can follow me."

Shaking his head, he picked out a suit. Held it up to himself and checked the length of the legs. Scowling, he slipped it on and fooled with it until he got it zipped without help.

Fascinated by his determination, Addy imagined she could be as fearless as he was. As he'd always been. Squaring her shoulders, she faced the glass doors as they slid open.

Mom led them into the room, voice muffled by the plastic between her mouth and their ears. "This is our number one test facility." She pointed to the first compartment. "Here we have a test subject. This is one who has been turned with no hope of regeneration."

Rounding the observation window, Addy gasped, stomach leaping into her throat.

Gerald, bound at the hands and feet against the back wall, growled and bit in their direction. Once icy blue eyes now cloudy and grey, a chunk missing from his neck, fingers withered and blackened.

Dad stood, eyes narrow, mouth set, hands balled into fists. Silent.

Watching him, Mom continued, "Fresh subjects are best for this part of the process. There's a lot of scientific jargon I'll skip. Suffice it to say, your friend has helped our research and his contributions will not go unnoticed."

He remained silent.

Like a strong, stone wall, her dad was.

But she? It felt like someone had punched her in the throat. Her vision doubled, and she blinked tears.

Reaching up to wipe them, she hit the mask instead.

Impotent, she balled her own fist and lowered her hands to her sides.

Mom led them to the next compartment, where men in white suits like theirs worked over microscopes and benches, vials of blood and other substances in racks before them.

"This is our sample lab," Melinda said, pointing through the glass. "Here, all the samples taken are tested for a variety of things. Virulence of the strain, effectiveness of the Cure on it, those sort of things."

Addy swallowed. The horde outside. Gerald inside. "Where do you get these samples, Mom?"

"I think you know the answer to that question, jellybean."

"Don't call me that."

Mom stepped back like she'd been slapped, eyes wide. Clearing her throat, she motioned them to the next window.

"Here, we have a group of test subjects. Each, a virgin canvas, if you will. People who have never been bitten."

Addy fully expected to see babies, lined up in a row. Wires sticking out from everywhere.

So convinced was she of the horrific picture, her brain couldn't make sense of what she saw before her until her dad let out an inarticulate shout.

Michael gasped.

Addy's reeling mind fought itself to make sense of what was in front of her. Her sight cleared, mental pictures vanishing like fog.

Six people in paper gowns, strapped to chairs. And on the end, a woman with half her long red hair shaved. Electrodes taped to the newly exposed skin.

Dad took two large steps to the door and jerked the handle. The door remained closed. He slapped it, trying the handle again.

"It won't open without an access card," Mom said.

He stepped toward her, tears standing in his eyes. "Open the fucking door, Melinda." Spit flew, splattering the inside of the plastic face mask.

Tim stepped between them, jester's smile stretching his mouth from ear to ear. "Don't touch her, Jackson. You step back or I'll throw you back in that cell to rot."

"Timothy," Mom said, laying a calm hand on his shoulder. "What have I told you about threats?"

He lowered his head, turning half his face to her. "Don't make them unless you can follow through. Yes, ma'am. But I won't let him hurt you."

"I know, and I appreciate that. But you don't need to worry." She patted his shoulder like a dog.

"Don't be so sure," Dad growled. "Open the god damn door."

"Jack, *baby*, I don't think you understand how important it is what we're doing here."

He glared, eyes skipping to Jane and back. "I don't give a fuck, Melinda. I really do not. Let her go."

Turning to the horrific picture again, Addy watched Jane's eyes roll under her lids. Her body jerked.

"Mom," she said, taking a step toward the window, "you have to let her go. Please. What are you doing to her?"

"Nothing, yet. She's simply sedated. But tomorrow we begin new testing. Maybe final testing."

"On a new Cure?" Addy asked, holding a hand up to the slick glass. It dented the gloves covering her fingers, pushing her back.

"No, Adelaide. Better than that."

Addy faced her.

Her mom smiled.

"On a vaccine."

***

Once the glass doors opened again, Adelaide ripped the hood off and charged through the double doors, but Jack remained behind. Taking deep breaths, he removed the hood and unzipped the suit with measured care.

If he didn't stay calm and breathe, he'd smash everything in sight. Break the window with his fists and pull her out of there. Shatter Tim's grinning face into pieces and leave him crying on the ground.

Leave his wife behind again. And, stranger or no, was that the right thing to do? Was it?

So he inhaled and exhaled, lungs working like a bellows, but calming the fire rushing through his gut rather than stoking it.

Melinda pulled off her hood as Michael fought his zipper. "Jackson, please, let me explain," she said, reaching for Mike's zipper.

Mike slapped her hand away.

His vehement disgust soothed Jack's troubled mind. If even Michael reacted with such anger, he must be on the right track. Greater good be damned, it was wrong to treat people like lab rats.

"We can rid the world of this illness," Melinda said, helping Tim with his suit. "Save the world from this disease. But you can't make an omelet without breaking some eggs."

Red filled every corner of Jack's vision. He rounded, taking one large step and staring directly into her face, nose to nose. "She is not an egg. She's my…she's…"

"She's family," Mike said, voice shaking. "We won't let you do this to her."

Backpedaling, eyes wide, Melinda bounced off the glass doors. She panted, cheeks flushed. "You don't understand. We're giving her the vaccine. When it works, she'll never turn. She'll never have to go through what I did. What your friend did.

Never know the pain of ripping someone's throat out with her teeth. Of killing someone she loves," she said, staring at Jack.

Blood rushed to his cheeks, forehead tight. Did she know?

He deflated. Wrinkled his brow. "Do I have your word the vaccine works?"

She looked at her feet.

All the answer he needed, he exhaled and stared through the glass.

"Mom?"

Without another word, Melinda brushed through them and out into the hall. Tim followed, eyes on her back.

Jack stepped to the glass doors, pressing his face and both hands into it. Cool and slick under his fingers, it felt thin enough to break. He knocked his forehead into it. Hard enough to feel the pain of it. Aiming for focus. A distraction from emotion.

What am I supposed to do?

His inner voice had no wisdom to offer.

"Dad?"

"Yeah, Mike." His breath fogged the window.

"What are we going to do?"

He sighed. "We're going to fix this."

"How? Which? I mean, a vaccine sounds like a good thing."

Jack closed his eyes. "I know, son. But there's a right way to go about it. And your mother, this company she works for, they're not. They don't have morals. Don't you see?" Opening his eyes, Jack faced his son. "That horde out there," he pointed in the vague direction of the doors, "that's their doing. They'll turn Jane; and all these people, into Dead Heads trying to find this vaccine."

"We can't let them do that. Not Jane."

His stomach flipped. No, not her.

"Let's find your sister. We need a plan."

***

"Adelaide!"

She stopped, halfway across the road, panting. Leaning over and resting her hands on her knees, she breathed deep as her mom caught up with her. The stars in front of her eyes faded.

"Addy, please," Mom said, feet crunching in the sand on the road.

A seagull cried, out there somewhere, drifting on the currents the ocean made from air.

Standing, sweating inside the plastic suit, she faced her mother. "Mom. I don't think it's right, what you're doing to Jane."

"I get that now, honey. I thought you'd be happy. I'm sorry."

"Happy? How could I be happy about this? Did Jane volunteer?"

"Not…exactly."

Addy growled. "You have to let her go. Don't do this."

Melinda reached for her shoulder.

The hand moved in slow motion. She had time to consider pulling back, running away, never looking back.

But who even was she anymore? Everything she'd been, all she'd built herself up to be, was a lie.

Mom gripped her shoulder. "It'll be alright, baby girl. It'll be alright, I promise. Look at me, here with you. They, the people running this crazy circus, they made it possible. I won't let them take your friend from you."

"Mom. Please," Addy said, taking Mom's hand and squeezing.

Mom squeezed back. "She seems to mean a lot to all of you. I really had no idea. Tim, he's an excellent intelligence officer, but he didn't tell me."

"Intelli— Mom. No."

Melinda shook her head. "What?"

"He's a snake. He's worse than a snake. He's repulsive."

To think she'd believed him over Dean. God, what an idiot.

Melinda's cheeks flushed. "He's shown me nothing but loyalty and kindness, Adelaide."

Sweat bunched around the collar of the suit, heat baking up into her face.

Her knees buckled.

Mom caught her, steadying her as they crossed the road. With gentle care, she sat her down in the shade of a tree.

Unzipping the suit, Addy pulled the sleeves off. The ocean blew gentle wisps of air over her sweaty skin. Her flushed face cooled.

"He's playing you, Mom. He's the worst kind of liar."

Melinda shook her head. "That's unimportant right now. What is important is you guys. I need you all to stay with me, now that you're here. You have to believe me," she paused, staring at the hospital. "We're trying to save the world here."

"Mom," Addy said, voice soft.

Dragging her eyes from the building, she made eye contact. Lifted a brow.

"At what cost? All those babies? Is that why you have people living here? Is that why you have prisoners? To be your guinea pigs? Explain it to me. Because—" She stopped, swallowing.

Melinda frowned. "Because?"

"Because right now, it doesn't look like you're on the right side of this."

"That's your father speaking."

Addy stood. "No. It's me. It's everything you taught me. Peace, hope, doing the right thing. For the right reasons."

Squinting, Mom smiled. "Hey, baby girl, wanna watch some Trek?"

Hell yes.

"No. No, Mom. You can't smooth this over with Star Trek and peanut butter like I'm twelve."

Melinda stood. "Let me know when you change your mind." Putting her back to Addy, she crossed to the hospital.

Eyes hot, Addy slunk into the house to get the rest of the way out of the sweaty suit.

CHAPTER 28

Turning every lock on the bedroom door, Addy stripped the plastic suit off. She balled it as small as it would go and threw it into a dark corner. Peeling off her sweaty clothes, she rooted through the dresser until she found a pair of pajama pants and a cropped shirt. She slipped them on.

A shower would be heaven.

She sat on the bed and stared out the window, eyeing the hospital.

Holding that baby, that had been something. She'd seen one or two but never held one, had no idea how it would feel.

And she'd really never considered the truth of thinking about them. Yeah, Jane talked about procreating. About finding the right person to repopulate with. But, real as that was for Jane, it was nothing but a daydream for Addy.

Consider having a baby? Wouldn't you have to have sex before you could do that?

Ugh.

She lay back on the bed, arm across her eyes.

Her mom had told the story of how she and Dad met so many times, Addy'd had it memorized by the time she was ten. What must it have been like, to live in a world where people just went to bowling alleys and hung out by the jukebox until cute boys came in?

To not have to worry about where the next meal was coming from. Not have to worry about where they were going to sleep. About getting eaten on a daily basis. Not have to learn to use a machete by the time they were four.

Knock.

Pause.

Knock knock.

Oh, excellent. Michael. Someone she actually did want to see.

Smiling, she peeled her sweaty back from the bed and stumbled to the door. Had she fallen asleep?

The door was already open too far when she found not Mike, but Tim on the other side.

He pushed his way in, closing and locking the door behind him. "Addy," he said, looming.

She backed up a step. Frowned. "Out."

"Please, let me explain," he said, taking a step toward her.

She backed up to match it.

He stepped toward her again, and again, she backed up. He continued until the bed hit her in the back of the legs. She fell onto it.

He sat next to her, hands folded between his knees, chin lowered almost to his collar bone.

"Out," she said, tensing to stand.

He put a hand on her knee. "Please, wait." Small, quiet. Like a frightened child.

Not falling for it, she told him again to get out.

Peeking at her from the corner of his eye, he frowned. A tear fell.

What?

"Listen, I have to tell someone, OK? I work for IRF."

"You. What?"

He nodded, looking up. Kept his hand on her knee. "I work for Iridium Flare. And I work for your mom's company, Talus Crest."

"That's what they're called?"

Nodding again, he smiled. "If you thought IRF was bad, you should check out Talus. There's a reason she didn't tell you their name. Wouldn't take long," he said, moving his hand up her thigh an inch, "to find out some really bad shit about them."

Her stomach curled. "I've never heard of them. Take your hand off me."

He did. Then smiled.

It was the most genuine smile she'd ever seen out of him. Even more so than that date all that time ago.

Could that have only been a month ago? Her head swam. "Tell me about them."

"I can't tell you much. I got as close to the general as I could, trying to get information. She's pretty tight-lipped."

"What can you tell me, then?"

"First, look, I didn't mean for Jane to end up in that room. I tracked her down last night after your mom called me in the middle of the night to find her. I don't know what happened after I dropped her off."

A pit formed in her stomach. Had her mom really requested Jane become a test subject?

"I mean, it'll probably be good for Jane, in the end. This vaccine trial is incredibly promising."

And the pit in her stomach became a rock, dragging it down to her toes. "What do you mean promising? Do you mean they don't know if it works?"

"Look, there's a lot we don't know. But what I do know is IRF and Talus are at odds. They want the same thing, but they're fighting over it. Trying to be the ones to release the vaccine first. If money becomes a thing again, and these people are convinced it will, they both want to be the one to have it."

"Money?" The word sounded foreign in her mouth. She'd never, ever used such a thing. Hardly even seen it. It seemed a ridiculous concept to have to give paper and coin to get things when you could just get them yourself. Or someone would help you in exchange for help getting what they needed.

But Tim was nodding, hair falling in his face. "I know, sounds ridiculous, yeah? But there it is. Money and power. The two things that once ran the world will once again."

The power thing sounded reasonable. "Why are you telling me this?"

Hanging his head, he spoke just above a whisper. "Talus sent me to Harkers Island to spy on Dean. Who IRF sent here to spy on Talus. But IRF also asked me to go there to spy on Dean, and on you, and find out how much you knew. How much he knew. And Talus asked me to spy on someone, but at this point, I don't even know what's going on anymore."

She stared, mouth open. She could hardly keep up with that sentence, much less who he was supposed to be spying on for what purpose.

Another tear fell from the corner of his eye. "And then there was the Task Force, and your dad, the general wanted me to get you all here, so I had to do all these things in the village. I had to turn that schoolteacher. And the deputy mayor. So your dad would be distracted. So we could catch him off guard."

"What do you—" She stopped, shoving a nail in her mouth. She spoke around her finger. "Did she really tell you to kill those people? Whose plan was that?"

"Does it matter? I don't even know what's going on anymore, Adelaide. It's driving me mad." He leaned over, lying his head on her shoulder and wrapping an arm around her waist.

She recoiled, bumping into the headboard. "Get off me, Tim."

Tears wetting her shirt, he shook his head. "I'm so confused, Adelaide. Your mom asked me for so much, and then IRF kept calling me to tell me where you were, and I sent those Dead Heads to the lighthouse—crashed a boat-full right into the beach—because I thought maybe they'd take care of Dean and I wouldn't have to worry about that anymore."

Her breath stopped. She ripped the nail down to the quick. It began to bleed. "You did what?" She tried to push him off, but his encircling arm tightened.

He lifted his face. Smiled. The old wolfish smile she'd come to hate.

"The night I killed Jane's parents, you know I chased her mom out into the street? Fuckin' had to strangle her right there in the bushes on the side of the house. Almost ran smack into you and Jane when I came back to check up on her dad. You looked so good in the starlight, though. I could hardly breathe."

Cold bloomed in her lungs, spreading to her fingers and toes. Her mind stuck, like those old CDs her mom used to play for them. "Jane's…Jane's parents? What are you saying? What did you do?"

He looked her over. "She said I could have you, you know. We need more babies."

All the wind left her gut. "She…you…what? Tim, get off me," she said, pushing his shoulder. When he tightened his grip again, an iron band around her waist, she put a palm in his face and pushed.

Smacking her with a shoulder, he ran her into the headboard.

Stars lit up her head. He flipped her so quickly it took her a moment to understand she now looked at the ceiling.

"What are you doing?" The high, desperate note in her voice wasn't familiar. She pushed at his shoulders.

He hooked a finger around the elastic waistband of her pants and shoved them down. They bound up at her knees.

"You know you want babies. I saw you holding that little bundle of joy." Clenching both of her wrists in one hand, he reached down with the other. His zipper rasped.

"Stop it! Let me go!" Whose voice was that?

He grinned, licking the side of her face again. "Mmm. Salty."

"Tim, look, we can, just, we can talk about this, OK?" she babbled. Twisted her wrists. The bones grated against each other, skin burning.

The screen door downstairs banged.

She sucked in a breath. "Mo—"

A soft, clammy hand slapped over her mouth and nose. "Ssshhh," he whispered. "I want to see if the honey is as sweet as the pot."

Struggling to suck a breath in her nose, she couldn't get air. Her head swam from the knock it'd taken on the headboard. His hand smelled like the inside of those suits. Like the antiseptic hospital lab. Like the torture they had inflicted on Jane.

Unable to breathe, her arms began to fall limp.

Releasing her mouth, he stuck a finger between her underwear and the skin of her hips.

The touch, light though it was, focused her thoughts like a laser.

Bucking with her hips, she ripped her wrists free and aimed a slicing punch at his Adam's apple. Connected.

He choked, grabbing at his throat.

Slipping a foot around his ankle, she bucked with her hips again. They both spilled to the floor. The breath woofed out of Tim as she landed on top of him.

His eyes focused on her and narrowed.

Rearing back, she aimed the top of her forehead at his nose. As the head-butt connected, his nose crunched. He grunted.

Aiming for the jaw, she punched him in the mouth with the heel of her hand. A tooth cut her palm, opening a burning, stinging gash.

He tried to clasp his ankles together and trap her.

She reared back with a knee and connected with his upper thigh, just beside the crotch. Missing the mark because her knees were still partially bound up in the pants.

Still, it was a good hit. He groaned, the muscles in his abs and legs clenching.

She rolled off and stood, fighting not to trip over her pants.

The door burst open behind her, splintering the frame. Pieces of wood pelted her shoulders and back.

Mom stood in the door, fists raised. Wide eyes took in the scene.

Tim in the floor next to the bed, nose swelling. Lip bleeding. Pants unzipped.

Addy standing, hair a wreck, hand bleeding. Pants around her ankles. Tears streaking her cheeks.

Melinda glared at the boy. "Get out, and never come back."

He stood, leaning on the bed, holding his pants up with one hand. "General, ma'am," he started.

She stepped closer, one measured step at a time, a hand falling to her sidearm. "If you aren't out of my sight in point five seconds, I will unload this clip in your chest. Allow you to turn. Then unload another in your brain."

He scurried past her, zipping his pants.

She kicked him as he passed, and he yipped like a struck puppy.

"Get off my island, Timothy. If I ever catch you here again, if I ever see your face," she said, drawing her gun, "I will not hesitate."

***

"I'll kill the son of a bitch!" Jack paced the living room, fists balled, head pounding.

Melinda flinched when he punched the wall. "He's gone, Jackson. He won't be coming back."

"I'll fucking kill him," Jack said again, rounding. He couldn't catch a full breath. Each one went shallow, charging back out through his nose as soon as he'd pulled it in.

"Dad," Addy said, crossing to him, "take a breath. I'm OK."

He looked her face over. Smoothed her hair and pulled her into a hug.

Eleven years of single parenthood had been tough. Each challenge greater than the last. But as much as he'd wanted to give up, he hadn't, and as he held his daughter close, he brimmed with pride. She could handle herself in so many ways. And so could Mike, both stronger and kinder than he himself was.

Perfect children, both of them. Everything he'd hoped for. More.

"Jackson," Melinda said, sitting down next to Mike.

Michael flinched.

"Melinda," Jack said, releasing Addy, "I need to speak with my children."

"Alright."

"Alone."

She closed her eyes and inhaled, lips tight. She left through the front door without a word.

Jack stepped to the window and watched her cross the road. Still just as perfectly hourglass as ever, he admired her shape without emotion. All the kindness, compassion, and empathy that'd been such a part of her in the past was just that: the past.

"Kids," he said, turning. They sat together on the couch, Mike patting his sister's back. Jack lowered into the chair next to them and leaned onto his knees. "We have to do something about this."

Addy sat up. "We have to get Jane. We've gotta get her, Dad."

He swallowed around the lump in his throat. "We do. Addy," he said, swallowing again, "there's some things I need to discuss with you. And you, Mike." He glanced at his son, unable to maintain eye contact.

Mike sat forward too, elbows resting on his knees, frowning. "What is it?"

Jack opened his mouth, but no sound came out. How much to tell? They would find out about him and Jane eventually, and sooner was better than later. Throat tight, he opened his mouth again.

"If it's about you and Mom, we know already," Addy said. "I mean," she said, glancing at Mike, "it's weird for all of us. I'm totally lost about it. I mean, I love her, we all do. But she's…"

"She's not Mom," Mike finished.

Jack shook his head. "No, that's not it. It— I—"

"But we can still save her," Mike said, reaching for Jack's hand. "We have to try."

Why couldn't he form a complete thought? Images raced through his head. The truck, Gerald's crimson lips, Jane's eyes, Melinda's reentrance into their lives.

"Michael, I—"

"He's right," Addy said. "We can save her. Get her to shut this place down."

"What if that doesn't work?"

"Well, then, we figure something else out."

Nodding, Jack set on the idea like a dog with a bone. Gnawed on it. Turned it over, eyes shifting back and forth with the thoughts that now raced through, hardly stopping to say hi before speeding on.

"Alright. If she won't help us, we take her key card. Not by force, though." He met each of their eyes. "This has to be a stealth operation."

Addy stood and paced. "We'll get back to Harkers Island after we get Jane, and we can come up with a plan with Scott. He's the leader there. A friend of Celia."

Mike stood, nodding. "Yeah. Yeah. We'll get them all. Right away. Shut this motherfucker down!" He raised a fist in the air.

Jack swallowed, looking up at him. His son never used foul language. Jarring, but effective. He stood with his children.

"Dad," Addy said, spinning, "I have to tell you what Tim said."

The mention of the boy sent his heart into overdrive. His blood pressure spiked, and red dots filled his vision. Clenching and unclenching his fists, he fought to maintain control. Silent, he listened as Adelaide explained IRF and Talus Crest.

And she told him about Dean, what he'd said about IRF, and Tim's double agent game.

"It drove him crazy, Dad. I think he was a good guy at some point. But playing all those sides, it was just too much for him."

Jack shook his head. "I don't care what his excuses are. If I ever see him again, I'll kill him. He tried to…he…"

"I know. But I'm fine."

"And the Dead Heads at the lighthouse. Your bite. Adelaide, you could have died. You could have turned."

"But I didn't. I'm fine. But there are forces at work. We need more. We need Mom. She knows."

He swallowed. His desire to tell them about Jane had passed, the moment lost, but it was still in the future. After they rescued her; after they got free. It'd break Mike's heart, but there was nothing for that.

Addy cleared her throat.

Startled, he looked up and found them staring at him. Lost in thought, they'd waited for him to return from his woolgathering. Here they wanted to rescue their mother and all he could think about was Jane.

Guilt wormed its way into his gut, his face hot.

"You're right. Let's get your mom back. If she won't help us, we'll convince her."

***

Addy waited on the porch until close to nightfall. The salty sea air curled her hair, made it into some kind of bushy creature she'd never met. The bite itched. Her head hurt.

Wishing for the calm Picard brought with him, she closed her eyes and imagined him standing before her.

Instead, she saw her mom, running across that sporting goods store, screaming to distract the Dead Heads.

The person Addy had become, so much of it built on that moment, the moment she lost her mom. That person was a lie. A trick of the mind. Made of paper.

So, then, who was she?

Feet crunched across the sandy drive. "Adelaide," Mom said, approaching. "Did you guys have a good talk?"

"I guess. Can I ask you a question?"

"Sure, honey." She mounted the porch and leaned against the railing.

"Will you come with us?"

"Where?"

Addy stood, taking her mom's hand. "Off this island. Away from all this. Come be a family with us again."

Staring into her eyes, Mom shook her head. "I can't leave what we're doing here. It's too important."

Eyes prickling, Addy dropped Melinda's hand and crossed her arms. She swallowed the tears. There'd be no more of those. After years of crying over her dead mother, she wasn't giving her any more. "We're important, too."

"Oh, Addy," she said, stroking her cheek, "you are. You are, honey. You're why I'm doing this."

Ah dammit. The tears came anyway.

"Mom," she said, voice shaking, "there has to be another way. Come with us, and we'll figure it out together. You know about IRF, right?"

Melinda spit. "They're no better. In fact, they're worse."

"Help us figure that out, then. Come with us."

Mom sighed. "I'd love to. I really would. But I just can't."

"Then let Jane go."

"The trial has already begun."

"What?"

"We moved it forward a little ahead of schedule. Don't worry about your friend, Adelaide. It's perfectly safe."

Addy couldn't feel her lungs, her feet, her hands. They'd gone cold. "How do you know?"

"We've tested this strain already. It's 92% safe. In fact, I'm very hopeful about this strain. With it, one day, we think we can create a synthetic immunity in newborns."

Head spinning, Addy fell onto the bench and stared up at her mother. "Mom. You've been testing on pregnant women?"

"Yes," Melinda said, sitting next to her. "It will take some…trial and error. Some of the fetuses won't survive the process. But the ones that do will be stronger, better humans because of it."

"Won't." Addy couldn't breathe. She huffed out the rest of the sentence. "Won't survive the process? *Babies.* You're talking about babies."

"We'll eradicate this disease within a decade like this, Adelaide. You can't make an omelet—"

Adelaide leapt to her feet. "Babies are not eggs! Oh my god, Mom. I'm gonna be sick." She doubled over, clutching her stomach. "I can't be part of this."

Melinda stood, pulling her into a hug.

She was warm, and soft, and smelled just like she always had.

What was wrong with the universe? How could it throw this at her like this, and then drop her?

Hugging her mom back, she cried more tears than she thought were left in the world.

"Addy, honey," Mom said, pushing her back, "you're not my prisoner. You're free to leave. Just don't try to come back with force."

She met her eyes.

Mom smiled. A brittle, broken thing. "You'll lose."

***

Walking between his children, Jack turned his back on his dead wife.

The front door slammed as they reached the end of the drive. The wind chimes tinkled.

Addy sighed. "Are you sure about this, Dad?"

"She's not coming with us. I'm sure about that."

Nodding, she sprinted down the road and to the head of the path that would lead them to the beach.

Being on opposing sides with the woman who'd once promised to be his partner through thick and thin was more of a blow than he wanted to admit. To them or to himself.

But it was as it was. Jack had to move forward. Despite how it should be.

He caught up to Addy and stopped, taking a long look at the prison.

A guard on the outer rim stopped, facing their direction.

"Come on," Addy said, tugging his hand. "Let's get down to the beach. We'll get the boats."

Allowing his daughter to pull him down to the beach, he trudged through the deepening sand. It tugged and pulled at his feet as they reached the shore, before evening out into smooth, packed ground.

"The boats are this way," Addy said, pointing toward the rising moon. It hung low over the edge of the ocean, orange and looming.

He thought of Jane, silhouetted in its full, silvery pink light. Felt the edges of the hole in his chest, exploring them with tentacles of emotion. It was shaped like her.

"I'm sorry, Mike. Addy. I'm not leaving Jane. I've got to go back," he said, squeezing Addy's hand.

She shook her head. "There's people on Harkers Island. They can help us. We'll come back with reinforcements."

"You and Michael go. I'm staying. I can't leave her."

"Dad," Mike said, laying a warm hand on his shoulder, "you'll get yourself killed."

It'd be worth it if he could save her.

"I have to, you guys." Shaking his head, he glanced back toward the prison.

A glint of light in the inlet caught his eye. Squinting, he pointed. "What is that?"

It moved closer, skimming waves.

"I think it's a boat," Addy said. She stared for a moment, and her breath caught. Eyes wide, she grabbed Jack's hand. "Dad. It's…" She stared into the inlet at the boat speeding for shore. One small flashlight at the stern, the boat slowed as it hit the breakers.

Pulling his arm almost out of its socket, his baby girl dropped his hand and ran down the beach, hair flying out behind her.

CHAPTER 29

Hair streaking behind her, sand flying from her heels, Addy ran down the beach.

The boat's engine cut as it hit the next breaker. As it washed closer, a man jumped from the bow and into the surf. He splashed toward the shore, sand sucking at his feet. "Adelaide!" His voice just louder than the pounding waves.

Butterflies rushed through her as she hit the water. After all the bullshit, double talk, and lies, splashing through the water toward him was the first uncomplicated decision she'd made. It was without thought, it was without anger, it was without doubt.

He caught her as she leapt on him, arms and legs wrapping around him.

She kissed him with everything she had. Teeth clashing against his and bloodying her lip, he mumbled "ow" and stretched his lips into a smile before they melted against hers.

A wave crashed in, hitting him in the knees. He wobbled, and she put her feet down. Holding onto him, she frowned. "What are you doing here, Dean?"

Her stern tone did nothing to dampen his grin. "Coming to rescue you."

"My hero."

He laughed, squeezing her.

Smiling, she watched as another man—the bartender?—dragged the boat ashore. "One measly boat?"

"The rest of them are right behind us. They brought the big boat," Dean said, glancing over her shoulder.

Dad and Michael stood at the waterline, Dad with his hands on his hips.

Chewing her lip, she grabbed Dean's hand and tugged. "Come on, let's get this over with."

Dean cleared his throat and followed her, high-stepping in the surf.

As they reached them, Dad stuck his hand out. "You the cavalry?"

He shook his hand. "I see you're really in need of help," he said, glancing around the empty beach.

"Dad," Addy said, "he says there's a boatful coming."

Dad flashed a fierce grin.

For a man whose life had just turned upside down, his smile came more easily than she'd seen in years. What had happened to him?

"There's a dock just the other side of the island," Dad said, pointing west.

Dean pulled a walkie from his belt. "Alpha team, come in, over."

"*Go for Alpha*," the walkie crackled.

"Is that Scott?" Addy asked.

Bobbing his head, Dean pushed the talk button. "Scott, there's a dock to the west of the inlet. We'll meet you there. What's your ETA? Over."

"*About twenty. Over.*"

Dean glanced at Addy. She nodded.

"We'll have to clear the dock, get the lights on," Dad said.

"I've got the Cookes with me. Meet you there. Over," Dean radioed.

"*Good. Find out about Celia. Over.*"

Dad shook his head. "She's probably in the prison. Your other friends, too."

Dean pushed the talk button. "Last known location is the prison."

"*Acknowledged. Over and out.*"

He handed the walkie to Addy.

Which she held out to her dad.

Pushing it back toward her, he shook his head. "Hold onto that, honey. I think you're a little more clear-headed than I am right now."

Her ego did a jig. Her heart stopped. And her feet moved west. On the way, she caught Dean up.

***

On her elbows in the sand, Addy surveyed the dock. Lit in one or two places, the landing itself was dark. The black sound stretched out behind it.

"Dad," she whispered over Dean's head.

"Should be a control booth at the head of the dock."

"I see five people down there," Dean said, lowering binoculars he'd pulled from the boat. He'd come with a whole bag full of supplies. Weapons, flashlights, you name it.

Addy held out her hand, and he slapped the binoculars down.

Peering through them, she also counted five. One of which walked into a building as she watched. Lowering the binoculars, she pointed. "One of them went into that building. I think that's a good place to check. Dad?"

"Let's round up the guards. We'll get the two on the left, you get the ones on the right. Meet in the middle. Take Dean and— Christian, right?"

"Yes, sir, Mr. Cooke."

"Jack, please. You and Dean go with my little girl."

"Anything you ask, Jack. Celia has a lot of good words to say about you. And I trust her judgment."

Addy flushed. Of course she did. There were a lot of good things to say. "Let's do it then," she said, crawling backward.

They followed, and as she stood brushing the knees of her pants, her brother surprised her with a hug. "Be careful, bean."

"I will. You too."

Dad nodded. "When they make land, first thing we do is split into two groups. One-third for the hospital, two-thirds for the prison. Dean, you said there were how many?"

"Couple hundred."

Addy slapped him on the shoulder with the backs of her fingers. "I thought Scott said they didn't have enough men."

Twisting a toe into the sand, Dean looked at his feet. "Yeah. I recruited people from some other islands."

Her heart fluttered. He must've gone as soon as she had left, gathering people to come get her back. Just in case.

She kissed him on the cheek.

Even in the dim light, his face reddened. "We going?"

They crept through the brush toward the dock, the hospital just across a large field.

Dad snapped his fingers at Mike, pointed, and they disappeared into the dark.

Addy led Dean and Christian across an open tennis court and into the shadow of a nearby, broken-down building. Three walls standing. Holding up a fist to stop them, she pulled an arrow from the quiver Dean had dug out of the boat.

Whispering over her shoulder, she asked where he found it.

"Adelaide, if you wanted me to rope you the moon, I'd get it done."

Grinning into the dark, she nocked an arrow.

The radio crackled.

Fumbling the bow, she managed to hold onto it while turning the walkie's volume down.

Too late. The guard walking by, rifle slung over his shoulder, turned toward the noise.

A stone hit him in the temple, and he fell, rifle clattering.

Mouths open, Addy and Dean eyed Christian.

He stood, slingshot braced on his wrist. Catching their stares, he shrugged. Reloaded from a pouch on his belt.

"Damn, Christian," Dean said. "You got any other tricks in that bag?"

Christian shrugged again. "Couple drinks. Let's go."

They crept from behind the building, Dean pausing by the guard to pick up the gun and check his pulse.

Addy raised a brow.

He nodded. "He's alive."

Footsteps approached.

They crept into the shadow of a building no larger than a well house. Another guard slouched past. One with a shock of red hair and a smattering of freckles.

Louis.

Putting a finger to her lips, Addy waited for him to pass. As he did, she jumped behind him and drew the wood of her bow across his throat. Pressed her lips to his ear. "You make any noise, I'll slice your throat with this bowstring."

Holding his rifle out by the barrel, he nodded.

Christian snatched the rifle and slung it over his shoulder.

"Good, Louis. That's good. Now, take us to the light switch for this dock," she said.

"Adelaide," he said, "I'll take you to Jane."

Shit. Jane.

No. The lights. They had to get the boat landed, or this whole thing was sunk before it began.

She pulled the bow closer. "The lights. Then the girl."

Breathing shallow, he jerked a thumb over his shoulder.

She passed him to Dean.

Catching him by the shoulders, Dean pushed the boy in front of them.

They edged up to the building she'd seen the fifth guard go into. A large picture window made up half of the front wall, lit from inside. The door had a slot for a keycard.

Addy pointed. "Slide your card, Louis."

A shadow detached itself from the sidewall. "I've been waiting for this," Dad said.

Without pause, he snatched Louis from Dean, socked him in the nose with a loud crunch, kicked him in the gut when he fell, and yanked the keycard from his belt.

The boy lay on the ground, crying and holding his nose.

"Dad," Addy said, round eyes staring at her father. While everything he'd done had been controlled, she'd never, ever seen him so close to the edge. His smiles weren't the only thing close to the surface.

Without a word, he edged past her and slid the card.

The door beeped. She and Mike flanked him, weapons drawn.

She felt more than saw Dean behind her.

Pushing the door open, Dad stepped into the small building.

A guard sat with his back to the door and window, checking displays and recording numbers on a clipboard.

"Hey, that you, Louis? Can you check the radar? I think—"

"Not Louis," Addy said.

Spinning, clipboard clattering to the ground, the guard reached for his rifle.

It was three feet away. He never stood a chance.

Dad snatched him by the collar before he even had time to inhale. He stood the guard up and held him on his tiptoes. "Lights."

The boy pointed to a large switchboard in front of the window.

Lowering him a fraction, Dad nodded. "Hit them all, Adelaide."

She eyed the board. There were a million switches. More than she'd ever seen in one place. "Dean?"

He stepped next to her, pointing over her shoulder. "Those look like light switches. Try 'em."

She flipped two large breakers. Air raid sirens wound up and went off.

"Crap. Crap. Crap," she said, flipping them back down. The sirens died with a wheeze.

"Those," Dean said, reaching over her. He flipped the first in a series of six green switches in a row.

One bank of outside lights came on.

She grinned at her dad.

He didn't see it. He stared out the window, squinting. "What is that?"

Following his eyes, she caught movement. Out in the black water of the sound.

With the flat of both hands, she flipped all the switches. Every light on the dock glared to life. The concrete shone. The water bounced light back into Addy's eyes.

She squinted.

A large pontoon boat, probably some kind of vehicle transport in a previous life, floated toward the dock.

At a high rate of speed.

The deck crowded, back to back, with Dead Heads. At least three hundred if it was one.

Dad released the boy and spat curses.

Adelaide stood, transfixed, as the boat slammed into the boat ramp.

Black, stinking water from the sound splashed around it. Metal screamed. Bodies flew.

At least fifty of them launched into the air. Some landed in the water. Some on land with sickening crunches.

Silence fell. The sound of her own breath filled Addy's ears.

Until they began buzzing.

The ones on the ground that were able untwisted their limbs and wobbled to their feet.

The ones on the boat bumped into each other and the sides of the boat.

Some fell into the water. Most stumbled off the boat and onto the ramp, gaining land.

In the wheelhouse, someone slumped over the wheel.

"Three guesses who that is, first two don't count," Dad said.

"We gotta get out of here. Come on," Dean said, tugging Addy's arm.

"The hospital. Dad," she said, grabbing his sleeve, "the babies. We have to protect them."

"We've got Louis's key card. Let's go."

***

Addy paused and lifted Louis to his feet outside the building. Setting him right, she pointed to the Dead Heads and took off after her father. Dean ran next to her.

She unclipped the radio. "Alpha Team, come in, over."

"Go for Alpha."

"The dock is full of Dead Heads. Proceed with caution." She waited. Oh, right. "Over."

"*Acknowledged. Over.*"

"We need the boat, Scott. There's children, babies. We have to evacuate. Can you get the Dead Heads away from the dock? Over."

"*Will do. Making port in two minutes. Be careful. Over.*"

"You too. Over and out."

She slung the walkie back onto her belt and they sprinted to the hospital, where Dad, Mike, and Christian had already gone inside.

Bursting through the front door, they found Christian holding the receptionist at gunpoint as Dad pounded the double doors to the left.

"Dad," Addy said, dashing across the space.

He spun, eyes red-rimmed, face flushed. "Fucking key card doesn't work on this door." He kicked it.

Hand on his arm, she pointed across the lobby. "What about that one?"

"Here," he said, holding out the card, "give it a try." Spinning back to the door, he reared back and kicked it again. It bowed and splintered.

As he shouted for Jane, Addy dashed back across the lobby. She swiped the card to the maternity ward, waiting for the light to turn.

Green.

Yanking the doors open, she whistled.

Dean and Mike joined her.

"Guys, Scott's team is landing in two minutes. They've gotta clear the dead, then we get these people to the boat. These babies don't deserve to be somebody's lab rats. You guys get them ready to go."

"Where are you going?" Dean asked.

"I've got to get Mom."

"Addy," Mike said, taking her arm, "she doesn't want to come with us. We already had that talk."

"I know," she said, pulling her arm free, "but I have to try. One more time. If she won't come, maybe at least she'll help. We have to get the prisoners out, too."

Dad shouted. "Give me that rifle!" A shot fired from the other end of the lobby.

Addy, Dean, and Mike ducked.

Dad cursed. "Bulletproof glass. Jane!" Dropping the rifle, he beat on the glass doors with both fists.

"Addy," Mike whispered, "is Dad OK?"

She stared at him, eyes wide. "No, Michael. I don't think he is."

Dad grabbed a chair and slammed it against the doors. It bounced. He dropped it, panting.

"Adelaide, go," Dean said, curling her palm around the haft of a knife. "We'll take care of him. And the babies."

Smiling, she brushed Dean's lips with hers and dashed out into the night.

***

"Give me that rifle!"

Charging back into the reception area, Jack snatched the rifle from Christian. He marched back to the glass.

Squeezed off a round.

It whizzed past him after the ricochet, blowing through a piece of the tile floor and sending shards of flooring into the skin of his leg.

The empty hole inside, his impotence before this damn door, pushed the stinging in his shin away from pain and into mere annoyance.

"Fuck! Bulletproof glass," he said, tossing the rifle. Shouting her name through the glass, so thin, yet too sturdy, he pounded it with his fists. Hoping they could prevail where the gun had not.

Stopping, panting, he looked around the room. Next to the closet for suits stood two chairs.

He snatched one up, slamming it into the door like he was swinging for the fences.

It bounced off the glass. Of course.

It didn't matter what he did. He'd failed her.

Dropping the chair, he pounded on the glass doors with his fists again, kicking at them. He bounced off the door as the chair had and fell over it.

It was impossible to get in there without the damned key card.

Paper gown.

Hair shorn.

Test subject.

Vaccine trial.

The horde.

His eyes hurt. He couldn't swallow the lump in his throat. Covering his forehead, he closed his eyes and let the tears fall.

Dean cleared his throat.

Wiping down his face with one hand, he turned his red eyes up.

"Jack, come with us. We'll get the women and children ready to evacuate."

He stood, hand against the glass for support. "Where's Adelaide?"

"She went to get her mom. Or at the very least, her mom's key card."

"Good Christ. I've got to go after her." He stalked toward the front door.

"Look," Dean said, grasping his shoulder, "you raised a good, strong girl. She'll be fine. Back before you know it." He shook him. "We need your help, here, now. When Addy comes back," he said, glancing through the glass, "we'll come back for Jane. She's not going anywhere."

Following his eyes, Jack looked into the clean room. She was just there. On the other side of the glass.

"You're right," he said, frowning at Dean, "the women and children have to get out of this madhouse."

"Come on," Dean said, jogging across the reception area.

Snagging the rifle, Jack slung it over his shoulder and followed Dean.

The receptionist, still at gunpoint, glared at him.

Jack nodded to Christian. "Let her go."

Frowning, Christian lowered the gun. Jerked his head at the door. "Go."

Without waiting to watch her leave, Jack entered maternity.

Dean, at the nurse's station, leaned over the counter. One foot out behind him, he pitched his voice low.

Was he…flirting to get what he needed?

Ha. Well. If it worked for women…

Jack approached.

Dean laid on his Southern accent as thick as he could get it.

The nurse giggled. "From inside you can get into the stairwell," she said. "But you need a key card from outside. I guess if you piggybacked—"

"Dean?" Jack laid a hand on his shoulder.

The younger man held up a wait-a-minute finger to the raven-haired nurse and glanced over his shoulder. "Yeah, Jack?"

"Now, please."

He winked. "You got it, boss." Pulling the gun above the desk, he aimed just left of the nurse. "Well, sweetie, we've got to get everyone checked out now. What do you say?"

Eyes wide, she put both hands in the air and pushed away from the desk. "Um. I don't think I can do that."

"Sure you can. It's real easy. Help us, or we tie you up and leave you here for the general."

Jack chuckled. "I used to be married to her. Trust me," he said, leaning an elbow on the desk, "you do not want to cross her."

Nodding, the nurse stood.

Dean frowned. "Get your friends."

She opened the door behind her and cleared her throat. With both hands in the air and her dinner plate eyes, no words were necessary to get the rest of the nurses out in the open.

Hand on the stock of the rifle, Jack motioned to Christian. "Check it. Make sure they're all here."

As he did, Jack took in the nurses. Caregivers. People who wanted to help others. Who loved babies.

He wouldn't like to hurt any of them.

"Listen, ladies. As my friend here says, we need your help. Don't freak out, but there's a horde outside, on the island, and we need to get these babies out before they become lunch meat. We'd appreciate it if you could help us. So would the babies."

Stone-faced nurses, including a tall redhead that reminded him of Jane in a non-specific way, nodded.

Jane. He'd get over there soon and pull her out of that damn chair and—

Focus, Jack.

Outlining a plan to get the babies and parents into the hallway, he split the nurses into groups and had Mike, Dean, and Christian lead them up the hall. Leading his own group to the end of the ward, he glanced at the green exit sign.

Stairs.

Andrew was up that stairwell.

So, there was one more thing he had to do.

After the babies, get to Andrew, Cure or kill, then Jane.

And once he got to her, he'd snatch her up, get her out, and just keep going.

Catching a glimpse of Dean down the hall, he grinned. Addy had found herself a partner. And turned into quite the leader herself.

And Mike. Michael was strong. Positive. Optimistic. He'd be fine. He might not understand at first, but he'd be fine. He always was.

Jack would just leave with Jane and never look back. It didn't matter where they went, as long as she was with him.

***

Head down, Addy sped across the road. The stench of the dead didn't yet overpower the salty sea, but the air came with an edge of decay. Eyes wide, knife drawn, she shot down the drive and up onto the porch.

She ran into the door, ripped it open, and charged inside. "Mom!"

The refrigerator kicked on. The hall clock ticked.

Wind chimes tinkled outside.

She called out again, tentative. "Mom?"

Nothing moved in the house. Nothing breathed.

She raced up the stairs two at a time.

Every room upstairs, including the one in which all their lives had changed again, sat empty. Bare. Still.

In the room that had been Mom's, the one with Star Trek and Star Wars posters on the walls and a giant print of the Milky Way tacked to the ceiling, a half-packed bag sat open on the bed.

Moving things inside the bag with the tip of the knife, she found rolled underwear, socks, a couple shirts. Flashlight, knives, a gun, and a few clips.

Frowning, she headed back downstairs. One thoughtful stair at a time.

So Mom had begun packing. Where was she going? Why was she going? Had she changed her mind? Was she coming after them? And if so, where was she now? Why had she left a half-packed bag?

Standing at the bottom of the stairs, she drifted, eyes unfocused.

Her feet turned toward the kitchen, making the decision for her. "I'll check the back. The beach. Just in case," she said to herself, mumbling through numb lips.

Creeping into the kitchen, she glanced at the table.

On it lay Mom's sidearm. And her key card. Squared up to each other and framed by the circle of light, equidistant from the edges.

Placed there with intention. A message.

She *had* changed her mind. She'd quit. This was her resignation.

Scooping up the key card, Addy dashed back out the front door.

CHAPTER 30

ashing back down the drive, Addy approached the trees at the end.

A half dozen 'Heads wandered in the field beside the hospital. Possibly drawn by the light spilling from the windows.

Slowing, she crept up to the one closest to her. It stank of the sound. Of old blood.

Of the antiseptic hospital.

A test subject. Part of the "large sample size."

Spinning, she drove the knife into its brain. Following it to the ground, she put a foot to its skull and slipped the knife free.

The next one was just as quiet. Just as simple. And still wore a paper gown.

Just like the one they'd put on Jane and the others.

She shuddered. Another test subject gone bad. The ground tilted under her feet. They'd already given the vaccine to Jane. What if it didn't work? What if she ended up like one of these guys?

Even if Mom realized her mistake, could Addy look her in the eye ever again? Could she forgive her?

A 'Head bubbled up behind her as she stood, paralyzed with thoughts of her mom, her best friend, her family.

Without looking, she switched the knife to her left hand. Sweeping across her shoulder, she buried it between its eyes. She let the 'Head drop with the blade deep in its cranium.

Bending, she worked the knife back and forth. It took more effort to slip this one free. Before it was fully disengaged, another bubbled up from her right.

Pausing her struggle with the knife, she kicked it in the face and sent it sprawling. Freeing the blade, she knelt and stabbed it through the head before it had a chance to get back up.

Panting, she glanced around the field. Still two left.

Man, but her arm and shoulder were tired. Throbbing with heat. 'Heads might go down like plastic people, but it was still a workout. She had sweat on her sweat.

Leaving the last two, she jogged back to the hospital.

The lobby stood empty.

The double door, the way to Jane, hung off a hinge. Though the glass had fogged where Dad shot it, the door itself remained intact.

The vestibule was empty.

Pulling the key card from her pocket, she charged into the maternity ward.

The ward bustled. Nurses called orders, men darted across the hall, up and back, and a few women in hospital gowns cradled little bundles.

Pulling the double doors closed behind her, she shouted. "Dad!"

The walkie crackled. "*Alpha Team to Beta. Come in, Adelaide.*"

She unclipped the radio. "Adelaide here, over."

"*We're landing. There's a couple hundred of them. Scattered. We're going to lure them south. Over.*"

"Roger that. ETA for evacuations? Over."

"*Uh. Calculating.*"

Waiting, she caught her dad's curly head bouncing across the hall, down at the end, near a green exit sign.

At a trot, she weaved through the nervous couples preparing their tiny babies for their first trip to the outside air. Some of them watched her as she skipped past. Some checked and rechecked supply bags.

Some sat, bags on the floor, staring into the faces of their little ones. Forgetting the commotion around them, engrossed in the little world that was just mom, dad, and baby.

Longing punched her in the gut. She lost her air again. This new desire, while not entirely unexpected, was what Jane had been preaching at her for months. She just hadn't seen it before. Hadn't felt it.

Dean, zooming out of a room, bag in hand, ran right into her.

Caught her before she fell.

Favoring him with a tight smile, she searched the hall for her dad again.

"Dad!"

"*Adelaide,*" the radio crackled.

Startled, she dropped the key card.

"Shit," she whispered, bending to pick it up. Someone kicked it out of reach as they scurried past.

"Crap," she said, pushing the radio button, "yeah. Adelaide here. Go Alpha. Over."

"*Give us about three minutes before you start coming out. It's, uh, it's messy.*"

Silence.

A hand fell on her shoulder.

Smiling, she turned. "Dean."

"Not so much," Tim said, grinning through a fat lip. Both eyes were black, and a gash had opened on his forehead, probably from the boat crash, releasing a sheet of blood down his face. It had crusted around his nose and in the corner of one eye.

Blinking, Addy backed up.

"You're worse than a bad penny, Tim," Dean said from behind him.

Tim raised his hands.

Dean socked him in the face, spinning him around.

Stumbling, Tim slipped on the key card and fell. It skidded away, again.

"Adelaide," Tim shouted, voice raw, "it's *him*! Not me!" He jabbed a finger at Dean.

She scowled. "Get the fuck out of here, Tim. Haven't you done enough already?"

He shook his head, lowering his chin and staring up at her from under his brow. He mouthed words without sound. *You wish.*

His lip curled in a sneer and he jerked a handgun from his belt.

He aimed past Addy and down the hall.

Jumping back, she followed his aim.

Mom stood just inside the exit door.

"Mom!"

All the activity in the hall slowed.

She tried to shout. Tell him to stop. Beads of sweat on his bleeding head dripped in agonizingly slow motion.

Dean lowered his head and rushed forward like a bull.

Corner of his mouth raising, Tim sidestepped and Dean charged past, skidding on the tile floor.

Taking aim, Tim squeezed the trigger.

Addy screamed.

The shot went just wide, punching through the drywall not three inches from Melinda's head, and sending a puff of dust and paint into her hair.

As her eyes widened, the activity in the hall crashed back into Addy's senses. Babies and mothers cried; voices clashed against one another.

Dean grabbed for Tim again, but he squirted away, scurrying to the end of the hall where he slammed into Melinda and came up with a handful of her hair.

Dad appeared at the end of the hall like a magician. He inched toward Tim.

Tim pressed the gun to Melinda's temple, twisting an arm behind her back. "Come with me, sweetheart," he said, licking her ear.

Movement caught Addy's eye. Using her peripheral, she watched Mike as he inched into the hallway, foot next to the keycard.

"Adelaide, my dear," Tim called, hiding behind Melinda, "it wouldn't have worked out between us. I like her better anyway. More mature, you know."

Melinda shouted as he wrenched her wrist into her shoulder blades. "Addy, honey, don't worry about me," she said, tears standing in her eyes. "Get these people and get out."

"Yeah, we'll be fine," Tim said, kicking open the door behind him. It led to the stairwell, where he dragged a silent Melinda.

Heart pounding, Addy turned to her dad.

He stood, fists clenching and unclenching, eyes flicking between her and the stairwell door.

"Michael," he said, eyes on the exit door, "pick up that card and go get Jane."

Without a look back, he slammed into the door and disappeared up the stairs.

***

Handing over a sleeping bundle to its mom, Jack smiled. It smelled like a newborn. Something he'd forgotten all about, newborn smell.

A radio crackled up the hall. Over the commotion, he couldn't make out the words. But Adelaide had the radio, so she must have returned. Hopefully, with the keycard.

He envisioned his next steps.

Get the key card.

Get the girl.

Get out.

Simple enough. His smile widened.

Heated voices floated down the hall. "It's *him*, not me!"

Oh, for fuck's sake. That boy was like a bad penny. Worse.

Feeling for the rifle over his shoulder, Jack noticed it was gone. When had he put it down?

He spotted it leaned against the wall in the room he'd just left. He must've put it down when he picked up the baby.

Carrying babies and daydreaming about a woman.

Great. Great job, Jack.

As he crept toward the room, his daughter screamed. A shot cracked. It punched through drywall with an insignificant *poof.*

All the hair on his neck stood, painful prickles all the way up to his skull.

Melinda stood next to the stairwell, Tim with a hand twisted in her hair.

She spoke to him over her shoulder. "What did I tell you, Timothy?"

He lowered his lips to her ear. "Oh baby, you know I love it when you talk dirty to me."

"Tim," Jack said, stepping into the hall, fists raised. Without the rifle, he was at a disadvantage. But he'd made a promise to his daughter he intended to keep.

Eyes widening, Tim spun Melinda at an angle, wrenched her arm between her shoulder blades, and pressed the gun into her temple.

"Adelaide, my dear," he called, hiding behind Melinda, "it wouldn't have worked out between us. I like her better anyway. More mature, you know."

Melinda shouted as he jerked her wrist into her shoulder blades. "Addy, honey, don't worry about me," she said, tears standing in her eyes. "Get these people and get out."

Tim kicked the stairwell door open, green light from the exit sign casting elongated, sickly shadows on his face. "Yeah, we'll be fine." He dragged Jack's ex-wife into the dark.

Breathing in through his nose, Jack tried to find the calm center between his eyes.

After killing his friends, turning his woman into some kind of lab rat, and trying to rape his daughter, Tim deserved no less than to have his heart ripped out, still beating, and then fed to Dead Heads as he screamed.

But there on the ground, there was the keycard.

Had Melinda returned it? Had she changed her mind?

It didn't matter, because here was his chance to get the card and rescue Jane.

He stood, breath short, fists clenching and releasing, eyes flicking between the stairwell door and the key card.

Andrew was still up there.

Adelaide searched his face, asking him without asking to save her mother.

Michael stood, foot next to the keycard. Probably with his heart set on the girl, as it had been for years.

It all crumbled. The visions of running away. They melted away like wet candy floss.

And so did anger. Desire. Fear. Love.

All that remained was duty. He owed them all, each and every one.

"Michael," he said, eyes on the exit door, "pick up that card and go get Jane."

Without a look back, he slammed into the door and disappeared up the stairs.

***

Last time Jack had been in this stairwell, it'd been lit.

Now it enclosed him in darkness as the door whooshed shut.

He seemed to have misplaced the flashlight as well. And he had no weapons.

Batting a thousand today, Jack.

Stopping to Listen, and to scent the air, he closed his eyes. Nothing moved. Nothing breathed. Nothing dripped murderous saliva.

Opening his eyes, for all the good it did, he crept up one step at a time. At the landing, he sniffed again.

Beneath the antiseptic hospital odor, there was a stench of old, dead blood. But, not. Off, somehow. Nothing had ever quite smelled like it.

Whatever else it was, it was unpleasant.

Creeping up the final few stairs, clinging to the wall railing, it came to him that he could see the shape of the door to the second-floor lab.

It had been left cracked, just an inch.

He crouched on the next set of stairs and eased the door open. Inhaling, he peeked just around it.

Bright neon lights bathed the room in white, hurting his eyes.

"The hell is taking you so long? Get this shit copied, already!" Tim, voice echoing from an enclosed office at the end, blue light spilling from the window.

Between here and there, the rows and rows of beds with their restraints, one or two with silent occupants. Still under the blinding white sheets.

Sliding through the door, he considered Army-crawling down the ward to the office. Thought about how his knees and elbows might feel about that. Reconsidered.

Crouching, he scooted between the beds in a kind of half-bent, half-squatting duck walk. He approached an occupied bed.

Face covered by the sheet, its occupant had legs too long for it. Their feet hung over the edge, naked.

Andrew.

The sheet twitched.

He froze, pulling in a breath and holding it. Waited for the buzzing to begin.

It didn't come.

"You bitch! Just get it done!" Tim's voice echoed off the ceiling tile, but the sheet didn't move again.

Exhaling with slow, thoughtful caution, Jack crept forward.

The sheet twitched again. A muffled and weak buzz whispered from beneath it.

He didn't stop. But after he took care of Tim, he'd have to come back.

Creeping up next to the office, some kind of drywall add-on, he crouched beneath the window. Back to the wall, he inched toward the door.

Holding his breath, he peeked over the lip of the windowsill.

Tim paced, back and forth. Computer keys clacked, Melinda with her back to the window, irritated and breathing hard.

"Are you fucking with me?" Tim's voice had crawled up to a whine. "Why is this taking so long?" He slapped her in the shoulder with a meaty thump.

"You don't have to hit me with that gun. I'm working as fast as I can."

"Move faster or the last thing you'll see is your brains all over the screen." Hands on his hips, he leaned into the screen.

With Tim's back to the door, now was the time. As Jack moved to peek around the door, the overhead lights went out.

Restraints rattled against a bed frame.

"What the hell now?" Tim shouted, pounding the desk.

"Tim, the computer is on an emergency backup. Calm down."

"You calm down. Dumb bitch."

Feet stomped toward the door.

Just as Tim reached the doorway, Jack stepped out, lowering his head and ramming his shoulder into Tim's waist. Like a football tackle, he drove the boy backward until his legs slammed into the desk. Twisting at the hips, Jack threw him sideways.

In the blue light cast by the computer screen, they both fell. Tim crashed into the wall face-first. His nose crunched. The gun flew into the dark. Melinda leapt from the computer.

"Sod ob a bith!"

"Oh Timmy," Jack said, releasing him to jab him in the kidney, "hurt your nose?"

"Jacksob," he said, straightening with one hand over the kidney, "dice to see you again." He snuffled blood up his nose. Hacked and spat a clump of blood and mucus onto the floor. "I see you chose your wife." He dropped a grotesque wink.

Jack's bile rose, burning the back of his throat. "I believe I have a promise to keep regarding you, Tim."

"What's that?"

"Well, I told my little girl I was going to fucking kill you. I'm a man of my word."

Tim swallowed. Glanced at Melinda.

Back to the window, she grinned, mouth stretching into something lupine, predatory. "Think I made you the same promise, Timothy."

A shape loomed behind her.

"Melinda," Jack said, pointing, "get away from the window."

She backed away from the glass. The 'Head approached, buzzing and bubbling.

Catching movement behind him, Jack turned in time to see Tim snagging the gun again. Too slow to stop him, he stood sideways and watched the approaching 'Head and the boy in turn.

"Melinda, my dear, if you would please," Tim said, pointing the gun at the chair. "Jackson, the door."

Grimacing, Melinda sat again as Jack snicked the door closed.

The 'Head stopped. Put a hand to the glass. The restraint from the bed hung off its wrist like a bracelet. Its very large wrist.

"Andrew," Jack breathed.

"Sucks about your friend, Jackson. Omelets and everything, I guess, huh Melinda?" Tim smacked her in the shoulder with the gun. "Last time I'm going to tell you. Faster. I want that information. We can all leave happy if you just give it to me."

"Tim," she said, swallowing, "I told you. It takes time to download the database. If you want it all, you just have to wait."

The 'Head balled a fist and struck the window.

Since when did they use fists?

"Faster, woman."

She laid a finger on the keyboard. Just one finger. Turned her face to his and lifted her lips in that lupine smile again.

Jack's blood ran cold.

"Oh, sweetie," she said, pressing the button, "I've just accidentally deleted it. All of it."

The computer's hard drive made an innocuous spinning sound and stopped.

"What? You bitch, what have you done?" He slapped her across the cheekbone with the gun. Her head whipped back, neck twisting almost too far.

Grunting, she slumped to the floor.

Pointing the gun in Jack's direction, he typed one-handed. "It's got to be here. Give it to me. Here we go. OK, password.

Bunnyrabbit16. OK. Let's go. I need this. *I need it.* No!" He slapped the keyboard.

The 'Head hit the window with that odd fist again.

Tim screamed, incoherent. Picked up the keyboard and beat it against the desk, keys popping off and flying in all directions.

And yet, he kept his grip on the gun.

Doesn't matter, Jack. You can take him. You have to.

As Jack readied for another tackle, Tim grinned at him.

"Oh no, Jackson. Not so fast. See, I think we need to have a talk, you and I. Now," he said, swinging the gun around in a flailing hand, "I like your daughter. She's perfectly delicious. And sweet and innocent. Did you know she's never—"

"Shut your mouth." The calm in Jack's voice surprised him. Cool and clear. "Drop it now."

Tim smiled. An ugly, cramped affair. "I like your wife, though. She's a strong woman. Did you know she likes to tie me up?" He leaned forward, winking again. The gun hung loose in his hand. "It's a power thing, you know."

"I know what you're doing, Tim. It's not going to work."

"That so?" Tim asked, raising the gun. "Looks like it has."

Steeling himself to leap, Jack bent his knees.

The door exploded inward, off its hinges, and nailed Tim. Launched into the wall, the door pinned him. The gun flew again.

Heart in his throat, mouth hanging open, Jack stared at the doorway.

Andrew stood there, bubbling, breathing hard, fists clenched. He opened his mouth, but instead of words, it only sounded like he was gargling blood.

Jack took a step toward him. "The hell have they done to you, buddy?" In the dark, it was impossible to see his eyes.

Andrew gargled. Pushed breath out past the plug of blood in his throat.

Groaning, Tim rolled from under the door and stood, brushing his knees. "Hey, Andy. Glad you could join us."

"Me too," Melinda said.

Aiming the gun at Tim's chest, she didn't hesitate.

Jack didn't even have time to tell her to stop.

She shot him through the heart. As he fell, she shot him again. And again. And again. Methodical. All to the torso.

The small office stank of blood and sulfur, copper and acrid gun smoke.

Jack counted nine shots before she stopped.

The 'Head in the door buzzed but didn't move. Breathed around the gargled blood and otherwise remained silent.

Staring at Andrew, Jack moved next to Melinda. She'd not shot Tim in the head, not once.

He eased the gun out of her hand and pulled the hammer back.

Taking careful aim, he delivered the killing blow.

***

"Andrew?" Jack stepped toward the door.

Snarling, the 'Head lurched into the room, reaching with blackened fingers for Jack's throat.

Head cool, Jack raised the gun and aimed between his friend's eyes.

Squeezed the trigger.

The hammer clicked. The gun was dry.

"Jack," Melinda said, tremble in her voice.

The 'Head wobbled closer, black fingers hooking.

"Jackson," Melinda repeated, tugging his sleeve.

Shouldn't his stomach be in knots? Shouldn't he feel anger? Disappointment? Sadness? Something?

Anything?

It was as though he'd left it all in the floor downstairs. With the keycard.

And here he was, facing one of his best friends. Turned into some kind of abomination, neither 'Head nor human. And he couldn't feel anything. Just a great gaping hole where emotion should be.

Andrew stumbled over Tim's foot and fell, landing in the spreading pool of blood.

He began to lap at it.

Oh, there it was. Revulsion still worked.

Swallowing his gorge, he grabbed Melinda's arm and tugged her out of the office. Stepping careful to avoid the blood, bits of drywall and door, and spilled papers, he pulled her out the door and toward the only other light—the green exit sign. "I'll see those damn signs in my dreams," he whispered.

The door on the other end banged open. A chorus of buzzing, cicada-like voices spilled into the room. Preceded by the stench of maggoty meat, their owners tumbled through the door. Fell over each other. Most wearing paper gowns.

"Shit, Jack, it's the remnants."

"The hell does that mean?" he asked, backing up.

"We have a, for lack of a better word, a holding tank in the back wing. Somehow they've gotten up here."

"Somehow?"

"I think we can discuss that later," she said, pushing him toward the opposite door.

They continued to spill into the room, buzzing and growling. Stinking. Old, dead flesh. Wasted muscles. Coppery, spoiled blood.

He swallowed. "How many are there?"

She cleared her throat.

One of them glanced in their direction. Probably. With only the blue light from the office, it was hard to tell.

"How many, Mellie?"

"About a hundred."

"Jesus Christ," he swore, pitching his voice low.

"I know. I'm sorry. Look. We have to get out of here. Back to the stairs."

The 'Heads inched closer, some tripping over beds. Like a wave, they swarmed into the room.

The other door swung open, banging into the wall.

Stomach sinking, Jack glanced over his shoulder.

Dead Heads coming through both doors. A stinking wall of them.

"And no bullets left," Melinda said.

Meeting her eyes, he took her hand. "I won't leave you to them again."

"You fucking better not."

The buzzing grew, hungry cicadas oozing into the room from both ends.

Andrew stepped out of the office. The blood around his mouth and down his front black in the blue light.

"Jack," he bubbled. "Jackie, run." He approached them, picking up speed.

Jack yanked Melinda out of the way as Andrew sped past.

He slammed into the 'Heads spilling through the door, scattering them like bowling pins.

Their buzzing didn't change. But Andy, Andy's heightened in pitch, growing and swelling like a wave rolling in.

He'd cleared a hole in the middle of the 'Heads. Jack saw stairs. "Mellie, come on," he said, tugging her hand.

"Don't have to tell me twice," she said, pacing him as he sprinted for the door.

Stepping out of the ward, leaving a snarling and chomping Andrew behind them, they flew to the first landing. Rounding the banister, they ran almost face to face with more of the horde.

"Shit," Jack said, skidding to a stop and kicking the closest one in the belly. It fell, knocking the others behind it back down the stairs.

"Up," Melinda said, pulling his hand.

Back up the stairs, she slammed one in the back so they could squeeze around the banister again. They took the stairs two at a time.

Jack's left hand flew across the scratchy railing, his right gripping Melinda's hand.

His mind projected the film of their escape from the apartment onto the backs of his eyes. Cradling his son with one arm, he'd squeezed her hand as they ran. She'd had to stop and kill one, stabbing her good kitchen knife right into its eye. She complained later about that knife about a hundred times before he found her another. In some department store somewhere, he'd nearly lost his head to a stealthy dead employee.

Stopping on the landing by the third floor, Melinda glanced in the window. The wing was dark. "They're all gone."

"I hope they got out," he said, glancing in the window over her head.

Frowning, she tugged his hand and drew him away from the door.

Snarls and growls, buzzing and choking drifted up the stairs.

"The roof," she said, pulling him.

The question of whether there was a way down from the roof once they were there crossed his mind, but the sound of the 'Heads climbing the stairs was enough to keep his feet moving.

CHAPTER 31

Watching her dad disappear up the stairs, Addy couldn't help but feel something had shifted. Something important.

"Dean," she said, watching Mike as he picked up the keycard, "we've got to get these women out now. I don't know why, but I feel like we can't stay here anymore." Swallowing, she looked up and down the hall. "We have to do this now."

Mike, standing with the keycard, held it out and stared at her.

Glancing at it, she grabbed his arm and handed the radio to Dean. "You call Scott. Get them on the boat. Send Scott to the prison. We're going to get Jane."

"Adelaide," Dean said, catching her arm.

She paused, one hand full of Mike's jacket. Shifting her feet, she gave Dean a tight smile. Now was no time for sappy love kisses.

He frowned, handing her his rifle. "Be careful. Get back to me in one piece, alright?"

One corner of her mouth turned up. "Only if you do."

As she and Mike reached the end of the hallway, Dean whistled over the commotion. It died, and he shouted it was time to go. Quietly. "Follow my friend Christian," he said, pointing at the round bartender.

Christian raised the hand holding his gun and waved it in the air. "This way ladies, gents, babes."

Leading them out the door, Addy propped it open and checked the lobby.

Empty.

"Let me check outside first," she said, dropping Mike's arm to jog to the front door.

About a dozen 'Heads had appeared since she'd last been out there. Just milling on the lawn.

Snapping a finger at Christian, she pointed to her eyes when he looked at her. Pointed outside. Flashed five fingers three times.

He nodded, dropped the clip, checked it, and reloaded. "We got it."

"Mike," she said, "let's get this done."

He glanced back at the women with their bundles. "You sure they'll be OK?"

"Yes. Dean's with them."

Mike slid into the glass vestibule and swiped the key card.

The doors hissed open.

Grinning, Addy dashed into the vestibule after him, eyes on the third room down. She tripped over the chair and it skidded into the space between the glass doors.

She managed to keep her feet by ramming her shoulder into the glass. She'd feel that tomorrow.

"Come on," she said, glaring at her grinning brother. "You don't have to always laugh at me."

"It's my job, bean."

Sidestepping the offending chair, she eased into the room. Though she eyed the third compartment, Mike stopped at the first one.

Feeling the cold, blank space behind her, she spun.

He stood at the window to the first compartment, so close to the glass, it fogged. He frowned. "We can't leave him like this, Addy."

Joining Mike at the window, she watched as what used to be Gerald struggled against his restraints. Snarling, growling, buzzing, it seemed like he could smell them on the other side of the glass.

She was certain of it.

Mike swiped the key card. The key panel on the door handle beeped green. He swung the door wide, leaving room for Addy to sneak through.

She did, creeping into the room as silent as her little feet would make her.

Still, the 'Head stopped, turning its dead eyes to her. They'd already begun their inevitable decline, showing the telltale signs of rot. Grey film over the pupils.

How did they see? How was it even possible?

It snapped and buzzed. Saliva dripped from its maw, splattering to the tile below.

She fought her gorge and won.

Mike remained plastered to the door. So it was her job.

As Gerald snarled and growled, teeth clacking, she flashed on Elizabeth in the hospital bed. Staring at the gaping hole in the side of Ger's neck, she couldn't forget the haunted, sunken look in Liz's eyes. That the only thing she remembered was doing that.

Aiming the rifle, she put a single bullet between his eyes.

Muffled screaming from down the hall followed as the body sunk, hands lifted above its head in some ridiculous parody of an icon.

"Addy," Mike said, voice dropped to a whisper, "let's go get Jane now."

Backing up, eyes still on Ger's face, she bumped into the wall before sliding sideways and out the door.

Mike, already halfway down the hallway, called to Jane. "We're coming, Jane. Hang tight." He dashed to the door and pulled at the handle. Nothing happened. "Crap, right. The key card."

He lifted it, locking it into the slot.

The lights went out.

The little red light on the door faded to nothing.

Mike swiped the card anyway.

No green light. No beep. No nothing.

He rattled the handle, shoving at the door with his shoulder. It didn't budge.

Running up behind him, Addy peered through the window. Pitch-black without the overhead lights, only the green exit sign at the end of the hall lit the room.

Mike reached in his pocket and pulled out a flashlight, flicking it on. He stuck it under his chin, grinning. "Who's the smartest one now, huh?"

"Addy! Mike!" Jane pounded on the glass from her side, her shouting muffled by the thick window. "They're all dead. All the others. Get me out of here."

Addy's heart skipped. If all the other subjects were dead from the "vaccine," was it only a matter of time before Jane was too?

God, I don't ask you for much. But I ask you for this.

He'd already given her mother back. What if he was fresh out of miracles?

Brow drawn, lips tight, she aimed the rifle at the door. "Michael, light please."

He aimed the flash at the door handle.

"Jane, stand away from the door," she called, cheek pressed into the cold stock of the rifle.

After giving Jane two seconds to get out of the way, Addy fired. Aiming each perfect shot, she created a half-moon around the doorknob. She fired until the rifle went dry.

The door swung. Mike rushed to it and shouldered it open.

"Jane, come on. Here, let me help you," he said, disappearing into the room.

Addy dropped the empty rifle and waited in the dark.

Mike came out, cradling Jane, her arms wrapped around his neck.

Addy gasped. "Are you alright?"

Jane nodded, eyes closed. "I think so. I think so. Let's get out of here."

At the glass doors, they found the chair had been bent between them.

"They tried to close automatically when the power went out," Addy said, stepping over the chair.

"Set me down, Michael," Jane said.

He did as he was told.

Struggling, she put one leg over the chair and stuck a hand out to Addy. The paper gown fluttered around her knees.

"This thing is fucking cold," she said, as she stepped over the chair.

Letting her go, Addy pointed at the closet. "There's some terribly stylish plastic suits over there."

Michael stumbled over the chair, dislodging it from the doorway. As Jane limped to the closet, the glass doors whooshed closed, catching his foot. Groaning, he aimed the flashlight at the closet so Jane could find it in the dark.

"Point that thing someplace else, Michael," Jane said, pulling a suit off the rack. He did, and plastic crinkled.

While Mike held the flashlight, Addy helped her zip up. Taking her hand, she smiled. "You look like a fairy princess."

Jane rasped her hand along the shaved half of her head. "The most badass one you know, sister. Let's get the fuck out of here."

***

Addy peeked into the front lawn. Dark shapes wobbled and bumped into each other.

"There's at least a hundred out there, maybe more." Hopefully, Dean had made it to the boat with the babies.

Jane clicked her tongue. "Is there light?"

"I think I saw some switches over here," Mike said, stepping behind the reception desk. A slight limp in his gait. "Ah. Here we go. 'Outside Lights.'"

Addy grinned at her brother. She opened her mouth but before she could get a word out, Jane tapped her on the shoulder.

"Anybody got a blade? I'm a little naked."

Flipping the one off her belt, Addy held it out to her. "Here, take this one."

Eyebrow raised, she frowned. "This your only one?"

"Sure," Addy said, shrugging, "but you take it." Looking past Jane, she spotted the bow lying on the ground by the desk. Whenever she'd dropped it there.

Jerking her chin at it, she retrieved it and reached back to count the arrows. Twelve. She flashed a grin. "Light 'em up, Michael."

He flipped every switch, one at a time.

Addy's pupils contracted and her breath fogged the glass as the lights came on. Giant floodlights at the top of fifty-foot poles, they lit the yard like daylight.

"I think we can work with that," Jane said, chuckling.

"We've sure as hell worked with less," Addy agreed. "Mike, let's do this." Spinning a hand in the air, she pushed the door open and the three of them slid into the bright night.

The air, salty and fresh before, hung with the stench of rot. Coppery blood mixing with the scent of flesh pulling away from bone. Sticking together in a pack, back to back to back, they crept through the grass to the first 'Head.

Mike pulled a machete out of his belt and separated it from its head.

As the body dropped, Addy whispered over her shoulder. "How come you get the big blade?"

"Big man, big blade, little sis."

"Blow me."

"Addy," Jane said, "six o'clock."

A 'Head stumbled toward them, gurgling and buzzing, blackened fingers outstretched.

If Jane was nine through twelve, and Mike was one through four, that made this one Addy's. Nocking and clearing the arrow before it was too close was a near thing, but the 'Head dropped, arrow protruding from both the front and back of its skull.

"Running out of room quick here," she said, nocking another and holding the bow upright.

"Hear you."

"Jane," Mike said, "ten."

Plastic suit crinkling, Jane sank the knife into the approaching 'Head's temple. Yanking the blade free, she wiped it on the Dead Head's paper gown and stood.

"Addy," she said, backing into the circle again, "why are they wearing paper gowns?"

"Uh. It's— It's a long story. Tell you when we're through here." She released an arrow into another 'Head.

Ten arrows left.

"What's the plan here, guys?" Mike asked, stepping out of the circle to separate another 'Head from its body.

"Get to the boat. Make sure Dean and the others are there."

Jane exhaled through her nose. "Where's Jack?"

"He went to get my mom. I don't know where he is now."

Jane sucked in another breath, whistling through her nostrils. Exhaling. Cool air hit Addy's shoulder as she stepped away.

Tackling the nearest 'Head, Jane punched it in the face and wrestled it to the ground. Stabbed it in the heart. It buzzed and buzzed, snarling up at her.

"Jane, what are you doing?" Mike hissed.

"Michael, your three," Addy said, stiffening as the 'Head reached for her brother. Wearing a paper gown, it had to be only about three weeks old. And fast.

"Crap," Mike said, stumbling on his bad foot and pulling the machete up a beat too late. The 'Head grabbed his shoulder, its teeth clashing together as it aimed for the only exposed skin it could see—his head and neck.

Too close for the arrows, Addy gripped the bow and swept it down, driving it across the 'Head's arms.

It released him, stumbling back.

He brought up his machete, sweeping it across and burying the blade in the side of its head.

It fell, taking the blade with it.

As he worked to free the blade, Addy glanced at Jane.

She stood over the 'Head, white plastic suit drenched in stinking, filthy blood. The 'Head lay on the ground in three pieces. Not only had she separated its head with god knew how many strikes, she'd also detached one of its arms at the bicep.

"Jesus, Jane," Addy said, stepping around the pieces and edging up next to her friend, "I wasn't turned around for more than thirty seconds. What the hell?"

She shrugged. "It's been a long couple days."

"It must've. You'll have to tell me about it when we get back to Harkers."

Jane's brow creased, mouth drawing into a tight frown. "It's over now, Addy. There's nothing to tell." Putting her back to Addy's, they circled to Mike.

"Let's get over to that little building there, other side of the field," Addy said, yanking Mike's arm. He stood, completing the circle again.

Sticking together like the rotating clock they were, they moved through the emptiest spots. Keeping quiet, only about fifteen 'Heads noticed them as they crossed the field. Never more than two at a time.

As they gained the shadow of the building, Addy pressing her back into the cool brick, shadows detached themselves from the trees.

Coming in quick.

"Guys," she hissed, nocking an arrow.

Their new visitors ran along the edge of the light until they hit a shadow in the space between two circles.

Dead Heads certainly wouldn't do that. Must be people. Question was, which people?

"Adelaide, thank god," Dean said, slinking out of the shadows, eyes on the field full of 'Heads. He gripped her shoulder. "Are you alright?"

She smiled. "Fine. Just another day at the office. Did you get the babies on the boat?"

"Yeah, no problem. These," he said, looking over her head at the horde again, "weren't here when we went out. It was pretty much smooth sailing all the way to the boat."

"What the hell, then?"

"I don't know, it—"

"Addy," Celia said, stepping in.

Grinning, Addy hugged her. The little woman hugged her back, at the same time making herself as small as possible.

"Where's your dad?"

"I don't know. He went to get my mom. He should be here by now," she said, the first fluttering of unease filtering from her brain to gut. "Who else is with you, Dean?"

Scott sketched a wave. "Good to see you, under the circumstances, Addy."

Lips tight, she nodded. Christian had come too, as well as Oren and Jeff.

Celia gripped her arm. "Your mom's the general, isn't she?"

"You knew?"

"I wasn't sure. But she looks like you. It's what I was going to tell you back on Harkers," Celia said. "I never got another chance to talk to you. Is she on our side?"

"I think so," Addy said, eyes darting around the little circle. "We can talk about it later. Let's clear this field."

***

Flashlight beam bouncing, Melinda hit the door to the roof running. Jack followed behind, closing and latching it. He looked around for some way to block it.

Nothing. Of course not. Just a plain hallway.

"Jack," Melinda said, halfway up the stairs, "let's go. At least two doors between us and them, it'll buy us some time."

Stomach churning, he followed her up the stairs. Bursting through the door to the roof, he locked the doorknob and slammed it closed.

Strong enough to fly a kite in, the sea breeze riffled his hair and the tails of his shirt. Floodlights bathed the roof in screaming white.

"Where to now, Melinda?"

She bit her lip. "Well…"

"Well what?" he asked, stepping away from the door.

"There's no way down."

"What do you mean? Isn't there a fire escape?"

"Buildings don't really come with codes, anymore."

He ran a hand through his hair. "Hell. There's got to be a way down." He stalked away, angled roof threatening to jerk his feet out from under him at every step.

Edging to the front side of the roof, Jack glanced over.

Crammed with Dead Heads, the field below breathed as they moved. Bumping into each other, growling, and buzzing. As he watched, a trio of people stalked through the crowd.

Melinda grabbed his sleeve. "Is that Adelaide and Michael?"

He squinted. Yes. And… "And Jane."

They stood and watched the trio edge its way through the 'Heads, working together in easy precision.

She tugged his arm. "I'm sorry I didn't listen to you guys. I just— I didn't realize she was part of the family. I'm glad she survived the trial." She favored him with a strained smile. "I should have listened to you about everything."

"Thank you. We'll talk about it later," he said, head swirling. "If we have a later."

With a grimace, he moved back across the roof. Perpendicular to it, another building touched the one on which they stood. "Can we get down that way?"

Melinda shrugged. "I don't know. I don't think so."

"Let's check it."

Crossing the roof with slow, measured steps, taking all the time he needed not to go ass over teakettle and all the way to the ground, Jack spotted a tower next to the other building. A radio or cell phone tower, from the looks of it, made of a lattice of metal bars. He spoke over his shoulder. "Mellie, I think we might be able to make that tower."

Melinda grunted.

A faint stirring of hope in his gut, he grabbed her hand and they crossed the roof together.

Stepping from one building to the next, he glanced at the tower again.

"Jack, that tower is too far away."

Shaking his head, he dropped her hand and worked his way to the edge of the roof. Looking down, he estimated they were at least thirty feet up. Probably a touch more. "Would you say that tower is about twelve feet away?" His mind spun with calculations.

"More like fifteen or twenty."

"Probably too far."

"Probably."

The door they'd come through slammed open, Dead Heads spilling onto the roof. Some wandered the other way, some stumbled across the roof toward them.

He looked her in the eye. "Shit, Mellie. We have to try."

Mouth tight, eyes flicking to the Dead Heads approaching, she nodded. Reached out and grabbed his hand, squeezing.

Glancing between the dead, the tower, and Melinda, he felt blank. Like a slate wiped clean. Like a black hole. No fear, no joy at her change of heart, no head full of cotton over how he still felt about Jane. No sadness over Andrew.

Nothing.

Eyeing the jump again, he let their slim chance at success sink in and wash over him. They probably wouldn't make the jump. It was simply too far.

The desire to feel something, anything, before he died overwhelmed him.

He met Mellie's eyes. His wife's eyes.

Staring back at him, she chewed her lip.

With one strong arm, he yanked her in and kissed her like he hadn't done for over a decade.

***

Kneeling beside the building, Addy nailed as many 'Heads as she could with the bow. The sound of fighting quieted, the bright lights focused her eyes to laser points. Her own breath the only sound in her head.

Exhale.

Ten. Through the ear.

Nine. Through the temple.

Eight. Through the jaw. Messy but it'd do.

Seven. Through the eye. Oh yeah, baby.

Six. Missed. Damn.

Five. Through the…oh wait. Through the scalp.

Four. Through the cheek of the same one.

Three. Up the nose. Ouch.

Two. Another through the temple.

"Addy!" Dean shouting her name snapped her back, the sounds of fighting crashing into her ears. "Behind you!"

Ducking, she rolled forward, slipping from under the grasping blackened fingers.

It stumbled after her, blood pooled in the feet, legs like a chicken. All the muscle wasted and drooping, skin bagging around the knees.

Sweeping a leg, she knocked its feet out from under it. She stood and kicked it in the jaw.

It buzzed and growled, reaching for her foot.

Lifting her leg, she swung her weight at the hips, drawing momentum from the shoulders down. Her boot crashed into its nose with a crunch. Again, she lifted and dropped her weight on the weak spot. Again. Again.

The buzzing stopped.

Spinning, she took in the field.

The eight others had cleared at least half of the field, working quickly. No time to savor the kill, no time to make it perfect, they'd hacked and slashed their way through like they were clearing weeds.

Spotting Jane near the hospital, she found Mike not far away. As she watched, they came together again, linking elbows and spinning like a whirling dervish. At least half a dozen 'Heads fell before they stopped to step away and handle a couple tricky, fast ones. Mike, limping, stumbled into her. Without looking, she set him right and impaled the 'Head in front of her. Grinning, he took his on.

Another approached from between them, and neither of them noticed.

Addy rushed to them. Squeezing between their turned backs, she reared back with the bow and cracked it across the 'Head's jaw. Its head spun and bone snapped.

It fell, head on sideways.

The air behind her crowded.

Jane and Mike stood to either side, staring down at the 'Head.

"Fuckin' A, Addy," Jane said.

"Holy crap, bean. You should do that more often."

Holding a hand over her shoulder, Mike slapped her five. She switched shoulders, and Jane did the same.

A 'Head fell from the roof less than two feet in front of her, meat sack splitting in two. It showered her in ichor.

Wiping a hand on her chest, she glanced up. Another fell, landing next to Mike. Its skin remained intact, and after a moment of stunned silence, it began to buzz again. It pushed an arm into the ground, broken ulna puncturing the skin and sinking into the sand as it raised itself.

"What the hell? It's raining Dead Heads," she said, pressing a hand to Mike's shoulder and shoving him away from the building.

Jane followed, and they backed away.

"Addy," Dean said, shouting as he ran across the field. He approached, breathing hard. "There's a bunch of them on the roof. I don't know where they came from, but we need to get back and regroup."

Several pockets of Dead Heads still left on the ground and dozens more about to fall on their heads. The path to the dock still clogged with stumbling, buzzing death, the only way they could go was back.

Shoving two fingers in her mouth and pressing her tongue, she whistled.

The others looked up.

She motioned them around the corner of the hospital. "We've got to fall back. Look for another way," she called.

Without waiting, she sprinted for the corner. It would be dark back there, and they could probably make the trees if they moved quick. Then work their way down to the dock.

Thin, but it was the best they had.

They caught up and she shared the plan, looking them over. "Scott," she said, eyeing the blood-drenched right arm hanging limp by his side, "what do you think?"

"You know the place better than I do, Addy. I say we do it."

One side of her mouth turned up, she led them around the corner of the building.

Jane gasped.

Addy followed her gaze to the roof, where her mom and dad stood, holding hands, discussing something. Dad kept pointing at the tower next to the building.

Calculating the distance, Addy knew they'd never make it.

She opened her mouth to shout they'd find another way, but Dad pulled her mom into a kiss. Mom wrapped her arms around his neck as though he was the only thing in the world.

Her breath caught in the back of her throat. As resistant as Dad had been, the flickering flame of hope she'd carried for her parents brightened.

"Good for him," Celia said.

Breaking her paralysis, Addy opened her mouth to shout at them. They'd never make the damn jump.

***

It wasn't what he'd hoped for, but kissing Melinda was enough to galvanize Jack. The way she kissed him back ignited his adrenaline, sent it racing through him.

He'd make the jump, pulling her with him if he had to.

The horde on the roof grew in size, though some fell off the sides. It was now or never.

"Let's go," he said, pulling her hand.

"Jack. Are you sure?"

"No."

They backed away from the edge, and he bent his knees to start running. He glanced at her, squeezing her hand.

"On three, we run," he said.

She nodded.

"One."

A roar split the air.

Flinching, Jack stared over his shoulder as bodies flew from inside the stairwell. It couldn't be.

Andrew appeared in the door, floodlights falling on his swollen face. On his split and bloody lips and red eyes. "Jackie," he growled. Grabbing a 'Head as it tried to bite him, he snapped it in half and tossed it away like a rag doll.

Jack choked, spit stuck in his throat. Not taking his eyes off his friend, he spoke from the corner of his mouth. "What did you do to him?"

"It's— That wasn't— We didn't mean to. It wasn't the intended result."

"Jesus Christ, Melinda," he said, eyes still glued to his friend.

Andrew swatted the surrounding 'Heads out of the way like flies. "Jackie," he gurgled again. Picking up speed, he jogged over the roof. His feet never betrayed a slip. He spread his arms wide, and before Jack could think to get out of the way, Andrew had slammed into them both, sweeping them into his open arms.

Feet spinning, Jack watched as the edge of the roof approached. Too fast. Too fast.

His heart jumped into his throat as they left the roof, Andrew shouting through blood.

The tower rushed at them. "Look out," Jack said, throwing an arm in front of his face.

Slamming into the tower, his shoulder bearing the brunt of the impact, his lungs compressed and forced the air out. Amazed he hadn't cracked his skull and unable to pull a breath in, he didn't think to grab onto the tower until Melinda shouted.

"He's falling!"

As Andrew slipped away from them, Jack looped an arm through the metal crossbars of the tower and reached out a hand to his friend. Finally drew in that breath. "Andrew! Grab on!"

Hand grasping, Andrew fell the fifteen feet to the ground and landed flat on his back.

Cursing, Jack disentangled his arm from the tower and climbed down as fast as his feet would let him. His shoulder screamed. Might have torn something.

Melinda descended next to him. As they reached the ground, Addy and Mike waiting at the bottom, she hugged each of them to her.

Grimacing at his children, Jack hurried past them, limping and holding the side that had hit the tower. Might have broken something in there, too. He stumbled and fell at Andrew's side.

The big man was still breathing, back arched in pain. He snarled and bubbled and breathed, moaning between breaths.

His bloodshot eyes found Jack's. "Hurts, Jackie. Hurrrts."

Wild-eyed, Jack looked around for Melinda.

There she was, standing with one arm over each child like nothing was wrong with the world and Jack's best friend wasn't writhing in pain, unable to die.

"Melinda, you have to help him."

Releasing the kids, she crept to his side, sinking down next to him. "Jack. The process is irreversible."

Andrew groaned, buzzing and gurgling. He closed his eyes. "Hurts, Jackie."

Eyes stinging, Jack let the tears fall. Why the hell not.

Dean appeared next to him, holding out a handgun.

Jack took it with a nod. Chambered a round.

Andrew opened his bloodshot eyes and growled at him. Fingers curling into claws and lifting to grasp at the air, he buzzed like one of them. Choking on the blood in his throat, he blinked. A tear rolled down his cheek.

"Hurts, Jackie."

Pressing the gun to Andrew's forehead, Jack let his friend go.

***

Letting the gun slip from his fingers, Jack lowered his head and breathed.

Inhale, exhale.

Not how I saw this month going.

A hand on his shoulder intruded.

"We gotta go, Dad," Addy said.

He laid his hand over hers. "You're right, baby girl. We gotta go." He patted Andrew on the sweaty, blood-drenched shoulder. "Thanks, my friend."

Putting his feet under him, Jack urged his tired knees to lift him from the ground.

Jane stood on the other side of Andrew, staring into his face.

Even painted in stinking blood with half her head shaved, her skin radiated its own inner moonlight.

A pang of guilt stabbed him in the gut. Had she seen him kiss Mellie? What must she be thinking?

Looking up, she met his eyes, then skipped past him to Melinda.

Who grabbed his hand and tugged. "Let's go, baby."

He turned to his daughter. "Which way, Adelaide?"

"The trees," she said, pointing behind the hospital. "We can follow them almost all the way to the dock."

As a group, they sprinted for the tree line, Addy in the lead. Just as they reached the trees, Jack stopped to take one last look at his friend. His friend, who, in the end, had finally gotten the chance to put those muscles to use like he wanted.

Like Jack had asked him to.

It was his fault Andrew was here, just like the rest of them.

Bringing up the rear, Jane tripped, throwing her hands out before she hit the ground.

He jumped, taking a step toward her.

His young, strong son was there faster. Gentle hands pulled her up. Though it was tight and strained, she smiled at Mike and dashed into the woods with his arm around her shoulders.

Spinning, Jack shrugged Melinda off and followed them into the trees.

Soft shafts of light fell between the trees, illuminating enough ground to steer his way around most of the hazards. Enclosed in the dark, the smell of dirt and salt crowded his nose.

He stumbled once or twice, but for the most part, they all sailed through the trees and approached the sound.

Clumping into a group at the edge of the trees, they watched the dock. Their ride sat moored on the far end. A group of thirty to forty Dead Heads milled about, a hundred feet or so from the dock.

Addy whispered over her shoulder to the grey-haired fellow. "Scott, are they ready to go?"

"They should be."

She handed him the radio. "Tell them to disengage from the dock, but don't start the engines. They need to be ready to go as soon as we're aboard. If that horde hears us, they could be right on our heels."

As Scott relayed her instructions, Addy turned to the others. "Stay low, keep quiet. Let's go." Without hesitation, she dashed out into the open.

Again, pride gripped Jack around the heart. She probably didn't even realize who she'd become through all this. Taking charge of the group without thought or effort, she'd all but led them out of this mess in relative safety.

Approaching the horde, he inhaled and held it without thinking. Made his footsteps soft and unobtrusive. Tried not to watch them as they buzzed and moaned.

So many of them in paper gowns. Too many.

Whoever this company was, they'd pay for all the damage they'd caused.

***

Addy's feet crunched over the thin sheen of sand on the concrete dock.

The horde shifted, their buzzing growing clearer. Increasing in frequency.

They'd been found out.

Whistling, she put on a burst of speed. Best to not look back.

At the boat, she leapt onto the deck and cut through the crowd of mothers and fathers, prisoners dressed in tan jumpsuits, and fighters from Harkers and the other islands. She spotted some people who must've been guards, too, and a couple kids she recognized from the Task Force.

She dashed up the stairs and burst into the wheelhouse.

"Get this thing started," she said, ushering Scott in and stepping back out onto the upper deck. Rounding the front of the bridge, she glanced at the rest of her group as they leapt onto the boat. Dean remained on the dock, helping the others board. Her limping brother was the last, and Dean gave him an extra shove to get him onto the deck. He unwrapped the mooring rope and threw it at the boat.

The horde approached, buzzing, groaning, reaching with dead fingers.

His name behind her lips, she nocked her last arrow and aimed for the closest 'Head. Held it, waiting for the right moment.

As the engines rumbled to life and the boat pushed back from the dock, Dean leapt. He caught the side of the boat and hung over.

Dressed in a paper gown, a 'Head leapt behind him, hooking onto and clutching his shoulders.

Shouting, he tried to buck it off. Dad and Michael reached over the side, both trying to dislodge the 'Head and pull Dean aboard.

Lifting the bow, she shut out the sound of his shouting. The sound of the horde buzzing. The rocking of the boat. Her breath crowded her ears. Her own heartbeat whooshed, calm and even.

Exhaling, she released the arrow.

Missing her dad by an inch and Dean by less, it flew home to the center of the 'Head's skull.

It dropped.

Helped aboard by Dad and Mike, Dean scrambled until he was over the railing and collapsed onto the deck.

Sound rushing back in, she took a few deep breaths and walked to the stairs. If she ran now, she'd start shaking. Taking each step one at a time, she rounded the bottom of the stairs as the bow of the boat pointed toward home.

Jane stood alone at the railing, hugging her elbows and watching the island recede into the distance. Addy paused, torn between her friend and her man.

Mike walked by and stopped next to Jane, hooking an arm around her shoulders. Though she remained stiff, she let him, and after a moment, she laid her head on his shoulder.

Nodding with a smile, Addy went around to the front to make sure Dean was alright.

CHAPTER 32

S o, you spent another two days in the infirmary, huh?" Addy stared at Dean as he sauntered up the walk. "That your new home?"

He chuckled, left arm in a sling. "This yours?"

Rocking in her chair, she looked over her shoulder. The one-story cottage, cute and small and squatting against the sunset, seemed to smile at her. "Looks like."

He grinned up at it, shifting from foot to foot.

"I've got an extra chair up here."

He struggled up the stairs, clutching the railing. Flopping into the wooden rocking chair, he rocked back and lost his balance, throwing his right arm out.

She caught his hand and helped him steady, grinning as he cursed. "How's your shoulder after that run-in with the boat?"

"I've had worse."

"Yeah, bet you have."

She let him keep the hand. They rocked for a bit on the south-facing porch, watching the sky darken over the sound.

Addy narrowed her eyes, imagining she could see the island across the sound. Some of the people from the hospital had called it Emerald Isle. "We went back over there, you know."

Dean's chair squeaked. "I heard. Kinda sketchy on the details, though."

"We mopped up stragglers. Wandering 'Heads and such. Got the rest of the prisoners."

"And the residents? Didn't you say there were like three thousand people there?"

She stopped rocking and turned her head, hair catching on a nail and yanking her scalp. "They're gone."

He sat up, chair doing its best to dump him onto the porch. "What do you mean, gone?"

She shrugged. "Like something came in the middle of the night and snatched them up. Every last one of them. Just. Gone."

Shaking his head, he squeezed her hand. "Like the Roanoke Colony. Any idea what happened?"

She ripped the hair free. Her scalp stung, and she sat back and began to rock again. "None. Dad's working on it, I think."

Holding her hand tight enough to turn his knuckles white, Dean frowned. "Scott lost the arm."

"Damn."

"Could've been worse. They had to Cure him again. He says that's like the sixth time. Your mom says he's lucky it worked."

Addy sighed. "I wish she wouldn't do that."

"What? Work in the infirmary?"

"Yeah. Given what she was responsible for, it's…well, it's a little creepy."

"Addy, your mom is a genius with this stuff. Besides Scott, she saved a few people we thought we were going to lose."

Nodding, Addy rocked. It made her twitchy, Mom working with sick people. Maybe she ought to take some time off.

"So, what about you?" Dean asked, rubbing the back of her hand with his thumb.

"What about me?" Turning, she caught his eyes.

"You gonna go work with Scott like he asked? Be his lieutenant?"

She scoffed. "No. No way. I'm not qualified for that." Dropping his hand, she stood. She walked to the end of the porch, staring into the sunset. Closing her eyes and cupping her elbows, half-moons of orange sunlight bounced off the inside of her retinas.

The other chair squeaked, and Dean clunked unevenly across the porch. A warm hand gripped the space between her neck and right shoulder, squeezing with fingers and thumb in a muscle-tingling massage.

Sighing, she rolled her neck. She should've known all along. This was what it was like to be touched by a sincere hand. Someone who meant what they said. Someone who was who they appeared to be. More.

He whispered in her ear. "How about us, then?"

Leaning back, resting her head on his shoulder, she smiled.

"I've decided to offer you the chance at a second date."

***

"Jack," Melinda called.

Closing his eyes, he stopped and waited for her to catch up. The last person he wanted around right now was her. Here she was anyway, jogging up to him.

"What is it? I'm a little busy." He crossed his arms over his cracked rib.

"Sorry, sorry. I just—" She stopped in front of him, out of breath. "I wondered if maybe we could spend some time alone together?"

"It's been three days, Melinda. I had to murder one of my best friends because of you." More accusation in that than he meant.

Oh well.

"I… Yeah. I'm sorry. I'm not sure how many times you want me to apologize for that, but if it's one more, and one more after that, and one more after that, I will. I'm sorry. I'm sorry. I'm sorry."

He sighed, dropping his hands. "It's not your apologies I want."

"Then what?"

"Time. Give me time. It's a lot to process, alright?"

She reached for him.

Flinching, he stepped back.

Brows creased, she dropped her hand. "Time, I can give you. But how much?"

"I don't know, Mellie. I'll let you know. Until then," he said, dropping his eyes, "I think you should consider stepping away from the infirmary."

Mouth a thin white line, she tried to hide her annoyance behind lifted brows. He'd seen it more times than he could count. "People keep saying that."

"People are right."

"I've done a lot of good there, Jackson. I've helped heal people they thought they were going to lose. And the babies—"

"Especially stay away from them. This is not me asking." He crossed his arms again. Hot pain seared through his ribs, but he kept the flinch on the inside.

She poked a pointing finger in his shoulder. "You do not get to. Order. Me. Around." Punctuating with pokes to the shoulder.

Frowning, he glanced past her.

Walking down the sidewalk, back to them, was Jane. She'd decided to do away with the rest of her hair. Even without the hair, he'd recognize the set of her shoulders, the swing of her hips, anywhere.

Grasping Mellie's hand, he lowered it. "We'll continue this conversation later. Excuse me." Leaving her fuming in the road, he hurried to catch his girl.

"Jane," he called, trotting to catch up. Just like he'd done to Melinda, she stopped but didn't turn.

His stomach sank, like a load of rocks had dropped in it. Still, he smiled as he caught her. Met her eyes.

They didn't dance. They didn't do anything. Just stared, flat and dry.

Off-balance, he stammered. "I— You— You cut your hair."

She crossed her arms. "Jack," she said, glancing at her feet. "I did. Thought about a Mohawk. Decided just to hit it head-on and shave it all." Kicking a rock, she kept her eyes down. Made herself small.

"Jane," he said, not reaching for her. He stepped into her bubble, though. "It's been three days. Are you going to talk to me?"

Looking up, the first crack appeared in her veneer. Chin trembling for a split second, she frowned, a crease forming between her brows. Opening her mouth, she drew in breath. Closed it. Opened it again. "I—"

"Dad!" Mike, shouting, jogged to them. He'd come out of nowhere.

Biting her lip, Jane backed up. Looked at the ground again.

The air where she'd been swirled, like a cold breeze had taken her place. The earth spun under his feet.

Jane gave Mike a quick grin as he approached and kissed her on the cheek.

Jack considered passing out. Thought it might not be best. Doing his best to cover shock and dismay with stoic silence, he glanced at his son.

"Dad, guess what!"

That boy used too many exclamation marks. "Yeah, son," he sighed, eyes on Jane.

Mike punched him on the shoulder, bringing his attention back to him.

"She agreed to go out with me," he said, voice a barely contained stage whisper.

Breath knocked out of him, it was all Jack could do to stare at his son. His ecstatic, jubilant, kind, and generous son.

Mike stared back, eyes widening in expectation.

Ah, yes. Words. He was supposed to have words.

"Good for you, son. Good for you." He patted him on the shoulder.

"Great! OK, I gotta go. They need me down at the dock. We're gonna go work on some towers across the sound. Get things up and running down here. See you later, babe," he said, giving Jane another warm kiss on the cheek.

Watching his son bounce away, Jack entertained a moment of happiness for him. He was the kind of boy the world should give things to.

He glanced back to Jane.

Not all the things.

Stepping into her bubble again, he reached for her face.

She grabbed his hand and gave it a gentle push. "Go and be with your wife, Jack."

As she walked away, the world still spinning beneath him, insides frozen, he tried to call her but found he didn't have the air to do it.

***

Knocking on the door to Scott's office deep within the Big House, Addy stepped back and waited.

Standing with her, Dean looked around. "This hallway looks just like the other one. How did you remember how to get here?"

"I guessed," she said, smiling.

Grinning down at her, he tweaked her cheek with a thumb. "You're cute when you lie."

Scott opened his door, nodding and standing back. "Normally I'd wave you in, but," he said, bouncing his armless shoulder, "that's not possible at this time."

"Thanks anyway, Scott," Addy said, leading Dean into the study.

A fire crackled away in the fireplace. Scott took one of the two chairs before it. Dean pulled up a third from the corner, and they all sat.

"What's on your mind, Adelaide?" Scott tucked his left hand under his chin and shifted the sling on his right shoulder.

She frowned. "A couple things. First, about my mom."

Scott sat forward, smiling. "Your mother is an inimitable woman, Addy."

"Right. That's true. But listen. Given, um, all she was responsible for, maybe it's best she not work in the infirmary."

"Oh," Scott said, sitting back, smile fading. He nodded, hand slipping back under his chin. "Yes. Yes, I see your point. But she's been almost indispensable. Did you know she got your dad's friend, Elizabeth, back on her feet and almost completely cured already? That sort of thing usually takes months! She's a genius when it comes to this disease."

"That's kind of our concern," Dean said.

Glancing between them, Scott shrugged. "I'm not sure I can ask her to step out. But I'll take your request under advisement. Now," he said, glancing at Addy, "I might be more inclined to consider it if it was coming from my lieutenant." He smiled, eyebrows raised.

"Consider it my first and only request as your lieutenant, then. Because I can't take the job. But if you make me, I'll take it for just long enough to ask you to get my mom out of the infirmary," Addy said, leaning forward.

"In that case, consider it done. I'll trust your instincts."

"Thank you. I appreciate that," she said, standing.

"I wish you'd reconsi—"

A knock at the door cut him off. Pushing himself out of the chair with one arm, he opened the door.

Dad charged in. "Oh good, you're here," he said to Dean.

"Dad?"

"I'm glad you're here too, sweetie. Listen, Scott," he said, closing the door, "I've got to talk to you about something."

"Go on." Scott sat again.

Dean offered her dad his seat. Dad crossed his arms. "My wife was part of a shady organization."

Scott nodded. "I know."

"But Dean here is also employed by one."

"I know that, too. Dean has been working to uncover what his company is doing behind everyone's backs."

"Exactly. With Tim gone, no one knows both sides. I see now, it was a mistake to kill him."

Addy scoffed.

"Little girl," Dad said, turning to her, "you laugh. But he could've given us valuable intel that now, we have to gather ourselves."

Her cheeks burned, stomach roiling. Of course, he was right.

"And now," Dad said, turning back to Scott, "we have to start over from square one. I suggest we get to work. Plus, we have to find out what happened to all those people over there. Thousands of people don't just get up and leave overnight."

Hand under his chin, Scott frowned. Firelight flickering in his eyes, he nodded. "I think you're right, Mr. Cooke. Tell me what you need."

Dad handed him a folded slip of paper. "A list of supplies. And," he glanced at Addy, frowning, "Dean. Would you help me?"

Addy jumped to her feet, eyes stinging, heart in her throat. "Are you kidding me right now? I just got you back, I just got Mom back, now you're going to take my Dean and leave?"

"Your?" Dad grinned with one corner of his mouth.

"You know what I mean," she said, arms crossed.

"Addy," Dean said, turning to her. The fire played in his green eyes, turning them a deep shade of emerald. "He's right. You know he is. I'm the best one there is to help him. I have to." He cupped her cheek.

Heartbeat in her throat, fluttering like a butterfly, she leaned into his hand.

Dad and Scott spoke behind her. Their voices came from far away, as though down a long hallway.

"But we didn't get that second date yet," she said. At least, for once, her eyes remained dry. That was a blessing.

Tugging her with the hand on her cheek, he kissed her for what could have been years. She sank deep into his warm arms and gentle lips, tingling all over.

He pulled back, lips still next to hers. "I'll be back before you know it."

"You get back to me in one piece, or it's your ass."

"I'll take good care of him, Adelaide. I promise," Dad said, from the door.

"I'll take good care of him, Addy. I promise," Dean said, whispering in her ear.

She grinned with one side of her mouth. "You better," she said, loud enough for them both to hear.

Following Dad out the door, Dean closed it behind them.

THE END

Acknowledgments

Thanks to everyone who put up with me while I was writing this. My family especially, my army of faithful (and brave!) alphas and betas, the world at large.

Special thanks to my editor, Michelle Rascon, for helping me make it shine. And to my cover artist, Jonas M. Steger, thanks for the most beautiful cover ever made.

Thanks for making me write this, Mel.

ABOUT THE AUTHOR

Bethany is a Southern transplant in the West, where she's made her home. She's been writing for as long as she could hold a pencil, and poetry has always been her first love. She lives with her kids, fiancé, and pets, as well as several hostages, er, houseplants she has not yet killed.

Reclamation is her debut novel, soon to be followed by book two, *Reclamation 2: Revolution*, and book three, *Reclamation 3: Reconstruction*.

Visit her blog to find out more about her interests and keep up with news. Sign up for the mailing list, where she won't send you anything except announcements for the next books in the series or other releases.

bperrywrites.com

RECLAMATION 2: REVOLUTION

EXCERPT

CHAPTER 1

A delaide's feet pounded the ground on the other side of the driftwood, spraying sand and leaves into the air. Not missing a step, she sprinted into the copse of trees ahead, pulling a breath through her nose and exhaling through her mouth.

Hot on her trail, her pursuer cleared the same driftwood just after her.

Listening for the feet to slip, hoping really, she twisted at the last second to avoid a scrubby bush in front of her.

Came out of nowhere, that thing.

Zigzagging, focused on pulling breath in through her nose and blowing it out through her mouth, she Listened again for her pursuer.

Silence behind her. Empty air.

Ducking behind a scraggly tree, she crouched on her heels and peeked behind her.

Nothing moved.

Nothing breathed.

The ocean, too far away to hear, salted the air with humid heat.

The middle of summer here was about the most awful torture she could imagine. Thick, heavy air crowded her lungs, filling all the space for breath. Water dripped from the air itself, as though she could take a handful and squeeze it.

Feet shuffled over sand twenty feet to her left. Here she'd been thinking about the damn weather and almost gotten snuck up on.

Dashing from her cover, she set her sights on a brick square. Could have been a store, could have been a house, could have been a who cares. It was more cover. Better cover.

No way to not be seen ducking in, she settled for getting there first. Stretching her legs to their burning limits, she sprinted for the building.

And where there was clear ground in front of her, then there wasn't.

Ankles catching the staff that had materialized, she tucked her shoulder as she fell. Landing flat on it instead of rolling, she exhaled a quiet *woof.*

Coughing, she rolled to her back and stared at the sky, cheek covered in sand. Hair in her mouth.

Sand in her teeth.

Of course.

"Score one for me," said a soft male voice. He leaned over her, angular cheeks curved in a smile.

"You son of a bitch, Yasuo," Addy said. "About broke my ankle."

Holding the end of the staff out to her, he laughed. "You should take better care of your surroundings, then, shouldn't you?"

Snatching at the staff, she pulled herself up and brushed away as much sand as she could get to. Spat until her mouth felt like the bottom of a dog's foot and frowned. "I thought you were back there. How'd you get in front of me?"

His smile fell. "Back where?"

"Back over," she said, pointing behind her, "there. That. Wait, that wasn't you?"

"You'd have to get up pretty early in the morning to get ahead of me, *pupil,*" Yasuo said, leaning on the staff.

"Oh, stuff it. You're what. Three years older than me? Two?"

"Adelaide, I may look youthful. But in reality," he said, leaning over the staff and whispering, "I am over six hundred years old."

"Shut up." Kicking at the staff, she caught it with a toe before he got it out of the way. "If that wasn't you, then what—"

The bubbling began, not five feet away. Stumbling through a bush, a Dead Head tripped over the lower branches and fell on its face.

"Nice going, Addy," Yasuo said, raising the staff.

The 'Head crawled toward them, feet tangled. Blackened fingers gripping handfuls of loose sand and clawing through it. Creeping closer, buzzing and growling, it could have been frustrated at its slow progress.

Addy knew better. There was no one home. Not anymore.

Unsheathing her machete, she glanced at Yasuo.

He frowned.

"I know," she said, looking at the blade, "you don't want me to bring blades for training. But you expect me to just walk around naked. No weapons." Hacking at the 'Head, she silenced its buzzing in one stroke. "I mean, what would we have done here? Just left it?"

Shaking his head, Yasuo picked up the staff and turned.

"Yaz, listen," she said, reaching for his shoulder.

Spinning, he took her hand. A sad smile lifted the corners of his mouth. "Adelaide," he said, "you can't tell me anything I don't know." He walked around the building and disappeared.

***

Returning to Harkers Island, Addy searched the dock as she berthed her canoe.

Not that Dad and Dean would come back this way, but she could hope. It'd been six weeks since she'd seen either of them.

Several boats took up space at the dock, but not their little silver skiff. Though Mike's boat was parked among them.

Back from the mainland after working the towers, undoubtedly already home with Jane. Who'd barely spoken to her in weeks.

She trudged to the Big House, limping over her sore ankles. Probably need ice later.

Scott had requested a report from the mainland. Even when she repeated she wouldn't be his lieutenant, he treated her like she was his Number One. That whole "not good with women" thing was a clever façade. The leader of this island was quite good with whomever he chose.

Hand on the doorknob of the Big House, weathered wooden sprawling monstrosity that it was, her fingers slipped off as someone opened it from inside.

"Oh, girl, I was just coming to find you," Celia said. Heavy-lidded eyes smiled.

"Celia," Addy said, pulling her into a hug, "I'm glad to see you." Pushing back, she smiled.

"You too, Addy. Hey," she said, tucking a stray hair behind her ear, "Scott's looking for you."

"I was just coming to see him," Addy said, stepping into the cool shade of the house.

Lazy fans spun on the ceiling, mixing hot air with not as hot air.

Sighing and fanning her face, Addy frowned. "What does he need?"

Stepping into the sun, Celia shaded her eyes and grinned. "You'll see."

Before Addy could open her mouth to ask, Celia pulled the door closed.

"Good talk, Cee," she mumbled, following the twisting, turning halls. The stuffed mallards on the walls pointed the way, if you knew how to follow them.

Which she did.

After knocking on the door to Scott's study, she stepped back and crossed her arms. She rehearsed what she would say after giving her report, whispering under her breath. "I can't do this job for you, Scott. I'm not telling you again, I—"

Slight squeak of the hinge.

Expecting to see Scott there, bobbing his missing arm, she couldn't process the man in the doorway until he stepped through it.

Wrapping his arms around her, Dean lifted her and spun in a circle. He buried his face in her neck. "Oh man, am I glad to see you," he said, breath warm on her collarbone.

Grinning from ear to ear, stretching her face so hard it hurt, she squeezed him back. Eyes closed, she held the back of his neck and head and breathed. He smelled like campfires and ocean.

He set her down, beaming.

"You're back. I didn't see your boat. Is Dad here?"

"Adelaide," Jack said, leaning in the doorway.

"Dad," she said, hand trailing away from Dean. "Are you OK?" Brow cocked, she looked him over.

"Yeah, baby girl. I'm alright." Hugging her with one arm, he kissed the top of her head.

"Adelaide," Scott called, somewhere deep in the study, "won't you come in? Bring your father and Dean, please."

Jack crossed his arms and cocked a brow, just like she'd done. "How's that not being his lieutenant going?"

Frowning, she stalked past him and into the study.

Though the fireplace sat dark today, every single lamp glared. Scott sat at his desk at the far end, surrounded by books. Catching her eye, he frowned. "It gets so horribly dark in here, with no windows. For today, we need the light." He motioned to the two chairs in front of the desk. "Please."

Ignoring the man dance behind her, Addy took a seat and waited for Dean and Jack to finish fighting over who got to stand.

After a few tense moments, Dean won. He draped his arm over the back of her chair and stood as Jack took the other seat.

"Scott, I—" Addy began.

He held up his only hand. "Adelaide, your father has important information. You'll want to hear this. Mr. Cooke?"

Jack cleared his throat and shifted. "Sorry, baby girl."

At least he could be polite for Scott when Scott clearly couldn't do it for himself. Was he incapable, or did he just not care?

"As I was saying before you got here, Addy," Dad said, angling his knees so he faced the space between Addy and Scott, "I think we've finally found the location of the Emerald Isle survivors."

Addy sat forward. A headache began behind her left eye. It always made such a nice accessory for the heavy cloak of guilt lying over her shoulders. Somehow, she'd transferred the fact that her mother had been responsible for all the experimentation and death on that island onto her own conscience.

Dean leaned over the back of the chair. "We had the hardest time finding them. After everything went down and they disappeared, it took us most of the time we've been gone just to pick up their trail."

Glancing up at him, she smiled with tight lips. "It was three thousand people, Dean. How could you miss a trail that wide?"

He frowned, brow creased above flat green eyes. "Addy, it was like they just disappeared. Vanished into thin air."

"I remember, I went back to the island the day after we left."

"They were just gone. Like they'd been picked up and taken in the middle of their meals," Jack said, turning to Scott.

Addy shivered. The pinprick of headache expanded into an ice pick. "It made no sense."

Dad sighed. "And knowing what we did about the experiments being done, the work on the vaccine, we had to find them."

"And you think you have," she said, rubbing her forehead.

A warm hand gripped her shoulder, a single-handed massage.

Too long since she'd felt that hand. Too long. The butterflies in her stomach threatened to flutter up into her eyes and become tears. Instead, she opened her eyes and stood. "So, where are they?"

"That's where it gets tricky," Jack said, turning back to Scott. Not before giving Dean a laden glance, steely blue eyes flashing in the lamplight.

Dean sat and leaned on the desk. "This isn't something we ask lightly, Scott, but we need more people."

Scott nodded. "Of course. Whatever you need," he said, looking between them.

"We've also discovered Iridium Flare might have had something to do with this," Dean said, pitching his voice low.

Addy crossed her arms, back against the mantel. Dean's company, IRF, involved in all this, too. He'd never let it lie. "When are you going back out," she said. Voice flat, more of a statement than a question. "After more than a month away," she mumbled, frowning.

The butterflies resettled in her stomach, but they weren't happy, fluttery butterflies anymore. They were "I think I'm going to throw up in your lap" butterflies.

Spinning in the chair, Dean tensed to stand.

Jack held a hand out to him. "We can't lose them again."

Arms uncrossed, she leaned on Scott's desk and stared into his eyes. "I cannot do this job. Not one more day. Not one more report. I am done."

Throwing a glance at her father and her, what? Boyfriend? After one date? Didn't you have to spend time together to be in a relationship?

Good lord, who knew.

She slammed the study door behind her.

www.ingramcontent.com/pod-product-compliance
Lightning Source LLC
Chambersburg PA
CBHW030826110726
47900CB00006B/1763